MW00474877

FROSTBITTEN

Also by Rebecca Zanetti

The Dark Protector series
Fated
Claimed
Tempted
Hunted
Consumed
Provoked
Twisted
Shadowed
Tamed
Marked
Talen
Vampire's Faith
Demon's Mercy
Alpha's Promise
Hero's Haven
Guardian's Grace
Rebel's Karma
Immortal's Honor
Garrett's Destiny

The Realm Witch Enforcers series
Wicked Ride
Wicked Edge
Wicked Burn
Wicked Kiss
Wicked Bite

The Scorpius Syndrome series
Scorpius Rising

Mercury Striking
Shadow Falling
Justice Ascending

The Deep Ops series
Hidden
Taken (e-novella)
Fallen
Shaken (e-novella)
Broken
Driven
Unforgiven

Laurel Snow Thrillers
You Can Run
You Can Hide
You Can Die

FROSTBITTEN

Deep Ops #6

By Rebecca Zanetti

Lyrical Underground Books
Kensington Publishing Corp.
www.kensingtonbooks.com

To the extent that the image or images on the cover of this book depict a person or persons, such person or persons are merely models, and are not intended to portray any character or characters featured in the book.

This book is a work of fiction. Names, characters, businesses, organizations, places, events, and incidents either are the product of the author's imagination or are used fictitiously. Any resemblance to actual persons, living or dead, events, or locales is entirely coincidental.

Kensington Books are published by

Kensington Publishing Corp.
119 West 40th Street
New York, NY 10018

Copyright © 2023 by Rebecca Zanetti

All rights reserved. No part of this book may be reproduced in any form or by any means without the prior written consent of the Publisher, excepting brief quotes used in reviews.

All Kensington titles, imprints, and distributed lines are available at special quantity discounts for bulk purchases for sales promotion, premiums, fund-raising, educational, or institutional use.

Special book excerpts or customized printings can also be created to fit specific needs. For details, write or phone the office of the Kensington Sales Manager: Kensington Publishing Corp., 119 West 40th Street, New York, NY 10018. Attn. Sales Department. Phone: 1-800-221-2647.

Lyrical Undergound Books and Kensington eBooks logo Reg. U.S. Pat. & TM Off.

First Electronic Edition: December 2023
ISBN: 978-1-5161-1127-5 (ebook)

First Print Edition: December 2023
ISBN: 978-1-5161-1128-2

Printed in the United States of America

This one is for my mom, Gail English, who somehow manages to kick our butts in Mah Jongg every week while maintaining that we should be nice to our elders. You're an amazing mom and Gaga to the kids, and we're so very blessed to have you in our lives. I love you.

ACKNOWLEDGMENTS

When Millie Frost burst onto the scene, I just knew she'd be a delight to uncover. And aren't we all thrilled that Scott didn't let the shadows claim him after taking that bullet for Angus earlier on? Whew! Thank you for diving into their tale. There's a whole squad of amazing people who helped bring this book to you, and if I've missed anyone, please know it's my head, not my heart.

Massive love and thanks to my incredible family - Big Tone, Gabe, and Karlina. You guys have been my rock, supporting me while I scribbled away in carpool lines, during practices, and even on those crazy family vacations. I adore you all and have so much fun reliving my college days through you. Sometimes I get all misty-eyed thinking about the days when you kids needed us to cart you all over the place. But wow, just look at you all now! I'm beaming with pride and awestruck by the amazing humans you've become.

A resounding thank you to my exceptional agent, Caitlin Blasdell, who has been my cornerstone and guiding star through many books and series. Your unshakeable support, priceless wisdom, and tireless advocacy have been the backbone of my career, and your editorial insights are nothing short of brilliant. I'm endlessly grateful for your companionship on this wild ride.

A monumental thank you to my phenomenal editor, Alicia Condon, who has diligently scrutinized every single word across a multitude of books, magically transforming my rough drafts into polished masterpieces. Your discerning eye, astute feedback, and relentless dedication have elevated each and every book to a higher level.

A heartfelt thank you to everyone at Kensington Publishing: Alexandra Nicolajsen, Steven Zacharius, Adam Zacharius, Lynn Cully, Vida Engstrand, Jane Nutter, Lauren Jernigan, Barbara Bennett, Elizabeth Trout, Arthur Maisel, Renee Rocco, Kristin McLaughlin, James Walsh, Jennifer Chang, Sasha Gross, and Sharon Turner Mulvihill. Thanks also to Jim Dorohovich, who came up with the perfect name for this series as well as how to improve on a Moscow Mule (change out vodka for Maker's Mark).

A gigantic thank you to my amazing assistant, Anissa Beatty, who has been the wizard behind the curtain, managing my social media and running my Facebook street team, Rebecca's Rebels, with unparalleled efficiency and flair. Your tireless efforts allow me to connect with readers in ways I never thought possible.

A heartfelt thank you to my Beta readers, Rebels Madison Fairbanks, Kimberly Frost, Heather Frost, Leanna Feazel, Asmaa Qayyum, Suzi Zuber, Jessica Mobbs, and Joan Lai.

A heartfelt toast to my steadfast support system and cherished family and friends, who have stood by me through thick and thin, book after book. Your constant encouragement, kind words, and unwavering belief in me have been a source of strength and inspiration. Special thanks to Gail and Jim English, Kathy and Herb Zanetti, Debbie and Travis Smith, Stephanie and Don West, Jessica and Jonah Namson, Chelli and Jason Younker, Liz and Steve Berry, and Jillian and Benji Stein.

Prologue

With four cups of coffee swirling in his gut, Scott Terentson rode the elevator up to the third floor of the investment bank, trying to banish the headache climbing from his neck to his skull. The elevator music was like the slow slicing of a knife across his nerves, but he kept his expression bored and his body relaxed. The residual pain of last year's gunshot wound echoed through his chest as always. He'd been in the hospital followed by PT for more weeks than he could count, so he just ignored the pain.

The door dinged open with a triple tinkle and he stepped onto plush, light blue carpet, facing a wide mahogany reception desk. There was so much woodwork around him, he wanted to puke. Instead, he plastered a smile on his face and strode up to the twentysomething behind the counter.

"Can I help you?" she asked politely, looking serene in a light beige suit and white shell.

"Yes, I'm here to see Werner Dearth." The guy definitely had too many *r*'s in his name. "I'm Scott Terentson."

The young woman, her dark hair pulled back in a severe bun and gold-framed eyeglasses covering pretty green eyes, lifted both eyebrows. "Do you have an appointment?" she asked in the way of corporate gatekeepers everywhere.

"No, but if he has half a brain, he knows I'm coming." More elevator music droned in the background, and he wondered how she didn't go crazy in this somber space.

"I see." She lifted the phone to her ear. "Hi, Gladys. There's a Mr. Scott Terentson here to see Mr. Dearth." She listened. "Very well. Thank you." She hung up. "Mr. Dearth will see you now." She pointed toward the closed doorway to the left of the reception area.

"Thank you," he said as a buzzer echoed and the door unlocked. He pushed it open to find a dark-haired woman in a red Chanel suit waiting for him. Her hair was up in a bun, and she wore no-nonsense, gray spectacles. "Mr. Terentson?"

Who else would it be? "Yes." He kept his tone polite.

Her gaze raked him, instantly taking in his Armani suit and green power tie. Pink tinged her cheeks and she warmed, smiling. "Very well. Mr. Dearth said to bring you on back."

"Thanks." Yeah, he'd worn the suit on purpose.

She ushered him through the hushed hallway with closed office doors and conference rooms on either side. The top floor of the investment banking firm had been done in a clean, modern design with a beige-and-gray color scheme to lighten all the mahogany.

He paused at an open doorway and glanced inside a mechanical room, and his body was electrified as a woman looked up. He blinked once. She blinked twice. She wore a light gray uniform with a logo for Al's Heating and Air Conditioning on the chest. Wild silver and gold streaks threaded through her temporarily red hair, probably from celebrating New Year's Eve a few days before. Her eyes shimmered a startling and unfathomable blue. What the hell was HDD Agent Millicent Frost doing playacting as an air conditioning repair person?

"Mr. Terentson?" Gladys asked.

He turned to her. "Oh yes. I thought it was a little chilly in here." It was damn right freezing.

"Yes." She threw up her hands. "There's something going on with the air conditioning. Hopefully they'll have it fixed soon." She raised her voice enough to be heard in the next office.

Millie rolled her eyes, grabbed a wrench, and returned to whatever she was doing.

Fascinating. Scott followed Gladys to the corner office, where she knocked quietly.

"Enter," a booming voice said.

Gladys smiled, interest in her eyes, as she opened the door for him. "Here you go."

"Thank you again," he said with as much charm as he could muster. His mind still reeled at the sight of Millie.

"What the fuck are you doing here?" Dearth asked.

Scott shut the door and advanced toward the man sitting behind the desk. A sprawling view of DC stretched out behind him. "You demanded an inventory of my client's jewelry, shoes, and, ah, what was it? Yeah. Purses." He sneered the last, even though he knew a few of those handbags were worth more than most cars.

"I wanted Julie to bring them." Crimson darkened Dearth's full cheeks.

"Too bad." Scott yanked an envelope out of his breast pocket and tossed it on the desk.

Werner Dearth looked like a wealthy banker, with his polished silver hair, sharp brown eyes, and ten-thousand-dollar suit. It was black and he didn't wear a tie. His belly hung over his pants, but he was still a broad man who could probably wrestle a full-grown bull if he wanted. Right now, his cheeks showed a ruddy tint, and his gaze a lethal sharpness. He reached for the envelope. "If she thinks she's keeping any of this, she's crazy."

"She's retaining her personal property, and I expect full disclosure of your liquid assets in addition to any real property you haven't divulged as of yet." The judge wasn't messing around with either party in this ridiculous divorce, but Scott's private investigators hadn't yet found the information he needed. Dearth was good at this.

Dearth shoved the envelope in the bottom drawer. "I wanted to speak with my wife and go over this list with her."

Actually, the man wanted to torment his wife. "She isn't going to meet with you alone ever again," Scott said smoothly.

Dearth's nostrils flared. "Your client's a real bitch, you know."

"Your soon-to-be-ex-wife is one of the kindest people I've ever met," Scott returned. She was also very good friends with his mother. "You breached the prenup and cheated on her."

"Prove it."

So far, Scott had been unable to do so. Anybody with information was more afraid of Dearth than Julie or even the judge. Right now, his entire case came down to he-said, she-said, and that was no way to go into court. "How about you stop being an ass and finish this thing?"

"Because she needs to pay," Dearth sputtered.

"That sounds like a threat," Scott said. "We all know that you cheated on your wife with an eighteen-year-old." One who had conveniently headed off to backpack around Australia, leaving her phone at home. "Just settle this and move on with your life." The last thing Scott wanted to do was put his client through a trial, especially since he had a proof problem.

"Like I said, prove it," Dearth said, his jowls moving. "I'm leaving that witch with nothing."

Not if Scott had anything to do with it. "You sound like a blowhard."

Dearth looked him up and down. "I investigated you."

How freaking boring. "So?"

"You're supposed to be an excellent trial attorney, but you don't do divorces. Is my wife doing...you?"

What an asshole. "Let's just make this a fair and amicable split, shall we?" He normally wouldn't touch a divorce with a fishing rod, but his mother had asked for a favor.

"I don't think so." Dearth frowned. "I will ruin her before we end this." He shrugged, moving his jiggling belly. "I don't think you have the chops for a real divorce trial. Since it's my third, I do."

Scott would have to schedule depositions, then. He didn't have time for this. "I've been playing nice so far, but that just ended. Do you get me?" He stared directly into the man's eyes.

For the first time, Dearth paused. "Yeah."

Scott had been a marine before he'd become a lawyer, and right now he was just pissed off. He didn't have many pet peeves, but somebody wasting his time shot right to his shit list. Add the fact that the jerk was an ass, and he shot right to the top.

A knock sounded on the door and Gladys poked her head in. "Mr. Dearth, your two o'clock is here."

Scott turned and strode toward the door, looking over his shoulder. "I'm more than happy to meet you in court. In fact, I prefer it." With that, he swept past Gladys, noted the door to the mechanical room was closed, and walked to the elevator to ride back down.

Dearth would prolong this stupid case just to mess with Julie. Shy and kind, she didn't belong in a courtroom. Scott shook his head, his headache increasing in force as he walked across the main floor and outside into the chilly January weather.

He'd somehow managed to claim a parking spot just a few yards down against the curb, so he walked to his SUV and leaned against it, waiting. About half an hour later, Millie Frost walked out, still in her cute little uniform. She caught sight of him and shook her head. He gestured toward the passenger side of his car.

She lifted her chin and started to walk away.

"Millie. I'll make a scene," he said quietly.

She halted, turned, then walked around to climb into the passenger seat, ducking down and slamming the car door. He could feel her eye roll but not see it.

He slid onto the driver's seat. "The windows are tinted dark enough that you won't be spotted by cameras."

"You know I'm on a case," she said with a cute huff. "You're a miscreant, Terentson."

"That seems to be the general consensus." He started the engine and pulled away from the curb. "Did you leave a vehicle nearby?"

"I planned to take the bus," she retorted.

He had no problem rescuing the pretty blonde from public transportation. "Do you want me to take you to headquarters?" The woman worked for the Homeland Defense Department.

"Yeah, that'd be great, considering you could've blown my entire case." She crossed her arms.

"What were you doing in the bank, Millie?" he asked.

She looked out the window. "None of your business."

She was probably one of the most intriguing women he'd ever met. She looked like Tinker Bell and acted like Q from the James Bond series. She was the gadget expert at the HDD and more specifically for Angus Force's Deep Ops team, the team that had gotten him shot. But every once in a while he helped them out anyway.

"What were you doing in the bank?" he asked again.

"I can't tell you that and you know it. It's an ongoing investigation," she replied. Her captivating, thick blond hair curled naturally to her shoulders. She barely came to his, adding to her compelling allure. She was a powerhouse in a very small package. With eyes as blue as pure sapphires and a notably pert nose, she captivated attention. When he leaned close enough, he could see a tiny smattering of freckles across it. He could admit to himself that he'd been intrigued by Millicent Frost from the first time they'd met. She unfortunately did not like lawyers, and he knew that because she had told him so herself.

He tried again. "I don't want to mess with your investigation, but I am representing Werner Dearth's wife in their divorce case, and the guy's a cad. Can you tell me anything about his finances?"

"Nope."

He pushed down irritation. "Come on, Millie. Just give me something. He's treating his soon-to-be-ex horribly, and his wall of lawyers want to destroy her."

"Stupid lawyers," she muttered. "Fine. I can't divulge anything about his finances. However, I will tell you that his secretary was blowing him before you arrived."

He jolted. "Gladys performed oral sex on Dearth in the office?" Gross. Just gross.

"Yep. I accidentally opened his door while looking for the AC unit. Good ole Gladys perched on her knees. But that's about all I can tell you."

Hmm, that was a start. "Thanks, Millie. I appreciate it." He pulled up to the HDD headquarters in downtown DC. "Are you still working with Angus and the gang?"

"Not on this one." She looked down at her hands. "I've been assigned elsewhere as I'm undercover for a bit."

He didn't like the idea of her out there on her own. The woman needed a team to back her up. "Just exactly what kind of bugs were you planting?"

She looked at him, her eyes guileless as she opened the door. "Planting? I have no idea what you're talking about."

He wasn't happy she was a good liar, yet he knew she was lying, so maybe she wasn't that accomplished. "Would you like to meet for dinner sometime?"

She hopped out of the vehicle. "Are you still a lawyer?"

"Yep."

"Then not a chance." With that, she exited his car and slammed the door, leaving the faintest scent of sweet magnolias behind.

Chapter One

Two months later

She wanted to kill Scott Terentson.

Millicent Frost sat in the witness chair, trying to keep from fidgeting. The wooden backrest felt like a hard iron bar that made her back ache all the way up to her neck. For some reason, even though it was only March, the heat in the courtroom had been turned off. She did her best not to shiver her rear end off; it was not yet nine in the morning.

The judge was a man in his sixties with thick gray hair, bushy eyebrows, and beady brown eyes. She disliked him on sight. The bailiff was a tall woman who seemed efficient and economical with her movements. Millie liked her. It was a bench trial, so there was no jury; at least she had that going for her.

That was all she had going for her right now.

Being back in a courtroom after all this time made her stomach churn. Hopefully the restroom was close.

The two lawyers spoke in hushed tones to the judge, gesturing wildly as she sat there and tried to listen. They argued over part of her testimony; the questions she refused to answer.

She took a deep breath and reminded herself that she was a grown-ass woman who knew how to blow up a boat with frayed twine and an old toaster, not a scared eight-year-old being kicked out of another foster home because she wanted to take apart engines rather than play with dolls.

Scott Terentson and his client, a stunning woman in her fifties with thick black hair, commanded one table, while the investment banker Werner Dearth and his lawyer, a high-powered-looking woman in a bright red suit, occupied the other table.

Unfortunately, in the rows of benches behind them sat HDD Special Agent Tom Rutherford, her immediate boss. As usual, he was dressed impeccably in a blue suit with a white tie. No expression marked his face, but heat rolled off him like steam from a volcanic vent.

Scott Terentson had probably just gotten her fired.

She wanted to march across the well and punch him in the nose. It'd be nice to make a lawyer bleed—especially that one.

Memories assailed her of all the lawyers through the years, those working for the state, who wanted her to keep trying foster homes instead of living with her aging great-aunt, until Aunt Mae was the only option. They'd kept her from happiness.

Damn lawyers.

The judge whispered something to the two attorneys, then everybody dispersed as if they'd been in a huddle and called, "Go team." She failed to read Scott's expression as he returned to his seat behind the table. His tailored suit gave him the look of a model—one too smooth for her taste.

She liked broad shoulders and muscle. Period.

"Now, as I was saying," the attorney for Mr. Dearth started. Named Lorraine Balbit, her style exhibited smoothness and calculation. Millie could normally anticipate the direction of an argument, so she tried to trace the pattern of the questions. It didn't bode well for her.

Lorraine cleared her throat. "So again, you snuck into Werner Dearth's place of business to spy on him for Julie Dearth and the government, correct?"

Millie swallowed. "No."

Lorraine stepped back. "Wait a minute. You do work for the government, do you not?"

"Yes," Millie said. She might lose her job, but she was not going to commit perjury.

"So why were you dressed as an air conditioning repair person on the day in question?" The lawyer pointed to a screen that showed a picture from the bank's security cameras of Millie in her bulky uniform.

There was no way out of this. "I'm sorry," Millie said, "but I am not cleared to speak about an ongoing investigation." In the audience, Rutherford dropped his head to his hand.

"Ongoing investigation?" The lawyer pounced. "Please tell me more."

"I just said that I couldn't," Millie said evenly. She'd never forgive Scott for this.

Lorraine looked at her client, then back at Millie. "Is the bank under investigation...or is my client being targeted?"

"Again, I do not have clearance to speak about an ongoing investigation," Millie said.

Scott stood. "Objection, your honor. The defense is going beyond the scope of direct examination. The witness was subpoenaed to testify as to what she personally witnessed, more specifically that she saw the defendant engaging in oral sex with his secretary, in clear violation of the prenuptial agreement. Period."

Oh, Millie never should have said a word to that asshat about what she'd seen.

"My client denies the slanderous accusation, and has a right to understand the reason for the witness's presence in his building, and more importantly, why she'd lie for the plaintiff's attorney." The lawyer tapped very red nails on her lip. "My questioning directs toward bias."

"Objection overruled," the judge said, sounding bored.

Lorraine smiled. "Let's see here, then. So we know from your earlier testimony, Agent Frost, that you work for the HDD."

"Yes," Millie said.

"And you've been known to work with Angus Force and his team, have you not?"

Millie didn't like where this was going. "Yes, I have worked with many teams during my time with the HDD."

"Many teams. How old are you?" Lorraine asked, her tone mocking.

"I'm twenty-nine." She appeared younger than her years, but she figured someday that would be an advantage. Right now, it didn't seem to be.

The attorney reached for a file and click-clacked on her four-inch heels across the well of the room. "Isn't it true that the attorney for the plaintiff has also worked with Angus Force, and what I understand is informally called his Deep Ops team?"

"I believe so," Millie said.

The lawyer looked up at the judge and then down at Millie as if she couldn't believe it. "So you're telling us that you and the plaintiff's attorney were not working together in order to entrap my client or, to put it rather more bluntly, blackmail my client into relinquishing his rightful share of property in this divorce?"

"I'm not working, and I have not worked, with the plaintiff's attorney in pursuit of this divorce case." Even the judge displayed a frown.

"Hmm. I've got to tell you, I don't think I like government personnel being used in this type of corruptive manner." Lorraine tsked.

Scott straightened his lithe body. "Is there a question there?"

"Yes." Lorraine moved closer to Millie. "How long have you and the plaintiff's attorney been lovers?"

"Objection." Scott shot to his feet. "Foundation, badgering, and damn bad taste."

The judge lowered his chin. "Objection sustained. Watch yourself, Ms. Balbit."

Lorraine's gaze remained on Millie. "I have to ask. Why do you have green streaks in your blonde hair?"

Millie sat back, her ears ringing. "Tomorrow is St. Patrick's Day." Duh.

The lawyer chuckled, and the sound was both throaty and kind of sexy. "I see. So you expect us to believe that even though you and the plaintiff's attorney have worked together for the government, you were both at my client's office on the same day for different reasons?" She clicked a button and a new picture came up of Millie and Scott outside on the day they'd met, then the screen advanced to show her getting into Scott's car.

The man had pretty much blackmailed her into accepting a ride.

"Yes," Millie said. "I didn't foresee running into Scott at the office building, and I don't see how he could've possibly known I'd be there the same day."

"I find that so very hard to believe. Why did you leave together in his vehicle?"

Millie's stomach cramped again. "He said he'd throw a fit on the street, and I didn't want to blow my cover."

Scott's gaze hardened.

Lorraine looked delighted. "Excellent. Now, let's go through this again." The woman then proceeded to question Millie about everything from her job to her qualifications to her relationship with Scott. By the end of the testimony, Millie almost believed she'd not only been dating Scott but had tried to set up Werner Dearth with him.

Finally, the judge excused her.

She walked out of the courtroom, a headache brewing behind her eyes. This marked a calamity. Rutherford waited for her, looking big and broad and way too polished in the dark hallway. Along the ceiling, at least five lights had gone dark.

"This is devastating," he confirmed curtly. He enjoyed a higher rank in the agency, and he had a standing as one of the Deep Ops handlers. The man didn't like any of the members.

A knot of tension balled up inside her. "I know."

"You just told our prime suspect that he's been under investigation."

"Agent Rutherford, the minute Scott Terentson subpoenaed me as a witness in this case, Werner Dearth must've known he was a suspect."

Rutherford sneered. "Now nothing will happen. We're not going to get him on tape, and all those people whose money he stole will go without justice." His perfect face flushed red.

She blinked. It was the most emotion she'd ever seen from her HDD handler. "I had to tell the truth."

"Of course. But you shouldn't have gotten in that car while on duty, Agent Frost." His chin lowered.

He was right, and she didn't have a defense for her actions. "I'm sorry."

"Too bad." Rutherford's eyes blazed. "I'm going to run this up the chain, and I will be in touch." He turned on his very polished loafer and stomped down the hallway and out into the overcast day.

Millie flopped onto a wooden bench, leaned her head back, and took several deep breaths. She normally loved her job, especially when she worked with the Deep Ops team. This undercover op had been her big chance. She'd been nearly guaranteed a promotion, which meant she could've chosen the team as her permanent spot, in addition to making more money to send home to Aunt Mae, who needed it.

How was she going to help her great-aunt without a salary? The woman had saved Millie, and she couldn't let her down.

All she'd done was talk to Scott that day in January, but she did get into his car, and she had been wearing her uniform. She hadn't considered that anybody would look at those surveillance tapes since she was undercover as an AC repair person—while actually planting surveillance equipment allowed via a valid warrant.

Dearth must've been watching Scott on his company's CCTV thread. God, she was an idiot.

She wasn't sure how long she sat there, but soon the door opened and Scott and his client strode out. The woman hurried into the bathroom, sniffing loudly. Millie looked up. "I take it the judge didn't like you?"

"The judge hated us all," Scott said wearily, sitting so close to her she could feel the warmth from his body. "I'll appeal, but my client might've just gotten screwed. I think the judge might be friends with Dearth, but I can't prove it."

"You screwed *me*," Millie said. "I think I just got fired."

Scott jerked. "Come on. The HDD can't be overreacting to that degree?"

"Yes. You have ruined everything." She closed her fingers into a fist, surprised at how badly she wanted to punch him. "Lawyers are the worst, and you're at the bottom of that oily barrel." For years, her aunt had fought to gain custody of Millie and her brother, and those state lawyers had fought every petition, asserting that her elderly great-aunt lacked the resources to raise two kids. So Millie and her brother had been separated until she'd turned eleven and JT had turned sixteen.

Then there wasn't anywhere else to go. Thank goodness.

"You're not fired." Scott reached for his phone. "I'll call Angus. He has juice with the higher-ups at the HDD after the success of the last couple of cases."

"No." Millie held up her hand. What an egomaniac. "I don't need your help. Go away and forget we met." The guy even looked like a rich lawyer. He had thick, dark blond hair and the most piercing and calculating blue eyes she'd ever seen.

Scott sighed. "I'm sorry. Honestly, I had no idea the HDD would be so hypersensitive."

As if it would've mattered. All he cared about was winning.

Scott's client came out of the bathroom, tears on her face.

"I have to go. I'll give you a call later." Scott seemed to hesitate. "I'll fix this."

"Great," Millie muttered. "I'm sure you'll just create a bigger mess." The jerk had chosen his client over her or what was right, just like a typical lawyer.

Scott tugged a business card from his pocket and shoved it into her hand. "Call me if they really try to fire you before I make amends." He turned and strode to his client, put an arm over her shoulders, and escorted her from the building.

Werner Dearth and his lawyer emerged from the courtroom, both laughing. Millie ignored them and hurried down the hallway toward the farthest exit.

She'd almost made it to the front door when Werner Dearth grabbed her arm, swinging her to a halt. Pulling free, she noted a vacant vestibule around them. Where was his lawyer? She glared. "What?"

He leaned in, his breath smelling like vodka. "You have no idea what you just unleashed, you bitch."

Millie took a step back from the vitriol in his voice. He was older than she, less fit, but twice her size. "Did you just threaten a federal agent?" She could see a bailiff down the hallway and would call out if necessary.

He snorted. "You won't carry that job title by the end of the week." His upper lip lifted in a sneer. "I take out my enemies, and you just became one. You won't see me coming."

Her phone buzzed and she pressed it to her ear, keeping her eye on the threat. "Millie Frost," she answered.

"Millie, it's JT. We have a problem. Aunt Mae might've had a heart attack."

Millie's entire life ground to a halt in that second. "What? Is she okay?" Her lungs stuttered.

JT's voice carried rough and low through the phone line. "I don't know. I'm headed to the hospital now."

"I'll meet you there," Millie said. It was a two-hour drive to the middle of West Virginia, but she could probably make it in an hour. She had to. Mae Frost was the most important person in her life. She'd worry about everything else later.

Dearth tightened his grip on her arm. "Don't ignore me," he snapped.

She shoved him hard enough that he took a step back and released her. "Touch me again, and you'll regret it for the rest of your life." She had to get to Aunt Mae. Ignoring the bastard, she turned and pushed outside into the frigid air.

Chapter Two

Tension pummeled Millie's temples and a heavy weight kept her pressed down. She tried to open her eyes but her brain failed to connect to her muscles. She tempted a swallow, but her throat turned parched as a desert.

The cloying smell of copper surrounded her, and her hands itched. A tacky texture enveloped them. She forced her eyelids open and tried to focus on the sunlight barely glimmering through blinds but not brightly enough to illuminate her immediate vicinity.

Where was she?

She moved and then yelped as she fell from a mattress onto the floor. Hazy darkness swallowed everything. Had she fallen in a puddle? What was going on? Fuzziness filled her skull.

Her hand hit some sort of table and she crawled up worn wood, fumbling for a light. Then the color red dominated her vision. Crimson covered her hands and arms.

She coughed. Was that blood? The liquid had congealed but was still slippery. Her eyes filled with tears, making the world blurrier.

What was happening?

She swiped the tears away, not wanting to touch her eyes with her bloody hands.

Looking down, she saw her nude body. Blood stained her chest. She opened her eyes wider, but the world remained murky. She clutched the mattress, her nails sinking into more blood, then balanced herself on her knees.

Bile rose in her throat.

She blinked several times, trying to focus. A man lay on his stomach on the bed, his bare torso visible. Wait a minute. Was that Clay? Clay Baker's face and profile came into view. His eyes bulged, and blood drenched his bare neck and torso.

She screamed, trying to wake up. This had to be a nightmare. Nothing changed.

Why was she in her ex-boyfriend's cabin?

How had she gotten there?

She hurriedly seized both the bloody mattress and the end table and forced herself to stand, swamped with vulnerability by her nudity. Her feet slipped in the pool of blood and she righted herself, gulping. "Clay?" She reached forward and nudged his shoulder. He didn't move. She looked around, trying to focus. What was wrong with her brain?

She struggled to form a thought.

Knowing he was dead, she pushed him again, ignoring reality. Her hand slid off his shoulder and hit something hard in the bedcovers. She grabbed something cold and gasped. She held a jagged-edged fishing knife, the one she had created herself with a handle containing survival tools—a fishing line and hook, a compass, and even a fire starter kit.

Why was her knife here?

Blood, already dried, covered the blade. She gasped and dropped the weapon. The knife fell half on the mattress and then slid onto the bloody floor.

She looked around. How did she get here? She hadn't talked to Clay in at least a year. She vaguely remembered driving to River City and seeing her great-aunt in the hospital yesterday, but then…nothing.

The morning light strengthened through the blinds, illuminating dust mites in the air. Had she spent all night with Clay?

Her clothes had been thrown over a wooden chair near the sliding glass door. Holding her breath, she crept as quietly as she could, just in case whoever had stabbed Clay remained in the cabin. Gulping, she yanked on her shirt, noting it was still buttoned up. The over-large flannel covered her at least to her thighs. She reached for her jeans and fumbled for her phone in the back pocket, leaving bloody handprints all over the light denim.

The wind rattled against the windows and she jumped. Then she shut the door as quietly as she could, searching for a locking mechanism. There was none. Her heart thundering, she grabbed the wooden chair and placed it in front of the door. If anybody lurked out there, at least she would know if they tried to get back in.

She still couldn't concentrate. The room spun around her, and none of this made sense. The itchy and heavy blood on her hands had crusted in her fingernails.

She looked back at Clay. With his one eye open, he appeared to wink. But his body lay still, and blood splattered all around him.

As reality started to return, she slid across the room and felt for a pulse. "Clay?" His eye had already gone partially milky. She knew he was dead, but she had to check for a pulse. There was nothing. In fact, his skin had already cooled.

She shivered and backed away, quickly punching in a number.

"River City Police Department," came a low voice over the line.

"Hi." Her voice trembled. "This is Millie Frost, and I'm out at Clay Baker's cabin." Her stomach lurched, and she turned to the side to vomit in the corner.

"Ma'am, are you okay?" She didn't recognize the voice, which was odd because she knew everybody in the small town, or at least she thought she did. "No," she said, coughing and wiping off her mouth. "Is the chief there? We have a problem."

* * * *

Scott sucked down his second cup of coffee as he dressed for the day, pausing in the midst of buttoning his shirt as the multitude of scars across his chest caught his attention. He gingerly touched the bullet hole and surrounding scar tissue, wondering how close he'd been to crossing over. Probably pretty close.

He didn't remember a light. He didn't remember a darkness. In fact, he didn't remember a damn thing except for pain, a lot of it. Putting his shoulders back, he reached for cuff links. He had a couple of court hearings that morning and then had to figure out his schedule, not that he felt any real interest in it.

All he did was go through the motions, but at least the law kept his brain alert.

The dog sneezed from his bed. "I hope you're not getting a cold," Scott murmured.

Roscoe sneezed again and then went back to sleep. The German shepherd had more problems than Scott did, and that was saying something. "I do not appreciate Angus dumping you on me before he and Nari left for Europe." They'd headed out of the country to attend a security conference, and Angus had needed a babysitter for the canine.

Roscoe snored loudly, his honey-brown eyes closed, his colorful muzzle buried in the blankets.

There was no doubt in Scott's mind that Angus was worried about him and somehow thought the dog would be good company.

Scott's phone buzzed and he pressed a button. "Terentson."

"Hi, honey. I heard about yesterday. Julie called me."

"Hi, Mom," he said, wincing as he tried to fasten the top button. Had his neck gotten bigger? He'd been fanatical about working out after he had finished physical therapy. He knew that muscles wouldn't stop another bullet if one ever came at him, but still, being stronger than the other guy could never hurt. "Yeah, it looks like we're going to trial. I can't really talk about the case with you, but you can get all the information you want from Julie."

"I'm not worried about Julie," his mom said. "I'm worried about you."

He reached for his coffee and finished the mug.

"Are you drinking coffee again?" Her voice rose.

"No," he lied and rolled his eyes. Though he'd reached his thirties, he still felt the need to lie to his mother.

"I can tell when you're lying," she muttered. "The doctor told you to lay off the coffee. You drink too much of it."

Coffee constituted his one vice. "Okay, Mom," he said instead. "I'm sorry I couldn't settle the case for your friend."

His mother snorted. "Like I said, she's a big girl and can handle herself. Don't let the tears fool you." She stopped speaking for a moment. "Julie is a nice person, but she's strong, Scotty. I'm concerned about you and not her."

He walked into his closet with his phone to his ear, viewing his various ties. "I'm wearing a blue suit today. What color tie should I wear?"

"Pink," she said instantly.

"All right." He didn't much care. He didn't much care about most things these days.

As if she could read his mind, she kept digging. "How's your mood?"

"I'm fine." But was he? The pleasure he'd previously felt in practicing law eluded him. The strategy used to entertain him. Now he just felt slow, as if he needed to find another path. "I have to go. I picked the pink tie."

"Don't forget dinner next week." She hung up before he could find an excuse to get out of dinner. Not that they weren't close— he just didn't want to face her questions because he didn't have any answers.

His phone buzzed again and his temper started to crawl up from his gut. The office knew not to bother him until he walked in the front door, which was usually earlier than anybody else. He was also the last person out the door late at night. Twenty-hour workdays were normal for him—at least they'd become so after he'd been shot. "Terentson," he snapped out. Apparently the time had come to get his butt to work whether he liked it or not.

"Scott Terentson? The lawyer?" The man on the other end had a gruff voice.

Scott stilled. "Who is this?"

"It's Chief Lawrence Wyatt from Shalebrook County."

"Never heard of it," Scott said. "What do you need, Chief?" He'd gotten so bad, he didn't even feel curiosity any longer. Even he knew that was a seriously bad sign.

The chief cleared his throat. "I found your business card in Millicent Frost's jeans."

The entire world locked into place with a metallic howl and then narrowed. Darkness edged Scott's vision. "Millie? Is she okay?" His breath heated his throat, and his temples throbbed. She had to be unharmed. Was this a notification?

"Yeah. Well, not really. She needs a lawyer."

Scott exhaled the breath he'd been holding. "She's alive. Good. Is she hurt?" His ears heated.

"No. She's unharmed, but I had to arrest her on suspicion of murder. She really needs a lawyer. Like right now."

Scott's hand shook on the phone. Actually trembled. "I'll be right there." He dropped his jacket and slipped on his shoes, hurrying out of his bedroom.

"We're in West Virginia." The chief gave him an address. "DC is about two hours away."

This made zero sense. He'd just seen Millie the day before. "I'll leave right now."

"Good. She said she didn't want a lawyer, so she's gonna be pissed I called you. Hurry." The chief clicked off.

Scott's brain reeled. Forcing himself to go cold, he whistled for the dog and jogged out to his Bentley Bentayga. The black vehicle ate distances when opened up. He let himself have a little luxury when it came to his vehicle.

"Let's go, Roscoe." He settled the dog in the back seat, jumped in, and drove out of the suburban area toward West Virginia, making a quick call to his office to reschedule everything he had that day. He drove faster than the speed limit, which he knew better than to do, but nobody stopped him. Soon he arrived in the small town of River City, his mind spinning. Who the heck would arrest Millicent Frost?

Large posters covered several storefronts advertising an upcoming Fishing Derby the following weekend, and the small town vibe confused him even more.

He pulled into the small parking lot of the River City Police Department. "I'll be back in a moment."

Roscoe, sprawled across the back seat, snuffled and gave him an encouraging nod.

"I'll get her, Roscoe. She'll be fine." Scott had talked to the dog the entire way, trying to work out what had happened. He knew Roscoe didn't understand, but still…

Scott jumped out of his vehicle and ran through the blustering wind to the front door. The building was a light red brick with gold lettering that said River City Police Department, and when he pushed open the glass door, a bell jingled. The waiting room was vacant of people but looked comfortable for a police station, with a leather sofa pushed against the far wall and three matching leather chairs next to it, all surrounding a table overflowing with fishing magazines.

An officer stood behind a reception desk dressed in a navy-blue uniform with a triangular patch on his arm reading River City Police. "Can I help you?" he asked. His shoulders were wide, his skin a burnished brown, and his eyes a sparkling black. He had to be in his forties, and his gaze was appraising.

"Hi, I'm Scott Terentson, and I'm here to see my client." Scott removed his ID from his pocket.

"She's back here," a man called out, coming into view down a long hallway. He appeared to be in his sixties, with thick gray hair and faded blue eyes. A chief's badge adorned his navy-blue uniform. "I'm Chief Wyatt. Lawrence Wyatt. Come on back. She's waiting for you."

Scott skirted the desk and kept his expression calm as he followed the chief past file cabinets and offices to reach two cells fronted by jail bars, the old-fashioned kind.

The chief paused. "Her bail transfer cleared, and we're issuing her paperwork now." His voice lowered. "The county prosecutor is headed this way, and he's out for blood. Just so you know." He unlocked and pulled open the barred door.

"Thanks," Scott said, waiting until the chief had walked away. "Millie?"

She huddled beneath a thick blanket on a cot at the end of the cell, her back to the wall, her knees drawn up. She wore blue sweats with a matching top that were much too big for her, as were the white socks covering her feet. "Scott Terentson." Her jaw dropped while those blue eyes raged. "What the blazes are you doing here?"

Chapter Three

Millie's heart rate increased until her ribs hurt. Of all the people to witness her sitting sadly in a jail cell, she would've chosen Scott Terentson last. "I asked you a question." Her voice shook from raw anger.

He scanned her, head to toe, leaving odd and irritating tingles in his wake. "Why are you in jail?"

Her breath heated. "Chief!" she bellowed. The man had left the door open and headed back to his office, out of her sight.

"You need a lawyer, Mills," the chief yelled back, too cowardly to return.

"Are you okay?" Scott asked.

She gulped. "I'm just fine. Do not think of calling in Angus Force or any of his team." She pressed her fingers to her forehead above both eyebrows and applied pressure. "Ugh. I have the worst headache."

"I don't like flying in the dark here, Millie. The chief said you were arrested on suspicion of homicide." Scott's tone exuded complete command, and his expression remained unyielding. "I'm not going anywhere, and if you don't start talking to me, I will call in the entire Deep Ops team."

As a threat, it was a good one. She didn't like this uber-controlled side of Terentson. "Fine." Maybe she could make use of his legal knowledge. The law had normally worked against her in the past, but he was an attorney, she needed one, and she could attest that he was ruthless. "I know. I mean, I guess I...I don't know. This is crazy."

He frowned. "What have you said to the authorities?"

"I haven't said anything," she said. "Well, I mean, except the truth."

His lips pressed together. "Did you speak with the police?"

"Of course I spoke with the police," she said, her voice rising. "I've known the chief my whole life."

One of his eyebrows rose. "Who died?"

Tears tried to well in her eyes and she battled them away.

"Wait, wait, wait," Scott said. "I need you to stay calm, no tears. Tell me what's going on so I can fix this." The tone held bite.

She sniffed. "Fine. So when I left the courtroom, my brother called to tell me my great-aunt, who raised us, was in the hospital with a heart attack."

"Wasn't a full heart attack," the chief called out. "She just needed one stent, and stress brought on the slight heart attack, no doubt. Probably because the economy sucks, and everybody in town is suffering. Don't you remember? You visited her late afternoon."

"I kind of remember," Millie returned. "But a lot of the day is fuzzy, and last night is blank." She'd already told the chief that.

Scott shifted his weight. "What do you remember?"

"I remember getting the phone call from my brother." She looked down. "But not much else. I came to town, and then I think we went to the hospital."

"You think?"

She looked up at him again and focused. "I can't remember much."

He looked closely at her head and eyes. "I see no signs of injury, and your pupils are not dilated. Tell me what happened."

"Apparently, according to the chief, last night I went to Snarky's Bar. I mean, it was St. Patrick's Day, but I don't remember anything."

Scott's probing gaze exacerbated her headache. "What is the first thing you do remember?"

"This morning, I woke up at Clay Baker's house in his bed."

No expression crossed Scott's face. "Who is Clay Baker?"

"He's my ex. We dated all through high school and broke up when I went to college." She swallowed. "It wasn't a good breakup."

"So you went home with him?"

She plucked at an embroidered figure of a donkey on the plush-looking blanket. "I don't remember," she said. "I woke up in his bed, and he was dead."

Scott sat back. "What do you mean dead?"

"He suffered a fatal stabbing with a knife I invented. It was definitely my weapon I found in the bed next to me. Blood saturated me as well as the blade."

Scott breathed out slowly. "You have no idea how you got there?"

"None," she said, her eyes filling with tears. "I don't remember anything."

"We're going to figure this out, Millie. So what happened then?"

She tried not to take comfort in his sure and matter-of-fact tone, yet her breathing leveled out. "I called the police and an ambulance. The chief came, saw everything that had happened and arrested me. I tried to call my brother, but I couldn't get ahold of him. I hope he's okay." JT had just returned home, and he seemed off.

"We'll figure it out." Scott turned to look at the open doorway. "Chief," he called out, "I want a blood test on her."

"I already took care of it," the chief called back.

Scott kept silent for a moment. "We need a rape kit, Millie."

Her chin dropped. "I wasn't raped and I didn't have sex."

"Millie—"

Heat flew up her neck to her face, probably turning her a bright pink. "I'm at the end of my cycle. Tampon, you know?" She coughed. "Besides the blood test, the hospital did perform a rape kit. The conclusion was no sexual activity."

Did his shoulders visibly relax? "Did you touch the knife?" he asked.

"I don't remember," Millie whispered. "I must've been drugged. As soon as they took my clothes and gave me these and let me clean up, the chief took me to the hospital to have me checked out. The nurse drew blood."

Scott rubbed his smoothly shaven jaw. The hard cut angle no doubt made jurors swoon. "Do you have any idea how much you drank last night?"

"No, but I usually don't drink much. I would've just had a beer." She shook her head. "Honestly, I can't remember a thing."

"Millie, we need to call in reinforcements for this."

Her head jerked back. "No," she said. "I'm already in enough trouble with the agency; it'll be a miracle if I don't get fired. Just forget all about this." She grabbed his wrist.

He flipped it over and captured her hand. "I'm not leaving you to deal with this alone."

Millie pulled her hand away, surprised at how much she'd wanted to leave it in Scott's warm palm. "Chief?" She stood and walked out into the hallway.

"Yeah, you can go," the chief yelled. "When you were being examined at the hospital, I drove your aunt home. You'd better make sure she rests."

An outside door banged. "Wait a minute here," a man bellowed.

Scott moved to partially block Millie with his body.

"Damn it," the chief muttered, reappearing from his office.

"I got here as fast as I could," Rupert Skinner yelled, his comb-over ruffled.

Scott's back vibrated. "Who are you?"

The chief leaned against the doorframe. "Shalebrook County Prosecutor Rupert Skinner, please meet Scott Terentson, Ms. Frost's attorney from the city. She has decided to remain silent."

No, she hadn't.

Rupert angled his head to look past Scott. "Millie? Can we talk?"

"No," Scott said curtly.

Skinner's beady brown eyes narrowed. "Talk to me, Mills. We go back a long ways, and I can help you here."

Yeah. She knew exactly how Skinner would help. He'd graduated from high school with both her and Clay, and he'd never hidden his interest in her. His advances had gotten so blatant that she'd avoided him completely last time she'd been home for the holidays. "I'm fine. Thanks."

His stringy brown hair stretched over the bald patch on his head, and he'd worn an impressive tailored brown suit. His gaze hardened even more. "Clay was one of my best friends. If you killed him, I will bury you."

Scott took a step toward Skinner.

The chief straightened from his relaxed pose. "That's enough."

"No. I told you not to release her," Skinner snapped. "I flew here from Charleston as soon as I could."

The chief gestured toward the door. "She made bail. Go home and check on Mae, Millie. I'll keep working the case."

"Thanks." She stood and brushed past Scott. His back vibrated like an animal's about to pounce. Then she leaned up and hugged the chief before sidling by Skinner and down the hallway.

Scott followed her, pressing a hand to the small of her back as they walked outside into the cold air.

Millie wearily climbed up into his fancy SUV and sat, her mind roiling and her stomach hurting. The chief never should've called the hotshot from DC. She had to get rid of him. Soon.

A snuffling sounded from the back seat and she turned. "Roscoe," she cried out, barreling over the center console to the back seat to wrap both arms around the dog as he sat up. He licked her face and she buried it in his fur, letting the tears fall. Roscoe was a good-size German shepherd with intelligent eyes and a sweet heart. He let her cry all over him as Scott started the engine and began driving down the main street of quaint River City.

"You don't have to move, Millie," he said. "But you need to give me some sort of directions."

She sniffled and lifted her head, still keeping her hold on the animal as if he could tether her to the planet. "Go two miles and turn right on Birch Road. Follow that for fifteen miles and you'll see another street called Riverfront. Follow that through the trees and turn left at Frost Outfitters." She cleared her throat. "Then you can go. I appreciate the ride, but I know you're busy in DC." Screwing up people's lives.

"I'm not leaving you while you're charged with murder," he bit out.

"Yes, you are." She was so done arguing with him. Then she leaned back and looked at Roscoe. "What are you doing here?" He licked her chin, almost looking as if he was smiling. She rested against the seat, letting the warm dog comfort her. "Why do you have Roscoe?"

Scott glanced at her in the rearview mirror, his hands large and appearing more than capable on the steering wheel. "Angus and Nari are in Europe, I think Berlin, for some sort of security conference, and they dumped the dog on me."

"Oh, they didn't dump him," she cooed, running her fingers through Roscoe's thick fur. He snuffled in agreement. Usually when Angus dropped Roscoe on one of his friends, he was looking out for that friend and figured they needed companionship. "What's going on with you? Are you having problems?" He had taken a bullet for Angus once, so she could be polite and ask after him.

He took the turn onto Birch Road. "I think maybe you should worry about your own problems right now."

She couldn't argue with that.

The rearview mirror reflected his piercing gaze. "I found it interesting that the chief of police, who arrested you, also gave you a hug when you left the station today."

Did disapproval deepen his tone? "It's a small town," she said softly. "I've known the chief my whole life, but he also had to do the right thing when he saw me covered in the victim's blood. Plus, the Baker family is a powerful one in these parts, and they're going to raise absolute hell."

"I can handle it, Millie, but no more talking to the police or anybody else about this, even if you've known them your whole life." His firm and rather unyielding tone made her bristle, but she couldn't fault his logic.

"I don't need you to handle anything."

Roscoe apparently figured out she was feeling better because he nudged her to the side, flopped all the way down, and put his head in her lap. She obediently began to stroke his head, and he shut his eyes, emitting an odd humming noise. She'd never thought a dog could purr, but this was close enough. "Thank you for not calling Angus or any of the team," she said grudgingly. "I just can't handle anything else right now."

"Totally understand," Scott said. "They're meddlers, and we need a clear path to figure this out. Tell me about you and Clay."

She winced. Discussing Clay Baker held zero appeal. "No."

Scott stiffened. "For the moment, I'm your lawyer, so you might as well bounce ideas off me. Or, to put it more succinctly, start speaking or I'm pulling over until you do talk." His tone had gone dominant hard.

She wasn't up to a fight right now. "Fine. As a nice kid in junior high, Clay turned into a butthead in high school. We dated throughout. He was a big football star and the president of the chess club. Smart guy. When I went to college in Virginia, he went to school in Charleston and eventually became…" She winced. "A lawyer."

"Ah," Scott said. "Became a lawyer, huh?"

She grimaced. "Yeah."

"So that's why you don't like lawyers?"

"It's one of the many reasons," she said curtly. "Plenty of lawyers screwed up my life until I was finally allowed to live where I wanted, which was with my great-aunt." Who had instantly given her tools and encouraged her inquisitive nature and propensity to blow up appliances.

Scott slowed down as a cow crossed the road. "I'm sorry to hear that. Keep going with the story," he ordered.

Whatever. "Clay and I dated on and off through high school and after graduation he asked me to marry him. I said no." She had fallen out of love with him at that point, if she had ever been in love. It made sense that a lost kid trying to find a home had felt stable dating the prom king—for a little while. Ultimately, they grew apart. "He had political aspirations and was an activist for many causes. He was extremely antidevelopment, which I always thought was odd."

"Why is that odd?" Scott asked, his gaze taking in the well-kept homes and large lots on either side of the road.

"His family owns an outfitting business," Millie said. "They run the rivers just like my family. There are a couple of new outfits that want to move in, and my aunt is all for it. The more the better. They'll help the town. But Clay quite publicly spoke out against more development."

Scott jolted and looked over his shoulder before returning his focus to the road. "Your family owns an outfitting business?"

"Yes. We provide guided fishing tours as well as whitewater rafting trips. There are a lot of rivers around here, and you can get to the New River in just fifteen minutes if you want a really spectacular experience."

Scott remained quiet for several moments.

"What?" Millie challenged. "You think I came from London?"

"Well, yeah. I figured you were raised by Scotland Yard to become the next Q," he murmured.

Quartermaster was pretty much her hero. "I was obsessed with James Bond books," she said. "But I've always had a knack for gadgets. You know, for sensors and bugs and everything in between. When I was a kid, I took apart all appliances in my vicinity, from toasters to engines to...well, the air conditioning unit at a hotel in Disneyland. Boy, did I get in trouble."

Scott chuckled. "I can just see you getting in trouble at Disneyland, Tinker Bell."

She blinked. "Tinker Bell?"

"Yep." He took the next turn, and the countryside turned to forest as he kept driving next to the local river. Soon they arrived at Frost Outfitters and he turned past the main lodge to a quaint white clapboard house with wind chimes tinkling in the wind. "This is where you grew up?"

"Mostly," she said, opening the door and allowing Roscoe to leap out. The dog ran to the frost-covered grass and started marking his territory. Scott exited the vehicle and looked around. Two fishing boats and a couple of rigs parked next to the bunkhouse.

"Do you know how to fish?" he asked.

"Yes, Scott," she said patiently. "I moved here when I was eleven. I know how to fish." Oh, for goodness' sake, it probably didn't fit her image as the gadget girl, but not only could she fish, she could guide.

He breathed deep. "What's the deal with Rupert Skinner?"

"He's a lowlife who most likely would've made me an offer that involved sex." She winced. "He and Clay were best friends, but he always made passes at me. His ego is fragile, and he'll be out for blood now that he knows I won't accept his help."

The front door of the bunkhouse opened and JT strode out.

Scott instantly put his body between Millie and her brother.

JT looked at Scott, glanced at Millie, then looked back at Scott. "Who the fuck are you?"

Chapter Four

Scott Terentson immediately took the measure of the man in front of him. The guy was dangerous—there was no question. Chilling shadows lingered in his eyes. He stood a few inches taller than six feet, his body broad and sharply muscled. He had dark hair, rather familiar blue eyes, and a scar that cut from one cheekbone across his mouth and down his neck. Although appearing unarmed, he looked as if he could take on a bear if necessary. Scott cocked his head and waited, not about to answer the rude question.

"JT," Millie protested, nudging Scott to the side and stepping up, her gaze appraising. "I know you've been gone a long time, but that is no way to greet a guest."

JT looked from Millie and up to Scott. "What kind of training do you have?"

Scott let his eyebrows rise and still didn't answer.

"JT—" Millie stomped her foot. "Knock it off right now. Where have you been anyway? I've been calling you."

The mysterious JT lifted one shoulder, his gaze remaining on Scott. "I went camping for the night and just got home so I can go pick up Aunt Mae. Lost my phone, or maybe I forgot it." He frowned. "I don't know."

"You are the worst with that phone." Millie threw her hands up. "The chief brought Aunt Mae home, according to him. But I haven't seen her yet." She took a deep breath. "Scott Terentson, please meet my brother, JT Frost. JT, this is Scott, who's a lawyer the chief called because I was in jail for the night."

JT's gaze immediately swept to his sister. "The chief arrested you? Why?"

She seemed to be biting the inside of her cheek. "It's a long story, and if you hadn't lost your phone, you would know all about it."

Scott looked from one to the other. They had the same blue eyes and that was about it. JT appeared to be a good five years older or perhaps more, but the hollowness in his eyes made it difficult to determine.

The tough-looking man scanned his surroundings as if seeking threats. "Whoa," he said, holding up a hand. "Now wait a minute. You have to catch me up here. Last night after dinner, you planned to have a drink with June Barbary at Snarky's. After being at the hospital all day with Aunt Mae, I had to get out of there, Mills."

"I know," she said, softening. She glanced at Scott. "Recently discharged from the military, JT doesn't like to be around people too much."

It was more likely that people didn't want to be around JT, but Scott kept that thought to himself. He walked forward, holding out his hand. "It's nice to meet you."

"All right." JT shook his hand, his gaze going to Roscoe, who circled the front lawn. "Did you get a dog, Mills?"

"No," Millie said. "Sort of. I work with a team in DC sometimes, and Roscoe kind of owns the team." She cut a look at Scott. "I don't think it's accurate to say that Angus or anybody on the team owns Roscoe."

"Totally agree," Scott said easily. Roscoe did what Roscoe wanted when he wanted. "If you bring him inside, we have to make sure the liquor cabinet's locked."

JT looked at his sister. "The dog drinks booze?"

At the word, Roscoe yipped and ran over to JT, where he planted his butt, looking up expectantly. JT stared at the dog. "Huh."

"He's got a little problem," Millie said.

JT reached down and scratched Roscoe behind the ears. "Alcohol's really bad for dogs."

"We know. That's why we keep it away from him. Though, to be honest, sometimes he secures a bottle anyway." She leaned forward. "He also has a slight problem with high heels," she whispered.

JT ruffled Roscoe's fur, making the dog lean into him more. "Lots of dogs eat shoes."

"No, he likes to wear them," Scott said.

"Huh," JT said again. That seemed to be his main mode of communication. "Back to you being in jail for the night. Did you get in a bar fight?"

Millie shoved her hands through her curls, making them even wilder. "No. Apparently somebody killed Clay Baker, and I was kind of found in his bed covered in blood with my specialty fishing knife next to me."

Oddly enough, JT's expression didn't change. He didn't even twitch. "If you killed him, let me know. We'll have to make provisions for you to get out of town."

"I didn't kill him." Millie threw both hands up. "Seriously, JT. Get a grip."

JT flicked his gaze up at Scott. "Did you kill him?"

"No," Scott said. "Did you?"

JT stood straighter and scratched beneath his jaw. "No. If I had, I sure wouldn't have left my blood-covered sister with him." That actually made sense. "A lot of people wanted him dead," JT said thoughtfully. "Did you go home with him?"

"I don't remember," she said.

For the first time, JT's gaze sharpened. "Were you drugged?"

She paled. "I think so, but we're waiting to hear the results from the hospital. They tested for everything."

"Huh. Call me the second you hear. For now, I'll take that fishing charter group out this afternoon. They should be here in about half an hour." He looked at Scott. "You staying for a while?"

"No," Millie said.

Scott had no idea. "Just until we figure this out."

JT looked at his sister. "Is he a good lawyer?"

Scott stared at the pixie. Would she lie?

She kicked a pebble. "Yes." Though she made it sound like a bad thing.

"Good." With that, JT turned on his heel and prowled toward the boats on the other side of the bunkhouse.

Scott glanced at Millie. "Your brother, huh?"

"Yep," she said.

His phone buzzed and he opened an email from one of his associates. "Ah, crap," he muttered.

She stiffened. "What now?"

He forced himself to meet her gaze. "We made the *DC Tribune* already—thanks to the Werner Dearth divorce case."

She kicked a pebble. "Fantastic. I'm sure my bosses will love that. What's the headline?"

He scrolled down to read. "HDD sets up husband in contentious divorce."

Millie let her head fall back. "Please say it doesn't name me."

He scanned the article, his gut churning. "It names us both, hints that we're doing the nasty, and ties you to Angus Force and his team. The article is partially positive about the team and their recent wins, but it does make note that they've been banished to an office outside of DC." This sucked. There wasn't anything litigious in the article, but it certainly painted them both in a bad light. "This is a gossip rag, Millie."

"I know, but everyone reads it." She visibly steeled her shoulders. "That's a problem for another day. I can only handle one at a time, Scott. Thank you for your help."

It was a clear dismissal.

So Scott had no choice but to set his stance. "Roscoe and I are staying here at least for the next couple of days. You need a lawyer, and Roscoe could use some country time."

Roscoe's ears twitched, and he turned to look at the house.

Millie crossed her arms over her chest. God, she was cute—and mad. Yet somehow it looked as if the green streaks in her hair had faded, as if the light was wisping out of Millie Frost. "I don't need a lawyer." Her eyes spit fire, but her tone rang hollow.

"The hell you don't." Scott shook his head. "Get on board or I'm calling in reinforcements." Yeah, he'd resort to blackmail if necessary.

The door opened and a diminutive woman walked outside. "Millie?"

"Aunt Mae." Millie rushed across the lawn and hugged the woman. "I'm sorry I wasn't there to bring you home."

Her aunt turned to study Scott as he walked across the grass to reach them. "Hello."

"Hi." He gave her his most charming smile. Or at least the smile his mom liked best. "I'm Scott."

"Mae." She held out a gnarled hand; her handshake was brisk and strong.

He kept his hold gentle as he studied the woman. She had Millie's blue eyes and stature, and light blue streaks ribboned through her curly white hair. Her flowered shirt and jeans were well worn and clean, and her back straight. A sweet smile lit her face, giving life to her papery skin. "Are you Millie's boyfriend?"

Millie made a gagging sound.

Scott tried not to take offense. "No, ma'am. I'm her lawyer. She needs one right now."

"I know." Mae's eyes widened. "The chief told me all about it on the way home."

"I do not require the services of a lawyer," Millie hissed through clenched teeth.

Roscoe wandered over and sat, looking expectantly up at Mae.

"Hello." Mae dropped to her haunches and scrubbed her hands through the thick fur on the dog's neck. "My, you're a handsome one."

Roscoe panted happily.

Millie patted her aunt's shoulder. "You should be resting."

"I'm fine. The stent made it all better. The chief said you need a lawyer," Mae said, still smiling at the dog. Then she looked up at Scott. "Are you any good?"

"I am," Scott said. The older woman was as enthralling as her niece.

Mae kissed Roscoe's nose and stood. "Do you accept payments? Like monthly?"

His heart warmed. "No payment necessary. Millicent and I work together with a team in DC, and this is a professional courtesy."

Mae's eyes narrowed. "Do you have an ulterior motive?"

Scott cocked his head, glanced at Millie, then focused back on Mae. "I really don't know. I mean, she's beguiling and gorgeous, but she's pretty prickly," he said thoughtfully. "Plus, she truly hates lawyers, and I am one." He had a feeling Mae could see past most baloney, so he saw no reason to hide the truth. "But she does need help, and I'm not leaving until I make sure the wild pixie isn't locked up."

Mae grinned, revealing a dimple in her left cheek. "I like you."

Millie groaned.

Scott matched her smile. "I like you, too."

"Good. Please stay and help my girl, even if she's not being properly thankful."

Scott's grin widened. "I would be delighted to be of assistance."

"Darn it." Millie turned and stomped into the house.

* * * *

Millie finished making sandwiches for her and Scott as Roscoe flopped on the country-kitchen floor, looking up at a couple of empty wine bottles holding dried flowers atop the fridge. "Those are empty," she said. She loved her aunt's kitchen. The walls were faded yellow, the floor natural wood, and the kitchen table handmade by her father years ago, before his death when she was only two years old.

Scott finished barking orders into his phone; it sounded like he was handing over almost all of his cases to his associates.

"I don't want you to give up your life for me, even though you did screw up my promotion." She'd needed that to help out her aunt financially. Even so, she found herself reluctantly impressed by how evenly Scott had dealt with her brother earlier. Most people couldn't look JT in the eye. Scott had not only watched him carefully, he'd extended his hand in friendship. That took strength.

"I can stay a few days and help you," he said easily, taking a drink of iced tea and looking around. "I like your house."

She placed the sandwiches on the cedar table, happy that Aunt Mae had finally agreed to rest for a while. "Don't tell me. It's cozy."

"Cheerful, I was thinking," he murmured. "What's the story with your brother?"

Millie sat and reached for her iced tea. "He's a little cranky."

"I noticed," Scott said dryly.

It felt weird having Scott Terentson eating lunch in her sweet country home. The guy could probably get a table at any high-end restaurant right now. Unlike her. She still wore the baggy clothing she'd borrowed at the police station. It felt like too much effort to go change.

"You grew up here with your aunt?" Scott took a man-size bite of the ham sandwich.

She probably did owe him some sort of background information. "Yeah—she's our great-aunt. My parents died in a helicopter accident on vacation in Hawaii when I was two and JT was seven," she said softly. "We were shuffled around for years because Aunt Mae was older, single, and usually broke. Finally, when nobody else would take us, Aunt Mae won and raised us both."

Scott's eyebrows rose. "So Mae runs this whole outfit herself?"

Millie nodded. "She hires help during the busy season, but she's always done it herself. I'm hoping now that JT has been discharged, he'll want to take over the business, but so far, he seems moody and undecided. We grew up helping in summers during college. Even now, I take a vacation during parts of the summer when Aunt Mae needs more bodies."

"Fascinating. I never would have thought that you liked the outdoors."

She chuckled, her body finally relaxing. "I love the outdoors, but I also love gadgets. So it's worked out."

"Your aunt didn't have to give me the spare bedroom," he said. "I know it's a small house. I don't want to move JT out."

"Oh no, JT doesn't stay in the main house. He likes sleeping under the stars, and only sleeps in the bunkhouse during rough weather. He actually doesn't like being inside very often."

To his credit, Scott didn't ask any more questions. Which was good because Millie figured if JT wanted Scott to know his story, he'd tell it himself. Her phone buzzed and she pulled it out of the heavy sweats.

"Millie Frost," she answered.

"Hey, Mills, it's the chief."

She put down her glass, the hair on her arms rising. "Oh, hi Chief," she said. "Did you get the results from the hospital?"

"I did. They didn't find anything in your blood."

Her shoulders dropped. "I was afraid of that."

"Yeah, me too," he said. "You still might have been drugged with GHB—it exits the body very quickly."

"I know," Millie said. "I've researched the drug before. There's a chance it could be in my hair, but there's also a chance it won't be."

The chief coughed. "I wouldn't waste time being tested since it's so late, but it's up to you. We'll figure out who killed him, Millie. I'm on it. But for now, you stay low and keep away from the Baker family. You understand me?"

"Gladly," she said.

"Also, be careful. Um, say hi to Mae for me." He ended the call.

Millie stared at the phone. Say hi?

Scott finished his sandwich. "I take it that was bad news?"

"There wasn't any trace of any drug in my blood."

He placed his paper napkin on the plate. "That doesn't mean you weren't drugged."

"I know," she said. "I had to have been drugged, because I don't remember anything."

Scott scratched his neck. "You could call Wolfe or Dana," he suggested, mentioning two of their Deep Ops colleagues. "They were drugged a while back, remember?"

"Yeah. I don't want to call Wolfe." She chewed on her lip.

"Probably smart," Scott agreed. "If you called him, he'd be here instantly, pregnant fiancée in tow. I'm uncertain whether he and JT would see eye to eye."

That could be a disaster, actually. So far, she was impressed that JT and Scott seemed to be getting along. For now, anyway. "I'm quite certain they wouldn't."

"All right," Scott said. "So who's this June that JT said you planned to meet for a drink?"

"June Barbary works at the Rapid Water Diner. We grew up together, and whenever I'm home, we hang out."

He reached down to scratch Roscoe behind the ears. "Let's start with her, then I want to retrace your steps from all day yesterday."

"I can do that." Millie tried to find her balance. Perhaps changing into her own clothes would help.

Movement sounded outside, and Millie craned her neck to look out past the flimsy curtains. A group of young women, all wearing bright pink sweatshirts, had just arrived with their fishing poles. JT strode to meet them to prepare for the expedition.

She needed to peruse the schedule to make sure that she didn't have work to do the next day.

"Are you in direct competition with the Bakers?" Scott asked.

"Yes." She fought a shiver. "His family is full of jerks. They'll be coming for me." How was she going to keep JT from destroying them the second they did?

Scott texted something into his phone.

"What are you doing?"

"I'm having a background check performed on them, on your friend June, and on your brother."

She sat straighter. "Leave my brother out of this. I mean it, Scott."

He stared at her. "If you say so." He texted something with his left hand, eyeing the rest of her sandwich.

She nudged the plate across the table. "Go ahead. I'm not very hungry."

"Thanks." He took the sandwich.

Roscoe looked imploringly at Millie. She reached for a little bit of the ham on the counter to toss to him. He snatched the piece out of the air easily.

"Softy," Scott said quietly.

"He's too sweet." She wanted to find amusement or even pleasure in the fact that she had gotten the city lawyer into the country to feed him a plain old ham sandwich. But the man seemed to be enjoying the simple meal, and he appeared more relaxed than he had the last several times she'd seen him.

Her abdomen warmed and instinct whispered down her back, the same feeling of excitement she felt when she found a new gadget without any directions.

Dread soon followed.

Chapter Five

As Scott stepped through the doors of the Rapid Water Diner behind Millie, warm, buttery air scented with fried bacon and freshly brewed coffee blasted him. Even though he'd eaten a sandwich only an hour before, his stomach rumbled.

She waved at a gray-haired woman behind the counter and walked to the right, past the vintage cream-colored booths, to one in the back. "June said she'd meet us here for a late lunch."

He gently reached for Millie's arm to make sure she slid into the booth first so he could put his back to the wall, and his gaze to the door. He instinctively clocked every entrance and exit out of habit in case they needed to leave quickly. The cozy place highlighted picture upon picture of fish on the walls. All different-size trout, sturgeon, and bottom feeders. No doubt they had all been caught in the nearby river. Some of the photographs had faded with age, and some appeared brand-new. Black frames surrounded each photograph.

He glanced at the other patrons, scouring for any sort of threat. An older couple sat in the booth down the way, and a lone writer scribbled in a notebook on a light pink bar stool in front of the counter.

The older woman bustled around the counter and delivered two sweating plastic glasses of water. "Millie, I'm so sorry about Clay. But he was a bonehead who deserved it." She leaned in, her eyes wide behind bottle-thick glasses. "I called the chief and said you stayed most of the night at my house."

Millie sighed. "Betty, that's so sweet, but we shouldn't lie to the chief."

Betty straightened her lemon-yellow uniform and patted Millie on the shoulder. "If necessary, Bob, Mart, Joshi, and I will tell the chief we stabbed Clay. They can't convict us all." She turned and sashayed behind the counter to wipe it down.

Scott just looked at Millie.

She shrugged. "Small town. I've been jury-rigging everything from air conditioning units to CPAP machines for folks my entire life."

"Who are Bob, Mart, and Joshi?"

"Two cooks and a handyman." She grinned. "They would confess, I'm afraid."

He had to stop this nonsense in its tracks. "Betty?"

Betty tossed the dishrag on the counter and brought a water pitcher over, even though their glasses remained full. "Hi," she whispered. "Should I confess?"

"No," Scott said firmly. "In addition, would you please spread the word that everyone just needs to tell the truth? It'll make it easier for the chief to find the actual killer."

Betty patted Millie's shoulder again. "Nobody would blame you if you had stabbed him, honey. That jerk kind of deserved it, right?"

Millie winced. "I didn't stab him."

"That's good. You keep saying that." Betty nodded vigorously, sending her short gray hair spiraling. "You never want to confess. It's good you have yourself a hotshot lawyer." She winked at Scott.

Was heat climbing into his face? "I'll do my best," he said.

"Good boy." She turned and hustled around the counter to refill the coffee carafe.

"Hey there." A younger woman bustled up with a spot of ice cream on her yellow uniform, her badge declaring her to be June. "You guys want anything to eat before I sit down?"

"Coffee?" Scott asked.

Millie shook her head. "No caffeine for me. How about a 7UP?"

"Great." June moved away.

Scott watched her go. She stood to about six feet tall with bright red hair and a smattering of freckles across her face with mellow brown eyes. She and Millie couldn't look more different. "How long have you known June?"

"For years," Millie said. "We've been best friends from the day I moved in with Aunt Mae. Her parents own the diner, and I think she's going to take it over from them. You'll like her, Scott."

"I'm sure." He couldn't imagine not liking a friend of Millie's. Well, except her brother. The jury was out on that one.

Millie looked over his outfit. "You didn't have to change to come to town."

The hell he didn't. "I'm much more comfortable, believe me." He kept a go bag in his vehicle at all times, and he'd changed into faded jeans and a comfortable, light green T-shirt. "It seems like, lately, my suits feel constricting." He paused. What prompted him to share that with her? She had enough to worry about.

"Just lately, or since you were shot?" she asked wisely.

Sometimes he forgot her brilliance. "I don't know. I think I felt unsettled even before taking that bullet," he admitted. But spending months in the hospital certainly didn't help. In fact, sometimes he could barely stand to be indoors. He suddenly felt a kinship with the mysterious JT.

"All righty." June hurried back, put a soda in front of Millie and a strong-smelling cup of coffee in front of Scott. She nudged Millie with her hip and sat next to her when Millie scooted over.

He held out a hand. "Hi, I'm Scott."

"I'm June." They shook. June sighed and looked over at Millie. "So, I've already heard."

"Oh, I'm sure." Millie took a drink of her soda. "The gossip is always all over town." She looked up at her friend. "Are you going to ask me?"

June leaned to the side and fetched a cup of coffee off the counter. "Of course not. I know you didn't murder that moron. I mean, seriously, if you had, you never would've stayed around all covered in blood."

"I appreciate that," Millie said dryly.

Scott cleared his throat. His chest ached right where the bullet had pierced his flesh. "What happened last night, June?"

June looked around. "You know, I'm not sure. We went to Snarky's. We played pool and darts, and we had a couple of drinks and some chicken wings, and everything was going fine. Clay and his brother Silas came in, and we decided to leave. But then, he asked to talk to you."

"He did?" Millie sat back, her jaw going slack.

"Yeah." June took a deep swallow of the coffee. "So you guys went over to the bar and you talked for a while. It was really weird." She placed the half-empty cup on the counter. "I hung out with Silas a little bit, but that guy's such a buffoon. I finally came up to you and said I wanted to leave."

Millie paled. "Please tell me I didn't want to stay with him."

"No, you didn't. He tried to get you to stay, but we walked to the door. Then Valerie and Verna came in."

Millie rubbed her left eye. "Valerie and Verna were there?"

"Who are Valerie and Verna?" Scott finished his coffee.

"They're twins about our age. It was always the four of us growing up. They still live in town," Millie said. "We were all friends in high school, and we keep in touch somewhat."

June nodded. "Yeah. In fact, since you're in town, you can come to Verna's baby shower next Saturday. I mean, once this whole mystery is solved."

Millie took a deep breath. "Verna is pregnant with their third, and she's hoping this one is a girl."

Scott didn't need the background. "What happened after the twins came into the bar?"

June twisted her coffee cup. "Valerie said she had an idea for some sort of medical device invention and wanted to pick your brain, Millie, and I needed to go home. You decided to stay with the twins for a little while. Verna said she had to leave by ten thirty and would give you a ride." June's eyes filled. "I'm so sorry. I never would've left you, but you seemed fine."

Millie definitely would've stayed if Valerie had an idea for an invention. She loved to work with friends creating new gadgets.

"That's all you know about the evening?" Scott asked, staring at June.

June tapped her fingers on the table. "Yes. Although, I *might* remember Millie coming home with me. I mean, if I needed to remember that."

Scott's chin dropped. "How about we all stick to the truth?" Was the entire town going to cover for the pixie? They would just screw up his case.

Millie touched June's arm. "How about you? Did you forget anything or have any memory lapse?"

"No," June said. "I went home, practiced yoga for a while, and went to bed. I figured you would reach home safely and we'd meet up again today. I'm so sorry." She put an arm around Millie.

"Have you seen much of Clay Baker?" Scott asked.

June leaned into Millie. "Oh no. He lives and practices law in Charleston. I know he comes home every once in a while, but I was surprised to see him last night at the bar."

"Tell me about his brother, Silas." Scott tried to form a complete picture in his head.

"He runs the outfitting business," Millie said. "They're located a few miles down the river from us. There are two other brothers. Lonnie works at the business and Glen is living in Richmond, I think."

Maybe the murder had to do with a family squabble over the business. "So, we have two brothers here." Scott pictured different scenarios. "And Clay, who often visits. Does Glen visit?"

"Not very often," June said. "I think they had some sort of falling-out and he went on his way."

"Hey, Millie?" a deep voice bellowed.

Scott partially turned to see a square-shaped bald man poke his head out from the kitchen. He wore a chef's apron and had a knife in his hand.

"Hey, Bob," Millie called out. "Smells great in here."

"Good. I just wanted to make sure you knew that I borrowed your fishing knife. The one with all the gadgets in it," Bob said.

Scott leaned his head back. These townspeople were going to be the end of him. "The same one that was used to murder Clay Baker?"

"Probably," Bob said, smiling and revealing a cracked tooth. "In fact, I think Mart might've borrowed it as well. When we get right down to it, most of the fishermen in town have tried that knife at one time or another."

"Thanks, Bob," Millie said weakly.

Scott shook his head.

She grimaced. "I know. I'll spread the word about telling the truth. The last time I saw that knife, it was in one of our fishing boats. It's true anybody could've gotten their hands on it."

That actually was good news.

Maybe Scott was on the right track. Anticipation at solving a mystery, a new feeling for him these days, rushed through his veins. He typed into his phone.

"Don't tell me, more background checks?" Millie murmured.

"Yeah, more background checks." He sighed. "We need to find Verna and Valerie."

June pulled a phone from her pocket. "I'll text them. Hopefully they can head down soon, and I'll sweeten the pot with free pie."

Scott smiled. "Thanks, June."

Something flashed in Millie's eyes and her chin lifted. Was that jealousy? Then they went blank.

Interesting. Very.

Chapter Six

Millie jumped out of Scott's fancy SUV in the dirt parking lot of Snarky's and walked up to the green metal door. With its weathered, wooden siding bearing murals of various fish, the bar had served as the main watering hole in the small town for generations. She knocked on the door.

Scott stalked up to her side, protecting her from the blustering wind. March was always chilly in West Virginia, and she should have brought a heavier coat. Instead, she'd just worn jeans, cowboy boots, and a green sweater that matched the streaks in her hair.

No sound came from within the establishment.

"It looks like they're closed," Scott said.

Millie rapped harder against the metal. "Oh, he's here."

"Let me." Scott leaned over her and pounded on the door, much louder and harder than she had. His scent of coffee and freshly cut oak washed over her skin. She'd recognize him anywhere without having to look. In fact, the first time they'd met, she'd dreamed of coffee for a week. Her abdomen rolled over slowly, and for a brief second, she thought about turning into his heat.

"Geez, what's the noise?" an irritated voice bellowed right before the door swung out.

Millie stepped back, and Scott instantly shifted her to the side, positioning his body in front of her.

"It's okay, Scott," she said. "This is Buck." She waited until Buck emerged into the cloudy day. "Buck, this is Scott. Scott, Buck."

Buck held out a hand to shake. "I've heard you were arrested," Buck said as Scott shook his hand, still watching him carefully.

"Yes." Millie looked up at the sixty-year-old bartender. She knew his exact age because the town had thrown a big bash for him last July. While he might be sixty, he looked about eighty, with his bald head, slightly stooped shoulders, and big belly. His kind eyes were a mixture of green and blue, and there were more liver spots on his hands than there had been the year before.

"I didn't kill anybody, Buck," she said.

"I figured." He turned and stomped back into the darkened interior of the bar. Scott cut her a look but then gestured her ahead of him. She walked inside to see bottle caps still littering the floor and boxes of alcohol on the top of the bar. To the far left pool tables and dartboards took up opposite corners. The bar lacked the space for a dance floor, but nobody seemed to mind.

"Did you see Millie here last night?" Scott asked.

Buck strode around the bar to begin opening the boxes. "Of course I saw her here last night. You're the lawyer, right?"

Scott lifted an eyebrow.

Millie whispered, "Small town."

"Ah," Scott murmured. "Yes, I'm the lawyer."

Buck crossed his arms. "How did he pass JT's tests?"

"There were no tests. I'm a grown woman and I can take care of myself, Buck," Millie said, the words ringing hollow in her head considering she'd been arrested for murder.

"Humph." Buck reached for a rag and wiped down the counter by the ice machine. "Even for a lawyer, you must be all right. No matter what Millie says, if JT had gotten a bad feeling from you, you'd be in the river right now." His gaze lifted. "Not swimming."

Oh, for goodness' sake. JT did seem a little darker lately, but he'd be himself again soon. Millie moved toward the bar and hopped up on one of the many green stools. Her memory remained a dark hole, and nausea rolled up from her stomach. Why couldn't she remember a darn thing? Scott felt like a solid wall of protection at her back, and she felt way too much pleasure in that fact. "I drank here last night. Did you see me interact with anybody?"

"Sure." Buck pulled out several bottles of Jack Daniels. "You and Junie hung together for a while. She left. You spoke with the twins. Valerie drank vodka and Verna club soda, 'cause she's pregnant again. Sure miss her working here." Then he pursed his lips. "That's all I know."

Millie picked at a scar on the wooden bar. "I'm sure Verna will return to work."

"She left during the holidays, and I needed her," Buck burst out. "We were slammed. She was always so cranky."

Millie didn't have time for this old argument but had to defend Verna. "She's pregnant, Buck."

Buck threw a hand carelessly in the air. "So? She's an excellent waitress, and they need the money. She could at least have worked through the season."

It was too bad that Buck couldn't get knocked up. Millie fought the urge to box his ears, mostly because she needed information. "Last night, did you see me speaking with Clay?"

"Yeah. You two talked right here for a few minutes. I couldn't hear what you were saying, but he looked earnest, which meant he was full of shit."

She forced a laugh when she wanted to put her head down and cry. Having an entire night lost to her was terrifying. "Yeah, I know. What did I look like?"

Scott waited silently behind her, providing that comfort and protection again.

Buck tossed the empty box into the corner and reached for the next one. "You looked more irritated than anything. It was the same expression you always had when you two were together. There was a fight over by the pool tables and I went and broke it up."

"Who was in the fight?" she asked.

"I don't know, a couple of out-of-towners who'd arrived early for the Fishing Derby." He opened the box. "They were arguing over some pool game. I tossed their asses out."

That sounded like a normal night. "Considering it was St. Patrick's Day, did I drink very much?" Millie asked.

"Not really. You had a beer with June and then you had a beer later on. You seemed fine to me, Millie. When I came back to the bar, you were gone." He looked down, his face flushed. "I honestly didn't think anything of it, but if that dimwit drugged you, I'd have killed him myself."

She patted his gnarled hand, unsurprised that the rumor of her being drugged had already reached the townsfolk. "You're not to blame."

"Did the twins remain at the bar late?" Scott asked.

Buck looked to the side, as if trying to remember. "I don't remember. I mean, it was St. Patrick's Day and we were slammed. I'll ask around for you, though, Millie."

"Thank you." She released his hand, making a mental note to bring him ointment for the liver spots. "I appreciate it."

Buck leaned to stare over her head. "She's not really in trouble, is she?"

Millie looked over her shoulder at the man standing tall as her current bodyguard. Scott's expression revealed nothing. "She could be. So please keep your ear to the ground, and if you find out anything, let us know."

"You've got it," Buck said. "I wish we had security cameras, but they're just too expensive right now. By the way, it's *entirely possible* you had too much to drink and ended up sleeping in the back room here."

She planted both hands on the bar. "They found me with the knife, Buck," she said gently.

"That's just it." He warmed to the subject. "I might've seen Clay with your knife—say he borrowed it and then left. You woke up this morning and I could've told you that Clay had your knife."

He leaned toward her. "So you went over there and maybe the real killer knocked you out with chloroform like on TV." He looked at Scott. "Right?"

"No," Scott said shortly.

Millie patted Buck's hand. "I appreciate it, Buck."

"Just keep my idea in mind," Buck said. "It'll be okay, Millie, I promise."

It was sweet that he was making promises nobody could keep. "Thanks." She hopped off the stool and walked out into the cloudy day with Scott on her heels. "I wouldn't have left with Clay Baker on purpose." She needed him to understand that for some reason.

"I got that impression," Scott said dryly. "Why don't we grab something for dinner, take it to your place, and talk this through?"

She couldn't believe Scott Terentson planned to stay at her house. But Aunt Mae had insisted, and there was no way around that woman. "I guess that's our plan."

Just as she started toward the passenger-side door, a dented gray Ford pickup careened around the corner and shot into the parking area, the driver hitting the brakes so hard they squealed. Two men instantly jumped out of the vehicle.

"Oh crap." She set her stance.

"You bitch," Silas Baker yelled, spittle spraying from his mouth.

"I didn't kill him," Millie said, looking at Clay's brother. Where Clay had been smooth, Silas was coarse. Oh, they both had started out as rough diamonds, but Clay had found some polish.

Silas had not. He stood about six foot four in a large red flannel shirt with a thick black beard matching his hair. He possessed beady eyes and beefy hands. "You slept in his bed all night." Silas's face turned red.

"I didn't kill him." She had to avert the disaster she saw coming as Silas glared over her shoulder at Scott. All of the Bakers were known to hit first and ask questions later. "I don't remember leaving. Somebody drugged me."

His brother Lonnie stomped around the other side of the truck. "Oh, we know you killed him. You've hated him for years."

"That stems from him being a jackass," she said. "But I didn't kill him."

It was the wrong thing to say. Silas immediately shot toward her and she held up her hands to defend herself.

With no warning, Scott nudged her with his hip and instantly stood between her and both men.

"Scott," she yelled, but it was too late.

Silas swung his monstrous fist toward Scott's head. She screamed, and then it was as if Scott became somebody else. He ducked the punch and volleyed a series of hits at Silas's midsection that had the man doubling over in pain and falling back against his truck.

Without even seeming to move, Scott jumped up, pivoted, and kicked Lonnie beneath the chin. Lonnie flew backward and landed hard. Scott performed a backflip in the air and landed on the ground, his stance wide and his body seemingly relaxed.

Silas roared and leaped up, hitting Scott midcenter, lifting him, and ramming him against the solid door. The metal protested with a loud crunch. Scott slammed both elbows down on Silas's shoulders, forcing the mammoth to drop him, then using elbows, fists, and knees, smoothly, almost gracefully, propelled Silas back against his truck. A perfectly executed roundhouse kick nailed Silas in the jaw, throwing his head sideways and slamming his temple against the vehicle with a loud thunk.

Silas dropped to the ground, unconscious.

Lonnie snarled, came up on all fours, and leaped at Scott. Scott, almost casually, looking bored, slammed his elbow on the back of Lonnie's neck. Lonnie flopped on the dirt, his mouth spitting dust.

Then silence.

Millie retreated a step. Her heartbeat thundered in her ears, and her abdomen turned over.

Scott turned around. His wild blue eyes contrasted with his calm expression, and his hands remained loose at his sides. "Are you okay?"

Her mouth gaped open. What in the heavens just went down?

Chapter Seven

Scott drove back to Millie's farmhouse almost in a daze, his mind spinning. Soon, he found himself seated at the comfortable kitchen table again with her looking at his bruised and busted knuckles, the dog snoring at his feet. Apparently the dog's day with JT had tired him out. "I'm not hurt." Scott attempted to catch her gaze.

She leaned down. "I think you hit Silas in the mouth. Do you have any idea how much bacteria is in anybody's mouth, much less a creep like that?"

The humor in her question caught him and he smiled. "I guess I never thought about it."

"Hmm." She moved toward a cupboard next to the pantry. "Let's see." She placed her palm flat against the wall and a panel slid open.

"Hey," he said. "That's pretty cool."

She looked over her shoulder and smiled. "Oh, this whole house is decked out. I'll show you some of it."

He had wondered. She was pretty much the Q of the Deep Ops team, and he had figured she had some fun gadgets of her own. It was yet another engrossing aspect to her personality. "Millie?" he asked. "I hope I didn't scare you." The last thing in the world he wanted to do was frighten her.

She reached far back in the cupboard and drew out bandages and a blue spray can. "I felt no fear." Turning, she walked toward him and took his hand.

Her touch nearly awakened the primal fighter he camouflaged with high-end suits. It was the first time she had really touched him. The sensation burned right through his skin to somewhere deeper, and he fought the real urge of taking her to the floor. "Are you sure?" he asked.

She sprayed the knuckles of his right hand. Pain instantly flared up his arm, but he didn't tense. She leaned over and blew gently on his injuries, and he tensed a lot, his cock jerking wide awake, ready to play. "I figured you were in the JAG Corps in the service," she said, looking up, her eyes an indigo blue.

"No." He shook his head. "I became a lawyer after my honorable discharge." Upon leaving the service, he'd been lost, and instead of burying himself in vodka or drugs, he'd forced his brain to learn something new. The law proved strategic and fascinating, and he had found himself again. Mostly.

"Did you go to school on the GI Bill?" She gently wrapped a bandage across his knuckles to fasten on the edge of his hand.

"No," he said. "I mean, I would have, but I had enough saved up." Truth be told, he had the trust fund of all trust funds. But he sounded like an ass when he said that, so he rarely did.

She leaned back and studied her handiwork. "I probably shouldn't ask, but what did you do in the military?"

He rarely discussed his time in the service, but he didn't want to close her off since she seemed curious. They needed to communicate so he could get her out of this mess. "I was in FORECON, and an expert in amphibious reconnaissance," he said quietly, memories slamming through him, pushing all thoughts of the law out of his brain.

She dropped into a kitchen chair. "You were in the Force Reconnaissance for the marines?"

"Yeah." Her surprise tickled him. "Had a mission go wrong and nearly drowned. If I'm having a nightmare, it's either about that moment or the recent one with my being shot."

"You've been through a lot. Your fortitude is impressive." She looked him up and down. "I figured you were born in a suit."

No need to lie to her now. "Close enough."

"I see." She checked out his other hand, decided it was good enough without intervention, and returned her supplies to the secret cabinet, which shut instantly.

Roscoe sneezed twice on Scott's boot, looked up at him, then shoved himself to all fours. He looked around and wandered over to nudge Millie with his wide head.

She chuckled and rubbed his ears. "You just ate, buddy."

"Why do you have a secret cabinet of bandages?" Scott asked, as curious as ever about her.

She rolled her eyes. "It's not secret. I just like..." Her voice trailed off.

"Contraptions," he supplied.

"Yeah." She walked over to the fridge. "I mean, take this. It looks like an ordinary fridge, right?"

The stainless steel fridge appeared to be just like the one in his ultramodern apartment. The apartment that seemed cold and boring compared to this charming home near the river. "That's a regular-looking fridge," he agreed, knowing it probably was anything but.

She tapped somewhere in the middle of the door and a panel rose.

Roscoe sat, his tail wagging on the wooden floor.

"Very cool," Scott said.

"Oh, you have no idea." She pressed a couple of buttons and blue letters came into view. "My fridge tracks inventory and expiration dates. Not only that, it'll suggest recipes based on what's inside." She looked over her shoulder at him and laughed, the sound musical. "My aunt thought it was crazy for a while. She'll never admit it, but she uses the recipe tracker all the time."

"How do you know?" he asked, enchanted.

She snorted. "I also might have installed a tracking device. So anytime she uses one of the recipes, I get a notice on my phone."

He threw back his head and laughed. "That's terrible."

"I know," she said, covering her mouth, mirth in her eyes.

She was even more likable than he'd thought.

Roscoe nudged her again, nearly knocking her over.

She opened the door and drew out sliced roast beef to give him a bite. He gingerly took the meat from her hand and stomped over to drop it onto Scott's boot, where he sat and began to eat.

Scott didn't bother moving his foot. The dog would just follow him, and Roscoe could outmatch anybody with stubbornness. Plus, it was nice having the animal close, which the dog seemed to somehow realize. "What else have you updated around here?"

"I tweaked the cooktop with a built-in thermometer and timer, and that back burner is the one that, for some reason, ensures the most even heat distribution." She sobered. "In addition, my aunt is getting older, so I have some safeguards in place. This place will never burn down."

Brilliant, sweet, and the woman wore cowboy boots like a pro. Oddly enough, he'd always had a thing for women in cowboy boots. Make them brilliant and more than a little quirky, and he became enthralled. Unfortunately, he felt so screwed up that he'd be an ass to make a move. It was a good thing she'd turned down his offer of dinner months ago. The woman had excellent instincts. "I like that," he said softly.

A pretty pink blush wandered over her cheeks. "I also voice-activated everything from the coffee maker to the dishwasher, which my aunt actually does enjoy," she said. She grabbed his good hand, sending a jolt of electricity up his arm. "Come on. Since I'm revealing at least some of my secrets, let's get you settled in before we bake a pizza."

She tugged him up the stairs, and they turned left at the landing to the guest bedroom. It was quaint with a hand-quilted white-

and-blue coverlet on the bed, flanked by antique oak tables that matched the dresser across the room. The place somehow smelled like violets.

"What do we have?" he asked, truly curious as Roscoe pushed past him, looked around, and jumped onto the bed.

"The bed first," she said.

Scott would not look at the bed, because the last thing he needed right now was to imagine her on it. She didn't need him to add to her stress. "What about the bed?"

She grinned, appearing younger than her twenty-nine years. "It's a smart bed with adjustable firmness settings and temperature regulations." She reached into a drawer and brought out what looked like a small microphone. "Millie Frost, 278345," she said.

"Affirmative, Millie Frost," came an automated voice.

"Here," she said, pointing the microphone at him. "Say your name."

He complied.

"Hello, Scott Terentson," the voice said, sounding a little sexy.

"There you go," Millie said, nearly hopping up and down. "Now you can direct the bed. You can make it as hard or soft, warm or cold as you want. In addition, you can set an alarm so it will gradually wake you up with a slight vibration. There's no loud, blaring sound." She was adorable.

All he could do was nod. "I think I love this bed."

Roscoe spread out, nose on his paws, and closed his eyes.

"I know, right?" she asked. "I tried to get Wolfe to let me install one for him, but he figured it'd be possessed or something."

That sounded like Wolfe. As the body man for the Deep Ops crew, Wolfe took danger to a whole new level. Yet like the rest of them, he had fallen under Millie's spell and would do anything for her.

Millie pointed to what looked like an innocuous bed table. "It's fully loaded. So if you put your phone or anything else that needs to be charged on the surface or in the drawer, it'll be charged by morning."

He grinned. "How convenient."

"In addition"—she pointed to the closet—"if you have clothes that need to be refreshed or unwrinkled, you just put them in there and push the blue button on the inside."

He couldn't believe it. "Anything else?"

She coughed. "Not that I'm going to tell you about...except for in the bathroom. In the guest bathroom, the mirror is a smart mirror with computer access as well as TV. So you can check your emails while you brush your teeth. And"—she rolled her eyes—"I installed a smart toilet. There are even some health monitoring features if you want to check your urine."

"I'm good." He backed away from her.

"That's what I figured," she murmured.

He had never in his life wanted to kiss her more, and he pretty much had wanted to kiss her since the first day they'd met.

"So," she said, rocking back on her heels. "Let's get that pizza going."

"Agreed." He waited for her to leave the bedroom first. Millicent Frost was too appealing and way too close to that bed. She shone with light and brilliance in a small package, and he was as fucked up as it was humanly possible to be. She deserved better than a burnout like him.

He'd protect her from this ridiculous murder charge and then get out of her life. As for his life, maybe he'd leave DC for a while. Perhaps go back to school. Books likely couldn't save him again, but at this point, did he care?

For now, he'd eat pizza with the most spectacular woman he'd ever met.

Chapter Eight

Millie placed the pizza in the middle of the table. While Scott had thought they would order in, if there was one thing she loved to bake, it was pizza.

"This looks amazing." Scott reached over to pour Cabernet into their glasses.

The moment felt intimate, with the wind blasting the windows and the house so warm and cozy. Millie hadn't felt off her game like this in a long time. She couldn't forget the sight of Scott defending her and how powerful he'd been, how dangerous. She never would've imagined the smooth lawyer would be able to fight like that. Oh, she'd never admit it to anybody, but it had been impressive, and frankly, a turn-on.

He looked up. "What are you thinking?"

"Nothing." She hustled to the back door, put two fingers in her mouth and let out a shrill whistle.

"Wow."

She looked over her shoulder and smiled. "What?"

He scanned her, his eyes betraying a spark of amusement. "That's quite the whistle you got there. It's a bit of a surprise."

"Yeah. It's how we communicate on the river."

An answering whistle came back and Scott chuckled. "That was a bit lower than yours. Don't tell me. JT's coming for dinner."

"JT would never miss homemade pizza." She moved to the cupboard to take down another plate.

"Good. I'd like to ask him a few more questions about what's going on in town and who might be here," Scott said, working his case, as always.

She paused. "I don't want you to let your other cases slide just because of me. That wouldn't be fair."

"I'm not. I have good associates, and if I'm needed, I'll drive back to town."

She cleared her throat. "That brings up another issue."

He looked up from pouring the wine. "What issue?"

"I haven't signed a retainer agreement and I need to know what your fee is."

He just looked at her then, his gaze thoughtful and his jaw set hard. "I'm not taking a retainer."

"You are." She leaned back against the counter as she let the cheese cool on the pizza. "Come on. I know that you're a very expensive lawyer, and we're going to be official about this."

"As far as I'm concerned, you're part of the team, Millie."

Her chin lowered. "Neither one of us is really part of the team."

The Deep Ops team was unique and they were a lot of fun, but she'd only been assigned to them for a brief time before her superiors had yanked her onto another case, and Scott just gave legal advice. Well, when he wasn't getting shot.

"We can discuss it later," he said.

She opened her mouth to argue just as the back door opened. JT strode inside, pulling along a smaller woman by the sleeve of her sweatshirt.

"Lila's going to join us," he said gruffly. "Lila? Meet Millie and her lawyer, Scott."

"Hi," Lila said, her voice quiet. "I don't need dinner." The woman ineffectually struggled against JT's hold.

Millie tried really hard to keep her mouth from dropping open. JT wasn't usually such a brute.

"Hi, I'm Millie." She held out her hand.

JT released the woman.

"I'm Lila." Lila looked at Millie's hand and slowly clasped it, shaking quickly and letting go. She had vibrant brown hair cut in a bob, tawny brown eyes, and a scar across her chin. "I've been helping your aunt with the business." She shuffled her feet. Her sweatshirt was overlarge and even her jeans looked baggy; Millie couldn't unobtrusively bend down far enough to double-check, but she was fairly certain Lila was wearing Millie's boots from a couple of seasons ago.

"Oh," she said. "Yes, my aunt mentioned that she had somebody helping out. I'm so glad you're here." Going on instinct, she grasped Lila's hand and pulled her toward the table. "I made pizza. It's my specialty."

The aroma must have hit Lila because a light pink flushed her cheekbones. "It does smell delicious."

"I'm Scott." Scott remained relaxed in his chair and didn't make a move toward Lila, as if instinctually he realized the woman wanted to bolt.

Millie pulled out a chair. "Please, eat with us." Her great-aunt had mentioned that she'd hired a woman to clean the bunkhouse for the upcoming season, as well as to organize a lot of the tackle gear. It certainly wasn't one of JT's skills, and Millie was too busy just now to come help.

Lila sat almost reluctantly, her hands in her lap. Millie cut her brother a look, but he ignored her and took a seat across the table. Was he trying to figure out what Lila was doing working for their aunt? If so, he didn't need to look so deadly sitting at the table.

Roscoe clambered off Scott's feet and lumbered toward Lila, who shrank back, her eyes wide.

"Hey." JT dropped his hand onto Roscoe's head and scratched behind his ears. "Stick with me, big guy."

As if he understood, Roscoe partially turned and leaned into the rub, his tail wagging on the floor and over one of Lila's boots.

The woman moved her feet to the side. Roscoe shoved his butt out, keeping his head beneath JT's vigorous rubbing, and shook his tail faster over both of her boots as if he wanted to include her. She watched him, and a hesitant smile tilted her lips. "I wonder how far he'd chase me with that tail."

"He'd stretch all the way across the kitchen if he could. Roscoe wants everyone to like him," Millie said, fetching two additional wineglasses before taking her seat and starting to dish out the pizza. "So Lila, where are you staying?"

"I'm staying in the cabin on the other side of the big sycamore tree," Lila said, reaching for her pizza and taking a bite. "Oh my gosh, this is amazing."

Her aunt hadn't told her she had rented out the cabin. It was another one that Millie had retrofitted with some special electronics, even though it looked like an ordinary small cabin from the outside. "How's the cabin working for you?" Millie asked. "I had a little trouble with the window shades last time I was home." She had them rigged to automatically move with the sun.

Lila smiled, transforming her face from pinched to pretty. "They're working well. Every once in a while in the middle of the night they spring open." She wiped her mouth with a napkin. "But it's just fun. For a while I thought the place was haunted until your aunt told me about your skills."

Millie smacked her hand against her head. "I'm sorry. I'll be out there to fix them when I can. I also want to take a look at the heated floor. It seemed to be on the blink last time I was home."

"Oh, it's always hot," Lila said, grinning. "I don't mind because it's cold for now. In July, it might be a disaster for whoever is staying there."

JT cocked his head and released Roscoe to reach for his wineglass. "You won't be staying there? I thought Aunt Mae hired you for the entire season?"

Lila reached for her wine and took a deep drink. "We'll see."

Roscoe turned suddenly.

"No!" Millie and Scott said in unison.

Roscoe snorted, looked at JT and then toward Lila for help. When nobody moved to share their wine, he sneezed, farted, and dropped onto his belly.

"I think he did that on purpose," JT mused.

"Definitely," Millie agreed. "Lila, I'll take a look at your floor as soon as I can." There was something wounded about the young woman, and Millie couldn't help but wonder about her taciturn brother's obvious distrust of the pretty brunette.

JT ate quietly as he always did. He finished his second piece and then looked up. "Mills, by the way, the clouds are parting if you wanted to look at the stars tonight."

It had been so long since she'd had a chance to look at the stars. She caught her breath. "I didn't know that. It looked to me like another storm was coming in."

He shook his head. "It'll pass. It'll be clear about ten tonight. Just thought I'd let you know."

"You like the stars?" Scott asked.

Some of the best times in her life had been sleeping beneath the stars with her brother around a campfire. He'd spent hours teaching her about the constellations, and she'd retrofitted a special telescope just for him. "Yes. We have a telescope."

"Don't tell me." Scott lifted a hand. "One that you tweaked?"

"Of course." She grinned. "I have star-tracking software on the telescope. It's pretty cool."

Scott's gaze warmed, and in response, her body heated wildly. "I have no doubt," he said.

JT, as usual, had been mostly silent through dinner. Finally, he focused on Scott. "What happened to your face and your knuckles?"

Millie looked closer. She hadn't really noticed, but a slight bruise darkened the area beneath Scott's left eye. The contusion would turn purple by the next day. She angled her head to study his neck to see three more bruises. Somehow she hadn't seen him get punched, but he had taken a fist or two.

"I had a run-in with Silas Baker and his brother Lonnie," Scott said easily.

JT sat back, his shoulders seeming to widen. "You had a run-in with the Bakers?" He looked Scott over, his gaze appraising. "You're still standing. How are they?"

"Unconscious." Scott shrugged.

JT just stared at him, but a new glint entered his eyes. Was that admiration or respect? Either way, it was an expression Millie wasn't used to seeing in her brother's eyes for any man she brought home. "Where are you from, Lila?" she asked, trying to defuse some of the tension.

Lila coughed and took a drink of her wine. "Denver. I was merely passing through town and chose to stay awhile."

"Really?" Millie asked. Now that was odd. Knowing her great-aunt, she'd taken Lila in instantly without asking a question.

"You don't sound like you're from Denver," JT said gruffly.

Lila jolted. "Well, I am."

Interesting. Sometimes people didn't want to talk about their past, and Millie understood that. She wished she hadn't dated Clay Baker all through high school.

JT looked at her. "Do we know who killed Baker yet?"

"No, and bloodwork revealed no evidence of drugs in my system, though I'm certain somebody did drug me." She still couldn't remember a thing, and she lacked injuries.

"You were definitely drugged." JT agreed with her silent contemplation. "Or you'd remember the entire evening."

"I know."

Scott finished his pizza and put his napkin on his plate. "Do you have any idea who'd want to kill Clay Baker?"

JT's gaze narrowed. "Pretty much anybody who ever met the asshole, if you ask me. I haven't been around for a couple of years, so I wouldn't know the gossip. I did hear earlier today at the hardware store that the brothers were in some sort of dustup over the family business."

"What's the gossip?" Millie asked quickly.

"There was a fight down at Snarky's Bar about two weeks ago," JT said. "The town was buzzing about it, apparently."

"I guess we start there," Scott said.

Lila placed her napkin, folded neatly, on her plate. "Thank you for dinner. You're a phenomenal cook." She stood.

JT instantly stood as well. "I'll walk you to your cabin."

"No, thanks. I'm good." Lila smiled at Millie and walked to open the door.

"Too bad," he said, following her out the door.

Scott looked at Millie. "That was interesting."

"I would say so." Millie stared at the still open door. "JT doesn't trust anybody, and he's overprotective when it comes to Aunt Mae."

As if on cue, JT poked his head back in the door. "Hey, I need you to cover the 5:00 a.m. guide tomorrow. It's only for three hours."

She blinked. "Sure. Why?"

"I have something to do." With that, he winked, shut the door, and disappeared.

"Your brother's an interesting fellow," Scott said.

Millie stood to start the dishes, surprised when Scott followed to assist. "I always thought you had a bunch of servants or something."

"No. My mother had a bit of a trust fund, but she was a stickler for hard work." His obvious fondness for his mother softened his words.

"That's sweet." Millie dropped a glass in the soapy water and sighed, reaching around for it.

Scott finished drying a plate. "Let me." He reached in and the bubbles covered his sinewed forearms. "This sink is deeper than most bathtubs."

Their hands met beneath the warm water, and fire zinged through Millie. "Um." She looked up to find him staring down at her, his eyes a glittering cobalt.

He moved then, ducking his head, his lips taking hers.

She sighed, leaning into him, stretching onto her toes. The running water faded to a hum as desire roared through her, pounding in her veins.

He cupped her jaw, his callused fingers rough on her skin, only adding to the multitude of sensations rippling through her. The man tasted of fine wine and impossible promise, and every inch of him was rock hard against her.

An engine started in the distance and she jolted.

Slowly, he opened his eyes and lifted his head, allowing his thumb one smooth swipe across her lips.

She shivered and drew back, only then realizing they were holding hands beneath the soapy water. Her mouth went dry and she hurriedly pulled free.

"I'm sorry." He tugged the glass out of the water and placed it on the counter, a muscle ticking along his neck. "I shouldn't have."

The best kiss of her life ended in an apology? She turned and dried the glass, her body wide awake with firing nerves. Oh, he was probably right that they didn't make sense and the timing sucked.

But that kiss. Oh, she'd dream about that.

Chapter Nine

Water pummeled Scott down to the jagged rocks at the bottom of the cave. He tried to move but couldn't. Excruciating pain tore up his legs to his abdomen, ripping through his skin, digging deep near his heart.

Gasping, he sat straight up in the bed, panting furiously, searching for his weapon. Sweat rolled down his forehead to drop onto the tangled sheets. Fuck, he hated the nightmares. He'd also left his gun in the Bentley. What had he been thinking?

A quick glance at the window proved it was still dark outside. Roscoe, being a brilliant dog, had obviously chosen to sleep with Millie.

The remnants of the nightmare pounded in his head. He'd been on mission in the South China Sea to recover a sunken prototype of a cutting-edge sonar system lost in a naval exercise. Enemy divers moved too close, so he hid behind the wreckage nearly too long, and to this day, could feel the water pressing down on him. Taking several breaths, he slowly pushed his nightmare away.

He swung his legs to the side of the bed and reached for the jeans he'd worn the day before. He had to get Millie straightened out today so he could return to his office, or at least to his closet. He stood, shoved his bare feet into boots, and reached for the sweatshirt Millie had given him the night before; no doubt it belonged to JT.

Silently, he opened the door, walking swiftly down the hallway and stairs to slip quietly out the kitchen doorway.

Heavy clouds rolled across the darkened sky, and he prowled through the dense mist toward the sound of water lapping in a hushed whisper onto the rocky embankment. The smell of a cigar caught him and he paused, turning to see the silhouette of a large man leaning against the bunkhouse.

"You're out early," JT said, taking a deep drag.

"Couldn't sleep," he admitted, stretching his back and moving closer.

In the early hour, JT Frost seemed more comfortable in the shadows than the oncoming light. He wore the same jeans and ratty sweatshirt as the night before.

Scott looked at the cigar.

"Don't tell Millie," JT said, taking another puff. "She gets irritated."

"No worries." Scott shoved his hands through his ruffled hair and turned toward the dark river. Droplets cascaded from the nearby trees, plopping onto moist earth. He hadn't heard it rain, but dampness and mist pervaded the entire world. Of course it was March in West Virginia, so at least the snow had passed. But crap, the cold hit hard. "I take it you couldn't sleep either?" he asked.

"I rarely do," JT admitted. "Millie hasn't told me much about you, but if you took on two of the Baker brothers and are still standing, you must have some training."

"Force Recon," he said quietly, finding the morning to be filled with more tension than he'd hoped. Another storm loomed in the distance.

JT just watched him, puffing on his cigar.

"What about you?" Scott asked, stretching his ankle. It twinged; he must have twisted it slightly in the fight the night before. He'd be fine.

"Navy SEAL," JT said, his tone curt and not inviting any questions.

Not that Scott needed to know additional details. He studied the dark moving water, seeing no answers in its unfathomable depths. Faint light was seeping into the landscape, fighting the mist, and the first sporadic calls of birds began to echo over the moving water.

"There's a guy in town," JT said unexpectedly. "He's somebody you can talk to."

Surprise filtered through Scott. "I'm good. I have somebody at home." Somebody he had spoken with after being shot this last time.

"How long you been out?"

"Long time," Scott said. "I had a handle on everything and then I took a bullet nearly center mass last year. It brought it all back."

"More than likely combined traumas," JT said. "Been there."

Scott hadn't realized he and JT would bond. "Yeah, it's all jumbled up in my head." Sometimes his entire body felt frozen and dull from being trapped under that heavy bulk of water for so long. But he'd survived, and the trauma had ended. Now he needed to get his head on straight.

The mist climbed around them as if alive, coiling toward the trees and shrouding many of the still-dripping branches. The scent of damp earth and the lingering smell of dead fish surrounded them.

"How much trouble is Millie in?" JT asked around the cigar.

"I don't know yet," Scott admitted. "It doesn't look good, especially since the county prosecutor seems to be excited about the case. But I do like that the chief of police believes she's innocent and has a fondness for her." One thing he'd learned during his time in the military and the courtroom was that personal connections meant everything when it came to witnesses.

JT puffed the cigar with intent. "The chief will still do his job."

"So will I. We may need to get a private investigator on this." Scott kicked an iced-over rock. "The Deep Ops team would be the best but they're a lot to handle."

"That's my understanding," JT said. "But if that's what Millie needs, that's what we'll do."

Scott really didn't want to call in the team as of yet. "Agreed— if I deem it necessary. Let's see what we can dig up today. I'm surprised the chief hasn't already found somebody else to look at. It seems a lot of people wanted Baker dead."

"I was one of them," JT admitted. "But if I had killed him, I sure as shit wouldn't have implicated my sister."

Scott hooked his thumbs in his jeans pockets. "You think it was one of his brothers?"

"I don't know," JT said. "I'm sure the guy made a lot of enemies in Charleston. He is a lawyer, after all."

Amusement ticked through Scott, even as an owl hooted a warning miles away. He hunched his shoulders against the chill. "There has to be at least one witness who saw when Millie left Snarky's. Do you have friends in town?"

"Not really," JT said. "Millie does, though. Everybody likes her. She's your key to investigating this. Don't go off without her."

"I'd like to speak with the chief on my own," Scott mused, calculating the best use of his time. "But other than that, you're right. She's how we get the entire town to help us figure this out. Although we need people to stop hindering the investigation by creating false alibis for her."

JT stood straighter, dropped the cigar, and ground it out beneath his thick boot. "What exactly are you and Millie to each other?"

"That's none of your business," Scott said instantly, even though he and Millie maintained a friendship, or at least a professional relationship. Were they friends?

"You seem like a decent guy, Scott," JT said. "But Millie's had enough loss and enough pain in her life. You seem to be a big twining ball of both."

Scott couldn't fault the guy's instincts, and he'd never blame him for looking out for his sister. "Your sister and I are work colleagues. Hopefully we'll be friends," he said. "You don't have anything to worry about."

"Good," JT said curtly. "I have something to take care of this morning and would appreciate it if you went out on the morning charter with her. They're out-of-towners and I don't know them."

"Not a problem." Scott had been planning on doing that very thing. He tried to convince himself it was to look out for Millie, but really he wanted to see her in a different environment. The more he learned about her, the more intriguing she became.

JT jerked his head toward several downed trees near an ax embedded in a large trunk. "When I can't sleep, when the demons get too loud, I chop wood. It's simple but it works." He turned and strode away, rapidly disappearing between the trees into the mist.

Scott scrutinized the pile of logs. As an idea, it didn't suck. Maybe he could banish the memory of Millie's sweet lips against his last night. He'd learned a long time ago in an ocean a million miles away not to wish for things that couldn't be.

He and the brilliant and pure Millicent Frost could never be.

* * * *

Snug in her parka and boots, Millie filled two cups with coffee as a strong gust pummeled the windowpanes. Grasping both mugs, she strode out of the kitchen door, hearing the thump, thump, thump of her brother chopping wood. The sound should be pleasing or heartwarming, but she knew the nightmares drove him to cut firewood when he had trouble sleeping.

Something rattled, and she partially turned to see the chief of police falling out of her great-aunt's window.

Millie pressed against the side of the house, the mugs heavy in her hands. What in the world?

The chief leaned back in, and her aunt reached out to kiss him.

Millie's jaw dropped.

The chief looked quickly around and then turned, plunking his cowboy hat onto his head and jogging across the far lawn to the main road.

Wow. Just wow.

Almost in a daze, Millie turned and stumbled toward the bunkhouse. Mae and the chief? Who knew? Apparently they wanted to keep it secret for some reason. Probably because JT tended to be so grouchy. Well, she'd keep their secret.

Her boots crunched over the frosty grass on her way to the gravel drive, and she kept walking to the bunkhouse, stopping cold when she realized that it wasn't her brother chopping wood. Instead, Scott Terentson, dressed in the borrowed sweatshirt and his jeans, rhythmically split the logs with animal grace.

The mist swirled around him, shrouding his expression. His rugged face was set in firm lines, while his piercing blue eyes concentrated on his task as if he were the only person anywhere near the river. The sinewy muscles of his arms and shoulders rippled with each swing of the ax, and his forehead glistened with a light sheen of perspiration, even though dawn had just arrived and the morning was frigid. His breath lightly panted out in puffs in the cool air.

Holy crap. Those tailored suits had hidden this raw strength. She'd had no clue.

At some point during his exertions, he had rolled up the sweatshirt sleeves, revealing powerful forearms better suited to a miner than a lawyer accustomed to high-end tailoring and marble courtrooms. He hadn't shaved and a light shadow of beard covered his chiseled jawline, making him look even more roguish than usual. His dark blond hair was ruffled and stood up in several places.

Her breath caught and fireflies winged through her abdomen. She swallowed several times and tried to remember when she'd pigeonholed him as a city fella. There was obviously a lot more to Scott Terentson than she'd realized. Not to mention that the kiss he'd given her the night before had pretty much blown her socks off. It had taken her hours to get to sleep afterward, and she had been tempted more than once to leave her bed for his.

Confusion blanketed her and she didn't like it. She usually knew exactly what she was doing, and if not, she could figure out how to create the right scenario around herself. A gadget didn't exist to help her figure out Scott.

As if sensing her, he stilled, struck the ax into the thick cedar trunk serving as the platform for chopping wood, and turned toward her. "I hope I didn't awaken you." His voice was a low growl that licked across her skin.

Her mouth went dry. Like desert dry. She gulped and made her way over the icy rocks to reach him. "I thought you were JT." She handed him the larger mug.

"Thank you." He accepted the cup, sniffed gratefully, and downed half of the liquid before testing the temperature.

She looked around the misty morning. "Where is JT?"

"He went to take care of errands about an hour and a half ago," Scott said, his hand looking large and strong around the coffee cup. "He also said to tell you to take me on the charter."

"You're welcome to come." The idea of spending the day on the water with him was far more appealing than she would've imagined.

A lock of his hair fell over his forehead, giving him more of a rebel look than a boyish one. There didn't seem to be anything boyish about the badass ex-marine turned lawyer. "It's been a while since I fished," he admitted. "But yeah, I think it sounds like fun."

Why had she invited him? Maybe he wanted a break from her. "Or you could call your office and get some work done." Guilt swamped her that she was keeping him from what he needed to do.

"No. I'd rather go fishing. What do you think we'll catch?"

She thought through the stretch of river she wanted to reach. "We're going to drive to the New River," she said. "This time of year, we should be able to catch some smallmouth bass as well as walleye. Do you enjoy fishing?"

"Yeah," he said, his gaze raking her body.

She warmed from head to toe in response to his lingering look.

"I used to fish with my uncle growing up," he said. "It was just my mom and me most of the time, but when Uncle Trace came through town, we'd go fishing. I kept it up during breaks for the last several years, but it's probably been, well, a while."

She could read the words he didn't say. It had been since he'd been shot helping out Angus and his team. Scott had been in the hospital for quite a while but had seemed fine afterward. Now she wondered. How could anybody go through something like that and remain unscathed?

"I find that fishing, especially fly-fishing, helps relax my mind," she admitted. "There's something about being out there in nature alone, or at least a distance from anybody else, that just calms and quiets..."

"All the noise," he finished for her. "Yeah, that's how I remember it as well. I think this'll be fun."

She angled to the side to look beyond him. "Oh, good. It looks like JT already attached the boat trailer to the truck. He's so helpful sometimes." Of course, JT always did that for her, but she was running out of things to say. So she rambled. "I packed the picnic lunch and several thermoses of coffee, hot chocolate, and water. There are only three people coming—it should be a good morning."

"How do you run a charter?" he asked. "I've never done anything like that."

She smiled. "As soon as the participants arrive, we'll take them through safety checks and make sure they understand the dangers. It's my understanding after reading the booking this morning that they're all experienced anglers, so they should have their own equipment and probably will just want to be guided to the good spots. It looks like tomorrow we have a charter for Running Creek, which is fun because we should be able to get some trout. But for now..."

She walked past him, feeling the heat from his body in a way that sent a shiver through her. Stumbling only slightly, she regained her footing and hopped onto a series of crates to look in the fishing boat. She reached in and flipped open the tackle box.

"What are you doing?" Scott asked, suddenly at her side.

She paused. With her perched on the crates, they stood almost eye to eye. "I'm making sure that JT remembered to pack the right flies. We have a difference of opinion when it comes to smallmouth bass."

"Oh yeah?" Scott asked, one eyebrow rising. "Tell me more."

"I think the Clouser minnow is the way to go. It mimics bait fish and I love the olive and white or the brown and yellow color options. I'm telling you, using them, we would catch smallmouth bass without question. But..." She rolled her eyes. "JT likes the crayfish patterns. I understand that crayfish are a good food source for bass, but they don't work as well. JT is just in love with the crayfish. I mean, the guy's nuts."

"God, you're adorable," Scott murmured.

The words caught her off guard and she nearly fell off the crate. "I am?" Most people thought she was weird. Sometimes interesting, but never adorable.

"Yeah." He reached out and brushed a knuckle across her jawline.

Her knees trembled. This was insane. Should she just tackle him and get it over with? That kiss the night before couldn't have been as good as she was making it out to be. Could it? "Um," she said.

The sound of tires on gravel drew her up short.

"Saved by the charter," he murmured, taking a step back and holding out a hand to help her down.

Her hand trembled slightly, but she accepted his, which was warm and strong around her knuckles. She hopped to the ground. "Let's meet these folks," she said. "And make sure they know what they're doing."

He turned toward what appeared to be a black SUV with tinted windows.

"Nice rig," he murmured.

Did Scott Terentson just use the word rig? "Are you sure you're not from the country?" She wanted to take his hand again.

"I'm sure, but I spent a lot of time with my uncle while growing up. He came from the hills of Kentucky."

She noted that he talked about his uncle in the past tense, and she opened her mouth to ask more when one of the SUV windows rolled down.

"Gun!" Scott yelled, tackling her to the ground.

Pain flashed up her hip to her shoulder before the chill frrom the scrub grass followed.

The sound of gunfire erupted through the misty morning, with bullets pinging off the metal fishing boat.

Chapter Ten

Scott instinctively tumbled Millie beneath the boat trailer, shoving her to the other side across the rough gravel. He could see beyond the firewood pile as three men jumped out of the dark SUV. The one firing abruptly stopped, and the silence clamored through his head.

"Damn it." He rolled to the other side as Millie began to stand. He barely peeked over into the boat and scrambled for the tackle boxes, grabbing two and yanking them down to dump their contents onto the ground.

"What are you doing?" Millie whispered, blood on her chin.

"Looking for anything I can use for a weapon." He grabbed a fishing knife off the ground.

Millie scrambled through the items and wrapped her small hand around the handle of a fillet knife.

"Don't suppose you have a gun nearby?" he asked, listening for advancing steps.

"No."

Going stone cold, he grasped the knife handle in his hand. The stainless steel weapon contained a six-inch blade, and while he would much prefer a gun, he'd make do. "Are there guns in the house?"

"Yes," she said, looking across the wide distance. "As well as some makeshift weapons I've created for fun." She gestured. "Come on. I have structured booby traps behind the bunkhouse and natural ones already set in the trees on the other side." Ducking, she scurried around the rear of the building near the river.

He didn't have his phone or a weapon other than the fishing knife. His mind quickly calculated the best way to get Millie to safety. He navigated around the building, pausing to look back. The shadows obscured the men's faces, but each one held a weapon, clad in all black. They sported no masks, which hinted at danger. They had killing as their aim.

He kept his back to the rough wooden siding and edged around toward the forest. No doubt the men would flank the building, approaching from both sides. Forcing emotion away, he gingerly lifted a dirty window and peered inside the small building. The main room held two sets of overlarge bunk beds, one strewn with clothing and a couple of books. JT's belongings. "Are there weapons inside?"

Millie peeked inside. "It's doubtful. I'm sure JT has weapons, but he'd keep them with him or hidden from the guests we let stay here overnight." She scrambled to open a utility chest set against the side of the building and pulled out several remote controls.

Scott craned his neck as the clock counted down. He could feel the men getting closer. "What do we have?"

She handed him a remote and leaned in to pull out what looked like three life-size squirrels to place on the ground. "Press the power button," she whispered.

He pressed the top button and the animals came to life.

"Good." She recaptured the remote and pressed a bunch of buttons. The squirrels turned around the corner. "I have them rigged to explode because I planned to play a joke on JT."

Fucking brilliant. He brushed his knuckles across her delicate jawline. "Stay down and out of sight."

She looked between the bunkhouse and the trees. "I've planted booby traps in the trees to protect the property."

He measured the distance. "What kind?"

"Poisonous herbs. If we can get those guys into the right patch, they'll be sorry."

Excellent. "I'll go around the other side. When I yell, you blow up a squirrel." He couldn't believe he'd just said that. "When I say run, you dart into the trees and lead the next guy to the poison." Which meant he had to take out two of them first.

"Got it. They're not expecting short Millie and her lawyer to be a threat." She crouched down against the structure, disappearing into the shadows.

He was counting on being underestimated. "I'll go up." He looked wildly around, then caught sight of the edge of the slanted roof. Moss grew over the rough shingles and down the wooden siding. Would the roof even hold his weight? This was such a fucking disaster, but he needed to get his eyes on the attackers.

He had to push fury to the background and go cold.

Shoving the knife in his pocket, careful not to stab himself, he reached up with both hands and flipped himself onto the roof, landing first on his elbows and then his knees so he didn't make a sound. The mossy shingles slipped beneath him and he stilled, waiting until they settled. From his vantage point, he could see the shadows of the men moving to the front of the structure. One would probably go inside. That left only one man to explore the rear of the building, looking for them.

Keeping as silent as he'd been trained, Scott maneuvered to the side nearest the river and looked down. A shingle slipped and he grabbed it, forcing the square back into place. The broad and tall man below him held the gun like he knew how to handle himself. Scott waited until the man had moved just beyond him and flipped over the side, slashing down with the knife as he dropped.

Shock stilled the asshole for a second, giving Scott time to clap his hand over the man's mouth and cover his scream. Then he shoved the blade farther into the guy's neck, ripping through cartilage and muscle. The guy jerked several times as blood spurted from his jugular.

Scott gently eased him down to the ground, stole his gun, and yanked his knife free to put into his back pocket. The body fell to the wet earth and bounced once. A rattle echoed from the guy's chest and he went still in death.

Scott peered down, realizing he held a Beretta 92FS. He appreciated the gun and knew it well. Making sure the manual safety was released, he took a deep breath and stalked back along the rear of the building toward the fishing boat where he'd acquired the knife. A quick glance confirmed nobody near the boat or various flies strewn across the ground.

"Where is she?" A rough voice came through the mist near the front.

Scott crept between the building and the metal boat to the front of the bunkhouse, keeping close to the building and in the shadows.

"Inside?" a man with a hoarse voice whispered, and the sound of the door being opened creaked through the morning.

Scott turned, weapon ready, only to be hit square on the arm by the butt of a gun. He dropped the Beretta and dodged forward, sweeping out with his elbow and forcing his adversary to lose his gun. Grunting, he punched the man in the face several times, driving him back. "Now!" he bellowed.

A squirrel dropped from an eave and exploded, throwing smoke in every direction.

Millie screamed from her hiding place, and he turned in panic, giving the man in black an opportunity to punch him in the face. Scott stumbled back, pain surging through his skull. The guy followed up with three hard blows to Scott's midsection.

He gasped from the swift torment, ducked his head, and charged, hitting the asshole in the gut and flinging them onto the wet earth. Millie shrieked, and the sound was farther away.

Another squirrel detonated, and the pieces hit his attacker. He yelped and fought furiously.

Landing on top of the rapidly striking attacker, Scott headbutted him in the nose, which splintered with a satisfying crack.

The man cried out, the shriek high with pain. Grunting, he wrenched a knife from a sheath on his thigh, sliced along Scott's rib cage, and lifted, struggling to find a position to stab.

Agony speared through Scott's flank. Snarling, pressing down with his body to keep his opponent pinned, Scott grabbed the man's wrist, twisted violently, and secured the knife.

Yelling, the man scrabbled with one hand on the ground and grasped his gun, lifting it. Scott slammed the blade into the man's neck, plunging it as deep as he could. The guy's eyes widened, he dropped the gun, and grasped for the handle as blood gushed from the wound.

Blood spurted onto Scott's face and he turned his head as the body shuddered several times and went still.

Scott smoothly rolled off him, snatched the gun off the ground, and charged around the cabin to see the last attacker running into the forest. "On your six," he yelled to warn Millie, pursuing him.

The guy caught Millie and threw her down.

She fought furiously and shoved what looked like bark in his eyes. The man on top of her lifted a knife, the jagged edge glinting evilly in the morning light.

Scott aimed and fired, hitting the attacker midcenter.

He stilled, his body spasmed, and he fell on her. A red rash already covered his neck and face.

Millie screamed and shoved at him with her hands, which were covered by her parka sleeves, her legs kicking the dirt.

Scott burst forward, grasped the guy by the shoulder, and shoved him off her.

She partially sat up and scrambled away, her legs moving furiously and her breath panting. Her hair was a wild mass around her head, her face pale beneath a cluster of bruises on her left cheek. Drops of blood dotted her chin and down her neck from the spray of the bullet.

Scott nudged the fallen man over with his boot. The guy rolled, his arm flopping uselessly on the ground, his eyes wide open in death.

Millie pushed herself to stand, her legs visibly shaking and her focus on the dead guy. "He was faster than I thought."

"Are you okay?" Scott asked, his senses automatically tuning into the outside area, searching for more threats. "There's blood on you."

She swallowed, not looking away from the guy. "No, but it's not my blood." Her teeth audibly chattered. "He's dead."

"Come on." Scott advanced toward her, keeping his movements slow and nonthreatening. "I saw you use the herbs. Did you hurt yourself?"

"No. I covered my hands." Was she going into shock?

They'd worked well together. He hadn't known they'd make such a good team. "Millie? I need you to take a deep breath and come with me." He had to get her away from the deceased man.

Wheezing, she took a tentative step forward.

"Honey? I think you're going into a panic attack." He reached her and gently slid an arm over her shoulders, using his most commanding voice, to which she seemed to respond. "Take a deep breath. In through your nose and out through your mouth. Now."

She did so, her small body trembling against him. Even so, she didn't look away from the body.

"Millie." Scott put bite into his tone. "Look at me. Now."

Shaking, she did so.

"There you go," he said calmly. "Now, we're going to walk out of these trees, contact the police, and call and cancel the group charter for the day. Understand?"

"Yes."

Good. Then he should probably get a bandage. As he escorted her from the cabin, he glanced down at his side.

Yep. A lot of blood.

Chapter Eleven

Sitting on the back of the ambulance, Millie pushed herself farther inside, but the rain still bombarded the lower half of her jeans and soaked her boots. The skies had opened up as if wanting to wash the blood away.

Near the bunkhouse, the local police secured one of her green tarps over the body outside the door as the rain pelted their water-resistant gear. The glare from the bright halogen floodlights obscured their expressions, but a somberness pervaded the scene.

A black-and-green truck rolled to a stop, and the chief of police jumped out to stride through the pounding rain, his gaze taking in the entire area. Millie's body felt numb and her head full of cotton.

"I don't need stitches," Scott growled for what had to be the third time.

"Yes, you do," Janet muttered back.

Janet had been a paramedic in the small town for at least thirty years, had been Millie's second-grade softball coach, and didn't like to be told no.

Millie shook herself out of her fog. "Scott, if Janet says you need stitches, you do."

"Slap a bandage on it," Scott said curtly.

Roscoe barked from the porch. Millie wiped rain out of her eyes. "Roscoe? It's okay, buddy," she yelled, fighting to be heard above the pummeling raindrops. "Stop barking."

Aunt Mae came out onto the porch and drew the dog inside. She'd tried to help Millie and Scott, but Millie had insisted she stay inside, out of the rain. Subsequently, the smell of freshly baked cookies soon wafted through the storm.

"Sorry I'm late," the chief said. "We had a lost hiker up on Tippy Mountain." He looked over at the SUV. "That's what the three were driving?"

"Yes, sir," Officer Locum said, the wind plastering his slicker to his body. Around forty years old, he played as the drummer in a local band called Riverbank Renegades, along with three of his cousins.

"We gave our statements," Millie said, her teeth still chattering. She couldn't believe three men had tried to kill them. Yet she and Scott had taken them down using her inventions and his training.

It was as if they'd worked together for years.

The drenched yellow crime-scene tape flapped in the rough wind, one edge breaking free to slap against the hunting lodge. "In fact, we gave statements to each of your officers." The police had immediately separated them to get the facts.

"I heard," the chief muttered. "I saw the SUV go by earlier when I grabbed coffee at Lulu's Diner before heading out." He looked at Locum. "Did you run the plates?"

"We did. SUV was stolen out of Charleston three nights ago."

The chief's shrewd eyes took in Millie. She didn't mention that he'd been at her house around four that morning sneaking out of a window. "I figured. You okay?"

"No." She huddled under a blanket, but she just couldn't get warm. The dead body on the ground caught her eye and she quickly looked away, noting the river swelling with the storm runoff as if it, too, had come alive like a frenzied serpent. The water threw debris onto the banks, its angry tirade echoing back from the hills.

The chief turned his gaze to Scott. "I thought you were a lawyer."

"I am," Scott said, not wincing as Janet none too gently slapped a bandage over his bleeding wound. He had taken off his shirt, and despite her brain fog, Millie had to admire his compelling chest. Taut skin blanketed raw muscle, and the multitude of scars marring his torso only added to the aura of violence he'd managed to hide until now. Several knife wounds created an almost-star on his left shoulder, and yet another bullet wound scarred him low on his right hip.

The chief examined Scott's torso. "Looks like the new scars will fit in with the rest. You were a marine, huh?"

Scott lifted one eyebrow. "I take it your officer reported everything."

"Yeah. You could say that. I had them read your preliminary statements to me on the ride in," the chief said. "Any ID on the bodies?" he called out.

A deputy near the entrance to the bunkhouse shook his head. He had introduced himself as Deputy Smise and he wasn't anybody Millie had ever met, so he had to be a recent hire.

"No, I ran the fingerprints with the mobile biometric device but the thing has a glitch. I'm still waiting," Smise said.

"Knock it against the wood a couple of times," the chief suggested. "That always works for me."

Amusement tilted Scott's lips. Millie shook her head. How could he experience amusement right now? They might've died. She'd had no idea he could be that deadly. He most certainly had saved her life.

She scooted a little closer to him.

"Are you warming up?" he asked, looking at her. She nodded. "No, you're not," he said, reading her easily. "Chief, do you need us right now?"

"Not if we have your statements," the chief said. "Real quick, any idea who would want to kill you?"

Scott slid an arm over her shoulders, tugging her into his good side. "No."

"Me either," Millie murmured, warmth enveloping her.

The chief studied the scene. "My guess is this would have something to do with the murder of Clay and you being found in his bed."

She could feel the blood draining from her face. "You don't think the Bakers sent an assassin team after me, do you?"

"I don't know, but I'll find out," the chief said. "I'm bringing them in today."

"I'd like to be there," Scott said quickly.

The chief studied him. "I don't think so."

Scott leaned forward. "As her lawyer, I have a right to be there."

"No, you don't," the chief said.

Millie thought through what she knew of the law. She couldn't figure out how Scott could demand to attend the interview, but she appreciated that he wanted to stay involved.

"Please, Chief?" She looked up at him, holding her breath.

The chief paused. "Millie, don't give me the eyes."

"Chief, someone just tried to kill me." Tears filled her eyes and they were not deliberate. She couldn't hold them back.

"You've got it. No crying." The chief held up both hands. "Terentson, you may come down to the station, and if the Bakers agree to it, you may attend the interview. That's all I can offer you. If they ask for a lawyer, we're out anyway. Though you should also know that Skinner is still in town and really wants Millie secured in a cell as we build a case against her."

Scott pulled her in even tighter, and she willingly let him hold her weight. Just for a moment. "Understood. For now, I'm taking Millie inside." It wasn't a question.

The chief shuffled his feet. "You probably haven't read the *River City Gazette* today?"

Millie's head dropped. "No. Why?"

"There's an article all about Clay's murder and you being found in his bed covered in blood." The chief's jaw hardened. "I have no idea who talked, but I will find out and can their asses." He sighed. "There's a chance the county prosecutor is chatting, trying to flush out information."

Scott figured the whole town already knew about the case. "Inside, Millie," he said.

The chief tucked a thumb in his jeans pocket. "I'll be in after I look at the scene. I called the county coroner and she wants to come out here, so we're going to do the best we can with the rain. For some reason, she wants to see them where they fell."

Scott jumped from the ambulance and reached to lift Millie down. His grip was firm and strong as he pivoted to put her on the ground, then set her on her feet. Obvious muscle played beneath his skin when he moved. "We'll be inside," he said. "Let me know if you need anything."

Millie faltered, her knees going weak. Without missing a step, Scott swung her up into his arms against his chest.

"Put me down." Panic choked her. "You're bleeding."

"I'm fine." He hunched his body over her to protect her from the punishing rain and strode swiftly across the grass and inside the warm home. He walked right through the kitchen to place her at the table. "I'll get you some coffee." Turning, he unerringly opened the right cupboard and drew down two mugs before pouring from the ever-full coffeepot on the counter.

Mae hustled into the room. "Are you two okay?"

"Yes." Millie tried to focus and noted he had already bled through the bandage across his rib cage. Her stomach revolted, and she took several deep breaths. While she often worked with badass agents, as their gadget girl, she normally remained safe back at headquarters. Not in the field with blood and dead bodies. "Here." She stood, her knees weak, and strode to the hidden cabinet to press her palm against the wood and reach far in the back.

"I don't think I need another bandage," he said.

"No, I have something that can stitch you up," she said, turning around. "Sit down." She tried to put force in her voice, but she sounded whispery. Must be the shock.

He sat and craned his neck to study the device in her hand, his brow furrowing. "What is that?"

"I created a quick-stitch tool," she admitted. "My brother's always getting wounded, and he won't go to the hospital. So I actually built this in high school." She looked down at the small handheld device.

Mae chortled. "I'm taking coffee out to the police. Don't even try to stop me." She grabbed the thermos and several mugs, quickly disappearing outside into the rain.

Scott leaned back in the chair as if the thing might bite him. "What's it made of?"

"Hard plastic," Millie said. "The device began as a stapler."

"Oh." He reared farther back, moving the chair a few inches.

Real amusement cut through her shock. "No, it's okay. I have fishing line and sterilized curved needles, as well as a chamber that releases antiseptic. It's spring-loaded."

He stopped moving, his chin still tilted. "All right." Leaning to the side, he tore off the bandage.

She winced. The gash appeared serious. Blood flowed down his ribs to pool on the waistband of his jeans.

"Oh, for goodness' sake." She reached for a kitchen towel to press against the wound.

He didn't so much as suck in a breath, but the pressure had to hurt. She wiped the blood off as gently as she could. "Hold very still," she said.

"No problem."

She immediately set the retrofitted stapler on one end of the wound and drew it gently across the entire gash. Her device stitched him up perfectly, spurting antiseptic as it went.

"That's fricking impressive," he said, looking down.

Parts of her started to warm finally. "Thanks." She returned to the cabinet and drew out another bandage. "Let's try this again, shall we?"

"Sure. Thank you." He studied his now-closed injury.

The sincerity in his voice caught her unaware. He was thanking her?

"You saved my life, Scott."

He looked up, his gaze predatory. "I promise, Millie, I won't let anything happen to you."

Chapter Twelve

Afternoon arrived before the police crime scene techs and coroner retreated from the property. Scott finished eating his lunch, his hair still damp from a shower as his mind calculated the steps necessary to ensure Millie's safety.

A knock on the door had his body going cold. Mae, in her room needlepointing, remained safely out of the line of fire.

"We need weapons. Stay back and run if I tell you to." He stood and stalked toward the kitchen door to find two nearly identical women beneath a bright pink-and-white polka-dotted umbrella.

"Hey," the first said, looking beyond him to Millie. "The world has turned upside down! I heard there was a murder here earlier."

Millie stood. "Oh, hi. I've been looking for you guys."

"We know. June called us," the other woman said. They were around Millie's age with light brown hair, green eyes, and full pink lips. They appeared almost identical, but the one on the left was pregnant and at least a couple of inches taller than her sister, who had shorter hair and was a bit curvier.

"Come in, come in." Millie gestured the women inside. "Scott Terentson, please meet Verna and Valerie Montgomery."

Thank goodness he didn't have to hunt them down. He moved to the side to allow them entrance. Verna shook out the umbrella and left it outside, leaning against the siding.

"What an adorable puppy," Valerie said, instantly sliding forward to drop to her knees and pet Roscoe's head. He obliged her by shuffling closer and resting his entire head on her knees. "Oh, he's so sweet."

"He's an old soul," Millie said. "Can I get you two anything to drink?"

"Coffee would be great," Valerie said. She glanced at the croissants on the counter. "But that's all. I've seen your aunt's recipe and I'm trying to stay away from carbs." She patted her rounded hip.

Verna sighed. "I'd love coffee but will have to stick with tea." She rubbed her protruding belly. "Although I'm happy with carbs."

"That's because you never gain weight," her sister muttered.

Scott leaned against the wall and surveyed them as Millie secured two mugs, taking out a tea bag for Verna.

Verna strode over and dropped onto a chair by the table as if she'd sat there a million times before. "Did a kill squad really come out here earlier today?"

Scott barely kept from rolling his eyes. Small town gossip always traveled fast.

"Kind of," Millie said, handing the mugs to the women. "What have you heard?"

Valerie's eyes widened. "That three men, all in black, tried to kill you." Her gaze slid to Scott, but she didn't continue.

Verna leaned forward. "Everyone is saying that you took out all three of them, Scott." Her voice lowered. "Is it true?"

Scott didn't answer.

Millie cleared her throat. "We shouldn't talk about the attack until we know more. I don't suppose you've heard anything about the identity of the guys with guns?"

The police hadn't been very informative after taking their statements. Maybe the small town gossip mill would help. "It'd be great if we could find that out," Scott added.

Valerie's face pinkened. "I heard that the chief is still trying to identify the shooters. The officers did run the fingerprints but are being closemouthed about the results." She rubbed her ear. "I'm friends with Liz Lathom, who's dating Officer Locum. I can call her later. She loves to gossip."

Scott turned his full charm on her. "That would be wonderful. Thank you."

Her blush intensified.

Even her pregnant sister blinked several times.

Millie made a sound low in her throat that sounded like a strangled cat. "For now, I need to talk to you both about the night of Clay's murder."

"That's what we figured," Valerie said, "after we heard everything." She took a big drink of the coffee. "Ah, this is good. It's your gram's recipe, isn't it?"

"Yeah," Millie said. Verna patted her rounded belly. Scott guessed she was probably around four or five months pregnant, but he didn't want to ask. He had learned young in life never to ask that question. "How are you feeling?" Millie asked.

"The morning sickness has abated somewhat," Verna said, kicking out her feet to cross her ankles. "But I'm swelling much faster this time than last time." She looked up at Scott. "This is my third. Alex and I have been married for about ten years and have two sons. I'm hoping this is a girl."

He smiled. "Congratulations."

"Thanks." Now she blushed even deeper than her sister had.

Valerie sighed and stood, walking over to take a seat. "Not me. Never been married. Can't seem to find the right guy." Her gaze raked Scott from head to toe. "What about you?"

Definitely unavailable ran through his head, and he couldn't help but look at Millie. "Never been married," he answered smoothly. Millie's lip twitched, and he wondered if she wanted to smile. "So you two visited Snarky's the other night?" he asked.

"Yeah. I wanted to see if there were any cute tourists interested in curvy girls." Valerie shook her head and looked at Millie. "We arrived just as June was leaving, but I asked to speak with you and promised you a ride home. We discussed my design for sleeping pods so patients can rest better in the hospital."

Millie rubbed her eye. "I don't remember any of that."

"Finally, I had to go home," Valerie said, turning her interested gaze on Scott again. "I work as a nurse at the hospital, and I had a 4:00 a.m. shift."

Verna nodded. "Right when Valerie left, Clay approached you, and the two of you ordered a beer at the bar. I couldn't believe it."

Millie wrapped her hands around her mug as if seeking warmth and safety. "Did I seem to want to talk to him?"

Verna sipped her tea. "Yeah. I was surprised because I thought you hated the guy's guts. But you sat there and talked, and I wanted to give you space."

Millie's shoulders slumped. "If someone drugged my drink at the end of the night, I might not remember the whole day before that."

Tears filled Verna's eyes. "I'm hugely pregnant and wasn't having a lot of fun in the bar, and Buck kept glaring at me because I don't want to go back to work after the baby is born. So I waited about ten minutes after Valerie left, and then you guys seemed to be talking, and I didn't want to interrupt. I mean, who knew? Maybe the guy had changed and you would be happy together. I ran to the bathroom, and when I came out, you had left." She flushed. "I'm so sorry, Millie."

"It's not your fault." Millie reached out and clasped her hand. "Apparently, no one paid much heed. I wish I knew when I left the bar."

"You left around eleven," Verna said. "I ran outside and saw you get into Clay's truck and scoot over to the passenger side." She wiped at her left eye. "I didn't see any signs of distress, or I would've done something."

Scott stiffened. "You saw Millie leave with Clay?"

"Yes," Verna said. "I'm so dumb. Why wasn't I suspicious?"

Valerie patted her sister's knee. "I'm surprised you didn't call me with that bit of gossip. It's huge." She blushed. "I mean, it would've been huge, if it had been true. Millie and Clay getting back together."

Verna winced and rubbed her rib cage. "You had an early shift and I figured I'd call you after." She sniffed. "I wish I had rushed over and said something. Anything. But you seemed fine, Mills."

Millie's eyes grew unfocused. "We need to get our hands on Clay's autopsy results. There is a chance he was drugged as well, but if so, how did he drive us to his place?" She started rubbing her temples as if being attacked by a raging headache.

"Who else drank in the bar that night?" Scott asked quietly.

The twins rattled off a series of names, and Scott made a mental note to track each person down to see what they had noticed, if anything. He also created a list of questions to ask the chief later. Too many blank holes existed not only in Millie's memory, but with the entire situation.

"Do you think you were drugged?" Verna asked.

Millie smacked her palm against her forehead. "I had to have been because I don't remember a thing. But some of those drugs aren't traceable, and the hospital didn't find any in my blood."

Valerie clapped a hand over her mouth. "I just can't believe it," she said through her fingers, the sound muffled. Then she reached for her cup again. "Seriously, you didn't look drugged. I never would've left you if I had even a hint."

"I know," Millie said. "Sometimes you can't tell with certain drugs like GHB."

"Is that a date rape drug?" Valerie whispered.

Millie swallowed rapidly as if trying to keep from vomiting. "Yes, but I wasn't raped. We didn't even have sex."

"Oh, good." Relief filled Valerie's face. "I was worried about that."

"Nope. I just awoke in a pool of blood next to his dead body," Millie said.

Verna gagged. "Who would want to set you up for murder?"

"Or who would want to murder Clay?" Valerie interjected. "A lot of people hated that guy. Maybe your involvement is just a terrible coincidence."

Scott had been thinking the same thing, but he wasn't willing to accept any one theory right now. "Verna? Buck said you used to work at the bar. Did you ever see Clay there?"

"Sure," Verna said. "It's the best bar in town. Any time Clay comes home, he and his brothers usually hang out there."

"Have you seen him with other women? Maybe leave with any?" Scott asked.

Verna tapped a finger against her lips. "Um, sure. He picked up women once in a while." She cut a look at her sister. "I think he expressed interest in June, right?"

Millie gasped. "June?"

"Yeah, but he chased anything in a skirt," Valerie interjected. "He caught more than a few, I bet. I'll ask around about that."

"Thanks," Millie said.

As the women began to chat about the town and the townspeople, Scott snapped his fingers at Roscoe. "Come on, Ros. Let's go outside and let you run."

Roscoe immediately jumped up and lumbered toward him. With that, Scott winked at Millie and strode out into the chilly March air, not any closer to answers than he had been before. The arrival of the kill squad had awakened something in him, something primal and dangerous, and whoever had sent them after Millie would pay.

Maybe he'd only been playing at being a lawyer. Perhaps he'd always be a killer.

If that kept Millie safe, then so be it.

Chapter Thirteen

Midafternoon, Scott slammed the SUV's door and loped into the police station.

The chief stood behind the counter this time. "Hey."

"Hey. You have the Baker brothers?"

"I do," the chief said. "Surprisingly, they're more than happy to have you sit in on the interview."

Scott frowned. "What does that mean?"

"It means they're not worried about shit," the chief said.

"Did you wait for me?" Scott asked, walking around the counter without being asked.

The chief snorted. "No. They're getting settled in there with coffee, and for some reason, Lonnie needed a candy bar." The chief rolled his eyes. "He's such a tight-ass, he should've asked for whiskey."

"I really appreciate this." It came as a surprise, considering Scott had killed three men that morning, but all evidence pointed to his actions being self-defense or defense of Millie, and apparently the chief didn't mess around. Scott liked that in a person. He really liked that in a chief of police.

"You bet. It'd be really helpful if you could tell folks to stop calling in with alibis for Millie. It's creating a backlog for me," the chief said, reaching for a mug of what looked like milk with a touch of coffee. "You want anything?"

Not if it was all cream and no coffee. "No, I'm good."

"You're missing out." The chief paused. "I need to tell you that a guy named Werner Dearth called this morning, saying he had evidence against Millie and that she could easily kill somebody."

Scott paused. So Dearth was making good on his threats of payback. "What kind of evidence?"

"Dunno. Just said that his investigators have turned up financial issues, a juvie record, and other, more personal problems. Guy sounds like an ass."

Scott studied the chief. "If she had a juvie record, you'd know it."

"She does. Accidentally blew up a fridge in a foster home and was charged with reckless endangerment. The conviction was expunged when she turned eighteen." The chief scratched his whiskered jaw. "Millie's a good person, but she seems to have a lot of enemies right now."

Irritation slammed into Scott's gut.

The chief coughed. "I do want to make sure Mae is safe. Are you going to be staying out there?"

"Yes. Until we figure this out." Was the chief blushing? No. It had to be the weird lighting in the hallway.

The chief turned and led the way back to an interrogation room where two men sat on the other side of a heavy metal table, waiting. The chief took a seat and Scott sat next to him. "You've met Scott Terentson. And again, I have to make sure you boys are on board with him being here."

"We're fine," Lonnie drawled.

Scott cut a look at Silas, who sat next to his brother. "Hello again." Silas still sported several bruises across his face and down his jaw, and no doubt his rib cage looked like somebody had taken a meat tenderizer to it. Scott didn't regret one punch and was more than a little surprised that Silas had agreed to speak with him. "It's nice of you to include me in this interview," he drawled.

Silas's nostrils flared. "That's fine. I just want to tell you face-to-face that I know that bitch killed my brother, and she will pay."

Irritation crashed through Scott, but he forced a smile. "Are you threatening her? Because three people tried to kill her this morning, and it sounds like you're confessing to sending them."

Lonnie rolled his eyes. He was a smaller version of his brother with thick, dark hair, light brown eyes and fit shoulders. Contrasting with Silas's beefy and overweight form, he boasted a sleek and muscular frame. They shared a similar blunt bone structure. "If we wanted Millie dead, we wouldn't send a squad of three," he said quietly. Scott instantly focused on the biggest threat in the room. While Silas appeared to be all bluster, his brother was not. His gaze held an intensity that warranted recognition.

The chief straightened as if coming to the same conclusion. "What proof do you have that Millie killed your brother?"

Silas's eyes widened. "Besides the fact that his blood covered both her and her knife when the cops arrived at the cabin? A weapon the little freak invented? You mean besides that, Chief?"

"Yeah, besides that, Silas." A hint of sarcasm thickened the chief's tone, and Scott took a moment to appreciate it.

"They left Snarky's together the night before, and my brother was dead by morning," Lonnie said. "We will pursue this. If you don't, we'll go above your head, Chief. In fact, we already spoke with the county prosecutor, and Skinner promised he's going to avenge our brother."

The chief leaned forward, a vein in his forehead turning dark. "I'll pursue this as well. I want to know not only who killed Clay, but who tried to murder Millie this morning."

"I don't know." Silas threw up his beefy hands. "The woman obviously is a trouble magnet. Maybe she's killed other people besides my brother and has a million enemies out there who want revenge. Have you thought of that?"

"I've looked into it," the chief said.

Scott masked his surprise. Even though the chief believed Millie, he was performing his due diligence in trying to find the murderer.

Scott had to respect that. "Did you see Millie and your brother leave the bar together the night of his murder?" Scott asked quietly.

"I wasn't there," Lonnie snapped.

"I left early," Silas said. "But we've heard all over town that they left together."

The chief took a deep drag of his creamer and coffee. "In whose vehicle?" he asked.

Silas shrugged. "I assume my brother's. From what I heard, his rig was the only one in his drive when the cops arrived that morning. Right?"

The chief nodded. "Right."

Lonnie flattened both hands on the table, showing slices across his knuckles. "Her guilt is obvious," he snapped. "They left, they ended up in bed together, she killed him by morning. I mean, connect the dots." Anger mottled his face a beet red.

Scott tilted his head. "What happened to your hand?"

"I might've punched a mirror when I discovered my brother had been sliced into pieces," Lonnie said darkly.

Maybe. Maybe not.

The chief took a deep breath. "Forgetting Millie for just a moment, is there anybody who wanted your brother dead?"

"No," Lonnie said. "He excelled as an attorney in the big city. People loved him. He had a good political career in front of him if he unwisely wanted one."

Silas reared up. "He wanted it. He had a good chance to go far in this world."

"Is there any possibility that someone in the political world wanted him dead?" the chief asked.

"No." Lonnie snorted. "He hadn't even really looked into that option yet. I'd say he was about five years away from it. He was enjoying being a lawyer. He was living large, winning cases, and making money."

"What about the family business?" Scott asked. "Rumor has it you all had a dustup."

Silas blew out a breath, filling the room with the smell of pepperoni. Old pepperoni. "There was no dustup. Clay wanted us to diversify, and we just want to do the fishing and guiding that we've always done. That's hardly a dustup."

"What about your other brother?" the chief asked.

"Haven't seen Glen in a couple of months," Lonnie said. "He wanted us to buy him out of the family business, and we said no. The terms of the trust don't allow us to sell to anybody else, so he found himself stuck."

"Hey, we're making money," Silas said, his voice rising. "I don't know why Glen refuses to take part in the business."

Lonnie cracked his knuckles. "I think he wants to start some other business, something to do with real estate. He wants to flip houses, and he needed seed money. I think he asked Clay."

Silas's jaw went slack. "He asked Clay? Did Clay give him money?"

"I have no idea." Lonnie tipped back his coffee, his tone bored.

"We're looking into his finances now," the chief said. "We'll keep you informed."

Silas looked from his brother to the chief; for the first time grief showed in his eyes instead of anger. "Great."

"Was Clay dating anybody?" Scott asked.

"No," Lonnie said curtly. Silas looked at his brother and remained quiet.

The chief stared at Silas. "What do you know? Don't hide things from me. I need to find out who killed your brother."

Silas's eyes darkened. "Clay worked as a hotshot lawyer in the big city and got as much tail as he wanted. Don't think he took any woman seriously, but I'm sure he didn't sleep alone very often. In fact, he had a goofy smile on his face the last couple of times we got together. I have no clue what chick occupied his brain, but he definitely made time with a woman or three. Who knows. Maybe four."

Lonnie placed his cup on the metal table with a loud thunk. "Clay wasn't looking for romance. He was a one-night-stand kind of guy, which is probably why Millicent Frost killed him."

"Huh?" Silas sputtered.

Lonnie glared. "Think about it. She's pining for him, they meet up at the bar, then they go to his home and fuck? Then he tells her he doesn't want anything serious. She's pissed and hurt, and she waits until he's asleep. He's helpless, and she goes for a knife."

Silas reared back. "That does make sense."

"Not really." The chief studied the two men. "I don't want to share too much about the investigation, but maybe this'll take the hot off your iron. I had Millie examined at the hospital, and they did not engage in any form of sexual encounter that night."

Silas swallowed. "Then why did she end up in bed with him?"

"Dunno yet," the chief said. "For now, the judge just granted me a search warrant for Clay's phone records. There's a backlog right now, though, and it could take a while. If you boys could ask around and get me information, I'd really appreciate it."

Silas drew both bruised hands down his equally bruised jaw. "I know that you like Millie, Chief. But you have to consider her a suspect."

"I do." The chief's expression softened slightly. "I arrested her and had her examined at the hospital. She's on my list, and if I discover she killed Clay, I promise I'll make sure she lives the rest of her life in prison."

Scott remained motionless. He knew Millie didn't kill Clay, but her fingerprints remained on that knife. She admitted to grabbing the handle out of shock that morning—moreover, she owned the weapon.

"I trust you, Chief," Lonnie said. "But we know who killed our brother. And believe me"—his gaze slashed to Scott—"she will pay."

Chapter Fourteen

Dinner proceeded mostly in silence, not due to mutual contentment, but because everyone seemed focused on a tension-filled internal dialogue. Millie could almost see the brain waves spurting around.

Aunt Mae had gone to her weekly bridge game, apparently feeling just fine with her new stent securely in place.

Millie's head ached, and even her bones felt weary. While JT normally kept silent, tonight he ate the spaghetti she'd quickly whipped up, and she could see the tension in his jaw and through his shoulders. Even Scott seemed edgier than ever before. Normally, he brought calm to all the chaos around them, but not tonight. His energy zinged around the room and added to the tension brewing behind her eyes.

Finally, JT stood. "I'm going for a run."

Excellent plan. "I'll clean up," Millie offered.

Roscoe leaped to his feet from his position beneath the table.

"You want to go?" JT asked.

In answer, Roscoe padded over to the door and waited. JT looked back at Scott. "Is it okay?"

"Absolutely." Scott jolted, as if he had been deep inside his own head. "He loves to run and he could burn off some energy."

JT opened the door and the two disappeared into the stormy night. Though the rain had stopped, the wind howled mercilessly through the trees, and thunder bellowed deep and loud in the distance. Every once in a while, the windows lit up from a jagged strike of lightning.

Millie shivered. "I'll clean up, Scott, if you want to go for a run, too."

He looked up, his eyes unfocused, then zeroed in on her. "I appreciate the offer. I don't require a run. I want to get organized." He stood and paused, looking around. "You wouldn't have an old corkboard around here, would you?" He carried his dishes to the sink.

"Kind of. I might sort of have a corkboard." She moved to the sink and looked over her shoulder. "I have a large digital touchscreen attached to a base with wheels so I can roll it around. I use it for planning more inventions, to be honest. Sometimes it's in my room, but when we had the wooden floors updated and polished, I put it in the garage and haven't taken it out."

"So you have a TV on top of a stand?"

She chewed her lip. "Not really. It was a touchscreen and now it has haptic feedback technology, so you can move or pin items. In addition, I equipped it with facial and voice recognition."

His lips ticked up. "I see. So, if I touch this thing, is it going to shock me? What kind of protection do you have on it?"

She had considered creating a shock-type response to protect the device but then decided against it. "No, just bring the screen inside. The board has voice and fingertip security. I had to take some cybersecurity precautions, and I'll tweak those so you can use all of the bells and whistles."

He studied her and her cheeks grew warm. "All right, thanks." He moved past the fridge into the garage.

She reached for the remaining plates on the table and dumped them in the sink. He returned in no time, easily hefting the large screen. She moved toward it and flattened her palm across the bottom right area. Lights instantly flashed, and she typed in what she needed. "Put your hand here," she said. He did so. "Say your name."

"Scott Terentson." His low voice carried through the quiet kitchen.

Lightning zapped outside, and she jumped. "You're good to go," she said.

"I'm taking this up to my room. Are you sure you don't need help with the dishes?"

"No, I'm fine."

"Good." He picked the screen up easily and quickly ascended the stairs on the other side of the living room.

"It'll automatically connect to Wi-Fi," she called out, "in case you need to access the internet."

"Thanks," he called back, the sound of his heavy footsteps a direct contrast to how silently he'd moved that morning to take out those three men. It was fascinating really, how much danger lurked in his scarred body.

She thought fleetingly about calling one of her friends from the team to help her make sense of her contradictory feelings. Nari was out of the country. Serena was still on a mission somewhere. But Pippa, Dana, and Brigid were in town, as was Gemma. While she didn't know Gemma all that well, the women were all dating very dangerous men, and she could use a friend right now.

Yet the second she called one of them, she ran the risk of the team heading to River City. She had enough to worry about right now without the unpredictable Deep Ops team descending on her.

Confusion didn't sit well with her. She was someone who deciphered puzzles and solved mysteries, and Scott Terentson was one she couldn't quite put into a box or handle with a gadget. His brilliant mind and his hard body had intrigued her from the beginning, but the easy way he maneuvered in her small town made him even more appealing. And then, of course, having witnessed how dangerous he could be, how freaking deadly, she was entirely enthralled.

She could admit that to herself and maybe to a good friend or two. But other than that, the attraction didn't make sense. As a woman of science and an inventor, someone so primal shouldn't have desire sliding through her veins so fast even her breath heated.

Having him one story away in the guest room was a temptation she didn't know what to do with, so she forced herself to finish cleaning the kitchen and then went through the reservation booklet her aunt kept by the phone. JT had obviously canceled a few charters, but they had to take the Derby reservations for sure.

She had canceled the charter scheduled for that morning and promised to make it up to the group during the height of the season with an all-day fishing trip. They'd seemed more than happy to swap the cold, rainy day for one in August, so at least that was handled.

Her phone buzzed and she lifted it absently to her ear. "Frost."

"Hi there, gorgeous."

It took her a second to recognize Werner Dearth's voice. "What do you want?"

"Just wanted to check in and see if you're still an agent." He laughed. "I can't stop thinking about you."

"Call me again, and I'll have you arrested for harassment." She ended the call, her heart thundering.

Then she waited for several moments. Finally, she couldn't sit still. She couldn't take a full breath, and her skin felt as if ants were crawling across her arms. She finally gave up and had just decided she'd go for a run when the door burst open and JT ran inside with Roscoe in his arms. "What happened?" she cried out.

"I don't know." JT placed the dog on the ground.

Roscoe looked up, gave her a doggy grin, and hiccupped.

"Oh no, you gave him alcohol?" Her eyes widened and she stared, stunned, at her brother.

"No, I didn't give him alcohol," JT said. "Well, I didn't mean to."

This was so bad. Panic caught her. "Explain." She hurriedly moved to the doggy bowl, made sure it was full of cold water, and shoved it under Roscoe's nose. "Drink this."

He lazily let his tongue loll out and started drinking.

Scott pounded down the stairs. "I heard yelling. What's going on?"

"He's drunk," Millie said, pointing at the dog.

Scott stopped cold, his gaze slashing to JT. "You gave him alcohol?"

"I didn't mean to." JT threw his hands up. "We went for a run, then I dodged into the bunkhouse to put on a warm sweatshirt. I don't know what fucking happened. The dog ran for my trunk at the end of the bed—I don't even know how he got it open."

"He's very talented," Scott noted.

JT scrubbed a hand furiously through his short hair. "Yeah, he had a bottle of Scotch open in no time and was tipping it back before I could blink." JT shook his head. "Honestly, I've never seen anything like it."

"I have," Millie said. "He's very determined sometimes." She scratched Roscoe behind the ears and he started to purr.

"What do we do?" JT asked. "Should we take him to the vet?"

Millie made sure Roscoe drank more of the water. "No. We'll watch his vitals and make sure he doesn't start shaking. Also, he has to keep drinking water." She sat down on the floor. "Unfortunately, he's done this several times, and Angus has had him checked out every time, and he's always been fine. Alcohol should kill dogs, but this one has been lucky." She glared at Roscoe. "You know better."

He farted and then hiccupped again, looking deliriously happy.

* * * *

"Thanks. I'll relay the message to Millie," Scott said, ending the phone call and studying the woman sitting on the sofa next to a peacefully snoring Roscoe.

She looked up, dark circles beneath her eyes. "Well?"

Scott exhaled slowly. "In the vet's opinion, since Roscoe drank all that water, is warm and not shaking, he'll be fine." Rain lashed the windows in the darkness as dawn arrived; the morning remained cold and shrouded outside. "Based on Roscoe's medical history and his current status as calmly sleeping, we still don't need charcoal or any intervention." Someday Roscoe's good luck would run out, but apparently not today.

She stroked Roscoe's coat. "I think I'll take him in once the vet opens. It was nice of Clancy to let us call him through the night."

"He sounds like a decent guy," Scott agreed, wanting more than ever to carry her up the stairs and to bed. To his bed. He was beyond furious that Werner Dearth had not only threatened her after the trial but had just called her. If necessary, he'd have a discussion with that man one on one. Soon. "Come on, Millie. Let's try to get a couple hours of sleep."

She pushed to her feet, patted Roscoe again, and ambled around a chair. "Good idea." Yawning, she held the railing as she took the steps.

He followed her, trying not to notice the sway of her cute ass in her tight jeans.

At the landing, she stumbled.

He caught her easily, his body wide awake.

For the first time, she didn't move away from his touch. Her eyes glistened with a mystifying shade of blue. "Scott?"

He kissed her. Holding her on the stairway, he leaned down and went all in, losing himself in Millicent Frost for the briefest of moments. Then he gently set her back on her feet on the landing.

She blinked, her lips still pursed. "I'm tired of fighting this."

He almost swallowed his tongue, several steps beneath her so he met her eye to eye. "Millie?"

She put her hands on her hips. "There's something here. Has been from day one, and this tension is driving me nuts. We need to get it out of our systems so we can concentrate." She reached for him, and he climbed a stair, lust careening through him as she planted both hands on his pecs. "It's not just me, is it?"

"No." Even his breath felt heated. Was she saying what he wanted? "Millie, I'm all sorts of fucked up." The woman deserved the truth. "Plus, the world is smacking you around right now, and you might not be thinking clearly." His thoughts deserted him entirely.

Her breathtaking eyes deepened to a mysterious indigo color. "We're both hot messes right now, Terentson. Planning anything would be insane. But I'm tired of pretending and wondering. Aren't you?" She caressed his chest, and her tongue flicked out to lick her bottom lip. "I was so scared about Roscoe, even though he's always been fine. But you never know."

"Me, too." Scott didn't want to admit it, but he'd grown fond of the eccentric canine. "Millie, I don't think—"

She leaned up and kissed him, her lips so soft he nearly dropped to his knees. He let her play and held his breath, his hands clenching into fists to keep from taking her to the landing in one motion. Swallowing, she leaned back, a peach color spreading across her pale face. "If I've misread you—"

"You haven't." He sounded like he'd been eating rusty nails. Lust poured through him, sparking his body on fire. He knew, without question, that JT was watching the house for the night, so they were safe. He could lose himself for a few hours and not worry about another surprise attack. Even so, he'd never take advantage of a sweetheart like Millie. "I'm trying to be a gentleman here."

"Forget that." She jumped toward him, her trust that he'd catch her landing hard in his heart. Both of her small hands tunneled through his hair and she kissed him again, her tongue sweeping along his lips and then sliding inside his mouth. She tasted like hazelnut coffee, and her warm little body felt soft against him.

That quickly, Scott Terentson, a man always in control and usually living in his head, was lost.

He tangled his fingers in her hair and took over the kiss, his body jolting with the impact. Sliding one hand beneath her butt, he secured her, still kissing her, and climbed up the remaining stairs, taking a left toward his bedroom. Her compact body moved against him, and he held her firm, letting the moment take them both.

The blood roared through his head and pounded in his ears, but he forced himself to be gentle as he laid her down on the bed, knowing without a doubt that she'd break his heart. No other way forward existed for them, at least as long as memories of blood and death trapped him. But he no longer cared.

She partially sat up and reached for the clasp of his jeans, desire flushing across her delicate features.

The chance to turn back had long slipped away.

Chapter Fifteen

Millie had never felt so out of control. As a woman who normally found her passion in challenging machinery and her own quest to invent, the intensity of her need for the hard-bodied protector shocked her even as it rushed through her. Leaning over her, he kissed her again, pouring intense fire down her throat to scorch each nerve on the way to her core.

She reached up and dug her nails into his shoulders, fighting to get closer to him. To feel him. All of him. More than passion emanated from his kiss. He harbored a loneliness that echoed through her body and matched the feeling in her soul. Both of them, lost, searching for something more.

Maybe it could be each other.

Warning ticked through the back of her mind, but her sense of control blasted away. Banished along with common sense and practicality. In its place, passion and desire made her breath catch in the back of her throat.

He released her mouth and nipped her jaw before dropping to his knees near the bed.

She looked up and stilled.

The tame lawyer was gone. Instead, the primal being inside Scott Terentson, the man who'd shed blood to protect her just the night before, lay revealed, raw and dangerous. His eyes were a shocking midnight blue, nearly black, and a dark flush heightened the rugged angles of his face. Slowly, deliberately, he removed first one of her socks and then the other, his touch firm and his thumbs massaging the arches of her feet.

Shocking electricity bolted through her legs, making her knees tremble. "Scott?" she whispered.

"I've got you." His voice had deepened, become rough with a tone that tortured her already sensitized nerve endings. He reached up and snapped open her jeans, smoothly sliding them down her legs without moving from his position. Then, as if he wanted to claim every square inch of her, he caressed her calves and placed a kiss on each knee.

Fire lanced through her.

She'd had no idea feet or knees could be erogenous zones. What was he doing to her? His teeth sank into her right thigh. Not enough to bruise or even really hurt, but with enough of a bite that she stopped breathing. For the first time, she realized how little she'd understood the high-powered lawyer. His cloak of professionalism, of sheer intelligence, truly masked the predator breathing beneath his skin.

This glimpse of him...was intoxicating.

He sucked on her other thigh, forcing blood to that small part, guaranteeing he'd leave his mark for at least a week. His gaze rose and met hers, showing pleasure. Dark masculine pleasure that she'd wear the brand—his brand—for a while.

Shocking need tugged low in her abdomen, and wetness spilled from her.

As if catching a scent, his nostrils flared. Then he found her. Moving slightly, he placed his mouth right on her core over her panties and sucked.

She cried out, arching against his scalding hot mouth.

"God, you're perfect," he rumbled, sliding the material down her legs, revealing all of her to him.

She squirmed. "I, uh, don't need that." Though man, she wanted it.

His gaze turned velvet over steel. "That's unfortunate, because I do need it. Want it. And that's what matters." The dominant hard tone expelled the oxygen from the room.

A faint feeling of vulnerability took her and then his mouth was on her, and she forgot all sense of reality. He went at her with that single-minded concentration she'd seen in him before, but not like this. There wasn't anything else in the world like this. His mouth, tongue, fingers, and teeth all forced unreal pleasure from her, and she shut her eyes, trying to ride out the storm.

He paused. "Look at me." His mouth was still against her, and the possessive words echoed throughout her body.

Sucking in air, she forced her eyelids to open. What she saw shook her and rushed need so quickly to her sex that she gasped. His expression was all male, harsh, lust glittering in his eyes. "Mine." Keeping her gaze captive, he lowered his mouth again and sucked her clit into his mouth. Then his tongue lashed her, rough and wet.

Even here, he was in complete control. It'd be intimidating if it wasn't such a turn-on.

She splintered, whispering his name, unable to keep her eyes open. The orgasm tore through her, ripping apart every nerve, exploding out from her core to reach every cell. He mercilessly flicked her with his tongue until she came down, unable to take any more. "Scott." She reached for him.

"Yeah." He stood and tore off his shirt. The battle wounds on his torso, old and now new, served to emphasize the cut muscle and raw strength beneath each scar. How had he survived so much? Unzipping his jeans, he kicked them somewhere else, leaving him in black boxers. Boxers he filled out in a way that had her mouth watering.

He was still in command. She didn't want that. She wanted him as out of his mind, as removed from his demons, as she was right now. So she reached for him, gratified when he put one knee on the bed and levered himself over her.

Finally, she could touch him. Humming, she gently traced the healed knife wounds on his shoulder, careful to avoid the fresh bandages on the other side of his rib cage. "So much pain," she whispered, trying to ease it with her touch.

"Don't feel pain." He grasped the hem of her shirt and pushed it up, forcing her to lift her head. Then it was gone. Somewhere across the room. His callused fingers slid beneath her bra, brushing her needy breasts. Suddenly, she wanted more. Then the bra was gone and his lips were enclosing one nipple. He scored her with his teeth and she clamped both hands on his head, tugging on his hair, moaning in raw pleasure.

This wasn't healthy. She wasn't even sure it was possible but happily gave up reality. Another moan tore from her.

He moved to the other breast, his heated breath flashing along her skin. "You taste like heaven."

"I don't taste like anything," she gasped, trying to think a little.

"You do," he countered, stroking her with his tongue.

It was too much and yet she needed more. She clamped her hands on his shoulders and pulled.

He lifted his head, his nostrils flaring. "You'll take what I give you." Then he sank his teeth around her nipple.

She gasped as pain and pleasure collided inside her. Who was this man? "Scott—"

He lashed her nipple with his rough tongue and lifted up again. "I'm in charge here, brilliant one. Get used to it." He then moved up her, the long, hard length of his cock pressing against her.

Her eyes might've rolled back into her head as her hips arched against him. She wanted him inside her more than anything else in the world, both of them barreling headfirst into pleasure. "Now, Scott," she ordered.

He stared down at her, and the primal lust on his face should've made her stop and think. "Begging is fine…orders are not." He reached down her body. Those strong fingers pushed inside her and then he flicked her clit.

She nearly came off the bed, more than wet and ready.

"Tell me you understand." His thumb stroked her clit, and shocking vibrations zinged through her. "Now."

"I understand." She reached down to shove his boxers out of the way.

His grin was wicked as he helped her, kicking them onto the floor. Then he pulsed against her, hard and full. "I like you compliant," he whispered.

The intensity of the moment made her question, just for a second, what she did want. Maybe there was more for them than just this one time. The depths of the man intrigued her. She leaned up and kissed his chest and then his neck, taking a slight bite out of his hard-cut jaw.

He reached to the side, digging into the wallet on the bedside table. A wrapper crinkled, he partially rolled to the side, and then he was back on her, body to body. His hands somehow found hers and he lifted her arms above her head, entwining their fingers and pinning her hands to the bed.

Jolting electricity arced through her. "Wait, I—"

"No. This is how I want you." Then slowly, his gaze on hers, he penetrated her. He was ruthless as he took her over, inch by inch, taking his time as her body adjusted to his size.

Her heart thundered. He finally embedded himself fully inside her, connecting them completely. Her eyes widened. Passion surrounded them and wildfires beat between them, but this went deeper. Somewhere much deeper than she'd anticipated. Vulnerability and a shocking need, one beyond the physical, swamped her.

Then he started to move. Hard and fast, giving no quarter, he pounded inside her. She gripped his hands, climbing toward the climax that might shatter her for all time.

He slowed. "Ask me."

She blinked, the blood pounding furiously through her veins. How could he just stop? She gripped him internally, enjoying the flash of lust filling his eyes.

He leaned down until his nose nearly touched hers. "Now you can beg." Slowly, he slid out of her and then drove back in.

Hard.

She cried out, so close to the precipice.

His dark chuckle sent tremors of need through her body. "I can hold you here forever."

She needed him. Now. "Please," she whispered.

"There you go." Dark power flushed across his face and he pulled out to drive back inside her, hammering hard and fast. Widening her thighs, she threw herself over that cliff, taking all of him. Wanting all of him.

Pleasure crashed through her like a pounding wave, consuming, taking all she'd ever be and giving her no choice but to ride out the most intense release she'd ever felt. Hot and wild, nearly devastating.

She almost panicked, then saw he was right there with her.

His entire body tensed and he drove deeper inside her, his fingers curling over hers. "So fucking amazing," he ground out, shuddering with his own release. He flattened his body even harder against hers, and she could feel his heartbeat racing.

Slowly, they both came down, and he released her hands.

She gingerly lowered her arms and smoothed her palms down his damp back, noting each ridge, hollow, muscle...and scar. Several she hadn't seen yet.

He leaned down and kissed her, levering his weight partially off her and onto his elbows. This kiss was different. It was sweet and deep, satisfied and...something else. Something male. A hint of promise and a claim of more.

She kissed him back, tasting him, her body still pounding.

He pulled out of her, stood, and moved to the bathroom to take care of the condom, before returning and sliding into the bed to curve his big body around her.

She couldn't find words.

"You're beautiful. Perfect. Beyond this silly world," he murmured against her hair, one arm banded around her waist, pulling her more fully into his warmth. His ripped abs felt solid against her back, and his cock remained partially hard against her butt. Surprising desire still lingered within her, which should be impossible.

She felt exposed in a way she hadn't anticipated. Vulnerable and even fragile. One night with him wasn't nearly enough. The more she got to know him, the more she wanted to be with him. Plus, she saw him so much more clearly now. He was always apart from the team, helping but not getting involved. She didn't want him to be alone. Everyone needed someone. These chaotic thoughts shimmered through her head, and she shut her eyes, wanting oblivion.

She'd thought sex with the tailored lawyer would be boring. Instead, it had shaken her to the core. His inherent dominance should give her pause and probably would when her brain started working again. Most likely the character trait was just an extension of his obvious need to be in control, but she'd figured that was inherent in his job and with intimacy.

She'd been wrong.

Her phone buzzed from the floor.

Scott shifted his weight, dropped an arm, and moved around. "Here it is." He pulled himself back up, settled around her again, and pressed the phone into her hand.

"Hello?" she answered, assuming it was the veterinarian calling from his office.

"Hey, Millie. Sorry to call so early but Rupert Skinner just left my office. The guy gets to work early," the chief muttered.

If her body wasn't so satiated, she'd probably stiffen. Instead she took a deep breath. "And?"

"You're being charged with first-degree homicide." The chief waited a moment. "The preliminary hearing is set for next week. You could probably get an extension, but talk to your lawyer. Is he still around?"

Millie gulped, barreling right out of her moment of bliss. "Um, yes." Her lawyer currently wrapped his nude body around her, his heated breath at her neck making her tremble.

"Good. Skinner is coming after you hard." The chief coughed. "I hate to say it, but all of the evidence is squarely against you. I don't have anything exculpatory yet. It ain't good."

"Thanks, Chief." She ended the call, her chest feeling hollow. Scott shifted against her. "What is it?" he asked sleepily.

She didn't want to ruin their brief moment of pleasure, but since morning light now slid through the blinds, she should return to reality. She could dream about him later. "It looks like I might be facing prison time." Oh, she'd fight it as hard as she could, but so far, she was in trouble. No matter what happened, at least she'd have this night to remember and keep her warm in the future.

"The fuck you are." Scott rolled gracefully from the bed, revealing a myriad of battle scars across his back as he reached down to fetch his jeans. "We might need to consider calling in your team."

Chapter Sixteen

Wearing only his jeans, Scott finished flipping the flapjacks from a frying pan onto a platter decorated with butterflies. His body felt the most relaxed it had been in months, if not years, and definitely since the last time he'd been shot. Yet his mind wouldn't calm.

He and Millie had tacitly agreed that the night before was a one-off and that they couldn't be together. Yet now that he'd had a taste of her, not one ounce of him wanted to let her go.

She finished a phone call with her aunt and placed her phone on the counter.

He looked over his shoulder. "Where's your aunt?"

"She met friends for breakfast, then thought she'd run errands before her follow-up appointment at the hospital." Millie smiled. "I wonder if seeing the chief is one of her errands."

Ah. That made sense. "They make a cute couple."

"I wonder why they're keeping it a secret."

"Maybe they're just friends with benefits." Scott turned and carried the platter to the table, where he had already set the plates and napkins.

He paused and studied Millie. Rosy cheeks graced her face and she had a hop in her step that hadn't been there the day before. He liked to think that he had contributed to her cheerful mood, but even her smile didn't banish the shadows from her eyes. The news from the chief wasn't good, and Scott hadn't been joking about calling in Angus and his team. He wouldn't allow Millie to go down the path to a criminal trial.

She poured two glasses of orange juice and sat. "This looks amazing."

"I can make pancakes." Truth be told, he could cook very few items. While he had some skills, cooking eluded him.

She dished up two plates. "It was nice of you to make breakfast." She reached for the syrup.

"It's the least I can do," he said, adding butter. He might have to work out longer the upcoming week, but butter on pancakes was a necessity.

She cocked her head. "What do you do for fun?"

Ah, they were at the talking portion of whatever had happened between them last night. For once, he didn't mind sharing his life. "In the fall I play touch football as a running back. Well, that's not true. I play tackle football in a league with other professionals in DC." He shrugged. "I think the league started out as touch football, but the game quickly evolved to us burying each other in the dirt."

Her eyes widened. "You wear pads, right?"

"And helmets," he said, grinning. "We're not stupid."

She lifted a shoulder in a cute challenge. "I had no idea you played football."

"It's not something I advertise. It's just something I do."

"What else?" she asked, leaning forward and reaching for more syrup.

Her interest in his life came across very sweet. He wanted to invite her to a fall game. Hopefully they'd still be friends. Would he always want more with her? Probably, but he was in no position to offer anything to a woman. "Once in a while I hang out with Angus, and so long as no one's shooting at us, that's fun," he said. "I also have friends I play poker with once a month."

"Also lawyers?" she asked.

He thought about it. "Not really. It's just an odd group of us who have known each other since our Georgetown days, and sometimes Wolfe joins in. One guy's in news, one guy runs a shipping company, and of course one guy is a dentist." He smiled. "Everybody needs a dentist in their poker club."

She laughed. "That's true." She looked around. "I make gadgets."

"No kidding. What else?" he asked, warming to the subject. There wasn't much that could make Millie Frost more likable, but he was willing to give it a shot.

She poured even more syrup on her pancakes. "When I'm in DC, I donate time at the Humane Society."

"That figures—you seem like a natural with animals. Anything else?"

She gave a cute smile. "I coach softball." She said the words quickly as if afraid he'd make fun of her.

He sat back. "You coach softball?"

"Yeah. I help a couple of friends with their kids' teams." She took a big bite of pancakes and then shut her eyes, humming in what could only be termed pleasure. Finishing, she smiled.

He couldn't imagine her as a coach. He'd bet she was tons of fun. "Tell me about your team."

Her eyes lit up. "They're in the third grade now but we started with them in the first grade. It's T-ball, but we have some girls who really could go far—maybe even get college scholarships someday." She hopped on her seat. "I structured different hitting and catching scenarios based on size and strength of each girl after creating specialty mitts for each of them. We're pretty good."

God, she was adorable. "I'm sure you are. I would love to see a game."

Her eyes lit up even more. "The season doesn't open for another few weeks, but you bet. I'd like to watch you play football." She chewed on the inside of her lip and looked down at the pancakes. "If I'm not in prison."

"You're not going to be in prison," he said. He'd break every law he had to in order to ensure her freedom. Putting Millie in a jail cell would be like locking up a firefly.

She rubbed both hands over her eyes and reached for her fork again. "How much trouble do you think I'm in?"

An intense amount. "You'll be fine. We'll figure out who killed Clay Baker," he said instead.

She sighed. "The chief said I could fight against holding the preliminary hearing next week since it's so early."

"You can, but I don't want to," Scott said.

"Oh." She sat back. "What happens at the preliminary hearing?"

He took a drink of his orange juice. "The state will give evidence and the magistrate judge will decide whether there's probable cause for charges against you."

Her face fell. "There's definitely enough probable cause, right?"

"Yes," he said.

She sighed. "What happens after that?"

After that? He had no intention of the proceedings getting that far. "After that, the case will be bound over to the circuit court and considered by a grand jury."

Her shoulders slumped. "Can't we just waive that and get to it?"

"No," he said. "We will not waive any of your rights in the interest of time. I want to hear all of the evidence. My plan today is to meet with the chief and prosecutor personally. I know the chief is an old friend of yours, but he also has a job to do, and we don't have all of the facts. The prosecuting attorney sounds like an ambitious bastard looking for headlines. We'll hear his evidence during the grand jury proceedings."

"Oh man." She dropped her fork. "Okay, then what?"

"If they return an indictment, you'll be arraigned and we can enter a plea, and then the trial process starts. We're not going to get that far, Millie."

She looked at her food as if she'd lost her appetite. "You think hypnotism would work to help me remember that night?"

"No," he said flatly. "If you were drugged, and we both agree that you were, then you won't be able to access your memories. I wouldn't put yourself through that."

"Fair enough." She looked small and defenseless.

"Trust me, Millie. I know what I'm doing." Even if they had to go to trial, he'd win the case for her. He believed whole-heartedly in her innocence.

Her phone buzzed again and she looked at it, frowning before lifting it to her ear. "Agent Frost." She sounded businesslike in an intriguingly sexy way. She slowly paled. "I understand. Yes, I'll be there." She ended the call and stared at the phone.

Irritation clawed up Scott's back, but he ignored it. "Who was that, Agent Frost?"

She placed the phone next to her orange juice. "It was HDD headquarters. Agent Rutherford called me in—I guess it's time to get back to work. I didn't think I'd be brought back in on the Dearth case, but it hasn't been closed, so maybe that's it?"

"Speaking of Dearth, what did you actually get on him?"

She looked away as if deciding what she could tell him. "We think he's been skimming profits from clients, but his paper trail has been expertly masked. It's a federal investigation and we received a valid warrant to basically bug his offices."

Scott sighed. "Unfortunately, since you got caught up in my divorce case, Dearth knows not to say anything in his office."

"Yeah. We're still tracing his financials," she said quietly. "It's just going to take longer than if we had gotten him on a recording and dragged his butt into headquarters." She sighed. "He's a real ass, isn't he?"

"Oh, absolutely. I can't tell you about the divorce because of client privilege, but if I think you need to know something, I'll speak with my client. Okay?"

"That's fair," Millie said, shrugging. "To be honest, Dearth is the least of my problems right now."

"Agreed," Scott said. The woman had more problems than she did curls. With the green fading from her hair, he wondered what color she'd go for next. He'd seen her with a multitude of different shades and once as a natural blonde. She sparkled sweet beauty in every circumstance.

His phone buzzed. He tugged it out of his back pocket. "Terentson." He barely kept the bite out of his tone.

"Hey, Scott," Tate Bianchi said. "It's Tate."

"Hey, Tate." Scott sat up straighter in his chair, wondering what the DC homicide detective wanted with him. "What's up?"

"We have a missing person case, and you're on record as representing her."

Scott stilled. "Who is missing?"

"Julie Dearth."

Scott rocked back in his chair. "Who reported her missing?"

"Her housekeeper, and there's blood at the scene," Tate said. "I conducted a quick search and found that you're her attorney of record in a divorce proceeding."

"I am," Scott said. He glanced at Millie. "I'm coming into the city today. I'll drop by and give you everything I have."

"Great," Tate said. "Thanks, I'll see you then."

Scott clicked off, his mind reeling.

"What is it?" Millie asked.

What had he overlooked? "Julie Dearth is missing." Scott couldn't believe it. He stood and carried his plate over to the sink. Werner Dearth was unquestionably a jackass and a criminal, but just what level of danger did he pose? "We have to get into the city."

"I just need to change into something official looking," Millie murmured.

The back door opened and JT strode inside with Roscoe on his heels. "We went for another run," he announced. "Dog's fine. Guy has a better tolerance for alcohol than a couple of my buddies from the service."

Scott reached for his orange juice. JT leaned back and eyed Scott from head to toe, taking in his bare chest and bare feet. Then he looked at his sister and his gaze hardened.

Scott met his eyes evenly and lifted an eyebrow in invitation. Did JT want to make an issue of Scott and Millie? If so, Scott could go a round or two. The morning had gotten completely out of his control, an unacceptable situation.

To his surprise, a slight grin lifted the right side of JT's mouth. He looked at him, patted the dog, and winked at his sister. "Good luck, Scott," he muttered, heading for the door.

"Wait," Millie said.

JT turned around. "What's up, Mills?" he drawled.

"I have to go into the city today but will drop by the doctor's office at the hospital for Mae's appointment. Can you keep an eye on her when she comes home? I don't like leaving her alone."

"Sure." JT turned around as if changing his mind and headed for the cupboard. "Do you still have those cookies you made the other day?"

"I have peanut butter left," she said.

He reached in and took out a bag of what looked like delicious cookies. "I need sugar." He strolled out, pausing to look over his shoulder once again. "You hurt her and I'll cut out your heart, Terentson. Just thought you should know."

The door shut quietly behind him.

That seemed fair.

Chapter Seventeen

Millie clip-clopped into the waiting area of the doctor's office attached to the small hospital to find Verna Montgomery sitting near her aunt, who had balanced a very pretty bouquet of pink peonies in a vase on the adjacent chair.

"Hey, Verna," Millie said, smiling.

Verna looked up and grinned. "Howdy. I brought some family paperwork to Valerie since she's on duty and dropped by to see your aunt Mae after her appointment."

"We've had such a good talk while I've waited for the pharmacy to fill my cholesterol medicine prescription," her great-aunt said, looking at Verna's belly. "She's so excited and hopes this is a girl. Wouldn't it be wonderful to be a great-great-aunt?" She slowly turned her head to Millie.

Millie rolled her eyes. "I am nowhere near to getting married, Aunt Mae."

"Hm, I don't know. That Scott Terentson is quite handsome."

"He really is," Verna said dryly. "I mean, I'm happily married and all, but I do have eyes."

Millie shook her head. "What did the doctor say?"

"That I'm fine." Aunt Mae touched the pretty petals. "Verna, you're always so sweet. How did you even know I was going to be here?"

"Valerie told me when I dropped off the kids' concert schedule, so I stopped into the gift shop. Valerie's helping out since I'm getting so large." Verna pushed herself to stand and walked over to Millie to lean over and whisper, "You have whisker burn beneath your ear, girlfriend." With that, she turned and headed into the restroom.

Millie tried not to blush.

Her great-aunt examined her. "You look nice. Where are you going today?"

Millie had worn her navy-blue suit with a bright pink shell and understated gold jewelry. This represented the height of her conservatism. She'd thought idly about removing the last of the green streaks from her hair, but then decided that Agent Rutherford could just bite her. "I have to go into the city for a while and get some work done."

"Good. I wish the pharmacy would hurry—I need to get back to work. We have a lot of charters for the Derby, you know."

"I saw," Millie said, guilt filtering through her. Her great-aunt needed more help to keep the business going successfully. "I have some funds," she offered quietly. "Why don't we hire you an assistant?"

"I don't need anybody to help me," Mae said, her blue eyes sparkling. "JT is home for good, I think, and now Lila's around. We haven't taught her to fish yet, but she's a fast learner."

"Speaking of Lila, who is this woman?" Millie asked.

Her aunt checked her cell phone. "She's a person who needed a place to stay. Where's Scott, anyway?"

"He's waiting in the vehicle with Roscoe."

Her great-aunt clapped her hands. "A dog's the first step in planting roots, you know."

Millie leaned over and kissed her great-aunt's papery cheek, happy to see the sparkle back in her eyes. "So they say. I have to go, but I'll be back as soon as I can."

"Let's talk about Scott."

Heat climbed up Millie's face. "Aunt Mae," she protested.

"That man has some very fine shoulders."

"Yes. He really does." Plus he was smart and apparently dangerous, as well as having chiseled features and rock-hard abs. "We're too different, Aunt Mae. He's not just a lawyer but one of the best, and I'm sure he has all sorts of ambitions and wants a wife who hosts garden parties or something."

"Garden parties?" Her great-aunt snorted. "Seriously? If he's smart, as you say, he wants a brilliant and charming woman who could make a house blow up by rigging a toaster with a mousetrap."

Millie winced. "That was an accident, and I didn't blow up the house. I merely started a fire in the kitchen."

"A big fire," Mae retorted.

"Sorry about that." Millie fought the giggle that wanted to get loose.

Aunt Mae smiled again. "Life should be full of adventure, and that man is smart enough to know it. I saw the way you looked at him."

If her great-aunt had any idea of what she'd actually done with him, she'd be relentless. "I love your romantic heart."

"I want great-grandnieces or even nephews."

"What about you and the chief?"

Mae blinked. "I have no idea what you're talking about."

"Uh huh."

Valerie walked in just then. "Here you go, Mae. Sorry it took so long." She handed over a paper bag.

Mae stood. "Thanks, Valerie."

Val nodded. "You also have to manage stress better, Mae. We all need you around here."

Millie ought to help out more at home. She thought about how she could rearrange her schedule as Verna emerged from the bathroom, looking refreshed with pink lipstick. "Hey, I'm glad you're still here," Millie said. "I have a couple more questions."

"I want to help," Verna said, her eyes a mellow green.

"Have you thought any more about when you saw me leave with Clay?" Millie kept getting a headache any time she tried to force memories into the black hole of that night.

Verna placed a hand on her protruding belly. "Not really. Why?"

"It just doesn't make any sense. I feel like I've lost a part of myself." Millie gulped. "Was I talking to Clay when you saw us?"

Verna frowned as if trying to remember. "I didn't really see your face. I just saw you get in his truck and scoot over. Then he got in after you." She shook her head. "You didn't seem like you didn't want to go, but no, I didn't see you talking. Oh man, Millie, I wish I'd stopped you or run after you or something, but I just figured you knew what you were doing."

"I know." Millie reached out and touched her arm. "I'm not mad at you. I'm just trying to remember. How did Clay seem?"

"He seemed fine. He shut the door and drove away. You don't think he was the one who drugged you, do you?" Verna asked, her voice hushed.

Millie leaned against the column. "I don't know."

Aunt Mae snorted. "He was such a jackass."

"His drugging you would make sense," Valerie piped up, rubbing her bare lips. "In fact, it puts things into perspective. If you really didn't like him, didn't want to go with him, why did you? You know, I heard rumors about Clay years ago."

"What rumors?" Millie asked, perking up.

Valerie tapped on her forehead. "I don't know. There's something. I swear this whole situation feels familiar."

Verna frowned. "I don't know what you're talking about. Are you sure you didn't just see a show or something? Sometimes you do that, Valerie."

Valerie scoffed. "I do. I mix up reality and TV sometimes, but no, I remember rumors circulating when Clay attended law school. I attended nursing school on the same campus, and we had mutual friends. I recall speculation about Clay and a woman who accused him of assault."

Heat rushed to Millie's ears. "That's at least something." She'd need to dig deeper. The excitement quickly turned to a pit in her gut. Time was not on her side.

Chapter Eighteen

The eleventh floor of the Henry J. Daly Building smelled like wood polish, fresh coffee, and ink over a slight note of body odor. With Millie and Roscoe in tow, Scott maneuvered toward the back of the floor beyond several hubs. It had been a bit of an ordeal to get the dog through security, but Tate had called down and made it happen. Scott owed him yet another one.

They reached the first bullpen, also known as the homicide division, where Tate already waited with a file in his hand as he leaned against the wall.

"Hey," Scott said, reaching out a hand.

Tate shook it. "Hi, Scott. Millie."

Millie smiled and leaned forward for a hug. "It's good to see you, Tate."

Scott remained passive. He hadn't realized the two had worked together before.

"You been practicing your game?" Tate asked, turning his attention to Scott.

"I'm ready anytime, boyo," Scott said, smiling.

Millie looked from one to the other.

Scott shrugged. "We play tennis once in a while."

"Huh," she said. "Interesting. Tennis and football, huh?"

Tate grinned. "I'm on the football team, too."

Yeah. One of the smartest things Scott had ever done was talking Tate Bianchi into joining their team about a year ago. Tate was at least six foot four and built like a linebacker, but he'd gone to college on a tennis scholarship and had natural grace as well. Besides being tall and broad, he looked like a badass with his dark skin, hard brown eyes, and bald head. He was quickly turning into one of Scott's best friends and it felt right to be standing there with Millie.

Tate dropped to his haunches and vigorously rubbed his fingers through Roscoe's thick fur. "Is he behaving himself?"

"No," Millie said shortly. "He got into some Scotch the other night."

Tate tsked. "Roscoe, when are you going to learn?" Roscoe licked his chin, panting happily. Tate chuckled and stood. "Come on. I have a conference room ready for us." He turned and led the way down the hall and into a smaller conference room with gray walls, windows facing the building next door, and noisy white tiles. He tossed a file folder on the table. "Come on, Roscoe," he called back when the dog hovered near a desk holding a platter of snickerdoodles. "No cookies for you."

Roscoe snorted, took one last longing glance at the cookies, and started their way.

Scott shook his head. "I swear, that dog."

All of a sudden, Roscoe paused, one foot up in midstride. He sniffed the air expectantly. He turned and looked across the bullpen, where a detective was taking a statement from a teenager. The teenager leaned forward with his hands in his pockets, his head up, and his eyes wide as he spoke. He took out his hands and gestured wildly.

Roscoe gave one short bark and leaped into the air, landing on a desk and scattering papers in every direction. His legs went out from under him and he scrambled, his nails clawing the desk. He toppled over a stapler and a cup of coffee, barked again, jumped on another desk and then another.

Several officers, both uniformed and in plainclothes, deserted their desks or areas near corkboards and rushed for the dog. One woman almost grabbed him, but Roscoe sprang gleefully onto a center table that held printouts, knocking them to the floor. He barked again and leaped straight for the kid in the blue sweatshirt. The kid was about seventeen with long black hair, angled features, and green eyes. He held up both hands, but it was too late.

Roscoe impacted him, knocking him back against the desk. With one fierce paw, Roscoe scrambled furiously in the kid's pocket. With a hard swipe, Roscoe flipped a bottle out of the pocket onto the ground, where it shattered.

The dog immediately dropped and started rapidly licking up the liquid. It took the scent a second to reach Scott, but he recognized vodka when he smelled it. Millie was already trying to scramble through the officers to get to the dog.

"Damn it, Roscoe!" Scott muttered. He jumped onto a desk and followed Roscoe's path to get beyond all the people crowding forward. Roscoe looked up, licked his lips, and shot through the legs of a uniformed officer, dodging left and right, knocking people over.

"Roscoe!" Tate yelled.

Millie ran around the other side, slipping on papers and going down.

"Millie," Scott bellowed, turning and heading for her. She grabbed the edge of a desk and pulled herself to her feet, paperclips stuck in her hair. Scott's irritation flashed to anger. "Roscoe!" he yelled at the top of his lungs.

The entire room stilled. Roscoe tried to halt on another desk but couldn't and ended up springing onto a copy machine. His paw hit the red button and the thing instantly started spitting out paper. Scott moved for him. Roscoe took one look at Scott's face and somehow jumped up and nearly backflipped to land on another desk—the one with the cookies. He devoured half of them, and just as Scott almost reached him, he turned and leaped toward the doorway.

A woman came out of nowhere and caught him in a flying tackle, wrapping both arms around the dog and turning so she landed on her back and skidded several feet, holding the animal but not hurting him. They came to a stop. Silence landed hard for several moments.

It took Scott a second to recognize Detective Buckle, Tate Bianchi's partner, with her long arms wrapped around the dog. Roscoe settled in, flattening himself on her, and licked from her chin to the top of her head.

"Roscoe," she snapped, rolling him to the side but keeping her hold on him. Wearing jeans and a green blazer now covered with cookie crumbs, she stood and pulled the dog up with her. Her gaze caught on Scott. "Are you kidding? What are you doing bringing him here?"

"Sorry." Scott winced as he bounded down from a desk and reached for the dog.

Roscoe panted happily and licked crumbs off his fur. His doggy gaze caught on Buckle's three-inch-heeled boots, crafted in black leather. He gingerly licked one.

"Oh no, buddy. I've heard about you and high heels," Buckle said. She looked at her partner. "You invited the dog in?"

Tate blanched. "Sorry, I wasn't thinking."

Scott cleared his throat. "Excellent tackle, Detective Buckle." The woman looked like a model at six feet tall with brown hair, lighter brown eyes, and an extremely stubborn chin.

She sighed. "Sorry, everybody. Pizza's on Tate this Friday." With that, she dragged Roscoe into the conference room.

Scott reached Millie and tugged a couple of paperclips from her hair. "Are you okay?"

"That dog," she said. She brushed dust off her clothes and followed Detective Buckle. Tate Bianchi leveled a look at Scott, but there wasn't much he could do about the situation, so he went after the women and waited for Tate to do the same. They sat at the table.

"It's always an adventure," Detective Buckle said, smiling and showing one crooked tooth that made her intriguing.

"Hi, Buckle," Millie said. "Haven't seen you for a while."

Detective Buckle wiped Roscoe's kiss off her chin. "I agree. Things have been good with you and the team?"

"Yes. We still have a pot going as to what your first name is."

Buckle laughed. "I don't think even Tate knows it."

"Oh, I know it," Tate said grimly, sitting down and reaching for his file folder. "Back to business." He tapped on a file. "We can't find Julie Dearth. Her phone must be off, and she hasn't used a credit card for a couple of days."

"There was a small amount of blood at her apartment near the door," Buckle said quietly. "We're canvassing the neighbors, but nobody has seen anything."

Fury lanced through Scott so quickly his throat hurt, feeling as if he'd swallowed a lit briquette. "She filed for divorce from Werner Dearth, and we're talking millions upon millions in the property settlement." He shook his head. "The guy's dangerous and he is a criminal."

"Do you have any proof of that?" Tate asked.

Scott glanced at Millie.

Millie wished they had proof. "The Homeland Defense Department is investigating him, but I don't know the status of the case. I'll find out later today and let you know."

"Investigating him for what?" Detective Buckle asked.

"Fraud and theft," Millie said. "We think he's been skimming client accounts, but the paper trail has been difficult to prove. The guy knows what he's doing."

Tate frowned. "A white-collar crime like that is a far distance from kidnapping, assault, or potentially murder."

"Oh, he hated her," Scott said.

"The guy's a real blockhead," Millie added. "I ended up testifying in their divorce case. He threatened me when I was leaving court and called me the other day. The moron thinks I'm his enemy now or something."

Tate rolled his neck. "We're executing a search warrant on Julie Dearth's house later today, and I don't have probable cause to bring him in for questioning. I am, however, asking him to come in." He turned his attention to Scott. "As far as you know, does Julie have any other enemies?"

"Not that I know," Scott said. "She's friends with my mother, and I need to check in with her today anyway. I'll ask her if she knows anything and call you if she does."

Tate shut the top file folder. "If you don't mind, would you please run me through everything you know about Werner Dearth? Both of you?"

Roscoe padded over and sat near Millie, placing his head on her lap. She started to pet him.

"No problem," Scott said. "I'm happy to tell you everything I know about that asshole." Was there a possibility that Dearth had harmed his wife? If so, how unhinged was he?

Chapter Nineteen

Millie didn't make it past the first floor of HDD headquarters before being told that somebody would meet her. She waited quietly in the visitor area by herself with her hands clasped in her lap. Security had refused to let Roscoe inside, so Scott had taken him for a walk around the block.

Maybe she'd be assigned to a different case. She wouldn't mind never seeing Werner Dearth again.

Agent Rutherford emerged from the elevator bank and walked toward her wearing his usual high-end suit. He wore a light gray pinstripe suit, complemented by a deeper gray tie. The ensemble flattered him. The guy had smooth blond hair, sharp blue eyes, and a jaw made to take a punch. She had wanted to land that punch more than once.

She stood, wishing she had worn jeans and a sweatshirt instead of this ridiculous suit that made her feel like an eighty-year-old schoolmarm. "Agent Rutherford, good afternoon."

He handed her an envelope. "We're in the middle of something right now, but here is the notice of your termination."

Her ears started to ring. What? "You're actually terminating me?"

"Yes." His face remained implacable. "You blew our case because of your relationship with Scott Terentson."

She hadn't had a relationship with Scott. Well, until last night. Shock zipped through her. "Sheer chance brought us together when I positioned those listening devices," she protested. Panic fluttered in her chest like a trapped bird battering her rib cage and seeking freedom.

"I understand that," Rutherford said. "Apparently, Angus Force and his crew have been a bad influence on you, Agent Frost. You used to be good at your job, but hanging around with that team has destroyed any objectivity you may have had."

Irritation snapped through her. "That's ridiculous. Angus's team has solved more crimes than any other unit here." Their unconventional nature led to their location in Virginia instead of the main headquarters. She actually missed the team and wished she could call Angus right now. A thought occurred to her. "Wait a minute. For a while, Angus was my direct supervisor. Don't you have to notify him?"

"He's not your direct supervisor right now," Rutherford retorted.

She looked down, trying to think, and caught sight of his shiny brown loafers. They probably cost more than her car. Not for the first time, she wondered where Rutherford earned all his money. It wasn't any of her business, and contrary to public opinion, she wasn't a computer hacker. She dealt with gadgets, not code.

"This isn't fair," she said, trying to keep her tone reasonable.

"I don't really care. You've received notice. The procedure is outlined in the papers I gave you. You'll have an opportunity to respond, and you may request a hearing next week. After that, a decision will be made." He stared at her, his gaze hard. "I can tell you the decision will be that you're out."

This was unbelievable. Nobody matched her talent with gadgets. "You're such a jerk," she said.

"Name-calling? That'll go in the report as well," he said.

"Oh please, like everybody who's ever met you doesn't know you're a jerk? I will fight this." Without waiting for his answer, she turned and walked quickly out of the first floor into the frigid

March day. The cold in DC currently surpassed that of River City. She looked both ways and caught sight of Scott and Roscoe headed her way.

"That was quick," Scott said, reaching her.

Roscoe panted happily, probably still buzzed from the alcohol he'd licked off the floor earlier. But the dog seemed to be fine, so she'd just keep giving him water.

She scratched behind his ears. "We need to get this dog some help," she murmured.

"I think he's seen a shrink," Scott returned. "Nari counsels him all the time."

"Nari gives him cookies," Millie retorted, shivering. "Come on, let's get out of the cold." Scott took her hand, which probably wasn't a great idea in front of the HDD headquarters. But at this point, she just didn't care.

"What's in the envelope?" he asked.

"My termination papers."

He stopped them cold, and Roscoe ran into the back of her legs. Only Scott's strong hands grasping her arms stopped her from falling over. "Millie?"

"I received notice of my termination," she said, her brain going numb. "There's a whole procedure, and I do want to fight it."

Scott claimed the envelope. "Oh, we'll fight it. Come on, let's get out of here. It's going to rain."

She walked with him to his SUV in a daze. Soon, they drove away from the city. "Where are we going?"

"I want to drop by and see my mom, if that's okay," he said. "I want to ask her about Julie."

Millie pressed a hand to her solar plexus. She'd forgotten all about Julie, the poor woman. There were more important things than a job. That didn't mean she wouldn't fight her termination, however. Then another thought hit her. "Your mother?" she asked.

He grinned. "You'll like her."

"Oh, I'm sure I'll like her," she said. How could she not? The woman had raised Scott.

"She'll love you," Scott murmured.

Somehow, Millie doubted that. She didn't fit the mold of the perfect politician's wife. Not a politician to date, Scott unquestionably exuded polish. Oh, he might be rough and tumble and dangerous, but most people didn't see that side of him. They saw the smooth lawyer. He'd probably earn a hundred percent of the vote if he ever ran for office. A politician's wife didn't have time to be inventing better bandages or dog bowls. "You said that your mom had a trust fund?" she asked.

"Yes. Her family came from the Russell Mustard Company."

"Wow." Millie just looked at him. "You're the heir to the Russell Mustard fortune?" She loved Russell Mustard. Everybody did. Supposedly, the family had sold the company about twenty years ago for buckets of cash.

He chuckled. "Yeah, I guess that's me."

She recognized his wealth, but he had far more than she'd realized. He was wealthy, like Richie Rich wealthy. "I see. Do you have a trust fund?"

He silently watched the road for several heartbeats. "Yes. A large one."

Great. How different could they be as people? Millie shopped at the discount store usually. So now she had to go meet some society lady who would look down her nose at Millie, and who most likely wouldn't want Millie anywhere near the heir.

They were so not a good fit.

They made the drive in silence, both seemingly lost in their own thoughts as Roscoe snored loudly from the back seat. He punctuated his snores with a growl once in a while as if he were chasing rabbits in a dream. Every few miles or so, he'd fart.

"That alcohol really messes with his system," Scott muttered, opening a window.

Millie rolled hers down as well and tried not to laugh. "God, no kidding."

Clouds gathered darkly above them, but so far no rain had fallen. They reached Old Town, Alexandria, and the historic charm of the neighborhood entranced Millie despite her misgivings. They reached a luxurious condominium on one side of the Potomac and parked in an underground parking area.

She jostled Roscoe to awaken him and helped him from the vehicle. He stood groggily for a moment, shook his whole body, then brightened. She could swear he smiled.

They followed Scott to the elevator, hopped inside, and rode up to the top floor. Oh man, this was worse than she'd thought. The elevator opened to an expansive and opulent vestibule with marble flooring, understated wallpaper, and one double doorway. Thank goodness she'd worn the uncomfortable suit. Roscoe looked around and headed right toward the door.

Scott followed, reaching for her hand. "Come on, Millie."

Oh man, she had to get her hand free. They couldn't walk into his mother's zillion-dollar penthouse holding hands. They were just too different.

He pulled a key out of his pocket and opened the door. "Mom, we're here," he called.

They entered a luxurious room, and the open-concept floor plan revealed both opulence and a judicious use of space. Natural sunlight streamed through the floor-to-ceiling windows, offering truly phenomenal and expansive views of the Potomac. The furnishings were high-end and light gray, yet in every direction hung paintings that delivered startling punches of color.

Millie appreciated the view, then was drawn instantly to a large abstract painting hanging over the sofa.

The work breathed with hues of red and yellow and gold, and it seemed to dance on the canvas. She had never seen anything like it. She leaned down to read the artist's name. "This is incredible." The movement made her feel as if she was in the middle of a kaleidoscope while also relaxing on a calm beach. "Truly wonderful," she whispered.

"Thank you," a female voice said.

Millie jumped and turned around.

"Sorry, I heard you come in." A truly stunning woman, probably in her late fifties, strode into the room, leaned up, and kissed Scott on the cheek. She stood several inches shorter than he but had his blue eyes and angled jaw. Her hair matched his shade of sandy blond, but unlike her son, she wore overalls over a white tank top and had paint...everywhere. On her knees, on her hands, on the side of her cheek, and even her hair.

"I take it you were painting?" Scott asked dryly.

"Yes. I'm working on a new series that encompasses the Rocky Mountains. I'm so excited. Do you want to come see?" She held his hand.

"Of course, we want to see. But first, Mom, this is Millicent Frost. Millie, this is my mom, Theresa Terentson."

Theresa grinned. "It's so very nice to meet you." She hurried forward and held out a hand. Millie shook it, surprised, noting afterward that her palm had different shades of blue on it. "Oh my," the woman said, digging into her pocket for a rag covered with more paint than her jeans. "This might help."

"No," Scott said. "Millie, there's a sink in the kitchen."

"Thanks," Millie said. Scott's mom surpassed him in the coolness factor, a notion that appeared almost implausible.

Theresa bent down. "Aren't you a handsome one?" The dog yipped and ran for her, hitting her midcenter and throwing her onto her back. She laughed and rolled with him. "Oh, I love you. You should get a dog, Scotty."

"Scotty?" Millie bit back a grin and looked at Scott.

He sighed.

Chapter Twenty

After a delicious dinner of grilled steaks, ultimate cheesy potatoes, and a mile-high salad, Millie wandered over to the wide windows in the living room to watch the Potomac churn beneath a tumultuous sky. Scott had headed to some office somewhere in the massive penthouse to work on his current cases, and Theresa had disappeared into her studio. The low drum of rock music pounded lightly through the floor, and curiosity grabbed hold of Millie, but first she had work to do.

She tugged her phone from her pocket and held it to her ear after pressing speed dial.

"Yo, Mills," Brigid Banaghan said by way of greeting. "Where are you? I miss seeing your pretty face."

"Hey, Bridge," Millie said. "I was undercover for a while but now I'm free." She didn't want to go into her probable termination from the agency right now. "I need a favor."

"You've got it. Anything you need," Brigid said. As the computer expert with the Deep Ops team, she could hack anybody at any time. She had started as a criminal, kind of, but had been cleared, kind of, and now worked for Angus's ragtag group of brilliant misfits.

Millie didn't want to get Brigid in trouble. "Where'd we come up with the team name anyway?" she asked suddenly. "Deep Ops, it's weird."

Brigid chuckled. "I think it was after several bottles of Leonetti Cabernet. We invented names because, for some reason, Wolfe thought we needed one."

"Who came up with it?" Millie asked, curious.

Brigid hummed. "You know, I don't completely remember. I think it might have been Pippa."

Pippa, an accountant, had agreed to marry Malcolm West, one of their operatives.

Millie had stalled long enough. "So listen, Bridge, I'd like to keep this between us, but I've had some trouble at home. It's all okay now and I'm protected. Please don't tell the team."

"Are you in danger?" Brigid asked. The humor disappeared from her voice.

Millie watched freshly darkened clouds race across the sky above the dangerous water. "No, I'm not. Honestly, Scott Terentson is with me."

"Really? What are you doing with our lawyer?"

Memories of what their lawyer had done to Millie shot heat into her face. "Our investigations crossed and then went south. His case involved a divorce, mine a securities fraud, and we probably blew both."

Brigid remained silent for a moment. "Are you going to get fired?"

"Probably," Millie said. "But that's not my focus right now, and I need you to keep this between us. An attack squad infiltrated my property back at home in River City and tried to shoot Scott and me."

"Are you okay?"

Millie started to wonder if this had been a good idea, but she needed answers. "Yes, I'm fine. We took down all three of them, and Scott did most of the heavy lifting." A warm flush spread over her body.

"Really?" Brigid drawled. "I knew he was an ex-marine, and since he plays football with Tate Bianchi, I figured he reached badass status. Plus, he did survive an attack that most people wouldn't have when he took that bullet near his heart during one of our cases. So, huh. What else is going on between you two?"

"I don't know," Millie said. "Probably more than I want to admit right now, but I have more immediate problems."

The sound of typing came over the line. "Fine, but you will dish on the hottie lawyer later. For now, tell me all about this attack on you."

Millie gave her all the details and also that she believed the chief held back evidence. Considering she had been a victim, she needed answers from him. "I'd like to know the identities of the attackers, as a start."

"You bet," Brigid said.

"Also, this is a crazy one." She told Brigid all about Clay, their relationship, and being found in his bed the other night. The story sounded incredible, even though she'd lived it.

"Oh my God, Millie," Brigid said. "We're heading out there right now. Oh damn. Everyone's out on mission."

Relief flowed through Millie so quickly, she reached behind her for the sofa and sat down. "Everyone's out?"

"Yeah. Angus and Nari are out of the country, and we have teams working on cases out of DC right now. I could call everybody back."

"No, no, don't call everybody back," Millie said. Finally, a break. "Just help me out, Brigid. We're safe. I'd let you know if I felt otherwise."

Brigid sighed loudly over the phone. "What exactly can I do for you?"

"Please conduct a background search on Clay Baker and his brothers. Determine if any women accused Clay of assault or drugging their drinks while he attended college and law school."

"That's no problem," Brigid said. "It may take me a little time because I may have to get on the phone. If I can't get answers, I'll head to the different campuses."

Millie stiffened. "Oh no, Brigid. I don't want to take you from other work."

"No, really. I'm just sitting here. People call in and I do computer research. I'm pretty bored, to be honest with you."

This might work out, so long as Brigid kept her request between them. "I owe you one," Millie said.

"No problem. Anything else?"

Millie shifted her weight and settled back against a plush light pink pillow. "Could you conduct a full background check on Werner Dearth? He's on the other side of Scott's divorce case, and his wife is missing. He also threatened me, and I'm wondering if he's an actual threat. The HDD has an active case against him right now, so there should be some background materials at headquarters, but you're better than their investigators."

"I appreciate that," Brigid murmured. "Now I have my to-do list. Are you sure you don't require backup?"

Sweet as the offer might be, Millie couldn't take team members off their missions. Plus, she felt safe with Scott and Roscoe around. "I'm positive. Just give me a call when you have anything."

"You've got it."

"Thanks." Millie clicked off.

She sat and stared at the river for a few moments before the beat of the music tempted her. So she stood and followed the sound, wandering through the high-end kitchen with its marble countertops, past an open door where she could see an office now occupied by Scott, to a wide double door. She knocked and nobody answered, but Theresa had told her to come visit, so she pushed open the door and then stopped, stunned.

The room, twice the size of the living room, boasted floor-to-ceiling windows. Natural light poured in those stunning windows as the panoramic view of the Potomac provided a still contrast to the wild room.

Paint streaked every visible surface.

A multitude of easels crowded one corner, with two more positioned against the far brick wall, obviously undergoing work. The colors and the splashes and the wildness characterized the entire room. The floor had been marble at one point, but even with drop cloths of different colors in every direction, paint could be seen everywhere. Glorious splotches of it.

The far corner held a massive cabinet with art supplies, including an impressive selection of premium paints and too many different brushes to count. A wide sink had probably been copper colored at one time, and now shimmered in a multitude of blues and greens. Music pounded through invisible speakers.

Her gaze caught on the woman who seemed to be painting in time with the beat. Theresa had her back to Millie as she worked on a mountain scene with abstract colors and forms that appeared to be about halfway finished. The painting exuded life, with mountains pulsating and shifting in harmony with the wild tune.

Theresa stepped back to survey her work, fresh paint smeared down her leg, her paintbrush in hand. She paused and looked over her shoulder. "Oh, hey." There were golds and pinks now on her neck and a fleck of white on her nose. Her beauty was a feminine version of Scott's ruggedness.

"Hey," Millie said. "I'm sorry to interrupt you."

"No problem." Theresa walked across the drop cloths to the sink and plunged the brush in a jar containing yellow liquid. She washed her hands and pressed the button above the sink. The music instantly cut off. "What do you think of my studio?"

"I love it," Millie said, honestly. She wandered over to the cleanup area. "What do you do with the liquid when it's done?"

Theresa wiped her clean hands on her jeans, smearing them with red and purple. "I try to recycle it as best I can."

"Really?" Millie ducked and opened the cupboard without being asked. "You know, I could rig this up for you so there would be a natural reclamation."

"You could?"

Oh, the challenge called to her. "You bet. In fact..." Millie started to think through her options, anticipation rippling through her veins. "I could create a system where you have different cleansers and water and a filtering system, so you could just move the brush from one to the other and the cycle would happen naturally."

Theresa clapped her hands once, spraying pink. "That would be awesome. Would you do that?"

"You bet. There's a lot I could do in this space to help you out."

Theresa leaned forward for an impulsive hug. "Millie, you're wonderful. Thank you."

Millie returned the hug and ignored the splotch of purple now on her suit.

"Oops," Theresa said, looking at the navy-blue jacket.

"That's okay. It adds something to this boring outfit," Millie said, grinning.

Theresa pushed a strand of her blond hair off her face. "You probably need clothes. I didn't even think of it. I'm sorry. Let's get you something comfortable." She put her arm over Millie's shoulder. "Scotty said you two were going to stay the night. For some reason, he's worried that Julie has gone missing."

"We're both worried."

Theresa propelled them across the room. "I find it sweet. You two are a perfect match."

"Oh, we're not dating," Millie said.

Paint dripped from Theresa's shoulder. "Huh. I have eyes and an artist's soul. Whether you two are smart enough to realize it or not, there's definitely something between you."

"I didn't say there wasn't anything between us," Millie admitted. "It's just things are complicated."

"Oh, pfft. Nothing like that should ever be complicated. Scott needs somebody full of challenge and adventure, and you seem just about perfect. You look like you could use somebody stable and strong. Believe me, my Scotty has both of those attributes tenfold. In fact, too much so. Did he tell you he's all but forcing me to fly to our Nantucket property tomorrow? Julie and I are close, and I have to admit, I did tell Werner Dearth to go to hell. The guy can't be that vindictive, can he?"

"Yeah." Millie winced. "I'm sure Scott just wants you to be safe."

Theresa pulled her back through the kitchen and living room to a stairway on the far end that led to the bedrooms upstairs. "He's lucky that I want to go paint there. It's the perfect time of year to capture the ocean." She nudged Millie with her hip. "So. Tell me all about yourself, Millicent Frost."

Chapter Twenty-One

Scott finished drafting his brief in support of a motion for summary judgment around three in the morning. He'd only been out of the office for a couple of days, and it shocked him how much work had piled up. He thought fleetingly about taking on a partner, but he didn't have time to deal with the vetting process right now.

Stretching his neck, he wandered through the penthouse and up the stairs to the guest bedroom he normally occupied. He walked inside to find Millie curled up on her side under the covers, barely making a bump. She slept peacefully and that pleased him. For several heartbeats, he just stared at her. Light streamed in the uncovered window now that the moon had finally banished the clouds for a short time.

She cuddled on her side, her hair a wild, curly mass over the pillow, still touched with green. Bruises still marred across her cheekbone from her fight with the guy he'd killed the night before, and irritation rippled through him that somebody had dared hurt her.

It took him a second to realize that Roscoe wasn't in the room. Scott had made sure the alcohol was buttoned up for the night, but there might have been cookies somewhere.

He looked in the other guest bedroom and found it empty. The dog hadn't been in the living room or kitchen, and while his mom might be a free spirit, Scott knew with certainty that she had shut the door to her studio to keep Roscoe out.

So he walked quietly into his mother's room, where she slept peacefully in her bed. Instinct had him stalking through the master bath to the enormous master closet. Inside, he paused. Roscoe lay flattened on the thick pink rug, his paws in a pair of bright green high-heeled shoes, and his nose between them.

Scott shook his head. "You are one odd chap," he murmured.

Roscoe looked up and smiled. Angus's theory posited that Roscoe had some sort of height insecurity, which didn't make a lot of sense for such a big dog, but apparently another soldier dog had been larger. Scott secretly thought Roscoe just liked the bright colors or sparkles that usually adorned heels.

"Come on, buddy, let's go to bed."

Roscoe stood, careful to slide his paws down so the shoes remained on. Scott angled his neck to see if the dog had found a pair for his back legs, and there was one purple and one red heel tipped on their sides.

"Leave the shoes here," he said.

Roscoe gave him a look.

"I mean it, Roscoe," he said, keeping his voice low with command.

Roscoe gingerly stepped out of the shoes.

"Thank you. Good boy."

With a sniff, it could have been disdain or just a doggy sniff, Roscoe padded past him and through the room. Scott followed, careful not to awaken his mother, and gently shut the door.

"You hungry?"

Roscoe gave one short yip.

Scott walked down to the kitchen to pour more food into the dog's bowl. He'd brought it inside after dinner, before their nightly walk. "Stay out of trouble," he ordered before heading into the unused bedroom and attached bath to take a shower, change clothes, and return to the office.

He wasn't going to get any sleep tonight, and he was fine admitting it was a blessing not to face the nightmares for a few more hours.

When the sun finally rose, he went into the kitchen and made pancakes for his girls. The thought went through his mind that Millie wasn't his girl. He had to get his head on straight and beat the nightmares before he could commit to anyone. But for now, he was her protector whether she liked it or not.

Both women emerged rather early, ready for the day, and he fed them, enjoying their light chatter. He had known they would genuinely enjoy each other, and it warmed something inside him that had been cold for a very long time.

He, Millie, and Roscoe drove his mom to the private airport and her plane. He wanted to keep the morning casual as long as he could. But as they neared, he looked over at his mother. Millie had insisted upon sitting in the back seat with Roscoe, who sprawled over the woman.

"Mom, I'm really sorry about Julie's disappearance."

Theresa patted his thigh. "Oh, thanks, Scotty. I already spoke with Detective Bianchi and told him everything I know, which isn't much."

"Do you think her husband hurt her?" Millie asked from the back seat.

"I don't know." His mom stared out the window at the rapidly darkening day. "The guy is a real meanie who cheated on her several times, which is why she finally filed for divorce. I don't think he ever hit her, but as a selfish oaf, he didn't want to split the property during the divorce."

Scott drove through the iron gates. "I've already conducted a background check on Werner Dearth. He doesn't have any sort of criminal record." He glanced in the rearview mirror at Millie.

There was no need to tell his mom about her ongoing investigation since it dealt with fraud and theft rather than murder.

Millie nodded as if agreeing with his silent thoughts. He liked that she could read him so easily.

He cleared his throat, needing his mother to take precautions. "Millie and I pissed Dearth off pretty bad. So if he is dangerous, Mom, I want you safe. I called the protection firm we used before and they'll be covering you in Nantucket."

Theresa rolled her eyes. "I think I'll be just fine in Nantucket, Scotty."

"I know you will," he said firmly, not willing to argue.

They reached the airport and he wound through to their hangar. The plane had already been pulled out, and the pilots waited outside.

His mom leaned over and kissed his cheek. "After you two wrap up all these issues you have going on, why don't you come visit me up in Nantucket?" She looked over her shoulder and winked at Millie. "I have plenty of room and the dog would love it."

Roscoe lifted his head and barked once.

"The dog's in," Theresa said, smiling.

Scott didn't look at Millie. They needed to talk soon, and he knew he wasn't right for her, but he was rapidly reaching the point where he wouldn't let her go.

* * * *

Millie's phone buzzed just as Scott pulled into the driveway of her Cape Cod–style cottage in Falls Church. She liked living close to DC in the quaint neighborhood, and more importantly, she could get home to her aunt Mae in just a couple of hours from there. She pressed the speaker button upon identifying the caller as the River City chief of police. "Hey, Chief," she said. "Is everything okay?"

"Depends how you look at it," the chief said.

Scott put the vehicle into park. "What does that mean?"

"It means the prosecuting attorney for the county wants to speak with you both."

"About what?" Scott asked tersely.

"Background on Clay's murder and the attack on you the other day," the chief replied. "I said I would extend the invitation. He's going to be here tomorrow going through case files."

Millie looked at Scott, and his gaze narrowed. "Sure, if he'll answer our questions as well."

Man, he sounded like a lawyer. For the first time, Millie found that to be a good thing.

"I think that's fair. Also, feel free to tell the entire town to stop confessing to the murder, would you? It's getting tiresome." The chief sighed. "It wouldn't hurt for you to bring your own attorney tomorrow. Just a warning." He clicked off.

Millie sighed. "This is getting more and more bizarre."

"I agree." Scott shook his head. "I'm having difficulty tying together all of the disasters coming at us right now."

Millie unfastened her seat belt. "Maybe they're not related to each other," she murmured. "I think it's possible that Dearth is unhinged and hurt his wife, in which case maybe he's angry at us as well."

"I haven't found anything in the guy's background that shows any sort of violence like this, or that he'd actually hire a hit squad to come after us." He looked at the cottage. "This isn't what I expected."

She blinked. "What do you mean?"

"I don't know. I expected some sort of high-end steel-and-chrome building with automatic sensors and booby traps everywhere." He grinned. "Maybe a contraption that would carry us from the car inside the house."

The guy lived in a penthouse and had a house in Nantucket. She'd had to scrape every dime together for her down payment. They didn't belong together. He owned a private plane, for goodness' sakes. "I wanted a place that felt more like the house where I grew up, but don't get me wrong, I do have a workshop with all sorts of booby traps and gadgets."

"I have no doubt." He stretched out of the SUV and opened the back door for the dog. "Come on, Roscoe."

Roscoe leaped out, looked around, and ran to mark the nearest bush on the other side of Millie's small lawn.

They had stopped by Scott's apartment for him to gather clothes before popping into his office so he could fetch several case files, and now they had finally arrived at her place to get clothing. She figured she'd need enough for maybe a week or two, but she also kept her closet full at her aunt's house.

She walked to the garage and placed her hand on the innocuous looking doorframe. The keypad emerged a foot lower than her hand, and she reached down to type in the code. The door slid open to reveal her compact Nissan. She wondered fleetingly if she should drive her own vehicle to River City but quickly discarded the idea because she liked traveling with Scott. Plus, the outfitting operation sported several work trucks she could drive if necessary.

Scott and Roscoe followed her through the pristine garage into her small, country-style kitchen. The appliances looked like they were from the 1950s and she had thrilled in finding each one at different garage and estate sales. Of course, she had updated and tweaked them with modern conveniences not imagined in the fifties.

Roscoe sniffed around.

Scott tilted his head to the side. "There's something off."

"What do you mean?" Millie looked around. The place felt as it usually did.

He moved past her to the comfortably furnished living room and glanced through the shades at the rain starting to fall. "I don't know. It's just a sense."

"Scott, believe me, this place is as safe as safe can get," Millie said. "Nobody could get in this house without me knowing it. I promise."

"I believe you," he said, frowning. "I did hear a couple of vehicles go by."

"I live outside of DC," she said. "Cars always go by."

"Yeah." He scrubbed his whiskered jaw. Oddly enough, his whiskers were darker than his hair, the contrast masculine. Tough and sexy. "But I heard the same clunking sound from a damaged muffler three times, with pauses in between as if somebody turned around at the end of the street. I'm probably on edge."

Just then, a battered blue truck drove by through the quiet neighborhood.

Millie listened. "You're right, that muffler has broken internal components."

Scott partially turned. "Get down!"

Projectiles blew through the front window, shattering the glass. Millie caught sight of something on fire and turned to run with Scott right behind her. The projectiles detonated in the living room, throwing the two of them across the kitchen and against the door leading to the garage.

Pain slammed down Millie's arm.

Several additional explosions sounded, and her cupboards flew open, spitting plates and glasses down on them.

Scott immediately rolled on top of her, wrapping both of his arms around her head.

Roscoe whined and shimmied up next to them, his nose on the door to the garage. Smoke poured from the living room, and crackling flames ripped gleefully through the morning. Scott stood in one swift motion, drawing her with him, and opened the garage door, carrying her inside with Roscoe on his heels. He slammed the door and opened her car door, pushing her across to the other side before helping Roscoe into the back seat.

He vaulted into the driver's seat. "Where's the key?"

"Just push the button. I always leave the key in," she gasped, her eyes stinging from the smoke.

"All right." He took a deep breath. "Where's the garage door opener?"

Smoke began to filter through the kitchen door and panic engulfed Millie. She'd secured her valuables in a safe, so they should be okay, but everything else she owned was going up in flames.

"We have to get out of here," Scott said.

"I know." She pressed the button on the dash.

"Duck down—I'm going to gun it." He ignited the engine. "As soon as the door opens."

She held her breath. The door rolled open and he punched the gas, swerving around his vehicle to the street. He paused and looked around. The blue truck had disappeared.

Millie stared through the window and watched as flames swallowed her home.

Chapter Twenty-Two

The fire took half the house. Scott leaned against the side of his SUV near where Millie perched on the hood, her legs dangling over the front. Roscoe had flopped next to her after having jumped on top, scrambling with his claws, then hunkering down with a sigh. Scott purposely didn't look at the damage because surely he'd have to get the hood buffed out.

Right now he didn't care.

They had moved the vehicles across the road to make room for the fire trucks. Acrid smoke still wafted through the air while debris gently rained down. Soot covered part of Millie's face, but even so he could see new bruises on her cheek and jaw. They appeared darker, more purple than the bruises from the other day, which had begun yellowing. He wasn't taking very good care of her.

"Stop worrying," she said, her gaze still on the house.

"I can't help it. I smashed you into that door pretty hard."

She turned to him and grinned, and he noted the right side of her lip had cracked. "Considering three projectiles exploded in my house, I'm rather thankful the blast threw us into the door and away from the flames."

He sucked in the stench of charred wood and scorched paint mingling with the choking fumes. The flashing red and blue lights of the emergency vehicles glowed eerily through the still-dispersing smoke, even as the firefighters rolled up their hoses. Their response had been quick and they'd managed to save half the house.

"I'm sorry about your belongings, Millie," Scott said.

She shrugged. "It's just stuff. I secured all valuables either in the safe or at Aunt Mae's house. I did like my bed, though." She rubbed the soot on her face and smeared the wet powder toward her ear.

Investigators had already arrived to examine the charred home, collecting evidence and snapping photographs. Tate Bianchi emerged from the front door and strode over the singed front yard and across the street. He had arrived only about twenty minutes ago, taken one look at them, apparently decided they were all right, and headed into the still-smoldering building.

"You sure you don't need medical attention?" he asked, soot on his bald head.

"No," Millie said, kicking out her feet. "We're good."

Scott wouldn't say they were good. In fact, if anything, he was downright pissed off. "What did you find?"

"Pretty much what I thought we'd find," Tate said, a small notebook in his hands. "Three shattered bottles with protruding wicks. Simple but effective. Tell me about whoever threw them through the window."

Scott frowned, the anger hotter inside him than the still-burning garage door, which had fallen from its track and now lay across the driveway. "Someone hurled the explosives from a blue truck with a damaged muffler. I noted one driver, but I honestly couldn't see clearly. Either dirt or a dark tint obscured the windows."

"What kind of truck?"

"Ford, early seventies," Scott said automatically.

Millie leaned down and scratched Roscoe's ears. "I heard the vehicle but I didn't see it," she said. "Everything happened so fast." She gingerly picked pieces of debris off her jeans and tossed them onto the pavement. The police had cordoned off the scene and neighbors had emerged from their houses to watch. Millie had waved at several of them, but had not yet attempted to speak with them, not that Scott would've let her move that far away from him right now.

He studied Tate. "You need to check into Werner Dearth."

"I already am," Tate affirmed. "Ever since Millie said that he threatened her, I've been investigating the guy, but I haven't found any suggestion of his having violent tendencies. As you know, he's a suspect in the disappearance of his wife."

The guilt at Julie's disappearance still felt like a fresh wound in his chest. "I do know that," Scott said. "Have you spoken with him?"

Tate looked up. "He's coming in later today with his lawyer. It took a while to arrange and he doesn't really need to speak with us, so I'm treading gingerly."

"I'd like to listen in on that," Scott said.

Tate's cheek creased. "I'm sure you would, but you're not going to. His wife is your client."

"Exactly," Scott said. "I don't have to be in the interview, but I currently represent her. The least you could do is ask Dearth's attorney if it's all right."

Tate slapped his notebook shut. "Fine. I'll ask Dearth's lawyer, but I wouldn't count on it."

"I don't know," Millie said thoughtfully. "Dearth seems like a narcissistic jackass. If he hurt his wife, I think he'd like nothing better than to brag in front of Scott."

Man, she was smart sometimes. Scott felt absurdly proud of her, which made absolutely no sense because they weren't even dating. Or were they? He needed to get his head on straight and his life organized before he even thought about beginning a relationship. So far, they'd been seeing each other for a few days, and she'd been fired upon and almost blown up. If he'd been faster or more alert, maybe she wouldn't be injured at all. He'd lost something when he'd been shot so many months ago, and he knew it.

"Whatever's going on in your head, knock it off." Millie reached out and punched him in the arm.

He jolted, surprised by the force behind the hit. "Watch yourself, baby."

She blinked. Twice. Shaking her head, she focused on Tate. "It's a quiet neighborhood but there may be some security cameras, Detective," she said. "I had CCTV, and as soon as you clear me to go back inside my workshop, I can pull the recordings for you. We should have something on the truck."

That figured. Even bruised and battered, Scott couldn't help but smile at her. "CCTV?" He looked around and still didn't see cameras.

"Yes, I placed the cameras in the trees," she said. "I also mounted one on the roof, partially hidden behind shingles." She craned her neck to look toward her house. "But that part burned up. However, the recordings transferred to a computer in the workshop, which is reinforced with solid steel and also holds my safe. We definitely have the arsonist on camera."

"Let's get them, then," Tate said abruptly.

Millie's eyebrow lifted in a cute and slightly haughty look. "I tried to go in when the first officers arrived but they wouldn't let me. We waited for you."

"Fair enough." Tate turned to look just as Detective Buckle strode out of the house, brushing soot off her shoulders. Today the tall detective wore black jeans, a white shirt, and a green pin-striped blazer. Her hair sat piled atop her head and her lips bore a light peach gloss. She looked at the still-burning garage door that had fallen onto the driveway, shrugged, and strode across the barely there grass toward them in spectacular, deep-chestnut-colored boots.

Millie cocked her head as if studying the boots, and Roscoe lifted his, whining softly.

"They aren't heels," Millie said quietly.

Roscoe lifted his head more, watched Buckle, then settled his muzzle on his front paws, remaining alert as the woman approached.

"This is a fricking disaster," she said, looking from Millie to Tate to Scott. "Someone apparently really wants you dead."

"We've noticed," Scott said. "The question is as to the target. We don't know if it's Millie, me, or both of us." He shook his head. "My guess is Millie because of the other case I told you about." He had made sure the chief shared the case file on Clay Baker with Tate and Buckle. "I wouldn't assume anything, however." The last thing he wanted to do was get stuck on one theory and be blindsided from a different direction.

Tate tapped his notebook against his hip. "Agent Frost, let's hit your workshop and find that recording. As soon as we discover the identity of this attacker, I think we'll find the hit squad that attacked you in River City."

Millie hopped off the SUV's hood, and Scott caught her before she could hit the ground. "Whoa," she said.

"Take it easy," he ordered, lowering her. "That was quite a blast you took."

"We both did," she said, reaching up to wipe off his cheekbone. "You're covered in soot."

The gentle touch careened through him, zinging past his balls and landing in his heart. "So are you." His gaze automatically scoured the neighborhood for additional threats. "Let's go view that recording." Then he planned to have a painful discussion with the driver who'd dared to hurt her.

"Hey," Tate said, his voice heavy with warning. "You have to let METRO handle this."

Scott just smiled. The time for waiting for somebody else to handle this had just concluded. After two attempts on Millie's life, he was done just being her lawyer. What he was, he didn't know.

Except, whoever had tried to kill her would soon wish they'd made different choices in life. Period.

* * * *

Millie sat in the control room looking through the one-way mirror as Tate Bianchi and Scott sat across from Werner Dearth and his lawyer. It hadn't been a surprise that Dearth had welcomed Scott's involvement, so long as he could ask questions as well.

Detective Buckle stood next to Millie in the small room, watching. "The guy's overly confident," she said quietly.

The attorney was the same woman who'd been at the trial, and she wore a light green spring suit with a black shirt. Instead of the jewelry she'd worn in court, today it was Van Cleef—and beautiful. Her hair glimmered beneath the yellow lights and her eyes sparkled a startling green, but her catlike smile clawed down Millie's back and made her want to rush in and smack her.

"What do you see?" Buckle asked.

"What do I see? I see a jackass and his lawyer."

Buckle shifted her weight. "No, go deeper. When you look at Werner Dearth, what do you see?"

Millie lowered her chin and studied the man. His high-dollar suit had been expertly tailored to flatter his well-fed physique. The true-black fabric contrasted with his gray tie, also streaked in black. His face was ruddy, his eyes beady, and his jowls pressed tight by his starched white shirt. He stared at Scott with a hard glint in his eye.

"I see a narcissist," she said, looking over at Buckle. "What do you see?"

Buckle tapped a finger against the glass. "I view a narcissist with his lips curled in a smug smile. Even his aura is overconfident." She tilted her head. "I don't know that I see him getting his hands dirty and killing somebody, though."

"I bet he could hire someone," Millie said.

Buckle nodded. "I think he could definitely hire someone." She reached over and turned up the volume.

"Run me through that again," Tate was saying. "Pinpoint your location the night your wife disappeared."

"My client already answered that question and stands by his statement," the lawyer said. What was her name? Oh yeah, Lorraine.

"He worked from home by himself planning a business trip to Berlin. It's that simple."

Tate leaned back. "We'd like to confirm that. Were you planning on your computer?"

"Get a warrant," Werner said bluntly. He looked toward the mirror as if he could see Millie. "You know, Terentson, I've been reading about you lately. You and that hot HDD special agent. Are you back there, Millicent?" he called out. Scott's entire back stiffened and rippled like a cougar bunching to strike.

Tate clapped an arm on his shoulder. "Calm down or you're leaving."

"I'm calm," Scott said, sounding brutally calm. Millie relaxed. He wasn't known as one of the best lawyers in the country for nothing. He could take Werner apart inch by inch if he wanted. But for now, apparently, he'd decided to attack with intellect.

"Your boy's got a temper on him," Buckle said.

"Yeah, but he controls it," Millie retorted.

"True enough," Buckle noted. Someone knocked on the door, and she turned to accept a stack of papers.

"What do you have?" Millie asked.

Buckle quickly read through the stack. "The video from your home captured the scene clearly, Agent Frost. The Molotov cocktails were thrown from a 1973 Ford F-100 pickup." She squinted. "There's dirt and I would have to say some very heavy window tint." She moved over to the computer bank to the right and quickly typed in several commands. The video came up. Millie had already viewed it briefly at her still-burning home, but Tate had quickly confiscated it.

Millie caught her breath and moved closer. The screen easily topped the one in her workshop. She watched as the driver passed by several times, then pulled into the driveway, rolled down the window, and threw the projectiles right through her front window.

"I need to invent a better glass," she muttered. "I don't like the current bulletproof because it's so thick. I bet I could do better." She needed to get on that as soon as possible.

"Do you recognize the thrower?" Buckle asked tersely.

Millie leaned closer to the screen. Dressed from head to toe in black, the attacker wore gloves, a hat, and a hockey mask. The bomber looked more like the guy from those *Friday the 13th* movies than anybody she'd ever recognize. The size of the person remained indiscernible, and the interior of the vehicle remained in shadow.

"I can't tell," she said. "The person had a good arm."

"That could be anybody," Buckle muttered, squinting. "They did a decent job of staying out of sight. It's shocking, really."

Millie didn't have much to go on. "All we know is this person can drive a truck and throw with pretty decent accuracy."

"I could do the same," Buckle said glibly.

"Yeah? You play softball?"

Buckle's lips turned down. "I have for years. I'm on a coed team. This coming spring, I think we're going to take it. We only got second last year."

"Sorry about that," Millie said, staring at the truck. Several dents and scratches marred the paint along with a smattering of rust along the side, which matched the old and worn tires. Buckle stopped the video, and they both looked at the spot where the license plate should be. It had obviously been removed.

"You don't recognize the truck?" Buckle asked.

"No, I've never seen it before." Millie looked closer. "I mean, it's old and obviously well worn. Chances are the arsonist stole it before heading to my house."

Buckle sighed.

Millie gave up on the truck and looked back at the interview. "I highly doubt that jackass drove an old truck or could even throw a Molotov cocktail."

"Agreed," Buckle murmured. "We don't have enough probable cause to obtain a warrant for his financials—there's no doubt he'd hire something like that out." She looked at Millie. "Since HDD has an investigation ongoing against him, surely they have his records?"

"It's my understanding that the techs are going through them now," Millie said. "I don't know that anybody at HDD headquarters will give me the information, but I have my sources on the outside." She needed to check in with Brigid soon.

Buckle refocused on the interview happening in the larger room. "Good. I'll make a formal request for that information, but my gut instinct is that you'll be able to get it sooner from your people than we will."

Millie liked that Buckle didn't ask about the source because she wouldn't have told her about Brigid anyway. Not that Buckle probably didn't have her own sources.

In the other room, Dearth pushed away from the table. "I'm bored with this. I have no clue where Julie is and couldn't care less." He rolled his eyes and then he winked. "Millicent Frost, if you're in there, know this is just the beginning. I'm truly looking forward to getting to know you better." With that, he smirked at Scott and sauntered his arrogant butt out of the room, his stride measured and calculated as if he enjoyed them watching him.

"What a twat," Buckle muttered.

"Yeah, but is he a dangerous one?" Millie murmured.

Buckle pushed hair out of her eyes. "I think he is, Millie. I don't know if he hired somebody to attack you, but there's no question you're in his sights. You need to take precautions."

As if he heard them, Scott looked over his shoulder. Even through the window, Millie could feel the punch of anger sizzling in his stark blue eyes.

"I think I'm covered," she whispered.

Chapter Twenty-Three

Passing a catering truck on the busy interstate, Scott barked out orders to his assistant as he assigned various hearings to his associates for the rest of the week. "I also need Bigsby to cover the Johnson deposition as well as the hearing with the county commissioners regarding rezoning plat fifty over in the third subdivision," he stated.

"Got it," Alexis, his assistant, agreed. "Anything else?"

"Yeah, switch the two briefs for the motions in limine for the Trasguard Incorporated trial from Bigsby to Lauren. She's a better writer, and I think she has a stronger grasp of materialmen's liens. Make sure she focuses on the hourly time requirement and not days. It'll make a difference in that one."

"All right."

He glanced over to where Millie slept peacefully in the passenger side of his vehicle, her head against the window and her mouth open slightly. He didn't need to look to know that Roscoe was snoring in the back seat, once again chasing something in his dreams.

Scott thought through his current cases.

"What else?" Alexis asked.

He paused. "I briefly read through Martin's pleadings for the shareholder derivative suit against the board of Mac May Industries."

Elevator music hummed in the background. "Okay," Alexis said.

"He needs to add claims for misappropriation of corporate assets and corporate waste. The rest of the causes of action are pretty good, but make sure he adds those and gets supporting affidavits. We're in front of Judge Katherine Sanchez, and she's a stickler for a strong foundation. He needs to get on that and have them done by Monday because I want to look them over before they're filed."

"Understood, boss," Alexis said cheerfully. "I don't know if you've looked at the press, but there's an article out today about Mrs. Dearth's disappearance that mentions you as her attorney. We've had the phones ringing off the hook."

He pinched the bridge of his nose. "Put Sharon in charge of vetting new clients, and make sure that she or Victor are careful with their conflict checks. I don't want to get into another situation like we did last year."

"Got it," Alexis said. "When will you be back in the office?"

He glanced at the sleeping woman, and a shocking feeling of protectiveness swept through him on the heels of what could only be termed possessiveness. "I don't know. For now, call me with any problems. Thanks, Alexis." He clicked off, reminding himself to give her an excellent bonus in July when everyone's contracts renewed.

His stomach rumbled as if unhappy with the fast-food burgers they'd grabbed for dinner on the way out of town. He looked in the back seat just to make sure that Roscoe was content. Scott had taken the bun off the dog's burger, but he figured burgers weren't that great for dogs.

He drove the rest of the way in silence, flicking on the windshield wipers when the rain started to gently dot and then cover his windshield. Darkness fell, and he made sure the vehicle remained warm enough for both woman and dog as he strategized his way through his remaining cases. He remained three weeks away from his next trial, so he figured his associates could handle all matters in the meantime. For now, he was right where he needed to be.

He drove through the small town of River City and continued on his way through the forest and along the river to reach Millie's picturesque little homestead. It still didn't completely jibe with the brilliant Q that he knew, but more and more he could see her living there. Hopefully, if they ever discovered who was after them, he could actually go fishing with her. It would be fascinating to see her out on the river, surrounded by nature. Though knowing Millie, she had a decked out fishing rod that would do everything from play music to serve cocktails.

Possessiveness gripped him as he drove up the dirt road to park near the driveway. It didn't surprise him when JT strode out of the bunkhouse, unheeding of the now drilling rain. Scott let the dog out of the vehicle before walking around to the passenger side.

"I've got her," JT said curtly.

"No, you don't," Scott retorted, opening the door and gathering Millie into his arms. She cuddled right in, not awakening. JT glared at him, the look hot enough to scorch Scott's already burning ears. "If we need to talk, JT," he said quietly, "I'll be out in a minute."

"Good," JT said shortly.

Scott didn't need this right now. He'd been fired upon and then nearly blown up. Subsequently, he'd spent too much time in an interrogation room with a complete jackass. Instead of letting any of that show on his face, he turned and strode through the rain and into the house. The door stood unlocked, an issue that needed to change rather quickly, even with JT on-site.

Millie barely stirred when he walked up the stairs and placed her on her bed before tossing a quilt over her.

He returned to the front door to see Roscoe waiting patiently. "All right," he said, moving aside. "She's up in her bedroom. Go up there and sleep." Roscoe stared at him, looked back at JT, and whined.

"We're fine, boy," JT said, appearing nothing like his sister as he stood tall and fierce in the pummeling weather.

They were anything but fine, but Scott didn't want to stress the dog. "We're fine. Go check on Millie and go to bed," he said gently. Roscoe, if it were possible, rolled his eyes and sauntered inside the house. Shaking his head, Scott shut the door and crossed his arms. "You have a problem?"

"What are you doing with my sister?" JT snapped.

Scott sighed. "Currently I'm keeping her from getting blown up." He related the events of the day to JT, whose expression went from pissed off to downright ferocious.

"Who the hell is after her?"

"I don't know," Scott said. "I'm doing my best to find out. But for now, we need to talk security. I know there are cameras, because Millie wouldn't live in a place without them. What else do we have?"

"We have guns and a dog," JT said. "The property is too expansive to fence in its entirety. We could plant additional booby traps, but we have charters and we have friends, not to mention the multitude of animals in the woods. I'd rather not blow up a bunch of deer with new gadgets."

Explosives didn't seem like a good idea. "There's only one way in, and you do have a gate. We certainly can't stop anybody from walking from the road to the property, but halting vehicles is a step."

"We can keep the gate closed except for when we're expecting a charter," JT said easily. "I can head to town and buy a chain and lock, but those still aren't much protection."

Scott didn't know how to broach the subject, so he didn't bother being smooth. "How well do you know this Lila?"

"Not well," JT said, a veil drawing down over his eyes. "I'd like to send her packing but Aunt Mae is being stubborn."

"I know I'm grasping at straws." Scott wiped rain off his face but didn't try to step under the eaves. If JT could stand in the rain, so could he. Plus, the droplets cooled his slightly singed flesh.

"Did you meet with the chief today?" JT asked.

"No. Something came up, like the explosion, so I called the chief and rescheduled for tomorrow. The prosecuting attorney seemed irritated, but apparently he wants a crack at us bad enough that he stayed overnight."

"I dropped by and spoke with the chief earlier today," JT said, his stance wide in the rapidly muddying ground. "Skinner has been asking around town for the last two days about Millie, about you, and about the Bakers. Just the way Millie was found in Baker's bed caused a sensation. Throw in the expensive lawyer from DC and her HDD connections? They're probably already casting for a movie of the week."

"I appreciate the analysis," Scott said wearily. "Have you heard anything from the townspeople?"

"No," JT said, "but I worked away from home for a long time. I wasn't around when Millie dated Clay, and I certainly didn't attend college with the guy. He's not very well liked by many people here, but it's my understanding he's the belle of the ball in Charleston."

Scott scratched a scab on his jaw and winced as it tore free. Multiple areas on his body had endured dents and battering. Too many areas. "What about in town? Have you heard anything?"

"Not really. Clay would come to town with his brothers. They'd usually kick up a ruckus in one of the bars, and he'd often take a woman home. That's not unusual."

"Got any names?" Scott asked.

JT kicked a rock off the grass into the dirt driveway. "A few, but nobody out of the ordinary. It's a small town, man. If Clay found himself in trouble, it happened back in Charleston. I've reached out to contacts I have there, but nobody knows much."

"We have our computer expert working on it as well." If anybody could track down the information electronically, it was Brigid.

JT sighed. "Are you armed?"

"Yeah," Scott said. "I picked up a couple of weapons at home. Are you?"

"You could say that," JT said dryly. "I'll shut the gate tonight, then we'll figure out something else tomorrow. We should probably invest in a gate that locks, but just having it shut seems to keep most looky-loos away."

Scott wouldn't get much sleep until he took out whoever wanted to kill Millie. How his focus had gone from his life to hers so quickly didn't concern him. "Did the chief tell you anything about the three attackers?"

"No. I asked, but he's close-lipped. They were obviously hired thugs, and not very good ones."

Yeah, but one had gotten to Millie before Scott could stop him. He'd hear the sound of her scream in his dreams for years to come, even though she hadn't been harmed. "They were good enough," Scott said.

"I heard you were better."

Scott swallowed as his chest ached and his body thrummed in pain. He needed rest, but his mind wouldn't stop. He only hoped he'd be as good next time, because danger unmistakably awaited them all.

Chapter Twenty-Four

After showering and checking the new scrapes, scratches, and burns on her body, Millie dressed in jeans and a mint-green sweater before stumbling down to the kitchen and the coffeepot. She poured herself a thick mug and drank half the contents before really looking around.

She'd been mildly disappointed to find that Scott hadn't joined her the night before in bed, and when she'd peeked into the spare bedroom, the room appeared untouched.

He had to be driving on empty, but she understood the demons haunting him. She'd had several nightmares the previous night that involved explosions, projectiles, and bullets aimed at her. How badly were his night terrors from his being shot with Angus combining with his obvious trauma from his time in the military?

She looked outside to see rain pounding the earth. The weather fit her mood. Where was everybody? She felt silly calling either Scott or JT via phone because they were obviously off doing something.

She hunted in a cupboard for something to eat. Hadn't she left Pop-Tarts in there a couple of months ago? The delicious treats lasted forever, so she rifled through different bins, trying to find them, until the sound of a vehicle caught her attention.

Straightening, she turned and walked to the door. Maybe one of the men had gone to town to get breakfast. She could only hope. She opened the door to see her friends springing out of an older white SUV. Her dismay at having her morning interrupted quickly gave way to gratitude as she noted the box of donuts in June's hands and the cardboard tray of lattes in Valerie's. As longtime friends, they were more than comfortable opening the gate and driving right in.

"Come in out of the rain," she called, opening the door wider, gesturing her friends inside.

They all laughed and ran through the rain, with Verna picking her way gingerly across the wet ground, her protruding belly leading the way.

Valerie landed inside first, and she gave Millie a half hug. "Hey, we figured we'd cheer you up."

"How did you know that I'd be home?" Millie asked, reaching for Verna to pull her inside and out of the rain. The pregnant woman's face was flushed and truly glowing.

"There are no secrets in this town," June said, smiling and placing the box of donuts on the table. She grinned when Millie mock-growled at her. "Fine. I saw you guys drive by the diner last night so figured you'd be in town for at least a day or two."

"Tricky," Millie said, accepting a latte from Valerie. "Oh, this is the best. I was just digging into the recesses of the pantry for a Pop-Tart."

Verna looked around and licked her lips. "Hey, where's the hottie lawyer from DC?"

"You're happily married and knocked up," her sister retorted. "Me, however..." She also looked around. "I'm single."

Millie ignored the flash of possessiveness that rippled through her.

"Oh, it's like that, is it?" June asked, her eyes sparkling. She removed a latte from the tray and took a big drink, moving over to take a seat at the table.

Millie had spent more mornings than she could count drinking coffee with June at that very table. "Sit down, my friends." She claimed her own seat.

"So?" June asked, her eyebrows raised. "Spill it about you and the sexy blue-eyed badass."

Millie shrugged. "I would if I could. I mean, if I knew anything, I'd tell you, but I'm not sure where we are or what we're doing."

"Ah, it's one of those." Verna sipped delicately from her travel mug.

Millie frowned.

"Don't worry. It's not a latte," Verna mumbled. "It's just herbal tea." She looked longingly at her sister's cup. "I would kill for caffeine."

Valerie snorted. "Soon enough. If you quit letting Alex knock you up, you could drink coffee again—and you get the full-cream ones and don't gain a pound. It isn't fair."

"Amen, sister," Verna said, her eyes twinkling. She leaned toward Millie. "Do we know who killed Clay yet?"

"No. I have nothing." Millie let the vanilla-flavored brew land in her stomach and warm her body. A needed jolt of caffeine cleared her mind. "We're supposed to meet with the chief today, but so far I have no idea." She exhaled slowly, forcing her body to relax, swiping a donut. "It's a long shot, but I am thinking about getting hypnotized. I need to remember."

"How about the guys who came here to shoot you?" June asked, her red hair up in a ponytail.

"Nope," Millie murmured. "The chief hasn't told me anything about them." A headache lingered behind her left eye just from the uncertainty. However, the sugary donut helped as much as the loaded latte. She looked at Valerie. "Did you track down anything about Clay's college days?"

"You bet I did. I've been on the phone constantly. Well, when I had time off from the hospital," Valerie said. "Both Verna and I have been calling people from college."

"Oh yeah," June said. "I forgot you went to nursing school, Verna."

"Yeah, for a semester," Verna said, shuddering. "Then I passed out when we had to inject oranges with a needle. Plus, Alex wanted to stay here near his family and then he got a job at the hardware store. So it just made sense to come home." A small smile played on her face. "Though I missed you, Val."

"I saw you every weekend," Valerie said, then she caught herself. "Oh, but I missed you too."

They all laughed. Millie missed her friends overall—how wonderful to be bouncing ideas off them again.

"What'd you find out?" she asked, eyeing another donut. She hadn't been working out lately, but stress did burn calories. Shrugging, she grabbed a pink custard covered in white sprinkles. The diner pastry tasted like sugary heaven. "Man, this is good," she said around the sticky frosting.

"I know, right?" June took a maple bar out of the box.

Millie reached for a napkin to wipe her face. "Please tell me good news, Verna."

"I didn't find out anything all that helpful," Verna said. "I talked to the few pals I made while briefly in school, but nobody remembered rumors about Clay."

Valerie eyed the donuts with longing. "I had more luck. I talked to a couple of friends who remembered rumors of accusations from a couple of women that Clay and his buddy, Frank Clubberoni, slipped drugs into drinks at more than one party on campus."

Millie sat up. "Really?"

"Yeah," Valerie said. "My friend remembered the women being members in the Delta Gamma sorority, maybe, but they couldn't recall names or dates. I called the school for you, and they failed to find any documentation, which could mean that nobody ever filed a report, or perhaps somebody redacted a report. One of my friends at nursing school remembered some sort of investigation, but she'd only heard rumors."

That was something at least. Maybe Brigid could get some answers. "I really appreciate it, Valerie," Millie said.

"No problem. I'm happy to help. Clay really was a cad."

Millie gingerly chose her next words. "Junie, somebody said that maybe you had gone out with Clay."

June coughed, then wiped her mouth after spitting out a small amount of her latte. "Hell no." Her eyes widened. "Millie, you and I have been friends since we were three. I wouldn't date that loser. I'm not saying he didn't come into the diner and hit on me, but he hit on anything that walked. I promise." She reached out and patted Millie's hand. "I never would've dated him."

Millie studied her friend's earnest face. June had never lied to her, so there was no reason to believe she would start now.

"Yeah, he hit on me all the time when I was still working at Snarky's," Verna said quietly. "I mean, he hit on everybody." She looked down. "Except Valerie."

Valerie snorted. "Yeah, we didn't mix. He called me chubby once, and I wished a curse upon him."

Verna sobered. "I certainly regret not stopping you from going with him. I'm so sorry, Millie."

Millie waved her hand in the air. "It's not your fault, and it's so nice of you all to bring me breakfast." How comforting to know that her friends trusted her. "Is the rest of the town buzzing over my guilt?"

"Not really. Nobody who knows you would think that," June hastened to say. "Everyone is still giving you alibis, I think."

Verna sighed. "Everybody knows that you really hated the butthead, Millie. Ignore the gossips."

Millie brushed crumbs off her jeans. "I didn't hate him. I just didn't want anything to do with him." Hate was much too strong a word, but if Clay had drugged her that night, she could go from not caring to dislike real quick. Whether he'd drugged her or not, it didn't explain who'd killed him.

A knock sounded on the door before Lila walked in with fresh flowers in her hands. She paused when she saw the women at the table. "Oh, I'm sorry. I'm not used to anybody being here." She'd secured her thick hair in a ponytail and wore an old T-shirt with ripped jeans. "I'm so sorry." She backed away.

"No, it's okay. Come on in," Millie said, pulling out another chair at the table. "Sit." She introduced everybody.

"We've met." Verna nudged the box of donuts toward the woman. "You came into Snarky's when I still worked there."

Lila flushed and sat with the blooms in her hands. "Sometimes when Buck needs extra help, I just clean the back room." She shook her head. "And maybe do a little inventory. I don't hang out at the bar or anything."

"You had a drink or two a couple of times," Verna noted.

Lila eyed the donuts. "What can I say? Buck pays me in cash and a beer once in a while."

"Have a donut." Valerie pushed the box even closer. "Seriously, if you don't, I'll eat them all."

Lila placed the flowers gently on the table. "I brought these for Mae. She loves wild roses."

"It's nice of you to help out around here," Valerie said.

Lila's eyes were veiled. "Mae has been very kind to me. I love the cabin and hopefully I'll learn how to fish soon. Although I don't think I ever want to guide." She reached for a chocolate glazed donut and took a bite, chewing thoughtfully. "These are fresh."

"I love the fresh donuts from the diner. They are the best," Millie agreed. "How often do you help Buck out?"

Lila swallowed. "Whenever he needs it. Maybe once a week, sometimes twice."

"You weren't there the other night when I was, by any chance, were you?" Millie asked, hope unfurling inside her. It'd be nice to get an answer—any answer to what had happened at the bar.

"I haven't worked for Buck in at least a week," Lila said, picking off another piece of the donut and eating it as if savoring every morsel. "He hasn't been as busy lately. I kind of expected him to call after St. Patrick's Day, but sometimes he likes to clean the place himself."

Millie cocked her head. "Have you ever met Clay Baker?"

Lila looked off to the side. "Yeah, a couple of times when I conducted inventory, he and his brother came into the bar." She looked down at her hands.

"Did you ever speak with Clay?" Millie asked.

"No," Lila returned. "I mean, he talked to me a couple of times, but I kept my head down and worked. He seemed..." She mulled it over as if thinking. "I don't know, slimy." She looked up at Millie. "I'm sorry. I know you dated him, and I mean no offense."

"No, slimy fit Clay perfectly," Millie said. "I hadn't realized that you'd met him also."

Verna snorted. "I don't think there's a woman in town who hasn't met Clay at least once. He hits on everybody, right?"

"What a jackass," Valerie said, sipping her latte.

The door opened and a very wet Scott Terentson walked in wearing jogging shoes, running shorts, and a tank top plastered to his muscular body.

June coughed, Verna gasped, Lila stared, and Valerie made a sound like a horny cat.

Millie's breath caught in her throat and her entire body heated, head to toe. "Morning," she managed to strangle out as her friends all erupted into giggles.

Chapter Twenty-Five

Around noon, Scott steered his vehicle competently through the rain and parked at the curb in front of the chief's station. Millie remained silent on the way into town, and he glanced over at her. "Are you okay? I mean, besides the obvious issues of stabbings, bombs, and loss of employment."

"Yes. Besides the obvious, I'm fine." She rubbed at a bruise on her chin. "What do you think of Lila?"

"I haven't given her much thought," Scott said blithely, jumping out of the vehicle and pushing through the wind to reach the passenger side. The rain had stopped for now, but a chill still hung in the air. "Let's get inside, Mills," he said, helping her out.

She let him assist her down and stood on the sidewalk looking both ways. The town appeared quiet in the late morning but even so, Scott ushered her inside the chief's office, not happy until she was off the street. At this point, he expected bullets from any direction. "Hey, Chief," he said as they walked inside, noting the man behind the reception desk.

"Hi." Today the man wore his customary uniform with his utility belt in plain sight, showing a sidearm, handcuffs, a radio, and pepper spray. "You're right on time. Rupert Skinner is in the interrogation room waiting for you." The chief's tone remained level, but a glint lightened his eyes.

Scott read him quickly. Good. He didn't want the chief liking the prosecuting attorney who wanted to put Millie away. "He does understand this interview goes both ways, right?" Scott pressed a palm to Millie's lower back and ushered her behind the reception desk.

"Yup," the chief said.

"Great." He leaned down to Millie. "Let me do the talking. I think he wants to trip you up, and it doesn't hurt for him to know you have representation."

"No problem." His girl looked adorable today in her green sweater and jeans, and he wanted to claim every inch of her body instead of dealing with bombings and murders. Instead, he settled into the moment and followed her and the chief to the interrogation room, where he took a position across from the prosecuting attorney.

Rupert Skinner's scalp gleamed between strands of hair under the fluorescent lights, and his drab brown suit seemed a size too big, hanging off his frame and making him look hunched over.

Scott had read a preliminary report on the guy created by one of his associates. He'd grown up poor, attended college and law school on scholarships, and reputedly held lofty ambitions. Scott hadn't found dirt on him as of yet, but if something untoward existed to be uncovered, his private detectives would find it.

Skinner looked up, ambition in his brown eyes. "Thank you for coming in." He stood and his red tie flopped on an untidy pile of folders on the table.

"Happy to discuss this," Scott said smoothly, pulling out a chair for Millie.

She sat and he did the same, waiting until the other two men sat across from him.

Scott looked at the chief, who had remained silent thus far. "Do you have an ID on the three men who attacked us?"

Skinner cleared his throat. "You mean the three men you brutally murdered?"

Ah, this was how the day would go. "Actually, we acted in self-defense and I think you know that, Skinner," Scott drawled. "So let's not play games. Do you have IDs?"

"We actually do," the chief said, without any file folders in front of him.

The prosecutor stiffened.

The chief looked at the guy and glanced back at Millie. "I have an investigation to conduct and I'm going to do it," he said blithely. "Millie, have you ever met a Bob Phillips, Gene Lightfoot, or Henry Halcomb?"

"No," Millie said, her face scrunching up. "I don't think so."

"What about you, Terentson?" the chief asked.

Scott shook his head. "Those names don't mean anything to me."

The chief reached over and snatched a darker brown file folder from somewhere in the middle of the pile of cream colored ones. "This is mine," he said. He flipped open the top and slid three photographs across the table.

Scott studied the pictures of the three men. "Yep. These three attacked us." Of course, they appeared a little different in their driver's license pictures. He looked up at the chief and banished his emotional reaction to killing three men. For now, anyway. "Who were they?"

The chief rubbed his shoulder. "They're known criminals from Charleston. Their records show some breaking and entering, some assault. They've all three done time."

Scott's shoulders ached. Had he torn something in the bombing the day before? "Were they affiliated with any criminal organization?"

"No," the chief said. "You sure you haven't seen any of them before?"

"Not until the other day," Scott said. He pointed to Lightfoot. "He started shooting as the first one out of the truck." All three men were big and they looked tough, but now they were dead. Because of him.

"Did they have families?" Millie asked quietly.

Scott kept from reacting. He didn't want the answer to that question.

"No," the chief said. "From the Charleston police records, they've gotten in trouble together since their teenage years."

Scott looked up at the chief. "Is the Charleston Police Department running their financials?"

"Yep," the chief said. "If someone paid them in any manner we can trace, we'll get it."

Scott made a mental note to contact Brigid. She'd be faster and had better resources than the local or state police. "Is there any connection between these men and Clay Baker?"

"Not that we've found," the chief said. "Except that Baker went to college and law school in Charleston, then lived there. We haven't found anything stronger than that to tie them together."

"What about with Werner Dearth?" Millie asked suddenly.

The chief flicked his gaze to her. "Not yet. I have requested a warrant for his phone records but probably lack probable cause on the local level."

Yet apparently Dearth's financials were even tripping tying up the HDD techs. "Any luck with your investigation of Clay Baker and possible criminal activity in college?" Scott asked.

Skinner sat up straighter and a strand of his thickly lotioned hair fell onto his forehead, revealing even more of his scalp. "Investigation of Clay? Clay was a great guy who didn't do anything wrong. Well, except get murdered. You're going to pay for that, Ms. Frost."

"It's Agent Frost," she said smoothly. "And I didn't kill him."

Scott shifted his weight just enough to let her know he'd do the talking as the damn lawyer in the room.

"Please walk me through how you ended up at Clay's house the night your knife sliced him into pieces?" Skinner asked smoothly.

"She's already on record and has signed her statement," Scott said. "She has nothing further to add at this point." He dismissed the county prosecutor and looked at the chief again. "Have you found anything about Clay's past?"

"He was in love with you," Skinner spat. "You knew that and you used it against him. Why would you kill him?"

"You're getting emotional," Scott said flatly.

Skinner leaned back, his eyes raging. "You're right." He stood. "The time for emotion is over. I'm sticking to the arraignment schedule already sent to you. It's my understanding you've already been fingerprinted. Now it's time to find justice for an innocent man. Do either of you have anything to add to either of these cases?"

"No," Scott answered for them both.

Skinner buttoned up his suit jacket. "Very well. You're on notice, Mr. Terentson, that charges are likely to be brought against you for the murder of those three men." He jerked his chin toward the pictures.

"Really? No self-defense, huh?" Scott asked. What a moron.

"No. I think these two incidents are tied together." He looked at Millie. "You lured Clay to his cabin and murdered him. I know that your career with the HDD isn't going well. I read in the paper how you two screwed up your last case. I think you took it out on Clay for some unknown reason."

Was this guy any good in court? "What about the three dead guys?" Scott asked, truly curious.

"I don't know, but I think somehow you set them up too. I will find a tie between you and those men," he said to Millie. "That I promise you."

"You seem confident," Scott said, going on instinct as he prodded for more information.

The prosecuting attorney smiled, revealing canines too long for his mouth. "Oh, I have a witness."

"What kind of witness?" Millie asked.

Scott cut her a look. She looked right back at him, defiance glimmering in her eyes.

"I have a witness who saw you making out with the deceased the night of his death," Skinner said, his smile widening until he was all teeth. "Not only that, but this same witness was good friends with Clay and knew that you two met up once in a while."

"Really?" Scott frowned. "They met up once in a while?" He repeated the words slowly. "Could you add a little more detail than that in case we end up in trial?"

"I can, but I won't. Except it's so good. This witness saw you get into a fight with Clay the night of his murder," Skinner said. "I don't have to tell you anything else right now, but believe me, this witness is extremely credible." He looked at Millie. "So I'm going to give you one chance and one chance only to revise your statement."

She crossed her arms and glared at him.

"There'll be no revision," Scott said. "You might want to turn this case over to somebody not emotionally involved."

"Not in a million years," Skinner said. "Enjoy your freedom while you have it, Agent Frost." He stormed out of the room.

The chief looked at Scott, then at Millie. "Tell me you don't have any ties to these men."

"I don't," Millie said, leaning forward to study the photographs. She tapped the picture labeled as Henry Halcomb. "There's something about him, though."

Scott's gut started to drop. "What?"

She peered closer. "I don't know. We need to find out everything we can about him. Maybe I've seen him before?"

Chapter Twenty-Six

Millie zipped her coat as she walked down the sidewalk with Scott at her side. He radiated a stalwart presence as he blocked the wind from chilling her. How easily she could become accustomed to him. Not only sexy and brilliant, but the man was downright likeable.

She forced her mind from the hottie next to her and surveyed her hometown. Excitement already buzzed in the small community on this quiet Wednesday. Colorful banners announcing the River City Fishing Derby already hung from every light post.

Artisans had already begun building their makeshift booths down several of the side alleys, hoping to sell everything from fishing equipment to crystals that brought magic and good luck.

"It looks like the Derby is going into full swing," Scott said, settling his arm over her shoulders. She sank into the feel of him against her but didn't want to explore her emotions at this moment. Her brain whirred with too many problems, and the idea that she could be facing prison time sent chills down her spine.

She shook herself out of her fear-based thoughts. "Yeah, we usually make a pretty good income with the Derby," she replied. "I don't want Aunt Mae to take out any of the scheduled charters, so I'll need to handle those."

Scott frowned. "You're not going without me. You've been shot at enough lately."

She chewed on her lip. "I'm concerned about our clientele as well."

He opened the door to the Rapid Water Diner, which already held a full-length poster announcing the prizes for the Derby. They ranged from custom-designed fishing poles to cold, hard cash. "You're concerned one of our enemies scheduled a charter?"

"No," she said. The tempting aroma of fresh apple pie instantly assailed her. "I'm more worried someone will shoot at us from a bank and hit one of our clients." She had a duty to keep them safe.

"That's a good point." Scott escorted her to the counter. "Let's grab lunch, then go figure it out."

Millie smiled as June bustled from the kitchen with a pot of coffee in her hand.

"Hey, you two. Out for a late lunch?" June asked, her eyes sparkling.

Millie looked around the partially full diner. Apparently, tourists had descended on the town early. "Yes. We'd like to order a couple of burgers to go."

"Sure thing." June had her bright red hair up in a high ponytail, and splotches of chocolate marred her faded yellow uniform. "I'll be right back. Let me put in the order."

"Thanks," Millie said gratefully, jolting as somebody tugged on her pants leg. She looked down to see Verna's son Lake pulling at her. "Hey there, buddy." She reached down and hefted the four-year-old against her side. "What are you up to?"

He smiled with chocolate smeared all around his mouth. He looked like his daddy but had Verna's pretty eyes. Millie glanced around to see the couple finishing tacos in a booth. She walked over, holding the snuggle-bunny. "I found something of yours."

The kid chortled and reached for his dad.

"Hey," Alex said, his eyes somber as he captured his son with one arm. A black cast covered his other arm. "Sorry about all the problems you've had lately."

"Thanks." Millie had attended high school with Alex, and he'd always been one of her favorite people. He stood to about six foot two with dark hair and light blue eyes. He and Verna had dated in high school and married soon after graduation. "What happened to your arm?"

"Broke it at work." Alex pressed a kiss to his son's head.

That sucked. "Where's Frankie?" Millie asked.

"He's in school." Verna patted her baby bump. Stress lines fanned out from her eyes, and she winced, pressing a hand to her side.

"Are you okay?" Millie asked.

"Yeah, I'm fine. Just having some cramps," she said, looking at her husband. "We'll be just fine."

Alex cuddled the toddler close. "The place is busy." He glanced at Millie. "How's your aunt Mae doing?"

How kind of him to ask. "She's good," Millie said. Her mind clicked facts and possibilities into slots as she sought a solution to their problems. "You know, Alex, I just thought of something. Do you have any extra time this weekend?"

"Time?" Alex grinned and looked down at his cast. "I have a lot of time. I got laid off at the store."

She reared back. "You did?"

"Yeah, but hopefully workman's comp is going to come in soon." He took a deep breath, his face pale. Did his arm still hurt?

"I don't want to ask you to do anything—" Millie started.

"No, really," he said quickly. "I'm free this weekend."

Verna leaned forward. "We've been brainstorming how to make extra money during the Derby. Do you need help?"

"We do. We need help with a couple of fishing charters. It's getting harder for Aunt Mae to be out on the river guiding. While I could guide, I'm kind of a distraction right now. What do you think about taking the charters for me?"

Scott approached on her right with colorful boxes containing the fragrant smelling burgers.

"I think it'd be great," Alex said quickly. "I could use the money and I've missed fishing this last year. We've been too busy to hit the river."

"It would be wonderful," Verna said, leaning over and patting Millie's hand. "Valerie can help me with the kids. They adore her, and it's not like she has anything else going on."

Thank goodness. "You'd be helping me a lot." She'd had no idea that Alex had been laid off. With two kids and Verna not working at the bar, surely they needed the money right now. "I really appreciate it."

"Excellent," Alex said. "When do you need me?"

She thought through what she had read in the schedule. "Actually, tomorrow first thing, if that works for you."

"You bet it does." He tickled his son, and the boy giggled.

Millie quickly introduced Scott, then said, "I'll see you tomorrow."

Verna smiled at her. "Thanks, Millie. You're a lifesaver."

"You bet." Millie followed Scott from the diner.

He opened the passenger-side door for her. "One problem down."

"Yes," she said, sighing. "About fifty more to go."

* * * *

Scott took in the bustling activity on the street as he started his engine. It'd be fun to visit River City for the Fishing Derby when he wasn't on the job. For now, he glanced at the quiet woman in the passenger seat. "I was thinking."

"Always an interesting prospect," she said instantly.

He grinned. "Seriously. Now that you apparently just hired Alex to help out with the guiding business, what do you say to taking a mini vacation?"

She looked at him, her eyes so blue his chest ached. "You want to go on a vacation right now?"

"Not exactly. I want *you* to go on a vacation." He thought through their available options. "Why don't you visit my mom in Nantucket? The house is large, and you could cobble together a workshop to build whatever gadget you want. Just for a couple of weeks."

She partially turned in the quiet vehicle and settled her knee beneath her. "Are you trying to get rid of me?"

"Not in a million years," he said honestly. "However, I am trying to keep you safe."

Her chin lifted. "I see. So I go off and hide in Nantucket while the big, bad men figure out this problem."

"Yes." The woman misunderstood him if she thought he'd allow her to be harmed.

The mellowness in her eyes morphed into anger. "I'm not going anywhere. Somebody drugged me and now is trying to frame me for murder. I'm a member of the HDD, and I know how to protect myself."

"I'm well aware of that fact," he said, holding on to his temper. "However, since you've been back in town, you've been drugged, framed, and fired upon. That's not even mentioning the fact that somebody bombed your house. I'm just saying that you need to seek safety for a brief time."

The thought of her being hurt clawed through him with a shocking force. So far, they'd been lucky and smart, but everybody knew that luck ran out at some point. Even if she survived nine out of ten attacks, that last one could kill her.

He would not let that happen. "Listen, Millie. I don't want to pull rank here."

Her head snapped up. "There's no rank for you to pull. You may be my lawyer, but you're not my boss. And frankly, you're not even my boyfriend, not that I would take orders from one."

"I'm not trying to give you orders." He didn't give two fucks about his status with her. If he had to kidnap her cute ass and haul it to Nantucket, he'd do it. He'd pushed his nightmares to the back burner because Millie's safety took precedence. Right now, the need to inflict violence on the bastards coming for her coursed through him, shocking in its intensity. "You need to be safe. Period. I'm certain JT would agree."

It was the wrong thing to say.

A bright rose flowed across her face, making her look fucking stunning. "Listen to me, Scott Terentson. We may have gone to bed, and I may have hired you to be my lawyer, which by the way we will discuss later because I will be paying you, but that's as far as this goes. If you even think of conspiring with my brother to send me away, you both will regret it with every fiber of your beings for the rest of your lives. Do you understand me?"

He could only stare.

She was glorious. "I can tell by your silence that you're too dumb to fully get me." She leaned toward him as if wanting a good fight. "I will invent something that will torture you till the end of your days. I don't know what it is right now." She looked around. "It could be a beeping sound that follows you wherever you go for the next fifty years. It could be that little pebble in your shoe that you can never rid yourself of. It could be the hordes of women who want to be in Scott Terentson's arms, somehow having access to you every second of every day."

He leaned back. The woman issued decent threats. "Millie, you're facing a spanking, and I don't mean an enjoyable one."

Her head jerked so quickly it was a shock she didn't get a migraine. "Oh no," she said. "I'm not done yet. Make sure you know exactly what you're doing if you decide to cross me." She slid around in the seat, facing forward, and crossed her arms.

God, her adorableness shone bright. He wanted to laugh but figured it would get him punched, and then he'd have to spank her in the middle of her town. "I'll think about it," he said dryly.

So far, he could cover her. For now. Her safety remained the most important thing in the entire world. If he had to kidnap her and take her to Nantucket, he'd do it.

She flashed him an irritated look. "We are finished with this discussion." To emphasize her statement, she huffed.

He pulled away from the curb. She might be brilliant, but the brat was dead wrong in this case.

Chapter Twenty-Seven

After dinner, Millie racked her brain as to who the mysterious witness could be. Who would lie about her like that? She said good night to her aunt and stared at the rain pouring outside the window while wandering through the otherwise vacant house. Scott and JT had better not be installing more booby traps without her. Such methods concerned her, but keeping Aunt Mae safe was far more important than anything else.

She caught up on paperwork and went through the company finances, her mind reeling. She also called Brigid two more times, but the woman didn't answer. Maybe she had been called out on a case.

Her phone buzzed. "Frost." Hopefully it would be good news.

"Agent Frost. Hello there. My investigators have informed me that you're in a world of trouble in your cute little town," Werner Dearth drawled.

Millie's lungs stuttered. "I told you never to call me again."

"Please. I think you love the attention."

She watched the storm outside. "What do you want?"

"I, ah, want to know if you've found my wife. I'm so worried, you know." He chuckled.

The cretin. If she reported his call, he could claim concern for his missing wife. "This is harassment, Dearth." She clicked off, surprised that her hand trembled.

Then she got back to work, irritated that neither Scott nor JT had checked in with her.

Around ten that night, the rain started to batter the ground as if the gods were trying to hammer through the soil. Tension rode the air. She couldn't breathe, so she stepped out onto the porch, surprised at the thick humidity that slapped her. She looked around and spotted Scott and Roscoe jogging from the gate.

"Where have you been?" she snapped, stepping into the wild rain. The droplets drummed against her face and she tilted her head to take more of them. Water had matted Scott's hair to his head and his light T-shirt to his hard, cut chest. Roscoe panted next to him and shook, sending water in every direction.

"Scouting the property," Scott said. "Go back inside. It's raining."

"You go back inside," she snapped, still angry at his high-handedness. Fury and frustration surged through her like a torrent, unyielding and hot. "I'm so tired of you telling me what to do." She recognized her unreasonableness, but the anger needed an outlet, and the man had threatened to spank her. Furious and confused, a part of her felt lost. Millicent Frost never felt lost.

"I'm your lawyer, and the man who was inside you not too long ago," Scott retorted.

"Not if I fire you," she snapped back, blinking water out of her eyes and refusing to acknowledge the second part of his statement.

He stepped into her space, bringing with him the scent of man and storm. "You're going to fire me?"

"Maybe." A surge of rage stole all her thoughts. "I'm tired of you playing games." She knew the second the words flew from her mouth that they were unfair.

"Games?" he asked, rearing back.

"Yeah."

Roscoe sat and panted, looking from one to the other, his tail wagging on the wet ground.

"Great. Now I'll have to give him a bath," she yelled.

"What is wrong with you?" Scott wiped rain off his face.

"You. You're what's wrong with me," she muttered. "I'm tired of this. Tired of the tension, tired of the uncertainty. I'm just tired."

He cocked his head. "Do you want to go for a run?"

"No, I don't want to go for a run." She shook her head. "I want to figure out who killed Clay, and we're not doing it here. I'm going into town, to Snarky's Bar, to see who's there. Maybe a regular or two will have something to say that'll remind me of what happened that night."

"There's a raging storm going on and if I just heard right, a tree came down at the far end of the property. You're not driving anywhere." Scott's face was a hard, unyielding mask.

Ire rolled through her like a runaway freight train. "Oh, if you think you can tell me what to do because we fucked one time, Scott Terentson, then you're crazy."

His eyes blazed an unholy blue.

Then he moved.

* * * *

Scott's ears rang as temper blasted through him to match the fury of the storm. Without thinking, he barreled toward her, tangled his hand in her hair, and yanked her head back. "What did you say?"

"You heard me," she snapped, her eyes an indigo blue and full of fire. Her lips were pink and full and too much temptation for anybody to resist, especially a man holding on to his control with both hands and losing.

He swooped in, his mouth taking hers. The storm around him paled compared to the wild hurricane of Millicent Frost.

Rain pounded all around them, beating in sync with the thundering of his heart against his rib cage. She wasn't a calm eye in the middle of the storm, but the very vision of turbulence, brilliant and dangerous and so sweet. He couldn't help but take them both away from the moment.

His lips moved against hers and he delved deep into her, allowing the flames to consume him in the middle of the downpour. Droplets trickled down her face and mingled with the heat of their kiss, contrasting violently with the passion unleashed between them. She tasted like fine wine and pure rain, and more importantly, like promise and hope.

Her fingers clenched in his soaked shirt as she rose on tiptoe, opening her mouth and giving him everything.

He pulled her even closer, consumed in her, lost in her, maybe even found in her. He drew back to catch his breath and stared like a man possessed. Her cheeks were flushed and her chest heaved as she panted out, but it was those eyes, those brilliant sparkling unfathomable blue eyes that nearly had him taking her to the ground. He swept her up against him, careful of the fresh bruises and cuts on her fragile body, and stalked through the deluge to the doorway, making sure the dog made it safely inside.

Then he kissed her again, taking what he needed. He positioned her so he could reach behind him and lock the door. The flimsy lock would at least warn him if anybody tried to get inside.

He then walked silently, still kissing her, lost in the feel of her tight body in his arms as he climbed the stairs and maneuvered into her bedroom this time. Wrenching his mouth free, he yanked off her shirt, pulling his head back just long enough to do so before he kissed her again, addicted to the feel of her against him. He set her on the bed, and her hands instantly went to his shirt, yanking it up over his head and forcing him to duck or get strangled.

She chuckled and the sound careened directly to his balls.

He was throbbing and he was hard, and never in his life had he felt this desperate. Even so, he had to make himself clear. So he once again tangled his fingers in her hair and drew her head back, keeping his grip firm to signify control. "Millie, you need to listen to me."

She blinked once, her gaze dropping to his mouth, then lifting again to meet his. "What?" she asked, unsnapping his jeans.

Desire morphed into lust in his veins, and the roaring of his blood nearly drowned out his good intentions. "I mean it." His throat felt raw. "I know you were angry and upset tonight, but you can't go off half-cocked like that." If he hadn't been there, she would've headed into town to try to solve the murder and could have quite possibly ended up dead herself. He would not tolerate her putting herself in danger. "Tell me you get me."

She slowly unzipped his jeans, challenge stamped hard across her face. "Terentson? You need to learn that I can take care of myself." She reached in and grabbed him, her hand wet from the rain and so soft, a low growl rumbled up his throat and emerged from his chest.

Triumph lifted her lips. "Now what were you saying?" she asked, stroking him.

He lifted his chin. Apparently he wasn't getting through to her. He'd have to try something else.

Chapter Twenty-Eight

Millie realized the very second she made the mistake. She'd underestimated Scott Terentson once again.

His chin lifted and his eyelids slowly lowered to half-mast. He looked dangerous and intent and shockingly sexy. "I thought I was making myself clear," he ground out, several octaves lower than his already low tone. "Let's try this again." With one smooth flick of his wrist, he unfastened the front clasp of her bra and the cups sprang open. He drew it lightly down her arms and leaned over, his mouth dropping to nip at her ear and to scrape along her jugular to her clavicle.

Need rushed through her, and her blood started to pound with a demand that far exceeded the storm outside.

He lifted his head suddenly with the bra straps just below her elbows and yanked her arms behind her back to quickly tie the bra together.

She jerked and pulled, stunned that he'd bound her hands. Looking down, she found her nipples rock hard, and her breasts *ached*.

His smile was beyond wicked. Then he dropped to his knees, unfastened her jeans, and pulled them down her legs along with her panties, revealing her.

Then his mouth was on her. She threw back her head and cried out as a shocking pleasure thundered from his mouth into her body. She whimpered and he nipped her in response, licking her, then lashing her clit.

He knew exactly what he was doing, pushing her higher, forcing her right to the edge.

She leaned against him, trying to find purchase, but her hands remained securely bound, and then he stopped. She opened her eyes and looked down. "Scott?"

"Yeah," he said, gently lifting one of her legs to pull her jeans and panties free before doing so with the other leg.

"What are you doing?" she asked, gasping, panting, needing.

He stood, scraping one hand along her ankle, shin, knee, and thigh to cup her mound.

She gasped and pushed into his hand.

He stood tall above her, his fingers sliding along her nape and entwining in her curls. His wrist twisted, forcing her head up, his eyes boring into hers with a hunter's intensity.

Her knees trembled and shook up to her core, and she tried to press against him, but he wouldn't let her.

"Are we ready to talk now?" he asked.

An emptiness growled inside her. "Scott," she hissed.

"Yeah." He slowly slid one finger inside her, sending rapture through her. She had to bite her lip to keep from whimpering. Her temper battled her desire and failed. She pushed against his hand, silently demanding more.

"Oh no," he murmured, all control, all male intent, leaning down and kissing her not so gently. "We're gonna talk, Millicent Frost. You get me?"

She bit his lip.

His eyebrows rose, then his gaze darkened. "You don't get me." He removed his hand and swiftly flipped her around, lifting and planting her on the bed.

She threw her head back. This would work.

Then his broad hand unerringly found its home on her behind. The slap was hard and sharp and rocketed flames through her. She threw back her head and, unable to support herself with her arms, fell forward onto the pillow. Swearing at him, needing relief, she turned her head to the side so she could breathe.

He spanked her several more times, hard, then his fingers found her core. She could feel the dampness on her thighs, and she mewled, pushing back against him. "Millie, we're still talking here." His teeth sank into her left buttock. She slid almost into an orgasm, but he moved his hand and squeezed her thigh, denying her relief.

She whimpered in frustration. "What?" she moaned. Who was this man?

"No more going off on your own. Are we clear on this point?" His voice was dark. Deep and primitive.

She'd agree to almost anything right now. "Yes, we're clear," she panted out, her voice partially muffled.

"Good." The rustling of clothing filled the silence, then the crinkling of a wrapper gave her hope. Strong hands grabbed her hips and she could feel him at her entrance. She tried to push back against him to make him hurry up, but Scott was in control now, and he apparently meant to keep it.

He slowly, torturously entered her, holding her on the edge without letting her go over. Soon he drove into her, balls-deep. "You okay, Tinker Bell?" he asked, his body a hot wall of muscle behind her.

"No," she sputtered. "Start moving or I really will figure out a way to kill you."

His chuckle was dark and more than a little amused as he spanked her several times. Raw nerves fired electricity through her, and she moaned. He reached under her and tugged on her nipples, his nails adding just enough bite to force a whimper from her.

He slowly pulled all the way out and drove back inside her, filling her more than she'd thought possible. His substantial length stole her breath, and yet she tilted her hips to take more of him.

His teeth raked the side of her shoulder blade, then all of a sudden he freed her hands. She scrambled to get them beneath her.

"Oh no, you don't." One of his strong hands manacled her wrists and tugged them above her head. "You keep them right there. Got me?" He pulled out and hammered back in.

"Yes," she whispered, curling her nails into the bedspread. She'd do anything to keep him from stopping.

"Good girl." One hand clasped her nape, then he started to move as his other one gripped her hip. He held her in place as he powered inside her.

Hard and strong.

Fast and wild.

Sure and intense.

Thunder ripped outside and lightning zipped close enough to light up the entire room, but she didn't care. She held on with her eyes closed, taking everything he gave her. This was far wilder than she ever would've anticipated. Nobody could have imagined this.

A desperate anticipation prickled along her skin and she tossed back her hair, pushing against him as hard as she could. Her heart thundered in her chest, but every single thought she'd ever had pinpointed on where they were joined.

He slowed.

She mewled, the thought slapping the back of her mind that she wasn't a woman who made that sound. Ever.

His hand came down hard on her butt, echoing through the room. She jerked, her thighs quaking.

His teeth latched onto her shoulder. "You're going to do what I tell you to do when it comes to safety. Period. No negotiation, no contingencies, and no arguing. I can do this all day until you agree." He spanked her again.

Her throat closed. A tremor started deep inside her. "Scott." She couldn't find another word.

"Promise. Now."

"I do. I promise," she rattled, so close to the edge.

"Good." He pulled out and drove inside her with such force the headboard smacked against the wall, hammering so fast that her body opened to take all of him.

She pushed against him again, then with a sharp cry, she fell over.

Euphoria blasted within her, more powerful than any bomb ever detonated. A thrilling surge of pleasure rushed through her. So exhilarating. She stopped breathing for one second, hanging completely suspended in time and space, then she crashed all the way, riding out the waves and murmuring softly until her body went lax.

Behind her, Scott tensed and powered inside her one more time. Holding still, he spasmed with his own release, whispering her name.

Gradually, she blinked back to reality as he pulled out and walked to the bathroom. When he returned, his footsteps projected strength and power. Fatigue engulfed her.

Chuckling, he lifted her, swept back the covers, and planted them both inside before drawing her near and kissing the back of her ear.

Her eyelids were already closing. "We're gonna talk about that whole bra thing later," she mumbled, settling her butt against his groin and allowing his strong front to warm her back.

He closed his lips over her jugular and pulled, no doubt leaving a mark. His mark. Then he kissed behind her ear. "Anytime, Tinker Bell," he murmured. "Anytime."

* * * *

The brutal water pounded down on Scott, burying him under tumultuous currents that somehow propelled rocks toward his head. He couldn't breathe. He could barely move, trapped deep in a watery grave.

The nightmare took him under, throwing him from the murky water into a rushing river, the one right outside Millie's home. The familiar setting twisted his gut, even as he fought the unknown currents, trying to keep his head afloat. He would pop to the surface every once in a while and draw in a deep breath before being dragged back down by unseen claws.

He fought as hard as he could, grunting, swearing, breaking the surface again, only to see Millie perched on a massive rock in the middle of the deadly current.

She wore a light pink sundress with her bare feet curled up and her arms around her knees. Her hair was a wild mass of bright green curls, and raw fear glowed in the blue of her eyes.

The sky above her morphed into an unreal, frothing mass, throwing bolts of fire at the ground. Several were aimed for Millie and impacted the water around her, causing the river to hiss out steam that partially obscured her expression.

He tried to swim toward her, holding his breath, using every ounce of strength he could summon. But the closer he got, the farther away her rock floated.

Armed enemies emerged atop the far bank, and flashes of light whipped through the stormy night as they fired bullets at her fragile body. She hunkered down. He bellowed and fought wildly to get to her as blood filled his vision.

An explosion rocked the entire scene.

He sat up in the bed, panting, sweat rolling down his shoulders. Lightning struck outside the house and he jolted, his gaze slashing to the open window. The barrage of rain pierced the night like runaway bullets. He scrubbed both hands down his face. His whiskers scratched his palms and he wiped back his hair, noting the slightly sweaty strands.

So now his subconscious wanted to fuck with him by combining his past military traumas with fear for Millie's life. Fucking wonderful.

Gulping, he turned to look at the silent woman next to him, sleeping quietly. She curled onto her side, her back to him with her hair a wild mass on the pillow. She slept peacefully, despite the violent storm outside.

He couldn't believe the nightmare. Bad dreams often haunted him, but the heaviness of this one felt like a warning about Millie. So far, he'd been lucky protecting her. But something was coming for him, and he knew it.

He silently slid from the bed and drew on his jeans before padding to the open window to look out into pure darkness. He heard only the staccato rhythm of rain striking the home, vehicles, and river. He took a deep breath and strode through the room to gently shut the door before descending the stairs.

Roscoe looked up from his spot on the sofa, giving a soft whine. He jumped gingerly to the floor and walked over to Scott to nudge him with his furry head. Scott petted the dog, finding comfort in the simple act. "I couldn't sleep," he said.

Roscoe snuffled against his legs.

"You want to go out?"

Roscoe turned, looked at the window, then snorted. Torrential rain poured down in buckets instead of streams. Scott should be upstairs in bed with Millie, keeping her warm, but he needed space.

The violence of the dream haunted him. But it was the ominous warning he'd felt during it that wouldn't allow him to get any more sleep tonight.

He hadn't been in control with her the night before, and that concerned him. He always maintained control. But he was also as screwed up as screwed up could be. How could he cover her if he couldn't even shield himself from the dreams?

He lumbered over to the chair by the window and fell into it, listening to the storm as it continued to rage. Roscoe padded to his side and slapped his big maw onto Scott's thigh.

Scott absently petted the dog and ran his mind through Millie's case. He didn't like the lack of other suspects. She'd not only invented but touched the murder weapon at the time of the killing, and she'd been found covered in the victim's blood, both of which concerned him greatly. Oh, he excelled in trial. But every lawyer realized the unpredictability inherent in every jury.

He reached for his phone, then paused before setting it down. The plans that he needed to make for her in a worst-case scenario shouldn't be traceable. He'd never broken the law in his life, but he would create contingencies in the event Millie's case didn't go the way he wanted.

For the first time, he put somebody above the vow he'd taken to the law. When it came to Millie, he harbored no qualms at blowing up his entire belief system. He would keep her safe. Period.

Chapter Twenty-Nine

Millie hummed softly to herself as she finished scrambling eggs and throwing in a copious amount of cheese. She'd also tossed in onions and peppers, so the concoction could be considered healthy.

She'd risen early to compile the picnic baskets for Alex's charter, then had assisted him with the safety checks for the anglers. One client hadn't purchased the correct fishing license, so she'd taken care of the requirement online.

JT provided a two-hour lesson on the riverbank with his usual gruff manner. The group of young teachers on vacation had seemed enthralled and must like the grumpy type of man.

Verna had dropped off Alex before taking their eldest to school for the day, and Millie wondered what it'd be like to have a family. She'd always seen herself getting married and having children. Aunt Mae would love to spoil the next generation.

Millie's heart warmed that she could help Verna and Alex. He'd thanked her profusely for the job before instantly charming his group of four couples, bowling champions from the next small town over. The assembled anglers appeared excited to hit the river, even though the rain would continue sporadically throughout the day. There was something truly enjoyable about a river after a wild storm like the one they'd had the night before.

As Alex had pulled the boat away from the property to head to the bigger river, she'd longed to go with the group. There was nothing like fishing a calm stretch of stream before the rain splashed it. But then she'd returned to bed, immediately falling into peaceful dreams until later that morning.

Now she looked out the window at the mellow, almost peaceful rain dropping to the earth; she couldn't see either Scott or Roscoe. They'd gone for a run at least half an hour ago, and she had started to make breakfast.

The night before had been both a little intimidating and a lot exhilarating. She had seen a side of Scott Terentson...hell, she had experienced a side of Scott Terentson that most people probably didn't know existed. In fact, until the night before, she hadn't realized the depths to that man.

She rubbed her chest. She was falling for him, and she knew it. How confusing. She felt both unsettled and vulnerable, and yet he'd intrigued the heck out of her last night. What kind of adventures could she find with Scott if she stayed with him? Not that he had proposed forever with him, but still. Considering whisker burn pinkened almost every square inch of her body, the matter bore contemplation.

Her phone buzzed and she looked down to see that the transfer from her bank account to the business had gone through. She didn't have a lot of available funds, but she was happy to share what she could. The Derby would bring in necessary cash flow, but she needed to pay Alex now.

She should check on her patents again. She'd invented a few fishing gadgets and had applied for patents, which should be coming in soon. Then she needed to somehow find a partner or a manufacturing firm, a matter beyond her experience. But after studying her great-aunt's finances, she realized she needed to step up and right now.

She heard the rumble of an engine before a black SUV came into view—so somebody had opened the closed gate. She didn't recognize the vehicle, so she rushed to the cupboard near the door and drew out her Glock 19, her heart hammering against her rib cage. She opened the door, kept her back to the frame, and swung out, pointing at the vehicle. Her great-aunt still slept peacefully, and Millie would shoot anybody trying to cause harm.

The SUV rolled to a stop and all four doors opened. She set her stance.

"Yo, Mills, put the gun down," Clarence Wolfe called cheerfully from the driver's seat as he emerged into view and shut his door. "I tried to find a latte place in town to bring you a treat but failed. Sorry about that."

Holy crap. She instantly dropped her arm.

Brigid Banaghan jumped out of the passenger seat, hauling several laptop bags with her. "Hey, Mills," she said cheerfully, not quite meeting her gaze.

Millie crossed her arms, careful to keep the gun loose. "Brigid," she said warningly, as the other two occupants of the vehicle, Ian and Oliver Villan, came into view. The twins had recently left MI6 and seemed a little lost to her.

Wolfe and Brigid walked toward her across the damp ground, while the twins moved to the back of the SUV to begin hauling out luggage and what looked like computer and surveillance equipment.

"Whoa, what is happening?" Millie put up her hands, momentarily forgetting the gun.

"What's happening is you should never point a Glock at me." Wolfe easily secured the weapon and tucked it in the back of his pants. "You look good." He leaned down and engulfed her in an all-encompassing hug. She hugged him back, unable to do anything else.

Wolfe was six and a half feet of pure, raw, dangerous muscle. He wore a torn shirt, a very worn leather jacket, and ripped jeans. He had brown eyes, short hair, and a jaw most certainly chiseled from solid rock. The scar cutting from his left temple down to his jugular gave him the aura of a wild man instead of detracting from his good looks.

"You can't be here." Millie stepped back.

He frowned, looking adorably confused. "I can't?" He looked around. "I'm pretty sure that time and space say I can."

"Did you just make a joke?" Ian asked, stomping forward with duffel bags over both muscular shoulders.

"I am hilariously funny," Wolfe said.

Brigid shoved the laptop bags inside the front doorway before leaning over to hug Millie. "Hi, my very, very, very good friend," she murmured, a slight Irish accent emerging. The rain had darkened her red hair, but nothing could dampen her sparkly green eyes, which reminded Millie of emeralds.

"Brigid, I thought we were keeping the internet search between us," Millie said.

"Nope," Wolfe said cheerfully. "Once a bomb went off at your place, the whole team was alerted."

Millie kept from smacking her head. That made sense. She should have realized they'd find out. "Wolfe, I thought all of you were out on mission."

"We were," Wolfe said. "The Villan boys and I decided to come on back. You're more important than anything else."

A wave of warmth coursed through her. "What about Dana?" His fiancée was at least thirty weeks pregnant.

"She's fine. She's with her family right now and is safe as kittens," he said. "Don't worry. As soon as we take care of who's after you, I'll fetch her and bring her home. Right now, she wanted to hang out with her sisters a little bit, which is okay, because the baby will be here before we know it."

The idea of Wolfe becoming a father still took Millie aback. He'd probably make a great one. Did he say safe as kittens? "Hey, speaking of which..."

"He's in the car," Wolfe said of his adorable cat. "He's snoring right now and I didn't want to wake him. I'll bring him inside as soon as we're finished arguing about whether or not we're going to stay here and solve your problems."

She wasn't up to an argument. Not with Wolfe, anyway. "Is there any chance I could win this argument?" Millie looked way up to his face.

"Nope," he said cheerfully, turning to scan the area. "Got any booby traps?"

"I already used my exploding squirrels but have irritating and poisonous plants in key places," Millie said, smiling as both twins drew nearer. "Hi there."

They had hazel eyes, black hair, and scarred, hard bodies. Oliver had more green in his eyes and Ian more blue, but other than that, it would be difficult to tell them apart without their individual scars.

"You two came to help?" she asked.

"Of course," Oliver said, hefting what looked like gun cases past her into the house.

JT suddenly emerged from down by the river, striding across the expanse between them, his gaze hard on the newcomers. "What's going on here?"

Millie instantly moved to position herself between Wolfe and JT. She adored both of them, but putting them in the same vicinity would be like tossing two lions into an elevator. It just didn't make sense.

The two eyed each other as JT neared, and Millie felt like taking cover away from them instead of stupidly standing in between them. They were about the same height, both scarred, both molded as warriors from long ago. She honestly didn't know who would win a fight, and she didn't want to find out. Her legs wobbled.

"Wolfe," JT said.

"JT," Wolfe returned, smiling, then they both moved forward into a quick man hug that involved some serious pounding on their backs before separating.

Millie's jaw dropped open. "What in the world?"

They both turned to look at her.

"Huh?" Wolfe asked.

"Yes?" JT questioned.

She looked from one to the other. "How do you two know each other?"

Wolfe frowned, his dark brows slashing down. "Seriously? I told you, I think of you as my eccentric little sister."

JT cocked his head. "And you *are* my little sister."

"And?" She drew out the word.

"The second I knew I had to protect you," Wolfe started, "I looked up your family."

She shook her head. "When did this happen?"

JT shrugged. "When was it, Wolfe? I think when I was home for the holidays for those two days. Besides, who cares?"

Wolfe nodded. "Yeah, we went fishing. Spent all day together. I know everything about JT. He knows everything about me. We're solid in our commitment to you, Mills. It's all good."

If the earth had opened up and tossed her in with dinosaur bones, she wouldn't have been more surprised. She looked over to see Brigid silently laughing. Oliver had not emerged back from the house.

Ian studied the group and lifted his nose in the air. "Hey, I smell something good. No wonder Oliver isn't back." He sidestepped Brigid and strode inside.

Millie wiped rain off her cheek. "Brigid, is Raider still out on a mission?" Brigid and Raider lived together and had for quite some time. It was unusual to see one of them without the other.

"Yeah, he's north of New York right now," Brigid said. "Don't worry. He knows where we all are. I had to let Angus and Nari know what's going on, too."

Wonderful. "I didn't want to get any of you involved in this," Millie said slowly.

Wolfe snorted. "Honey, you should have called us the second you were in trouble." His voice remained gentle but a hard glint darkened his eyes.

JT stared up at the sky. "I told her to call you, but she didn't listen."

Shock slammed through her and she gave her brother a look. "You did not."

"Yes I did," he said easily. "Like I said, you didn't listen."

She questioned whether JT and Wolfe should be friends. She lowered her chin. "Jack Trawler Frost. You tell the truth right now."

Wolfe paused and swiveled his head to face JT. "Jack? Your first name's Jack?"

"Yeah," JT growled, his frown fierce. "But most people never, ever use it."

Wolfe looked up at the cloudy sky, then down at his boots before focusing on his friend again. "Jack Frost. Your name is actually Jack Frost."

JT sighed and gave Millie a glare that promised retribution. "My biological father died before I was born and our mother married Samuel Frost. He adopted me."

"Huh," Wolfe said. "Cool. I like the name Jack Frost."

Just then, Scott and Roscoe jogged out of the forest, and Scott took in the scene before pausing, his chest heaving and sweat mingling with rain on his face. To his credit, he then continued walking toward them instead of running away, as anybody with an ounce of sanity would've done.

When he reached them, Roscoe panted happily and ran around Wolfe's legs.

Wolfe leaned down to pet him. "Hey, buddy. You been staying sober?"

"No," Scott said, curtly. "We're trying, but he's, erm, talented."

"True that," Wolfe said, scratching a deliriously happy Roscoe, then standing. "Hey, Terentson. How are you?"

Scott stepped closer to Millie as if making a claim, no expression on his handsome face. "I'm good, Wolfe. It's nice of you to come help."

"Absolutely," Wolfe said, his smile widening until it reached his scar. "I brought the Villan twins and Brigid."

Scott looked from Millie to Wolfe, surprisingly at ease. "Well, then," he said. "We'd better get started."

Chapter Thirty

Millie's great-aunt radiated an adorable charm. Scott smiled widely as she handed him another chocolate chip cookie before bustling out of the living room. He couldn't help but feel superior as he munched happily on the treat while Wolfe glared at him. Oh, Millie's aunt Mae had been generous with everybody, but he had gotten the extra cookie. Obviously the woman would love to see Millie settled down and happy. Right now, he seemed to be the best possibility.

Millie had settled Brigid in Scott's former room and the twins and Wolfe with JT in the bunkhouse. He had every intention of staying with her, and apparently she was of like mind because she helped him move his possessions into the light pink bedroom.

He wanted to be near her, not just to keep her safe, but because she was quickly becoming his everything. If he could just get his head on straight, maybe he could be somebody she deserved.

For now, Brigid quickly set up her command center in a makeshift desk area against the stairs, and the rest of them gorged on chocolate chip cookies and sinfully good cinnamon rolls.

Wolfe had brought in Kat, who was an eight-month-old white cat with one mangled ear and heterochromatic eyes—one blue and one green. As a kitten, the animal had burrowed into Wolfe's pocket quite often, and now that he was bigger, he sometimes lounged on Wolfe's neck like a fur stole. At the moment, he was sniffing around the room, detouring every once in a while to beg for a bite from someone's cookie.

Millie's Aunt Mae hovered near the stairs. "If you all are good for a while, I may go take a little rest." The woman wore a pretty flowered skirt and pink sweater and had nicely curled her hair. She looked healthy, but her shoulders had begun to stoop.

"You do need to rest," Millie said smoothly around a big bite of cinnamon roll. "We'll be fine, Aunt Mae. Okay?"

She winked at her. "If you all get bored, go see what Lila's up to, would you?" With that, she turned and strode into her room.

"Who's Lila?" Wolfe asked, still eyeing the remainder of Scott's cookie, so he shoved it hurriedly into his mouth.

"She's someone who helps Aunt Mae around the place," Millie said.

"All right," Brigid said, turning around, at home in her element with two screens in front of her. "Here's what we know." She ran down the facts from both cases. "Let's start with the Clay Baker murder. I might have hacked the local chief's computer, and I'm printing out a list of the patrons that he knows frequented the bar that night. We need to speak to each of these people and find out who else was in the bar. I don't believe the list is complete."

She then typed rapidly on her keyboard, and the other monitor flared to life. "I'm hacking into any CCTV I can reach in town, but frankly there's not a lot. It's entirely possible to get to and from Snarky's Bar and Clay Baker's cabin by the river without going past one camera, I'm afraid." She shook her head as if the idea seemed unbelievable. "So when talking to witnesses, we need to make sure to ask them about Clay's truck and if anybody saw it that evening."

She glanced at Millie and winced. "Your fingerprints were found on your knife. And so far, there's been no other physical evidence found. Your blood and his blood are the only DNA at the scene, but I'll keep digging."

"Time of death?" Scott asked.

"Coroner estimates death occurred between midnight and 4:00 a.m.," Brigid said. "The police files are fairly inconclusive. The chief of police interviewed Clay Baker's brothers, and the two who live in town have alibis for that time frame."

Millie straightened. "They do?"

"Yep. Silas hung out with a woman named Trix Jackson all night. I guess they met at the bar and he took her home."

"Oh," Millie said. I know Trix, and if she gave Silas an alibi, it's solid. She teaches kindergarten and could do so much better than him."

"What about Lonnie?" Scott asked.

Brigid turned and clicked a couple of keys. "Lonnie was actually out of town, and the chief has confirmed his flight to Atlantic City and his return the next day after he heard about the murder." She read closer. "Said alibi has been confirmed via CCTV from a casino. Apparently the chief is pals with the owner and got the feed easily." She cleared her throat. "I may have hacked an email or two."

That was beyond illegal. "Brigid, let's not get you into trouble," Millie said.

"We don't have anything on the fourth brother yet. What's his name?" Scott asked.

"Glen," Millie said quickly.

Brigid kept reading. "Glen was at home in Richmond. According to the chief's notes, at least the ones that he typed in, he doesn't consider Glen a very strong suspect. Thus far, there's been no effort to corroborate Glen's alibi by use of CCTV or anything else."

"We need to go speak with him," Ian said, looking at his brother. "Sounds like fun."

Brigid shrugged. "Currently, the chief lacks any other suspects, and I'm sure the prosecuting attorney has access to those files. Also there is no mention of a star witness, as described by the slimy county prosecutor."

Scott cracked his neck. "Let's stick to Clay Baker for a moment. Have you discovered anything from his college days? I'd like to confirm his habit of drugging women. At least that would explain who drugged Millie, although it doesn't help us find who murdered him."

Brigid turned, tapping her fingers on her mouse. "Two women filed complaints against Clay and his buddy Frank Clubberoni, claiming they were drugged during their college days. I had to dig deep to find them because both victims retracted their statements."

"Why?" Millie asked.

"I don't know. I can only tell you what I found. But I'll print out their names and addresses. One lives in Charleston still and the other moved to Charlottesville after graduating."

Ian looked at Scott. "Charlottesville is on the way to Richmond. Two birds, one stone, all that. We'll talk to her and then go talk to the Baker brother."

"Good plan," Scott agreed. "Anything else on Clay?"

"No," Brigid said. "I've done what I can. But unless we open an investigation, and since one of our agents is involved we might have jurisdiction to do..."

"It's a state crime," Scott said. "We don't have jurisdiction."

Millie leaned into his side, and he slid an arm over her shoulder, not caring that everybody in the room would witness the intimate act. Unless they were complete morons, the group already saw the connection. Why play games with some of the best investigators in the world? "Do you have anything on Werner Dearth?"

"Yes," Brigid said. "Because HDD is actively investigating him, I spoke with a couple of friends at headquarters. They're narrowing it down with his financials. The guy is pretty good at hiding transactions and committing fraud." Brigid turned and typed again, bringing up a series of documents. "So far, we haven't found anything that would indicate payment to the hit squad of three that attacked you. I have their backgrounds, but according to Scott, you guys already heard all about them."

Wolfe leaned forward and snatched another cinnamon roll off the platter. "We need to discover who hired them and then knock down their door."

Scott shook his head. "Dearth is the only person who comes to mind. I mean, I've worked several cases with your HDD Deep Ops team, but I can't think of anybody who would hire a hit squad to kill Millie or me."

"Me either," Millie said. "Dearth did threaten us, and he has called me a couple of times."

Brigid blanched.

Scott stiffened, his instincts rising. "What?"

Brigid looked at the papers again. "Late yesterday afternoon, Werner Dearth filed a complaint against the Homeland Defense Department and is going to file additional pleadings next week, suing for harassment."

"Harassment?" Millie's head snapped up.

"You're specifically named," Brigid said. "He said you two conspired and colluded to entrap him and that you, with the full force of the federal government behind you, bugged his offices in order to help your lover with a divorce case."

Millie dropped her face into her hands. "Oh, for Pete's sake," she muttered.

Scott sat back. "I take it he'll be filing a complaint with the Bar Association?"

"Already did," Brigid murmured. "You should receive notice any moment."

"Wonderful," Scott said. "We'll deal with that later. For now, we need to know if he hired the hit squad."

Brigid grimaced. "So far, I've got nothing."

Scott cleared his throat. "Let's split into teams. Wolfe, Ian, and Oliver, you go speak with one of the possible drugging victims in Charlottesville and then track down Glen Baker in Richmond. Millie and I will seek out the other potential victim in Charleston, and I'd like to speak with relatives or known associates of Clay

Baker and the three men from the hit squad since they're all from that city." He glanced at his watch. "It's not even noon, so we could rendezvous back here for a late dinner tonight?"

Wolfe watched his cat pounce on Ian's knee near his plate of cookie crumbs. "I'm going with Millie." His jaw visibly hardened. "I know you're tough, but people keep shooting at you. Together, we can flank her better."

Millie shook her head. "I'm armed and can take care of myself."

"Didn't say you couldn't," Wolfe replied, snagging the cat off Ian's leg. "Also not negotiating." He stood and moved into the kitchen, taking a bowl from the cupboard and milk off the table.

Millie glared at him, then turned her attention on Scott, her eyebrows up in clear question.

Scott wanted Wolfe's company if he allowed Millie to go. "We might need to split up in Charleston if there are enough associates of the three men from the hit squad, and I'd like to do a broad search. It makes sense for Wolfe to accompany us." He tilted his head. "Brigid? Are you solid staying here and running a sort of headquarters?"

"I am, and I'm armed," Brigid said breezily. "I'll cover Millie's aunt Mae until JT returns."

"I really appreciate it," Millie murmured, her voice thick.

Brigid nodded. "No problem. Why don't you all hit the road, and I'll text you names and addresses? In addition, if possible, I'll call ahead and see if folks will meet with you."

"Sounds good." Scott stood and stretched, catching Millie watching his chest muscles. Interesting. "Let's roll out in ten minutes."

Brigid's phone buzzed and she glanced at the screen. The redhead stiffened, turning toward the television mounted above the white stone fireplace. "Um, Millie? Can you turn on the Prism Media Network station?"

Millie reached for the remote control and brought up PMN, with its rolling lower banner showing current stock prices. "Sure."

Scott looked up, cold dread slithering along his spine up to his neck. "What is it?"

The commercial flipped from a guy crooning about motor oil to a news report featuring Nanette Grandelle, the nation's legal expert for news. "I can't stand that woman," Millie muttered.

Neither could Scott. She sensationalized every case she covered, immediately punching any defendant hard and smearing them with half-baked legal theories.

A picture of Millie slid into view and Nanette went into great detail about the gruesome murder of poor, innocent Clay Baker, a man she portrayed as either the next saint or the next president of the country. "Although our federal agent here looks spritely and innocent, she's known as a brilliant and deadly strategist, and if she wanted to commit a murder, she'd make it as confusing as possible for law enforcement," Nanette purred, her blond hair frizzy around her head and her deep-set blue eyes spitting with manufactured fury.

Scott kept his temper at bay until Nanette caught HDD Agent Tom Rutherford leaving the headquarter building. When pressed, he admitted to Nanette that the agency had put Millie on leave as it investigated all crimes.

Millie groaned.

Nanette then took up the whole screen, the crow's feet near her eyes deepening as she squinted. "We'll follow this case closely, I can assure you. Coming tonight are more details on this agent's lover, well-known DC attorney and heir to the Russell Mustard fortune Scott Terentson, who quite possibly used the federal government to help him investigate a divorce case." She leaned even closer to the camera. "His client, by the way, is currently missing, and police are investigating the possibility of foul play." The screen flashed to an advertisement for garden hoses.

Scott looked at Millie. "I have plans in place no matter what happens. I promise you will be safe."

Wolfe caught his eye and gave a short nod. At least they were on the same page—legal or not.

Chapter Thirty-One

Millie had always liked Charleston. As the capital of West Virginia, it had everything a city could offer, including phenomenal shopping and a wonderful theater. The Appalachian Mountains rose in the distance, providing a sense of shelter to the vibrant municipality.

Millie sat in Scott's running SUV listening to Brigid on speakerphone as Wolfe stretched out in the back seat. They had parked in front of Clay Baker's law office, which was, surprisingly, a modest one-story brick building outside of town. No light shone from the windows, and a sense of desolation blanketed the scene.

"There's nobody here," Millie said.

Brigid sighed. "I'll send you a list of his employees. He didn't have many, and apparently they've already moved on. The chief of River City did speak with a couple of them on the phone, and they didn't have helpful information. I'll try to track the remaining folks down."

"Thanks," Millie said.

"Absolutely. And good news. HDD has the CCTV from Werner Dearth's condominium building and his place of employment pursuant to a valid warrant on the security fraud case, and I now have a copy on my hard drive. I'm going through footage of the day his wife disappeared, and we'll see if he left the building."

Scott tapped on the steering wheel. "Do you have footage from the weeks leading up to the murder?"

"Yes. I have two weeks before, but I could probably get more. What's up?" Brigid asked.

Scott turned down the heat. "I'm curious who might've visited Dearth. He isn't the type to get his hands dirty, and I don't think he'd be dumb enough to conduct shady business over the phone or internet. So if he hired somebody to kidnap Julie, or if he hired the hit squad that attacked us, he would've done so in person."

"Gotcha," Brigid said. "I'll start by watching the hours upon hours of people visiting his office and home, then I'll track the occasions when he left and see if I can trace his movements. We do have a warrant for his phone and GPS, but my gut says he's smart enough to leave the phone at home for anything illegal. This will take me quite a while." Instead of discouragement, pure glee lit her tone.

Millie shared a grin with Scott. Brigid loved computer work, no matter how tedious. "Thanks, Bridge." Millie looked at her phone to scan the information Brigid had sent. "For now, we'll go speak with one of the possible drugging victims." The woman lived across town, and Millie gave directions as Scott drove.

Wolfe's phone buzzed, and he clicked it on. "Hey, honey. You're on speaker with Millie and Scott."

"Hi," Dana said, and they could hear the sound of women laughing in the background.

Millie turned to look at Wolfe. "You sound like you're having a party."

"No. It's my sisters. We're shopping for shoes online," Dana said. "How's your case going?"

"Fantastic and boring," Wolfe said, shooting Millie a look. "There's nothing to worry about. How are you and my son?"

Dana chuckled. "Your daughter and I are just fine." The background laughter rose in volume. "I just have a second but wanted you to know that I reached out to my journalist friend who attended Charleston University at the same time as Clay Baker."

Millie grinned at Wolfe. She hadn't even thought of pursuing that line of inquiry. As an accomplished journalist, it made sense Dana had contacts in good places. "What did you discover?"

"There were a series of rumors about date rape drugs on campus during that time, but no recorded cases. Most people didn't report, unfortunately," Dana said. "My friend is going through old archives at the paper since he works as a professor there now, and he'll call me if he finds anything interesting. He figures there might be some notes or the beginnings of articles that didn't pan out and thus weren't published. I'll keep in touch."

"Love you and be careful," Wolfe ordered.

"Love you, too." Dana clicked off.

Wolfe's eyes hardened.

Millie gulped. "Wolfe? You don't have to work this case with us. I'd completely understand if you wanted to fly out to be with Dana." The man rarely left Dana's side, and it had to be killing him to be across the country from her.

"She's fine for now," Wolfe said, his chin lowering. "We need to get you figured out, sister."

Sometimes he was so sweet.

Millie turned back to the front and watched Scott from under her lashes. What would he be like in a full relationship? As perhaps a husband? When she'd first met him, she'd thought he was kind of a smooth playboy. But the more she had gotten to know him, the more she'd realized that wasn't the case. In fact, he was the opposite of a playboy. Almost too distant and too wounded.

Could she save him?

They soon reached a subdivision nestled into the rolling hills. Based on a preliminary background check hurriedly conducted by Brigid, the first victim, Wilma Johnson, worked as a nurse at a local family doctor's office. A quick call from Brigid had confirmed the woman had today off.

Scott parked at the curb. Millie turned and looked at the charming two-story home. The outside was painted a light yellow with dark blue shutters. A girl's bicycle lay tipped over on the grass near several budding crocuses.

"Maybe I should go in alone," Millie said.

"It's not a bad idea." Scott looked back toward Wolfe. "I can see a woman being more willing to speak with Millie than either of us."

Wolfe cracked his knuckles. "True that. We should have brought cookies with us." He showed love by giving sugar.

Millie rolled her eyes and jumped out of the vehicle. "I'll be back." She walked across the grass and up to the front door, where she knocked.

A pretty woman dressed in jeans and a ratty T-shirt beneath a well-worn cardigan instantly opened the door. Her black hair was up in a bun, and wire-rimmed glasses covered her dark eyes. "You must be Millicent Frost," she said.

"I take it my friend Brigid reached out to you?"

"She called about half an hour ago." Wilma gestured her inside. "Come on in."

So far so good. Millie walked inside a comfortable-looking living room with a deep green sofa and chair set. Barbies scattered across the fireplace hearth and several footballs and basketballs made a pyramid in the nearest corner.

"The kids are all at the park with my sister right now," Wilma said, gesturing her to sit. "Can I get you anything to drink?"

Millie's shoulders eased. "No, I'm fine, but thanks." She had worried that Wilma wouldn't speak with her. "Sorry to bug you on your day off."

"That's okay." Wilma sat on one of the chairs as Millie took the other one. The artwork above the mantel featured a series of pictures of various kids—two boys and a girl who all resembled their mama. Knickknacks also adorned the mantel, ranging from crystal football players to butterflies. The collection sparkled.

Wilma looked out through the main window at the SUV. "Your friends can come in too."

"Nah, they're fine in the vehicle." Millie crossed her legs. "It's nice to have a break, to be honest."

Wilma laughed and fluffed a pillow next to her to rest her arm. "Sorry. I banged my elbow the other day at bowling, and I'm still sore."

"Bowling's a thing these days, isn't it?" Millie asked. "It seems like everybody's into it."

Wilma shrugged. "Yeah, it's something to do. You know, date night gets a little tedious. If you're competitive, it's still fun. And the beer's always cheap."

Millie swallowed. "Man, I'm uncomfortable asking you this. But when you were in college, obviously studying nursing?" When Wilma nodded, she continued, "You filed a report with the campus regarding Clay Baker."

"I didn't file a report," Wilma said. "My roommate did."

Millie paused. "Your roommate filed the report about you?"

"Yes." Wilma looked down at her hands. "This was so long ago. But yes, I attended a party that night."

"Did a fraternity throw the party?" Millie interjected.

"No," Wilma murmured. "I attended a party at Clay Baker's apartment that was not Greek related. I went with a bunch of girlfriends from my sorority and...I don't know. I lost the night." She looked up at the pictures of her children. "We goofed off all night, and the next thing I know, I wake up in the morning and I'm in Clay Baker's bed."

The scenario sounded familiar...except Millie had awakened to a pool of blood. "Do you think somebody drugged you?"

"Now? Yeah, I think I was probably drugged. At the time, I just didn't know." Wilma shook her head. "That time took place before all of the news reports about date rape drugs. Even though I studied nursing, I didn't know a lot about illicit drugs."

Millie thought back to her college days. "I can understand that."

"There was a chance I drank too much, which had happened before. But I just didn't remember that night, and I still don't." Wilma looked back out the window. "You know, I'm at peace now. I went through counseling. I've worked hard. I truly have accepted that I'll never know what happened that night."

"Do you think Clay drugged you?" Millie asked.

Wilma rubbed a smudge off the table holding a crystal lamp next to her elbow. "I have no idea. Now, you know, being older and being able to look back, I believe I drank some sort of drug. But I can't even say Clay Baker drugged me. I have no idea."

Millie glanced at her phone to read the report from Brigid. "Wilma, did you know a student by the name of Bobbi Jones?"

Wilma frowned. "Bobbi Jones? That doesn't ring a bell. Did she attend the nursing program?"

Millie read more of the notes sent to her by Brigid. "No. Actually, she studied economics, and it looks like she filed a report against Clay two years after yours."

"Oh," Wilma said, her face clearing. "My roommate filed that report my senior year. So I would've been gone by the time this other woman filed hers."

Millie cleared her throat. "Why did you retract the report?"

Wilma settled the pillow more comfortably on her leg and placed her arm down. "Because I didn't remember anything. The campus police spoke with Clay and his two roommates. They all denied any wrongdoing. They said we'd done shots, which we may have done, and that I had stayed willingly. Their recollection was just as good, or frankly better, than mine." She rubbed her left eye. "I didn't have a case. I was about to graduate, and...I don't know. I was young and the whole thing was embarrassing."

"I understand."

Wilma sighed. "Honestly, at the time, it was possible, at least in my mind, that I had done a bunch of shots and just couldn't remember what happened. I partied quite a bit in those days."

"Whatever happened was not your fault," Millie said instantly.

Wilma smiled. "I realize that now." She looked up. "I saw in the paper that Clay Baker was murdered and your friend Brigid confirmed it on the phone when she set up this meeting."

"I didn't kill him," Millie said. At least, she didn't think she had. She thought it was highly unlikely that if she had been drugged, she would be strong enough to stab anybody. And besides, there weren't any marks on her hands or body. If she had stabbed Clay Baker with a knife, she would've surely cut herself at the same time. "I don't know who killed him," she said, "but I'm trying to find out."

Wilma lifted her shoulder. "I can't say I'm sorry he's dead, even though I have no idea if he drugged me or not. The guy was a real boor. He acted like a rich big shot with a bunch of money but just lied."

Millie glanced at her watch. "I appreciate your talking to me." She stood, and Wilma did the same. "Real quick? You mentioned Clay Baker had a couple of roommates. Do you remember their names?"

Wilma pursed her lips. "Yeah. They were a couple of weird dudes. One guy's name was Frank Clubberoni. He actually died two years after I graduated in a car accident on campus. It threw the campus into shock."

Millie mentally crossed him off her list. "Any other roommates for Clay?"

"Just one; a slimy man."

"Do you remember his name?"

Wilma tapped her foot. "His name was Rupert Skinner. Always gave me the creeps."

Chapter Thirty-Two

Scott watched Millie as she walked across the lawn and skirted the sparkly pink bike. She opened the door and climbed up into the SUV, bringing with her the familiar scent of magnolias. He breathed deep, his shoulders relaxing now that he could shield her if necessary.

She looked into the vacant rear seat. "Hey, how did you lose Wolfe?"

Scott ignited the engine. It would be impossible to actually lose the big man. "He called for an Uber. Brigid got hold of Clay Baker's office manager, who agreed to speak with us, so he went in that direction."

"Excellent," Millie said.

Scott pulled away from the curb. "What'd you find out?"

"Not much. Wilma doesn't remember anything from that night. But she told me that Rupert Skinner was one of Clay's roommates and backed up Clay's claims that they were all partying and that she stayed willingly."

"That prosecuting attorney," Scott retorted. "He's too personally involved with all of this."

"We did know they were friends in college, so it doesn't surprise me that they lived together." She reached for her phone, pressing speed dial.

Scott slowed down as a dog ran across the road.

"Hey there." Brigid's voice came through the speaker system. "You find out anything?"

"Not really," Millie said. "However, will you conduct a background check on Rupert Skinner? He lived with Clay Baker in college, and I'd like to know if anybody filed claims against him."

Smart. Scott kept an eye out for more dogs. If they could find evidence against Skinner, maybe he'd be more forthcoming with facts about Clay.

"You've got it," Brigid said as the sound of typing came over the line. "Anything else?"

"No, we're just going to meet with Henry Halcomb's girlfriend. Are you sure she's willing to talk us?"

Considering Halcomb had tried to kill them as part of a hit squad, it was surprising anybody would talk. Scott took a left turn, driving slowly through a new neighborhood.

"Yes. Her name is Nancy Wilcox, and I texted you her address. She sounds young," Brigid said.

Scott glanced up at the gathering clouds. Great. More rain. "Thanks, Brigid," he said.

"Happy to help," Brigid said cheerfully. "I'm sorry, but I haven't found any relatives or acquaintances of Bob Phillips or Gene Lightfoot yet. Apparently, they met Henry Halcomb in prison. Phillips is from Montana and Lightfoot's from California, but so far they're just loners."

"Loners make better members of hit squads than people with full families," Scott said grimly as he drove around town and away from the nicer homes.

"True that," Brigid said, parroting Wolfe. "Also, your aunt Mae is up and baking again. We're having enchiladas for dinner." Brigid clicked off.

Millie looked at Scott. "You are in for a treat. My aunt makes the best enchiladas in the world." His stomach rumbled as if on cue. Millie looked at him as he drove toward the other side of town. "How are you doing, anyway?"

He blinked, surprised. "Fine. Why?"

"You were pretty restless in your sleep last night. Were you having nightmares?"

He thought about lying to her. "Yes."

"I'm sorry. I've had nightmares before too. It's probably normal after the other night, right?"

"I don't know what's normal," Scott admitted, driving through an older commercial part of town.

Millie's phone dinged and she pressed a button. "Hello?"

"Hi. It's Chief Wyatt."

Millie stared at the dash. "Hi, Chief. You're on speakerphone with Scott and me. What's up?"

"I finally got ahold of Max Crouse at the gas station at the edge of town. He handed over the VCR tapes for his CCTV for the last two weeks."

Scott's jaw dropped. "Did you just say VCR tapes?" He hadn't met a soul the last five years who hadn't switched over to NVR.

"Yup," the chief affirmed. "The system is ancient, but according to Crouse, it works. He has time-lapse recordings."

Millie sighed. "So there are about thirty hours per VCR tape, then. Are you sure he still has the night of Clay's death? Those old tapes record over themselves."

"Yes, I'm sure. Crouse saves ten of them, then recycles. The problem is that he doesn't label the damn things and apparently he dropped them and mixed them all up before bringing them to me. So it's gonna take some time."

Millie cut a look at Scott. "Please tell him thank you, and call me if you find anything."

"I will. It's a good thing I have an old VCR back at my place." The chief ended the call.

Scott turned the vehicle toward a residential area. "I take it the gas station is on the way to Clay Baker's river cabin?"

"Yeah." Millie leaned over and turned up the heat. "When this is all over, I'm building Crouse a state-of-the-art recording system and not charging him a dime. Even if his recordings don't help us any."

"That's nice of you." Her quick brain had captivated him from their first meeting, but her heart? Well, now. That fucking enthralled him. He kept his thoughts to himself, turning down a street and noting garbage lining the side. Soon, they reached a utilitarian-looking apartment building, a skeletal structure with a patchwork of faded colors stained by the passage of time and years of neglect. There were no shiny pink bicycles on the still-frozen patch of grass that ran the length of the cracked cement sidewalk.

Millie glanced at her phone. "She's in apartment number two." She craned her neck to see through the window. "It's over there."

Scott followed her line of sight to the apartment nearest a rusty fire escape clinging to the side of the building. He stepped out of the vehicle and drew on his leather jacket to hide the weapon at the back of his waist. "Are you armed?"

"Yep," she said, patting her overlarge purse. She jumped out and walked next to him across the barren ground to knock on a dented gray metal door. The place smelled like fast food and old plaster. The door opened and a woman peeked out. She couldn't be more than eighteen. Her belly was swollen with child and her blond hair was pulled back in a ponytail. A yellowing bruise marred her chin.

"You must be Millie and Scott," she said slowly, quietly. Even though the spring of March chilled the air, she wore a sparkly pink tank top over her protruding belly above matching sweats. "Come on in." She opened the door and gestured them inside.

The interior of the depressing apartment held threadbare green carpet and a torn sofa. Newspapers and beer bottles lined the dented coffee table, and a small kitchenette near the back door smelled like burned tomato soup. "Have a seat," she said.

Millie sat on the sofa and Scott followed suit while the woman dropped onto a disheveled gray rocking chair with burn marks along the bottom.

Millie smiled. "You must be Nancy."

"Yes, I am. I'm Nancy Wilcox." The girl folded her hands on her thigh. "Henry and I loved each other." Her gaze landed on Scott. "Are you the one who killed him?"

"Yes," Scott said, unwilling to lie to her. "I didn't want to kill him, but he didn't give me a choice."

Her eyes filled with tears as she looked at the dirty screen door that led to what appeared to be another dismal patch of what used to be grass. "Henry had problems. He had his good side, though, you know? But he had a real bad temper and he drank way too much." She gestured toward the beer.

"How old are you?" Millie asked.

Scott stilled, but it was a valid question.

"I'm nineteen," the girl said. "Henry and I have been together for a couple of years. He was only thirty, you know."

Scott took the hit to the gut. He'd killed a thirty-year-old. There hadn't been a choice at the time, but he wished it could've been different. "I'm really sorry for your loss," he said, meaning it.

"Thank you," Nancy said, chewing on a thumbnail.

Millie cleared her throat. "I don't know how to ask you this, but do you know who might've hired Henry to come after me?"

"I have no idea," Nancy said, her eyes wide. "He didn't share his business with me." She looked away.

Scott remained silent for several beats. "I think you do know, or at least you know something."

The girl looked up at the ceiling. "No, I really don't," she said, going at her torn thumbnail as if she hadn't eaten in way too long.

"Please don't lie to me." He put command in his voice this time.

She dropped her gaze to his, and her eyes widened. "I'm not lying?" She made it sound like a question.

"You're not in trouble," Scott said, going on instinct. "But we all know that somebody hired Henry and his two friends to kill us, and I need to know who that was."

"I honestly have no idea," Nancy said. This time, he believed her. She shifted uncomfortably. "However..." She looked down at her feet.

"What?" Millie prodded.

Sighing, the girl reached into a cupboard beneath the old coffee table and pulled out a rumpled paper bag. She turned it upside down, and two stacks of cash dropped onto the table. "He was paid ten thousand dollars in cash." She looked at Scott and then Millie. "I don't know who hired him, but he hid this here and left that night."

Scott eyed the bills. "You have no idea where he got that?"

"No." The girl shook her head. "But I sure could use it for the baby." She rubbed her belly. "Henry didn't have family and neither do I, and so it's just me and this little one."

"You can keep the money," Scott said. "Did you know Bob Phillips or Gene Lightfoot? They tried to kill us along with Henry."

She tore off the rest of the nail. "I'd only met them but never spent time with either Bob or Gene. I don't think Henry had paid them yet. Is some of that money theirs? Or their families'?"

Scott didn't bother telling her that the money shouldn't be anybody's at this point, considering it was payment for a hit. "No. It's all yours."

"Can you name any of their acquaintances?" Millie asked.

"No," Nancy said. "Honest. I stayed out of Henry's business as much as possible." She rubbed the bruise on her jawline. "He really didn't like me to ask questions."

Scott wanted to gather the girl up and take her home, but that wasn't his place. Instead, he reached into his pocket and drew out an old receipt. "Do you have a pen?"

"Yeah," she said, fumbling around in the same cupboard and handing him a ballpoint pen.

"I'm giving you the name and number of an organization I sometimes work with. They help unwed mothers with baby planning and job training." He wrote down the name of the organization and a contact person. "Why don't you give them a call? You and your child don't have to be alone in this."

Her hand shook as she accepted the paper. "Thank you. I appreciate it."

"You bet. They're headquartered in DC, but they have satellite offices everywhere, including here in Charleston. They'll help you out, Nancy."

Millie stood. "Thank you for speaking with us. It was nice of you."

"I don't feel like I helped much," Nancy said, clinging to the receipt as if it were a lifeline.

"You did. At least now we know for sure that somebody hired Henry and his friends and paid in cash," Scott said, also standing. Now, he just had to figure out who.

Chapter Thirty-Three

As they drove up to the garage, it took Millie a second to recognize Valerie and not her twin sister sitting on the front porch. Millie climbed out of Scott's SUV as Scott and Wolfe did the same.

While Wolfe had met with two of Clay's former employees, neither had much to say. It was a bust, according to him. He looked to where JT unloaded one of the fishing boats near the river. "JT needs help." He quickly strode away.

Scott turned and took one step after him before halting.

"Go ahead," Millie said. "Go play with the boys. I'll check on the timing for dinner." Her stomach rumbled, so hopefully Aunt Mae had the meal finished.

Scott winked and followed his friends. She turned and watched them all. What was it about boys and boats? Chuckling, she walked over the wet grass to reach Valerie.

"Hey, what are you doing?" She plopped down next to her old friend.

Valerie watched the men as they tossed materials out of the boat. "After shopping for all of the baby shower decorations, I told my sister I'd pick up Alex. They only own the one car, and Verna needed to take Frankie to baseball tryouts."

"They only have the one car?" Millie asked. "I thought they owned two or three vehicles."

"Things have been rough," Valerie said. "The economy's not doing anybody any favors, and then Verna unexpectedly became pregnant again. So she doesn't want to work at the bar, and I don't blame her. Of course, then Alex broke his arm at work. I give her whatever funds I can spare, but I'm not loaded, either."

"We really could use the help around here." Millie just had to figure out a way they could pay Alex and keep the lights on.

Valerie rubbed dirt off her knee. "I'm surprised you haven't invented something and made a billion dollars by now."

Millie couldn't agree more. "Since I'm paid by the HDD, all of my inventions belong to the government, but I have applied for a few patents that have to do with fishing. If those ever go through, or rather, if I can figure out a way to get my creations manufactured in a way that doesn't cost a fortune, then I could sell my specialized fishing poles. I'm working on it." So far nothing had panned out, but she hadn't really given it her full effort either. Plus, perhaps Scott's legal background could be beneficial, even though he mainly worked as a trial attorney.

Valerie grinned. "That would be so cool." She straightened as Alex drove through the gate, pulling the other fishing boat. "Oh, good. I'm working in a couple of hours and wanted to be able to grab some dinner."

"You're welcome to eat here," Millie said, watching her old friend draw near. Hadn't Valerie and Alex dated in junior high? Then he and Verna fell hard and fast in high school. Apparently that wasn't odd for any of them.

"Thanks," Valerie said. "I have to see what Alex wants to do. He might want to watch baseball tryouts, if I know him."

Millie watched him turn around and back the boat in perfectly next to the other one. "He's a good guide. We could really use him around here."

"I hope so," Valerie murmured. "Sometimes I wish Verna had stuck to nursing school with me. I make a decent living and my benefits are great, but she just didn't like blood."

"Or needles," Millie chimed in.

Valerie looked at her feet and used one tennis shoe to wipe mud off the other. "Very true. So you and June haven't kept in touch much, huh?"

Millie looked sideways at her. "What do you mean? I talk to June at least once a week." Maybe that wasn't as close as they used to be. Millie needed to make more of an effort to stay in touch with her friends. "She's okay, isn't she?"

"I think she's lonely," Valerie mused, her gaze tracking Scott. "She and one of the Fremont brothers dated for a while, but they broke up about six months ago. She hasn't gone out with anybody since. Is your Scott taken?"

Jealousy spurted through Millie. "I don't think he's her type."

"Gotcha," Valerie said. "The way you two looked at each other, with the whole lust thing in your eyes, I hoped true love had hit you."

"We'll see." Millie didn't know what kept hitting her, but the thought of saying goodbye to the badass lawyer made her solar plexus ache. She considered the situation, watching the clouds billow in from down the river. "We do have a couple of guys on our team. They're British."

"Ooh," Valerie said. "I love British accents. Are they both single and does at least one like a curvy girl?"

"Yeah. And they're twins."

Valerie frowned. "That's kind of weird. I don't think I want to date a twin. Being a twin is enough."

Millie chuckled. "That's a really good point. I'm sad June hasn't dated anybody else. She always loved to go out."

Valerie kicked at a pebble.

"What is it?" Millie asked.

Valerie stiffened. "Nothing."

"Tell me."

Valerie sighed and zipped up her windbreaker. "June and Clay got together. I know she said they didn't date, but she left Snarky's with him at least two times a week during the last three or four months. Maybe they didn't officially date each other, but they bumped uglies together."

Millie's insides twisted. "June actually dated Clay?"

"Dating is probably too strong a word, but she stayed the night out there plenty. I don't know why she lied to you. Maybe she feared upsetting you."

Hurt swept through Millie. "I don't understand. She can tell me anything." Maybe Millie hadn't been a good friend the last few years. She had gotten caught up in her work and had often gone undercover, but she had met up with her friend every time she came to visit her great-aunt, which occurred often. "I feel terrible about this." Millie said. "She must have been really lonely to turn to Clay."

"No kidding," Valerie agreed. "I considered him the biggest dumbass in the world."

"Me too. And I dated him." She'd have to reach out to June soon.

Valerie stood as Alex loped toward them, appearing more relaxed than he had the last several times Millie had seen him. "It looks like he had a good day. I hope this works out."

"Me too." Millie pushed to her feet. "I don't think we can afford health benefits or anything like that. At least not right now." She wondered if it would be possible to expand the business. They'd always been pretty content with the two boats, but if she set up a corporation and hired more guides, they could expand. Although she wasn't certain either JT or her great-aunt would go along with that plan.

"Hey there," Alex said as he approached. "I take it Verna has the car?"

Valerie tucked her thumbs in her front jeans pockets, a light peach filtering across her cheekbones. "Yeah. You're stuck with me. We've been invited to dinner, but I figured…"

"Oh no. I want to watch baseball tryouts." Alex once again looked like the carefree high school kid Millie had known. Maybe it was a good thing she'd come home. He looked at her. "By the way, one of my anglers today brought the paper with him. Are you being arraigned next week?"

"I am—on Thursday. Unless we can figure out who really killed Clay," Millie said.

Valerie slipped an arm over Millie's shoulders. "Everybody who knows you, knows you didn't kill Clay."

"Yeah, but Rupert Skinner thinks I did. Or at least he wants justice for Clay because they were old friends. But who knows? The chief has some videotape from that night. Maybe there's something on it." It was highly doubtful, however. Everybody took that same road and she couldn't imagine anybody driving by with a murder weapon right on their dash.

Alex wrinkled his nose. "Skinner was an idiot as a kid and apparently hasn't changed any." His chest filled. "I can say you stayed with us that night."

"No." Millie held up a hand. "No more alibis. The chief is losing patience."

"Fair enough." Alex looked at his watch. "Hey, we have to get going." He leaned down and kissed Millie on the top of the head. "I had fun today. Thanks a lot."

"You bet. You up for another run tomorrow?"

"Absolutely. I'll be here at the same time." He turned and hurried toward Valerie's vehicle. "Come on, Aunt Valerie," he called back. "You can watch tryouts as well."

"Oh, goody," Valerie whispered under her breath, sliding a smile toward Millie. "He has no clue. I'm dropping him off and heading home."

Millie laughed.

Valerie walked toward her car and looked over her shoulder. "Get going on those British twins, will ya? I just changed my mind. I am so bored."

"Absolutely." There was nothing Millie liked more than matchmaking. Except inventing. "Hey. Just a sec." She dodged into the house and ran back out with a gray knit hat in her hands. "Alex," she called out.

He half leaned out of the car. "What?"

"Tryouts are outside, aren't they?"

"Of course they're outside. It's baseball." His grin made him look years younger.

She tossed him the hat.

He scrutinized it. "Thanks?"

"You bet. It's activated by wetness, so if it starts to rain, there's a miniature umbrella that'll pop out the top and cover your head." She clapped her hands. "Let me know how it works, will you? I'm applying for a patent, probably next month."

"You've got it. If this thing strangles me, I'm suing, though."

She laughed. "That's fair." She turned as the other men strode up from the boat area.

Wolfe grinned. "Aren't we having enchiladas?"

* * * *

They finished a late dinner close to ten, and Scott wished fleetingly that his mother could be there to enjoy the fun. The team had assembled and all reported back on their activities. Ian and Oliver had spoken with the other potential rape victim from Clay Baker's college days, a Bobbi Jones, and her story sounded similar to Wilma's. She couldn't remember anything even though she had awakened in Clay Baker's bed.

His roommates had sworn along with him that they'd taken shots of tequila all night, and she couldn't remember whether she had or not, so she dropped the case. Now a successful accountant, the woman apparently had found a good life. She didn't seem sorry about Clay's death, however.

Unfortunately, Glen Baker hadn't been home on the twins' way through Richmond, so Scott needed to track down the final Baker brother on his own.

Clay Baker was being laid to rest this coming Sunday, and Scott wanted to attend the funeral to see the mourners. He had resolved not to let Millie go. The threat level for her remained too elevated. "Dinner was wonderful," he said to Millie's great-aunt.

She laughed and waved a fragile hand in the air. "Oh, you're such a sweetheart, Scott."

Wolfe rolled his eyes.

Mae removed an apron from a drawer to pull over her head. "I'll clean up. You kids go work on your case."

Scott caught sight of the pattern on the front of the apron at about the same time as everyone else. Millie gasped and the room fell silent.

Mae turned. "What?"

As one, they all swiveled to look at Roscoe, who lounged by the refrigerator. If any one of them had been wearing that argyle pattern, the dog would've leaped across the room and sunk his teeth into the material. Instead, he crouched and gingerly padded across the kitchen as if he'd turned into a stealthy predator.

"Roscoe," Millie said in warning.

The dog didn't react but instead continued toward Mae. Then he gingerly sank his teeth into her apron. He didn't pull or unbalance her in any way. He just patiently waited.

Mae looked down at the dog. "What in the world?"

"It's that pattern." The pattern was a crisscross of argyle. Millie reached over and untied the apron. "Duck your head, Aunt Mae."

Her great-aunt complied, and Millie drew off the offending garment. The second the frock came loose, Roscoe growled and tore the apron away from the women to run across the kitchen and attack the fabric.

Mae's eyes widened. "What is happening with that dog?"

Millie shook her head. "We don't know. An explosion injured Roscoe when he served as a soldier, and somehow he saw this type of pattern in the area. Angus believes the design covered the vest of another soldier, but regardless, whenever Roscoe sees the pattern, he shreds the material. He must really like you, Aunt Mae. I've never seen him react so calmly before."

Scott watched the dog obliterate the fabric. "He is getting better, isn't he?"

"No," Wolfe murmured. "I wore socks with the design, and he nearly took off my ankle last week. He showed only gentleness with Mae." Wolfe winked. "We should all be gentle with beautiful women."

"Oh you." Mae threw out a hand. "You're just too sweet." She reached into the cookie jar. "Would you like another cookie, Wolfe?"

"I would love another cookie," Wolfe said, on his best behavior.

Scott's back teeth ached from Wolfe acting like a choir boy. "Mae," he said. "Let me clean up. You cooked dinner. You get to go rest."

While the woman seemed cheerful, her eyes betrayed fatigue and her shoulders slightly stooped. "Oh, no."

"Oh, yes," he said firmly, gently taking her by the shoulders and turning her toward the living room. "Otherwise, I'll feel absolutely useless."

She hesitated. "In that case—"

"I do need to earn the cookies," he said. "You gave me several."

"I'm so glad you like my cookies, Scotty." She patted his chest. "Maybe I will go rest."

Millie shot him a grateful look and put her arm around her aunt's shoulders. "Come on, Aunt Mae."

JT stood and sidled to the kitchen door. "So long as you're cleaning up, Terentson. Have a good night." Without waiting for a response, he disappeared outside.

"Smart guy," Brigid said, smiling. "I'll help you, Scott." She stood and carried several of the plates to the sink.

"I'll pick a movie," Wolfe said, standing and prowling as only he could toward the living room. "I've had enough of work today. We're done working. We're going to watch a movie."

Scott didn't have the appetite for a movie, but he was weary of thinking about murder and suspects. He could be honest with himself that he wondered about Wolfe's choice of movies.

He and Brigid rapidly set the kitchen to rights before he wandered into the living room, where Millie had saved him a seat next to her on the love seat. A thump echoed through his heart. It had been a long time since he felt a part of a team like this. Even at his law office, he stayed in charge, and he often felt alone. This was different.

He sat next to Millie and put an arm over her shoulders. "What are we watching?" he asked, almost afraid of the answer.

"*Maverick*," Wolfe said happily. "I've only seen it fourteen times."

"Good choice," Scott mused, pulling Millie to him and extending his legs on the ottoman. He could get used to this.

Chapter Thirty-Four

The sound of a phone buzzing and bouncing across her bedside table had Millie blinking sleepily awake. She'd fallen asleep in the middle of the second movie the night before, something to do with a dog on vacation. She yawned, not remembering how she'd gotten to bed.

"Answer that, would you?" Scott mumbled sleepily from behind her.

Passion surged within her from his sexy voice, making her fingers tingle. "Yes." She reached for her phone and lifted it to her ear. "Frost." She didn't have the bandwidth to use her whole name or title.

"Hey, Millie. It's June." Panic rose in June's voice.

Millie sat up. "What's going on?"

"I don't know, but a bunch of emergency vehicles have been roaring by for the last fifteen minutes, headed to the chief's house." June lived a mile down the dirt road that led to the chief's house, which was nestled at a turn in the river.

Millie wiped sleep from her eyes. "What kind of cars?"

"All of them. I'm talking fire truck, paramedics, every cop out there. Something's happened, and considering the only case he's working on right now is yours, I thought I should call you." She coughed quietly. "I figured you could find out what was going on with your government contacts, right?"

"Yeah, I can get us some answers." Millie pushed herself from the bed. "Thanks, June, I'll let you know."

Scott was already standing and reaching for his jeans, his broad back still bare. "What's up?"

"Something about the chief." Dread engulfed her insides. "Maybe it's a coincidence, but he's the only one who lives along Downey Road other than June, and she said a bunch of emergency vehicles have sped by."

"Do you want Brigid to monitor the frequencies?"

First Millie needed to find out what was happening. Had she gotten the chief hurt as well? "No," she said, "let's not get her out of bed. I mean, this is River City. Let's just go up there." She still had a badge she could flash if necessary.

"Okay."

They hurriedly dressed and quietly exited the house to drive the twenty miles outside of town toward Shady Mountain. Millie pointed to a small wooden A-frame set back from the road as they passed it. "That's June's house." The lights blazed from every window.

They followed the twisting road another five miles and reached the chief's sprawling cabin. The world was a cacophony of red and blue swirling lights. For once the clouds had parted and the stars twinkled down with the moon high and full, illuminating the chaos.

Scott stopped and jumped out of his vehicle, running toward a clearing where many of the deputies used buckets to throw dirt and water from the river on the burning building. Activity buzzed around the fire truck in the driveway, and the three volunteer firefighters battled with angled hoses, pouring water onto the flames.

Millie caught sight of the chief on a gurney being loaded into an ambulance. She ran toward him. "Chief!" He lay still beneath the blankets with his eyes closed.

"He's been shot twice," Janet said tersely, helping to heft the chief into the ambulance.

Millie looked back toward the flames. "Shot, and then a fire started?"

"Looks like it," Janet said grimly.

"Chief," Millie whispered, looking at the gnarled man. He'd already been strapped in, and burn marks showed on the side of his face. "Please call me when he's out of surgery." She pivoted, running to grab a bucket.

She worked tirelessly with Scott and the other volunteers until finally the fire died out, quieting from a deafening roar to a smoldering crackle. She turned her head and coughed.

Next to her, Officer Locum dropped his bucket. Soot covered his face and his sweats. He must have jumped right out of bed when he got the call. "You okay?" he asked.

"No." She looked around. "Who would shoot the chief?"

"I don't know, but we'll find out. We have two deputies covering him at the hospital." Counting the three fighting the fire, that included pretty much everybody.

"Was he working on any other cases besides Millie's?" Scott asked tersely, wiping soot off his forehead.

Locum nodded. "Yeah, we had a B and E yesterday at one of the outfitting stores. Somebody stole a bunch of fishing poles. We're thinking a tourist took advantage of the busy day."

"Anything else?" Millie asked.

"No, it's been pretty quiet. Things usually heat up around here in summer, as you know."

Millie craned her neck and looked at the still-smoldering building. As the firefighters rolled up the hoses, the smell of burned wood and metal clouded the air along with debris. She coughed, her lungs heaving.

Scott looked at Officer Locum. "Could we investigate inside real quick? The chief had some evidence, and I'm just wondering..."

"The VCR tapes?" Locum asked.

"Yeah." Scott placed his dirty bucket on the battered ground.

The officer shook his head. "Usually all evidence has to stay at the station, but the chief wanted to go through those tons of tapes on his own time. I can't let you into the house because it's a crime scene." He looked around and his jaw firmed. "But I'll run inside and look for you. I'll be right back."

"Be careful," Millie said.

"No problem." Locum jogged around the back of the structure where it appeared the fire hadn't spread too badly.

"Are you burned?" Scott asked, brushing more debris off her cheek, being gentle with the bruises on her face.

She panted. The acrid and invasive smoke singed her lungs. "No. I just...I mean we can't assume somebody shot the chief because of my case. It's just that he doesn't have a lot else going on right now."

"This could be personal or it could have something to do with an older case," Scott said. "Although my gut instinct says your feelings are probably correct. I don't like the coincidence of him bringing those VCR tapes home and getting shot the same night."

Locum returned in about ten minutes, shaking his head. "I couldn't find the box containing the VCR tapes."

"Are you sure?" Millie asked, her heart thundering.

Locum nodded somberly. "Yep. I found the VCR, which he'd set up in the living room, but there's no box of tapes anywhere. Whoever shot him took that evidence."

* * * *

Dawn slowly illuminated the horizon as Scott drove away from the ruined building. He and Millie had worked furiously to finish extinguishing the flames and every bone in his body hurt. He couldn't imagine how sore she must feel right now.

His phone vibrated in his back pocket and he yanked it out and tossed it on the dash, clicking the button. "Terentson, and you're on speakerphone," he said.

"Hey, it's Wolfe. Where are you guys?"

"Long story. We're on our way home," he said, surprised that he'd called the place home.

The sound of movement came from Wolfe and a door slammed. "Is Kat with you?"

Scott paused and looked at Millie. "No, why would Kat be with us?"

"You never know. He's independent."

Millie's eyes widened and she leaned toward the dash. "You can't find Kat?" Her voice, still rough from smoke inhalation, rose sharply.

"No, and there are several open windows. Usually he just crashes somewhere in my room, but I think he is gone. He doesn't know this area." Normally unflappable, Wolfe's voice had deepened with emotion.

Scott sped up. "We're on our way."

"We'll help you find him," Millie said, clicking off. "Has he ever lost Kat before?"

Scott shrugged. "I don't know enough about Wolfe to answer that question, but my guess from the sound of his voice is no. I figured Kat was a free spirit."

"I thought so too," Millie said, scrubbing both hands down her face. Streaks of soot from the fire covered the already faded green stripes in her hair. She sneezed.

"Bless you."

"Thank you," she said. "He wouldn't jump in the river or anything, would he?"

That cat could've gone anywhere. Scott eyed June's still well-lit house. "Did you want to pop in and tell June about the fire?"

Millie hesitated. "No, I need to have a longer talk with June and now's not the time. Let's help Wolfe. I'll text her real quick and give her the lowdown, but that's as far as I want to go right now."

"Okay," Scott said, waiting until she had completed the task. "What do you and June need to talk about?"

"She's been dating Clay and for some reason lying to me about it."

His mind ticked through the new information. "You don't think she would've gotten angry enough to kill him?"

"No," Millie scoffed. "She doesn't have a violent bone in her body, but I'm bothered she didn't trust me enough to tell me the truth. Maybe I haven't been as good a friend to her as I needed to be."

Scott doubted that very much. He concentrated on keeping his vehicle on the road when all he wanted to do was punch his hand through a wall.

They soon reached Millie's home, where the light poured from every window on the main floor.

Wolfe met them, striding out of the house with Brigid on his heels. "Hey, JT and the twins already started searching the forest," Wolfe said, all business now. "I'm headed in the other direction."

Millie could feel his pain. "Scott and I'll search across the river just in case Kat headed that way. There's a walking bridge a mile up as well as several shallow places he could have crossed on rocks."

"I usually don't worry about him," Wolfe said. "He's free to do what he wants, but..." An owl hooted loudly in the distance and Wolfe's shoulders went back. "There are predators out there the cat doesn't know."

"It's okay." Millie quickly went in for a hug.

Scott's heart thumped hard. She was a sweetheart and they had more important problems right now than a cat, but apparently the feline was part of the team. When somebody on the team found trouble, they all focused on rescue scenarios immediately.

He returned to his vehicle and dug in the glove box for a flashlight. "All right," he said. "Millie, you're with me."

* * * *

After failing to find the cat, the somber group finished a late brunch, with Brigid typing away on her computer in the living room. Wolfe and the twins immediately headed back out to search for Kat while Millie and Scott cleaned up. Her great-aunt had gone back to bed, upset about the chief being shot. She said she just needed a little rest.

"Hey, I found something," Brigid called from the other room.

Millie wiped her hands on a dishcloth and hurried into the other room. "What's up?"

Scott stood in the kitchen and leaned against the wall, looking tall, dangerous, and somehow sleepy. It was an intriguing look on him.

Brigid looked over her shoulder. "I couldn't sleep last night, so I used my laptop in my room. I wish I had heard you guys leave."

How sweet. "There wasn't much you could have done at the fire. We just provided some man power," Millie said.

"Understandable," Brigid said. "I worked on Werner Dearth's financials all night."

"Did you find something?" Millie asked, her breath catching.

Brigid tapped on her screen. "Kind of. He withdrew five thousand dollars a week ago."

"Five?" Scott asked. "Henry Halcomb had double that amount. We need to trace a ten thousand dollar payment."

"Yeah, but Dearth has withdrawn a lot of money the past two years in various amounts, ranging from five hundred dollars to a thousand. It's probably walking-around money, but he could have saved up and come up with that ten grand pretty easily, based on these withdrawals."

Millie wiped her hands on her jeans that were still wet from doing the dishes. Those darn dish towels didn't work. She should invent a towel that truly dried everything. "Rubber bands secured the stacks of money we saw at Nancy's house. It's not like they were official from a bank or anything," she said. Not great evidence, unfortunately.

Scott nodded. "I'll tell you what, I don't think they need more people looking for Kat right now. Why don't you and I drive over to Richmond and see if Glen Baker will speak with us before heading into DC? I think it's time we had another discussion with Werner Dearth to tie him to that hit squad."

"You think he'll talk to us?" Millie asked.

"Yeah, I think he's arrogant enough to speak with us," Scott said. "I'll go in casual instead of looking like a lawyer, so maybe he'll feel superior."

As a plan it wasn't fantastic, but at the moment it was the best they had. "I'll run up and shower and change into something more appropriate," Millie said.

Brigid coughed. "Hey. I'm still looking through CCTV from Dearth's buildings, and a lot of people go in and out. I'm nowhere near the day of the murder."

"You're doing a good job, Brigid," Scott said, turning and studying Millie. "Millie? While I'm going casual, why don't you go full-on HDD badass agent? Look like somebody who wants to challenge him."

"I like it," Brigid said. "Get into that twit's head."

Now that was a plan. "I'll be ready in about fifteen minutes," Millie promised. Part of her wanted to stick around to help find Kat, while another part wanted to invite Scott Terentson into the shower with her. However, he was right. Enough people searched right now for the wayward feline, and they didn't have time for a shower interlude.

For now, she needed to track down who had shot the chief and wanted to frame her for murder.

Chapter Thirty-Five

Glen Baker lived in an apartment complex outside Greentown Community College, where the doors were red, the outside stucco, and the roof metal. A hodgepodge of different vehicles parked near the building, most of them sporting Go Blue Dog stickers. A dumpster over to the far right of the building overflowed with beer cans, fast-food wrappers, and what looked like a copious number of vodka bottles.

"How old's this guy?" Scott asked, stretching out of his SUV and looking dangerous.

Millie shivered in the cool spring air. "He's in his early twenties. Nice kid, if I remember right. We'd hang out with him once in a while when I dated Clay in high school."

"Is he in college?"

"I don't think anyone's really done a background on the guy," she said thoughtfully.

Scott took her hand as they walked toward the nearest stairwell and climbed three stories to the top floor.

The feel of his strong hand bracketing hers had her shivering for an entirely different reason. "According to Brigid, he's in number fourteen," Millie mused. She had to stop lusting after Scott's hot body. They had work to do.

They wandered through the hallway, stepping over bikes, more beer bottles, and what looked like part of a canoe before reaching the correct door. Scott rapped on the heavy metal. Something fell inside. He knocked again.

"Just a second," an irritated male voice called out. Seconds later, the door opened to reveal Glen Baker, his thin frame in jogging shorts and a green tank top with a college logo on it. His hair was ruffled and his eyes sleepy. "Why are you here so early?" He yawned widely.

Millie glanced at her watch. "It's noon."

He looked at her. "Huh. Oh, whoops. Guess I missed class. Who are you? Wait, Millie, is that you?"

"Hi, Glen," she said. She hadn't seen him in about five years. They'd somehow missed each other when she visited home. "Are you attending college?"

"Yeah. I'm earning my business degree. Since my brothers wouldn't go into real estate with me, I figure someone has to take over our guiding and rafting enterprise who at least understands how to count." He scratched his belly and opened the door. "Come on in."

Millie introduced Scott.

"Hi." Glen shook hands with him.

Millie walked inside, holding her breath, then released it in surprise. She had expected more of a frat house vibe. Freshly vacuumed carpet cushioned her feet, and knickknacks sparkled absent of any dust. A leather sofa and chair sat in the living room in front of one of the widest TVs she'd ever seen. A quick peek in the kitchen showed bright yellow countertops, white cupboards, and no mess. "Glen, your place is pretty decent," she said.

"Thanks." He grinned. "I'm not stupid. If I party, I party at somebody else's house."

"Nicely done," Scott agreed.

So far, Glen's openness surprised Millie. She sat on the sofa and looked toward the young man she had known as a kid. "I didn't kill your brother and I'm sorry for your loss."

"Yeah, thanks," Glen said, loping back to sit in the chair as Scott planted himself next to Millie on the sofa. "Clay and I weren't close," Glen admitted. "But I'm sorry he is dead."

"Do you have any idea who might have wanted to kill him?" Scott asked.

Glen's focus landed on Millie. "No. I know he was rude to you, but I also remember you from when I was young. You came to all my soccer games."

"It was fun to watch you play," she admitted.

Glen cracked his knuckles and blinked as if he couldn't quite awaken. "You were found in his bed with blood all over you, Millie. The prosecuting attorney called me and said your fingerprints were on the knife."

She gulped. "I know, but I can't remember anything from that night."

Glen's bare toes scrunched into the thick gray carpet. "Skinner said that you're lying about that and trying to set up some sort of defense."

"Do you know Rupert Skinner?" Scott asked.

Glen rolled his neck, cracking a vertebra. "Clay and Skinner were good friends, so I've met the guy. Can't say I was impressed."

Fair enough. She clasped her hands in her lap. "I'm telling the truth." She drew in air. "So far, I have no memory of leaving Snarky's or going to Clay's. We broke up a long time ago, and I had no intention of ever seeing him again. It just doesn't make sense."

Glen studied her, his gaze finally focusing. "You don't seem like a killer."

"If not Millie, then who do you think killed your brother?" Scott asked.

"Couldn't tell you," Glen said. "Like I said, I haven't been home much in the last few years. I figured they'd need help at some point and I'd go home, but honestly, it's been nice being away."

Millie cleared her throat. "You seem to be doing well." She fidgeted and forced herself to relax. "I don't know how to ask you this, but I think there's a chance your brother drugged me. Do you think that's possible?"

Glen looked down at his legs and back up. "I think there's a good chance my brother drugged you." He flushed. "Clay got real drunk one night a few years ago and told me if I ever wanted to score, he'd found the foolproof way. I asked him what he meant and he hinted he could obtain drugs."

"Did he actually say he used drugs?" Scott asked, his tone dark.

"No, but he alluded to it," Glen said.

Millie cocked her head. "I'm sure the police searched his house. If they had found drugs, I'm sure we would've heard."

Glen shifted in his seat. "Maybe. I haven't been back to his place, but when we were kids, anytime we wanted to hide something, we did it in a tree outside our home."

Millie had never heard that, even though she'd dated Clay for years. "In a tree?"

"Yeah. It was a stupid game we played as kids. The tree was visible from the house, and once you looked for it, you couldn't miss it." He shook his head. "I don't know if that'll help you or not, but if my brother had anything to hide, it wouldn't be in a safety deposit box. He was too suspicious for that."

Millie leaned over and patted his hand. "I really am sorry for your loss. I know you weren't close, but he was still your brother."

"Thanks," Glen said. "If he did drug you, I'm so sorry, Millie."

Millie stood and walked toward the door. "Thank you. Will you be attending the funeral on Sunday?"

"I will," Glen said. "But you should probably skip it. While I don't think you're guilty, Silas does, and you never know what he's going to do. He is quite the hothead."

Millie paused and turned. "You don't think he would've hurt the chief, do you?"

"The chief? No. That guy's invincible. Nobody would hurt the chief."

Not true. If he only knew.

* * * *

They were halfway to DC when Scott pulled over to take a phone call from his office. From his terse replies, it sounded as if he was disagreeing with a proposed settlement in some sort of breach-of-contract case.

Millie took the moment to study him. He sat easily in the driver's seat, one hand on the steering wheel and the other holding his phone to his ear. He stared straight out the window as he spoke, his profile all fierce lines. She moved her gaze from his hand up his sinewed forearm to his muscled biceps. While not bulky, his body undeniably showed sleek strength.

Her breath quickened and her thighs softened.

His hair had grown, the darker blond mixing with the light. The whiskers on his chiseled jaw were even darker, contrasting with his deep blue eyes. As she listened and tried not to watch his firm lips move, he took over the conversation in that way he had, soon issuing orders in a calm and no-nonsense rumble as he tapped callused fingers on the steering wheel.

The strategy he outlined was most likely brilliant, but the roaring of blood through Millie's head drowned out the meaning of his words.

What was she going to do with him?

She'd dated men before; her eccentric ways initially drew interest that ultimately turned to irritation. She could lose herself in her workshop with her gadgets for days. For some reason, she didn't think Scott would mind. He seemed to lose himself in the law. Well, not the law, but in strategy. Yet she could tell from the few glimpses he'd allowed her into his thoughts that the nightmares plaguing him were holding him back.

Finally, he ended the call and turned to look at her.

Desire lingered in the depths of his eyes as if he'd been reading her mind the entire time, and they moved as one. He grasped her arm to haul her onto his lap as she reached for his neck.

Then his mouth was on hers, his tongue sliding against hers. He tasted like mint and something unidentifiable. Something all Scott. Spicy with a hint of danger.

She moaned and pivoted, straddling him. He was defined and hard against her thighs, and she gyrated closer, shoving both hands through his thick hair and pulling back. His kiss turned fierce, and his fingers flexed at her hips before sliding to cup her butt. He squeezed, sending sparks of fire through her entire body.

This was insane. She didn't care. Her nipples hardened to desperate points and she rubbed against his hard chest, seeking any sort of relief. One of his hands caressed up her hip and slid beneath her shirt, moving to palm her breast over her bra.

She gasped, but he didn't relent, still holding her mouth captive with his.

He kneaded her breast, plucking her nipple through the cotton.

She tried to get closer to him and he unsnapped her slacks, sliding his hand inside her panties. Yes. She opened wider for him, not knowing it was possible to need a man this much.

Then his fingers found her. He flicked her, sliding one finger inside her, then somehow twisted his wrist until she saw stars. He forced her to ride his fingers as his other hand clamped on her hair, dragging back her head, so he could kiss his way down her neck. Something had been unleashed in Scott, and she reveled in it.

She panted, climbing, then cried out when he pushed her over the edge.

The climax rippled through her, stealing her breath. He kissed her even harder, adding to the pressure and sending her spiraling.

Finally, she came down with a soft whimper and slowly returned to reality. She exhaled as he removed his hand and gently zipped up her pants and engaged the snap. What had just happened? She'd lost all sense of time and place. They were on the side of the road, for goodness' sake.

She leaned back to look at him, stunned. His eyes were the blue of the bottom of the sea, dark and mysterious, with a glittering lust glowing from within. He looked like a wild animal.

Her lungs stuttered.

Then he smiled, the sight primal as he lifted her off his lap and settled her carefully in the passenger seat. "Keep that thought, Millicent Frost. We're definitely finishing this tonight."

It sounded as much a threat as a promise.

Chapter Thirty-Six

Just as they reached the investment bank, another light rain began to fall. Scott eyed the unrelenting sky as he parked at the curb. "When this is all over, I'm taking you to Mexico." Gut instinct told him she remained safer here with her team for now, so he wanted to look to the future. The idea of her in a bikini on a beach certainly warmed the chill always in his gut.

Her eyebrows lifted. "Mexico?"

"Yeah. Cabo. Somewhere warm where they'll give us drinks with little umbrellas. You know, someplace nobody shoots at us or commits arson."

An impish grin lifted her lips. "I'm pretty sure there are fires in Mexico once in a while, but I get your meaning. Are you ordering me to take a trip with you, Scott Terentson?"

Well, he could've asked more graciously. He had broken up with more than one girlfriend when she suggested taking a trip with him, but with Millie, everything felt different. "Yeah, I'd love to go on vacation with you." He meant every word.

"You're on. I mean, if I don't end up in prison." She reached for her door handle just as her phone rang.

It took him a minute to place the tune. "Is that the Darth Vader theme?"

"Yes." She flipped the phone onto the dash and pushed a button. "Hello, Angus."

Scott cocked his head. Angus Force led the Deep Ops team with control and humor. As an ex-FBI profiler who could punch, he strategically knew how to make the hit land for maximum effect.

"Millie." Controlled anger vibrated through Angus's tone. "I just got off the phone with Agent Fields from HDD."

Millie stilled. "Oh, I thought Fields was on vacation."

"He's just back today. Apparently you're being terminated, and two of my agents have taken unexpected leaves of absence."

Millie's mouth dropped open. "Wolfe and Brigid took leaves of absence?"

"Yes. They asked for time off and were told no, so they basically put in for accrued vacation time," Angus muttered. "Would you like to tell me why all this is happening?"

Millie looked at the phone as if very sorry she'd answered the call. "It's kind of a long story."

"No, you misunderstand me. I don't want the story. I want to know why nobody has called me."

Millie shrank back against the seat. "Because you're in Berlin." It sounded like a question and she looked beyond adorable.

Scott straightened, in case he needed to step in.

Angus remained silent for a moment, but raw tension vibrated through the phone. It was a rare talent. "Agent Frost, you are on my team. That means anything that affects you affects me and the team as a whole. Why didn't you call me?"

She gulped. "I didn't want to bother you. I figured I could handle this and I did seek help from Brigid. But honestly, Angus, I didn't know that she and Wolfe were using their vacation time. I'm sorry."

Was that a growl? Scott could swear he just heard a growl. It was pretty good. It wasn't quite a Wolfe growl, but Angus had some chops. There was no question.

"What is this about you being found with a dead body?" Angus bit out.

Millie quickly gave him the rundown.

"Good Lord. Have you at least called Scott?"

Scott fought a grin. "I'm here, Angus." How affirming that Angus knew Scott would protect her. Of course, Scott had been shot for the guy.

"Are you going to get her out of this mess?" Angus asked without preamble.

Hopefully, and if not, he'd get her out of the country. "I'm working on it," Scott said.

"I would've expected you to have called me, Terentson, considering you're involved."

Scott glanced at his watch. "Didn't even think of it. I'm not actually part of your team."

"The hell you're not," Angus said, his voice tinged with threat. "Apparently, I haven't made that fact clear. I'll call Wolfe in just a moment and make sure that he can smash that point home."

Millie slapped her hand against her head. "Not Wolfe."

"Oh yeah," Angus said, obviously warming to his subject. "If anybody can remind the two of you that you're part of my team, it's Clarence Wolfe. Expect a real nice, cozy sit-down with him soon. Until then, I want full reports from both of you regarding this entire situation, and don't leave a thing out."

Amusement, for some odd reason, bubbled through Scott. "I don't work for you, Force."

"You all work for me," Angus bellowed, clicking off.

Millie snorted. "Is it just me or does he have some serious control issues?"

Scott threw back his head and laughed. Truth be told, he wanted the entire team working this case. Between the chief getting shot and Kat's disappearance, his plate was absolutely full.

Millie smoothed down the navy-blue slacks that matched her blazer. New splotches dotted the fabric. Her breasts pressed nicely against a pretty white shirt adorned with pink flowers. She looked young and fresh and definitely official. The green streaks had all but faded from her hair, leaving thick blond curls.

"How official do you want me?" she asked.

He wanted her in any way he could take her. "Maximum official."

She reached in her bag for a clip and unfortunately secured all those curls atop her head. While still adorable, she now looked like a prim librarian, just ready to let loose. "How's this?"

Pretty fucking perfect. "You look great." He opened his door, his boots splashing water on the pavement as he exited the vehicle and walked around the grill to assist her out.

"You want to lay odds that we'll actually make it to his office?" She looked up at his face.

"Sure. I give it 80 to 20, especially because you look delicious." Taking comfort in her quick smile, he ushered her inside to a guarded reception desk. He gave their names and made sure the security cameras captured good views of them.

The security guard called up, waited, listened, and nodded. "You can go on ahead."

Millie blinked. "Huh. That's a surprise." She placed her hand at his elbow and they went to the elevator bank to ride up to the top floor. "Last time we worked in this building, I was undercover and we both nearly ended our careers."

"Ah, good times," Scott said as the door opened.

They walked out into the plush reception area, where Gladys waited, this time dressed in a vanilla colored St. John suit with surprisingly sexy red heels.

"Mr. Terentson, Ms. Frost." Her frown was such that it melded with her chin. She obviously didn't approve of their visit. "You may come this way," she said primly, walking behind the desk and down the long hallway Scott remembered from last time.

Millie coughed into her hand to mask a cute giggle, one he wanted to hear again. Instead, he kept his expression stoic as they walked past all the closed doors and the conference rooms to reach that corner office.

Gladys knocked.

"Enter," Dearth bellowed.

This time Millie rolled her eyes.

"Knock it off," Scott whispered, nudging her with his elbow and feeling like a kid sneaking out on prom night.

"You knock it off," she retorted predictably.

He needed to get a grip. This should not be enjoyable, but she had a way of adding light to the darkness always present around him. They were facing jail time for her, or at the very least, loss of employment, somebody wanted them both dead, and yet, he was having fun. He'd been missing this type of interaction during the last year.

They walked into the ostentatious office. Werner Dearth sat behind his massive wooden desk, definitely in the power position of the room. "You have a lot of nerve coming here," he sneered.

"We really do," Scott agreed, putting his hand to the small of Millie's back and directing her to the chair on the left. If Dearth made a move toward either of them, Scott could intercept him easily from the other chair. They sat.

"What do you want?" Dearth asked.

Scott didn't see any reason to go slow. "We want to know why you paid Henry Halcomb ten thousand dollars to kill us."

Millie sat up prim and proper, looking like any tough government agent. "Do you have the balls to tell the truth, Dearth?"

"I have never heard of Henry Halcomb." Today Dearth wore a severe, oversize black suit with a pink tie and a dark green shirt. Once again, he'd buttoned it up too tight and his jowls hung over. Was the guy just trying to fit into his spring wardrobe? Even his eyes bugged out. Sometimes a person just had to get a bigger shirt.

"Sure you have," Scott said. "We're tracing the money to you now."

Dearth fumbled for a shiny gold pen and twisted it in his fingers as he eyed Millie. "I think you just wanted to see me. Are you obsessed with me?"

She snorted.

"Halcomb told everybody in his little world of petty crime and aggravated assault that you paid him ten grand, and the minute the deed was done, he planned to blackmail you for more. He called you a fat cat," Scott lied.

Dearth swallowed. "If you had any proof of this, the police would be here right now."

An unfortunately true statement.

"Why do you want me dead?" Millie asked, sounding truly curious.

"I don't want you dead. I want you broken," Dearth retorted. "You don't seem to understand that when you decided to become my enemy, I would treat you as such."

She crossed her legs. "That's psychotic."

An apt diagnosis. Scott drew Dearth's attention back to him, not liking the guy's gaze on Millie. "We're also tracing your movements. Why'd you harm your wife?"

"You know I didn't harm my wife. I have an alibi. The police checked it out."

Scott narrowed his gaze. That alibi had been too quick to roll off the man's tongue. "Oh, I have no doubt you paid somebody to kill us. You have more withdrawals from other accounts you think we don't know about." It was a shot in the dark, but Scott felt comfortable taking it.

Dearth sat back and paled slightly. Aha, so the man hid more accounts.

"Are you sure you don't want to set things right?" Millie asked. "Your sins have to be eating at you."

Dearth shook his head. "That's it. Get out of my office," he yelled at the top of his lungs, spittle flying from the corner of his mouth.

As if she'd been waiting just outside the door, Gladys swung it open. "You must leave or I'll call security."

"Fair enough," Scott said cheerfully, pulling back Millie's chair and making sure she walked in front of him, just in case Dearth grabbed a gun or did something equally ridiculous.

Something didn't sit right here. Scott looked over his shoulder. "Where's Julie?"

Dearth glowered. "I have no idea. Ask your mother. Those two are thick as thieves."

Scott strolled down the hallway, then took the elevator to the lobby with Millie. They emerged into the rain outside.

She looked up at him. "You think we rattled his cage enough?"

"Oh yeah," Scott said. "We definitely rattled his cage." He glanced down the street to see two of the private detectives he often contracted with, waiting patiently to follow Dearth wherever he went. Brigid was on it with a computer and she would trace him electronically. "I think he's going to screw up and soon."

With that, Scott ushered Millie into the car and drove away quickly. He wanted to ensure she didn't get caught in the cross fire.

Again.

Chapter Thirty-Seven

They returned to River City just after dinnertime, and the entire town hummed with excitement. The Derby started the next day and the party had spilled into the streets.

Scott dropped by the hospital on the way through town to find the chief still in a coma. The doctors had successfully removed the bullets, but their patient hadn't awakened. A deputy was stationed at his door and he promised to call as soon as the man awoke. So far, they didn't have any clue who had shot him.

Mae sat by his bedside, looking wan and tired.

"Come on, Auntie," Millie said, trying to get her to leave.

"No." Mae held the chief's hand. "We've been together for years, just playing it safe. Why didn't I tell him how I felt?" She looked up at Millie. "Visiting hours are over shortly, then I'll head home."

"All right," Millie agreed reluctantly.

Scott ushered Millie out. "Are you hungry? We could grab a burger."

"Not really." She looked over at him. "Are you?"

He needed to get some color back into her pretty face. "No."

"I'm worried about the chief, and I also don't like having Angus pissed at me," she admitted. "It reminds me of when JT gets mad. You never know what's going to happen."

"Oh, I know what's going to happen," Scott said dryly. "I'm certain Angus Force is on his way here right now." Even an angry Angus investigated matters with an impressive focus, and another set of eyes would help.

Millie cut Scott a look beneath her lashes. "I'm not hungry and you're not hungry. What do you say we check out Clay Baker's cabin?"

Scott had been expecting the request. "It's still a crime scene, isn't it?"

She shrugged. "I'm already the defendant. Could I really get into much more trouble if we went?"

"Yes," he said curtly. Yet he couldn't blame her. In fact, she'd remained remarkably calm and sensible under the circumstances. He didn't think he'd be able to hold it together to such an extent and probably already would've punched anybody in his way.

If she wanted to investigate, he wasn't going to stop her. "What the hell," he said. "We're already in trouble on every front right now. Let's go to Clay's."

They made the drive mostly in silence. Millie's phone rang and she glanced at the face, then ignored it.

"Is it Angus again?" Scott asked. "I can call him if you want." He had no problem telling the man to leave her alone.

"No, it was June," Millie said. "I don't want to talk to her right now. Maybe I can carve out time to see her after Verna's baby shower tomorrow."

"You're still going to the shower?" he asked.

She nodded. "I feel like I've ignored my friends here too much. I promise I'll be safe."

He knew she'd be safe because both he and Wolfe would cover her. Perhaps he didn't need to tell her that. "I'm sure it'll be a nice time," he said. He wound along the country road, crossing the river several times and finally reaching what had been Clay Baker's refuge from the city.

The night was now pitch-black and yet the cabin cut an ominous silhouette, as if carved from the darkness itself. The rain periodically splattered against his windshield as thunder crackled in the distance. Another storm barreled toward them.

"Let's be quick about this. We're about to get very wet." He reached into the glove box and took out his industrial-size flashlight for Millie. "You take this. I'll use the flashlight on my phone." He exited the vehicle before she could argue and crossed around to meet her on the other side.

Lightning flashed in the distance, highlighting her pale face. "You sure you want to do this?" he asked.

"Yes," she said, looking toward the flapping yellow crime-scene tape attached to the front door. The rest of the tape had broken off and lay tangled and wet on the muddy ground.

"All right." He took her hand, finding comfort at his gun nestling at the small of his back. He led her around the cabin to the rear, figuring it'd be better to break and enter from that point.

Surprisingly, the back sliding glass door was unlocked. He flashed the light inside, then Millie did the same, her beam reaching the far recesses of the main room. She shivered. He didn't ask again if she wanted to leave. Instead, he stepped inside. The furniture had been overturned, no doubt as the investigators had searched the place. Cushions remained on the ground and fingerprinting dust covered every surface.

A chill permeated the room and the smell of blood still thickened the air, scenting it with copper. He looked around and caught sight of a lone reclining chair that faced the TV on the far wall above the fireplace. His long legs ate up the distance to the chair and he sat, staring at the TV.

"What are you doing?" Millie asked.

"Pretending I'm Clay. Glen mentioned his brother would want to see his secret hiding place." Scott looked around the room and out the sliding glass door. Several trees could be seen from this vantage point, but not as many as he would've expected. "Come on." He bounded out and took her hand, gratefully exiting the dismal cabin and taking several deep breaths of the chilly but fresh night air.

Holding her hand, he scouted the area, then walked across the deck and down the stairs to the marshy grass. "Those four trees there," he said, pointing. "Those are the only ones he could see from his recliner."

He hurried toward the cluster of four tall pine trees, noting the boot prints all over the yard. The officers had already searched this area, but had they paid any attention to the trees? He moved toward the closest one as Millie examined the one next to him.

"What are we looking for?" she asked, her voice hushed.

He patted down the bark, then brushed away pine needles at the base, not seeing anything. "I have absolutely no idea." He gingerly prodded up some of the dirt and found more dirt. "Huh," he said, moving onto the next tree as Millie did the same.

"Just because the brothers hid things in trees when they were kids, that doesn't mean they're doing it now," she muttered.

"Totally agree," Scott said, feeling foolish. "I don't know what I was thinking." He patted down the fourth tree and stood back just as something caught his eye. The bottom of the trunk had loose bark partially sticking up. Shrugging, he reached for it and tore it free. "What is this?" Leaning closer, he dug deeper and his nails hit something metallic.

"What do you have?" Millie whispered, coming up on his right.

He kept digging and she reached in to help, one hand holding the flashlight steady so he could see. They soon unearthed a square, dented metal box. He pulled it all the way out of the earth and brushed it off, noting the old-fashioned number lock on the side. "If Clay used three numbers, what would they be?" he asked.

"I don't know," she said. "666?"

He tried it. It didn't work.

"Try 000."

He did so. Nothing. The sky opened up as if angry at their failure and pummeled rain down on them, soaking them almost instantly. Millie yipped and put her hand over her head.

"Come on," Scott said, grasping her hand and starting to run.

She ducked her head and ran with him, her kitten heels sticking in the mud every few steps. Soon they reached the SUV, where he lifted her inside before jogging around and settling himself in the driver's seat. He handed the metal box to her. "Let's break into that at home."

Damn it. Home. He'd said it again.

Just then both doors were wrenched open, and brutal hands ripped him out of the vehicle.

* * * *

Millie yelped and dropped the metal box on the floor as a man tore her from the SUV. She immediately kicked out with her kitten heel, grateful for its pointed edge.

"Yo," a man yelped.

She looked up. "Lonnie, what are you doing?" She struggled in his arms and he pivoted, putting her against the truck.

"What are *you* doing?" he yelled, his face lowering to hers, his cheeks blazing red.

For good measure, she kicked him again. "Looking for evidence that your brother drugged me the other night."

He still had his hands on her arms, so she shoved him in the midsection. "Let go of me, Lonnie, before I really hurt you."

He swallowed and took a step back, apparently reading her intent. Yes, she had been about to kick his balls through the roof of his mouth. Behind her, a series of grunts and growls echoed. Pushing Lonnie even farther away, she hustled through the pounding rain to see Scott and Silas locked in battle.

"Knock it off, you two," she yelled.

They didn't heed her. Silas punched Scott in the jaw, throwing him back against the vehicle. The metal crumpled with a loud protest. Scott instantly dashed forward, punching Silas in the face and several times in the gut. Silas doubled over.

Oh, that was enough. Somehow, her purse was still over her shoulder. She yanked out her 9mm, pointed it in the air, and fired several shots. Everybody froze. Slowly, both Scott and Silas turned to look at her.

"Knock it off," she said again, this time letting her voice rise above the storm. "Silas, you're being a complete ass. You know I didn't kill your brother."

Silas's hands curled into fists and his chin lowered. "I don't know that."

"Of course you do. You've known me most of my life. Yes, Clay and I broke up a long time ago, and yes, I somehow was drugged and ended up in his bed. But you know me, Silas." She could see the turmoil in his eyes, but she didn't have time for this. Lonnie stood at her side, his hands in his pockets, silent in his grief.

"You guys, I'm really sorry somebody murdered your brother." She looked at the two. "But I think, even through your anger, both of you know it wasn't me. I'm trying to figure out who did it."

And then in front of her eyes, Silas crumpled. He dropped to his knees.

Sympathy hit her hard, and she moved to him, only to have Scott pivot and put his body between them.

"He's okay," she said gently, pressing her hand against Scott's flank. "I've known him a long time." With that, she moved forward and placed her hand on Silas's shoulder. The skies opened up even more, drenching them.

His heart-wrenching sobs echoed through the night. "He was my brother and I didn't save him."

She wanted to kneel and hug him, but the tension in Scott's body stopped her. Instead, she leaned in and slid an arm over his shoulder. He pressed his face to her dress pants, and sobbed. "He was my younger brother."

"Do you have any idea who wanted to kill him?" she asked softly, as the rain plastered her hair to her head and her suit to her body.

Silas sniffed. "I have no idea. It doesn't make any sense. He was the one who got out. He was the one with the good future." Silas looked over at his other brother. "Not that I don't love it here, because I do, but..."

"I know," Lonnie said, tears on his face. "I get it." He walked forward and hefted an arm beneath his brother's shoulder to lift him up. "Come on, Silas. Let's go get seriously drunk."

"Do you want a ride?" Millie asked.

"No, thanks," Lonnie said. "We're going to walk. Silas's place isn't too far down the river. The rain will be cleansing."

Silas's shoulders straightened and he turned to look over his shoulder. "I'm sorry, Millie. I know that you didn't kill my brother. I've just been so angry."

"I understand," she said softly, meaning it. "We'll find out who did. I promise you."

Scott cleared his throat. "Did you or did you not hire the hit squad that tried to take out Millie the other day?"

Lonnie rolled his eyes. "Of course not. Where would we hire a hit squad?"

Millie's heart ached for the brothers. "I believe him."

Silas looked at her. "I've been angry, but I would never try to kill you, Mills. You know that, right?"

"I do," she said, hurting for him. "Don't worry. If it's the last thing I do, I'll find out who killed your brother." The brothers walked away to be swallowed up by the forest. She had to keep that promise. No matter what.

Chapter Thirty-Eight

The SUV windows fogged up on the way back to Millie's place, and Scott turned up the heat. Then he made the mistake of looking at her.

Holy fuck. Her hair curled wildly around her smooth face, and her wet shirt plastered to her breasts, showing clear outlines.

She turned toward him, her gaze running over his wet torso.

He sped up, driving quickly to slide to a stop in front of the house. The tension in the vehicle slipped beneath his skin, pounding with need.

She jumped out and ran through the rain into the house, and he followed her, feeling like a predator chasing his cute little smartass but sweet prey.

He had more bruises than he could count, but nothing compared with the pounding in his dick. He'd gotten hard the second Millie had planted her sweet ass on him in the truck earlier, and the sound of her orgasm kept filling his head. Then to see her after the rain soaked her, he wanted to lick every inch dry.

She was everything, and he had to figure out how to keep her safe.

For now, he walked up the stairs with her to her bedroom, his heart thundering. When they landed inside, he shut the door and looked at her. "You good?"

"I'm fine. You're the one who just got into a fight." Her beauty prodded at the darkness in him that wanted to take her down to the bed and now.

"You should ease my hurts." Without waiting for her to flirt back, he was on her, his hands on her hips and his lips taking hers. She tasted like sunshine and spice, and her scent of magnolias drifted around him, sliding through him, landing hard in his heart.

Her sweet hands somehow scorched his skin as she tugged his shirt out of the way and filled her palms with his abs, humming softly as she did so. Her electric touch zipped right to his balls.

The idea that somebody wanted to hurt her roared fire through him that he had to calm before he allowed himself to continue. Gently, he caressed her back, then tangled his fingers in her hair. "I love your hair," he murmured against her mouth. "It's wild and unpredictable, like you."

She pulled his shirt free. "I love your chest. It's hard, unyielding, and strong. Like you." To punctuate her words, she kissed and nipped his pecs, her fingers tracing the dips and hollows of his abs. "You could be airbrushed, Terentson." She released his jeans and reached in, sliding her smooth hand along his length.

Desire shot through him so quickly his ears rang.

A sweetness lived in Millie Frost that stole his breath every time. But this side of her, the passionate and free side, that one owned him. Had since the first time she'd glared at him upon discovering he was a lawyer.

A primal possessiveness clawed through him with the need to take her and make her his. Forever. To keep her and explore the world with her.

She leaned up on her toes and nipped his jaw before nibbling his mouth. The woman was temptation, sin, and pure innocence all at once, and he tried to shut down ideas of forever. They hadn't even discussed right now. But for once in his life, words weren't of the utmost importance. This was. Touching her. Learning her. Loving her.

Leaning back, she licked her swollen red lips, and removed her blazer. "We have to be quiet. Brigid is just down the hall."

It took a moment for her words to register.

Then a wickedness rose in him. A playful side to him that nobody else in his life had ever brought out. "Oh yeah? Let's test that rule." He lifted her and tossed her on the bed.

She bounced and chuckled.

Before she could claim a full breath, he bent down and pulled the shirt over her head. She helped ditch the bra. Then he slid her pants down to the floor along with her panties, knelt, and tossed her legs over his shoulders. He had to taste her.

Now.

He licked her, humming along her clit.

Her entire body trembled. "Scott," she whispered.

Yeah. She drove him crazy every minute, and at least here, he'd keep control of them both. So he went at her, giving her just enough bite with fingers and lips that soon she moaned restlessly against him.

"Quiet," he whispered, chuckling against her core.

For an answer, she grabbed a pillow and yanked it against her mouth.

"Don't think so." He reached up and easily snatched the pillow free, tossing the silk over his shoulder.

He kissed her again, driving her up with his tongue until she was panting and begging. Then he stood, removed the rest of his clothing, and rolled on a condom he'd had in his wallet.

She watched him, her cheeks rosy, need in her eyes.

He grasped her arms and pulled her up, sitting, then settled her on his lap so she straddled him. "Told you we were going to finish this." He lifted her, gently placing himself at her entrance, and let her work her way down to his thighs. He held her arms to help her balance. "Go slow," he whispered, as her body slowly accepted him.

Defiance lit her eyes and she shoved down on him, gasping as her body trembled.

She winced.

"Told you." He clasped her arms and lifted her, only to slam her back down. She threw back her head, elongating her graceful neck. Then he did it again.

She gasped and clawed her nails into his chest, starting to move on her own. He kept her on the edge, slowing her down just as she got close, until once again she was panting and working against him. Fire lanced down him, shooting through his balls. So he released his control and let her pound, helping her when they needed more speed.

Her body stiffened and she broke, gripping him with her internal walls so tightly that he saw stars. He exploded, shattering inside her, electricity racing down his spine as he jerked with the most powerful release he'd ever experienced.

She went soft against him, her face falling against his chest. "I think we were quiet."

He chuckled, holding her tight. The woman had been much louder than she realized. "Then we'd better try again," he rumbled, proceeding to do just that.

* * * *

With her body pleasantly sore after a wild time with Scott in her bed, Millie chose to ignore the other aches and pains from her various run-ins with shooters and explosives as she wandered down to the darkened kitchen to fetch a glass of water. She had woken up to a quiet house; hopefully everybody was asleep.

As she poured herself a glass, a figure on the front stoop caught her eye. The door was open with only the screen protecting the house from what appeared to be an oncoming storm. She padded barefoot to the front door, grateful she'd pulled on a pair of leggings and a tank top.

"Wolfe?" she asked, stepping outside.

He huddled on the front porch, his long legs extending all the way to the ground as he stared into the night. Her heart hurt for him. She pressed a hand to his shoulder and sat, adjusting her weight on the smooth concrete.

"What are you doing?" she asked.

The rain had drenched his hair and clothes as he'd apparently searched all night for Kat. "Just looking," he murmured.

"No luck, huh?" she asked.

"None." Palpable tension rolled off him, and in profile, tension turned his jaw rock hard. "I don't know how I could have lost him."

She stared into the night, barely making out the silhouettes of the boats by the river. The cloud cover had finally thinned and the moon valiantly tried to shine down, without much success. "He's a smart cat," she said lamely, trying to zero in on any sound besides the wind through the trees and the river lapping against the banks.

"He's never been gone this long," Wolfe said. "He doesn't know this forest. You have everything from coyotes to owls out there, and they all would like to take a bite out of a cat."

Millie rubbed her chest. How discouraging that they hadn't found the cat by now. "Yeah, but he's quick."

"I shouldn't have let him out," Wolfe said. "Or maybe I should have pushed him out more. I don't know. He spent so much time in my pocket and my house that maybe I let him get complacent." He glanced at Millie. "I would never let you get complacent. We train all the time when you're with the team."

She'd learned some deadly moves from Wolfe. "Training with you is fun. I think you've been good with the cat."

"Have I?" His voice remained low and tortured. Wolfe never raised his voice. He could be scary without adding one decibel to his rough tone. "I don't know, Millie. I have a kid on the way. I can't even take care of a cat. What if something happens to my kid?" His pain tightened the atmosphere around them.

Even though she wanted to cry at losing Kat, her heart warmed for him. "Listen, Wolfe, you're going to make a great dad."

"Am I? You don't understand. I've wanted to lock Dana and this babe down since the first second I learned of the pregnancy. You know she's in California with her family now, right?"

"Yes," Millie said. "That just shows you don't hold on too tight."

He remained stiff next to her. "Millie, I have six buddies of mine from the service on a rotating schedule around that ranch. Honestly, a foreign army couldn't invade."

Millie winced and pushed curly hair out of her face. "That might be a bit extreme."

"I know, and that's just the beginning. The kid hasn't even been born yet. It's a good thing we live in the compound."

Millie patted his wet jeans, trying to offer reassurance. "The compound is very safe." Angus Force and his team owned several miles of property outside of DC where they were building houses in a nice little cul-de-sac. A fence enclosed the entire area, and she had no doubt that cameras and booby traps covered the perimeter.

"Speaking of which," Wolfe said. "We don't have enough booby traps yet. We need you to start creating some that won't harm wildlife or possible kids running around."

"No challenge there," she murmured.

He nudged her with his shoulder and nearly knocked her off the porch. "If anybody can do it, it's you."

"You're not wrong," she agreed, already formulating plans in her head.

"Oh, and I'm not sure if you knew this, but one of the lots is yours."

This was news. "Huh?"

"Yeah," Wolfe said. "Since Serena sold her house to Gemma and the Brit, we platted out another house for Serena. Then we figured we'd start a foundation for yours next to it. You'd be across the street from Ian and Oliver."

Millie jolted. "Are Ian and Oliver aware they have homes?"

"I don't know." Wolfe lifted a shoulder. "But they certainly are on the plat."

"Wolfe, I'm not sure I want to move that far out."

He stretched his neck. "Didn't your home just blow up?"

The wind picked up and she shivered. "Yes."

"Well, then, there you have it." As was Wolfe's way, he turned as if finished with the conversation.

It might be nice to live in a small neighborhood with her friends. She fleetingly wondered how Scott would like living there, then banished the thought. Even though the night had been incredible, they certainly hadn't spoken about the future.

As if reading her mind, Wolfe continued. "Does Terentson have many good friends?"

"Um, I think so. He's good friends with Tate Bianchi because they're on the same football team, and I know he plays poker with some guys."

"Oh, I play poker with him sometimes," Wolfe said.

Of course he did. She looked at him. "Why do you ask?"

He shrugged. "I just think it'd be fun to be in a wedding. So far, none of our crew has gotten married. I mean, everyone's engaged, but we all keep getting caught up in cases, and there haven't been any weddings planned. Mine's probably the first, but Dana doesn't want to get married till after the baby's born. Don't ask me why. I don't get it."

Millie did. Dana seemed logical, but was also a dreamer. "She probably wants the fairy-tale wedding with the beautiful dress."

"I just want to marry the woman," he said. "But I'll give her time." He glanced at Millie. "Not a lot of time."

She smiled. "I understand. For the record, I think you're going to make a wonderful father."

"Maybe. I'll try," Wolfe said, looking out. "I can tell you nothing's going to hurt my kid or my wife."

Millie didn't bother pointing out that even Wolfe didn't have control over the entire world. It was nice that he sometimes thought he did.

He took a deep breath. "I'm going to head back out to the woods."

"Clarence Wolfe," she said, grasping his wet flannel. "You need sleep."

He looked down at her, his gaze more tortured than she'd realized. "I'm not sleeping until I find that cat, dead or alive."

Chapter Thirty-Nine

Before Millie could offer to hunt the woods with Wolfe, Scott opened the screen door and stepped outside. She jolted and looked up at him. "Hey, Scott." A pretty pink blush wandered over her face.

"Hey." He held out a hand, waiting until she accepted it before pulling her up to place a quick kiss on her nose. "You go back to sleep."

She looked down at Wolfe. "Oh, but..."

"I've got it," Scott said. His mind kept spinning and wouldn't stop. He couldn't get Dearth's statement out of his brain.

"You require sleep too," she retorted, looking at the fresh bruises on his face. "You got in another fight tonight."

"It barely qualified as a scuffle," he countered. "Silas wasn't really into it. Honestly, I pulled my punches." He hadn't wanted to cause serious injury to a man so obviously angry and grief-stricken. "Get some sleep, Millie. You have that baby shower tomorrow, and both the arraignment and your termination hearing at HDD next week." The poor woman needed her sleep. He hadn't gone easy on her earlier, either.

She hesitated.

"We've got this, Millie," Wolfe said, pushing his bulk off the porch. "I didn't mean to keep you up."

"You didn't," she said, patting his shoulder. "I'll see you two tomorrow."

Scott opened the door for her and she disappeared inside. "Where do you want to search tonight?" Or rather, this morning.

Wolfe partially turned, his thumbs tucked into his jeans. "I've got this, Terentson. You don't need to go with me."

Every instinct in Scott's body whispered that Wolfe required backup. The man was obviously on the edge and needed a friend. "No, I'm good," he said. "My mind won't stop spinning, which means the nightmares are coming for me anyway. I'd rather help you look for Kat." It was charming how worried the big brute was about the little feline.

"Okay," Wolfe said, lifting his shoulder. "I've looked through the forest and the bunkhouse and all along the river, so I thought to head out toward the main road this time."

"It's a good idea." Scott had thrown on jeans, boots, and a sweatshirt with a hood, which he drew over his head. Rain began falling again, which in his experience meant the skies would soon crack wide open and drench him. "I wonder if the weather's always like this out here."

"Seems like a normal spring to me," Wolfe said, loping into a walk. "What's on your mind?"

Too much. "Besides the obvious?"

"Yeah."

Scott rolled his aching neck. "Werner Dearth. He's an ass, and he seems to want to harass Millie, but something he said bothered me."

"What?"

"He said to call my mother." Scott ran through the last few days with his mom. Her best friend had been missing, yet she'd calmly gone to Nantucket. "Damn it." He yanked his phone from his pocket and dialed.

"Hi," Theresa said. "What's up, Scotty?"

His instincts started to hum. "Where's Julie, Mom?"

Her silence was telling. He waited her out. Finally, she sighed. "She's here. Safe and sound."

"What about the blood at her place?"

"Werner demanded to see her that night, then threw a vase at her after a fight, so we decided she should get out of town."

Scott pinched the bridge of his nose. "She didn't need to run. I would've kept her safe."

Theresa chuckled. "She's perfectly safe. In fact, her disappearance has upped the heat on Werner, that ass, and we've enjoyed that. Don't be mad."

He didn't have time to be mad. "We'll talk about it later. Love you."

"Love you, too. Bye." Theresa hung up.

Wolfe chortled. "I only heard half of that, but I find the situation funny."

Scott wouldn't say that. "Humph."

"So. Millie and I were just talking about your wedding."

Scott tripped on a rock and quickly regained his footing along the dirt driveway. "Really? What did Millie say?"

"She suggested that I'd make a great groomsman," Wolfe said, swiveling his eyes left and right as he scanned for the cat.

Scott figured the cat's white coat would show even in the darkness, so he did the same, hoping to find the animal soon. "You would make a great groomsman," he agreed.

"Thanks. I'll take that as an offer." Wolfe's teeth flashed in the dark. "You're going to do right by my little sister, aren't you?"

Scott stepped lightly over a pothole and made a mental note to take a look at the driveway the next day. All this rain caused too many holes that required filling. "I think one brother of hers is enough for me to worry about." JT had been cordial, but he had every right to be protective of his sister.

"Oh no, buddy. She has two," Wolfe said. "The minute I decided she was a sister, she became a sister, you know?"

Scott sighed. "I know."

"What are your intentions?" Wolfe asked.

"Well, I don't know." He surprised himself by giving the man the truth instead of saying something smooth or glib. "I like her a lot. In fact, it's pretty obvious I more than like her, but I'm as fucked up as can be. I can't get rid of the nightmares, and sometimes I wake up afraid that I'm going to punch a pillow or somebody near to me."

Wolfe stepped onto the grass, studying it closely. "Have you ever done that?"

"No," Scott admitted.

They walked through the gate and Wolfe paused, looking one way down the quiet country road and then the other. "Then you probably won't. Besides, Millie knows how to defend herself. I taught her. If you ever get that lost in a nightmare, she'll kick your ass." Wolfe shook his head. "I'm serious, man. Don't ruin the rest of your life because of shit you've gone through. We've all gone through too much crap to count, and if we let it beat us, or keep us from living, where would we be?"

The man made a good point.

"And it's not just that," Wolfe said, starting to walk toward town.

Scott fell into step beside him. "What do you mean?"

"You're bored, Terentson. You're tired of fighting about contracts and worrying about associates. You've finally found something exciting and intriguing in Millie, and you're afraid that she deserves better, that you're just using her to find some inspiration."

Scott nearly stopped in his tracks as the truth of the statement hit him. He hadn't even thought of it that way. He looked again at this man who had become a friend. Even though they spent a few hours a week together working on cases or playing poker, he truly hadn't witnessed Wolfe's depths. "I didn't realize that," he said.

"Sure," Wolfe said easily. "Let me tell you, that's not it. It's not the excitement of Millie. It's actually her. She's one of a kind, man, and something in you recognizes that. Even though being a lawyer seems kind of dumb sometimes, you're not stupid."

"I think I appreciate that?" Scott murmured.

Wolfe clapped him hard on the shoulder, jarring his bruised ribs. "Good talk. Now, let's find my cat."

* * * *

Early in the morning, Millie handed everybody Pop-Tarts as Scott and Wolfe rummaged for iced coffees in the back of the refrigerator.

"I'm headed out again," Wolfe said, drink in hand as he strode grimly out the door where Ian and Oliver already waited.

JT and Alex had taken out the charters early that morning. The Derby was in full force.

"You two didn't uncover anything?" Millie asked, munching on her strawberry-frosted Pop-Tart.

"No." Scott took a deep drink. "We searched up and down the main road, but found no sign of the cat. Wolfe's getting really worried."

"I know," Millie said, her gut aching. She looked at the metal box on the table. "We have three ways to open this thing. I could try every possible combination or invent some sort of device to open it, or we can just break in."

Scott reached into his back pocket for a screwdriver. "I grabbed this from the bunkhouse. I say we go for brute strength."

"Agreed," Millie said. "I don't really care about saving the metal box, but I'm dying to know what's inside it." The way things were going for them, it would probably just be Clay's diaries recounting his good old days.

Brigid wandered down the stairs and into the kitchen, yawning. Today she wore jeans and a cream-colored sweater that made her hair look even redder than usual. "Doesn't anybody sleep in around here?" she mumbled, wandering over to the coffeepot to pour herself a deep mug.

"Sometimes," Millie answered. "Aunt Mae is still asleep."

Brigid yawned again and looked at the metal box. "What's that?"

"We found it at Clay Baker's cabin." Scott rummaged in the junk drawer and drew out a hammer. "Everybody step back." Nobody moved. Shrugging, he leaned over, shoved the screwdriver near the lock, and started pounding.

Millie finished her Pop-Tart while Brigid drank her coffee with a happy hum.

The box sprang open. They rushed forward to look inside.

"Huh." Scott pulled out three vials of liquid. "What do you want to bet?"

"GHB," Brigid said, taking the vials. "I'll run these to the post office and send them to DC."

"It should probably go to the local police," Scott said. "It's their crime."

"Oh fine," Brigid said, shaking her head. "They'll probably just use our lab anyway."

Scott lifted an old and faded piece of paper off out of the way. "Oh," he said, whistling.

Millie looked at VCR tape upon tape lined up neatly inside the box. Labels on each held names and dates going back nearly five years. Alarm filled her chest.

Scott picked up a tape and looked at it. "Dora, from three years ago."

Millie nodded. "Those are from an old-fashioned video recorder."

"A handheld one?" Scott asked.

How had Clay turned into such a monster? Millie coughed. "They used tapes instead of digital."

"Smart," Brigid muttered. "There's too much of a footprint with digital. These old tapes are the way to go if you want to hide something."

"We are definitely not going to like this," Scott muttered. "Do you have anything that'll play these?"

Millie didn't want to view the content on those tapes. "Yes. I have tons of old video recorders in my workshop," she said. "I used to take them apart and create everything from kaleidoscopes to small detonators. I'll be right back." She walked through the kitchen to the garage and her workshop at the far end, rummaging through boxes until she found what she needed. She returned to discover Brigid making more coffee and Scott lining the tapes up according to date.

She hesitated.

Scott looked up, his gaze intense. "Your name isn't on any of these."

Relief flowed through her and the breath that she hadn't realized she was holding whooshed out of her lungs. "That makes sense," she murmured. "Clay and I broke up after high school. All of these tapes date to his college days." Yet the latest one was dated only four weeks ago. So it appeared Clay *had* drugged her the other night. But who had killed him?

"Here you go," Scott said, handing her the tape labeled with Dora's name. "I also have tapes for Wilma and Bobbi, the victim Ian spoke with."

Millie gagged, then shut down her emotions to maneuver Dora's tape into the out-of-date video recorder. She flipped open the screen.

Brigid remained across the room, watching her.

A woman came onto the screen, stumbling across what looked like an apartment. Beer cans covered nearly every surface, and a flag for the college that Clay had attended hung over a leather sofa.

The scene moved and Clay smiled into the camera, looking about eight years younger than the last time she'd seen him. He winked. "Dora decided to visit," he murmured, then laughed, turning to film a woman who stared blankly around. Her eyes were hollow and her movements jerky. She fell onto the leather sofa, tilting to the side, obviously drugged.

Another man laughed in the background. Millie stiffened as the camera panned to Rupert Skinner. "Son of a bitch," she muttered.

"Skinner is there." Nausea rolled through Millie, and she watched as long as she could before slapping the video screen closed.

Brigid had gone pale, even though she hadn't viewed the tape from across the room. "I don't want to see it," she said.

"Neither do I." Scott's jaw looked as if it had been carved from granite.

Millie fought to keep from throwing up. Clay had basically filmed the entire night, which included rape by both him and Rupert Skinner.

She gulped.

"I'm going to take these to the police station myself," Brigid said.

"Let's catalog them first," Scott murmured, holding up a hand, fury turning his eyes a cobalt blue. "I don't want to see any of these, but I do want to make a spreadsheet of names and dates just so we keep track." He secured a pen from the drawer. "This does open up a whole group of possible killers. Not that Clay didn't deserve it—because he did."

Millie sat at the table, her Pop-Tart swirling in her gut. "We need to get Skinner, now."

"Oh, don't worry," Scott said darkly. "He'll be arrested before the end of the day."

Chapter Forty

After a lunch of chicken casserole, Millie hustled around the kitchen, yanking open drawers. "Where are the... Oh, here they are." She found the bows to plant on the voluminous baby present she'd bought for Verna.

Her phone buzzed and she reached for it, finding a text from June.

Can you talk?

She glanced at her watch and quickly texted back.

Not really. Let's talk at the shower.

While she loved June, she still wasn't sure what to say about the lies her friend had told.

Please, Millie. I really need to speak with you before the shower. Can you swing by my house?

Millie chewed on her lip. She didn't have time to drive all the way out to June's house—it lay in the opposite direction from Valerie's cabin. Also, she wanted to conduct one more search for Kat in the bunkhouse just in case he'd sought refuge during the night.

She sent another text. *I don't have time.*

Please, Mills. It's important. Can you meet me at Valerie's just twenty minutes early? I really have to talk to you.

Scott looked over her shoulder. "Is June always this pushy?"

"No." Millie's temples began to ache. "I wonder if she knows that Valerie told me she'd been dating Clay."

"It doesn't sound like dating in the public sense," Scott said. "They might have just hooked up once in a while."

Millie didn't care what they'd been doing. "She's been a friend of mine for a long time, and I don't understand why she'd lie to me." She shot off another text.

I'll try to get to Valerie's fifteen minutes early, and then maybe we can grab a drink after the shower.

Scott cleared his throat. "I had Brigid run June's financials just to double-check."

Millie turned around to face him. "You did what? June's been my friend my entire life."

"I know, but she's in financial trouble."

"Most of this town's in financial trouble right now," she said, instantly going hot.

Scott zipped up his windbreaker. "I'm aware of that, but June had her new SUV repossessed a month ago, and she's three payments behind with the mortgage on her home. I'm just saying, Millie, sometimes people who need money do things you'd never suspect."

That made no sense. "So, what? You think she fell for Clay and then killed him because she was broke? That he promised her money or something like that?"

Scott shrugged. "It's possible?"

"Not June. I've known her my whole life, and if something's going on with her, she'd tell me. She's been trying to talk to me for a couple of days."

Scott's lips pressed into a firm line. "You're not going to her place."

"No, I'm meeting her at Valerie's, and I actually need to get going if I'm going to arrive early. I'll be home in a couple of hours."

His smile would appear charming to most. "You're not going by yourself."

She planted her feet. "You are not invited to the baby shower."

"I'm aware of that. However, I am driving you. I'll remain outside in the car." He glanced at his watch. "Believe me, I have plenty of work to do. One of my associates just screwed up a deposition."

Millie looked at the still messy kitchen.

"I'll clean up," Brigid called from the other room. "As soon as I'm finished conducting this internet search."

Scott's phone buzzed and he read the screen, a dark smile crossing his face. "Rupert Skinner is in custody in Charleston."

"Good." Millie finally breathed easier. He deserved to pay for his sins.

They'd enjoyed a luncheon of chicken casserole made by Millie's great-aunt, who now napped. She had wanted to attend the baby shower, but Millie had insisted she take it easy because the woman had yawned wildly several times. "All right," Millie said. "I will be back." Then she jogged outside and climbed into Scott's SUV, not having the energy to argue with him.

She held the baby present on her lap as they drove the twenty minutes to Valerie's cabin. The nurse owned a couple of acres along the river and had made good use of them by building a greenhouse nestled in the cottonwood trees.

Millie stepped out of the vehicle, holding the brightly wrapped green present. "Are you sure you're okay sitting in your car?"

"I'm positive," Scott said, leaning over to grab a notebook. "I think it's better you don't hear me rip this guy a new one before we move on to other cases." Even though Scott hadn't gotten much sleep the night before, his eyes shone with alertness and his shoulders remained wide and open.

"Try to stay out of trouble. I'll bring you a cupcake." She shut the door and walked toward the quaint home, noting June's battered old black truck already parked by the side of the garage. The truck had been in her family for years; Millie knew how much she had enjoyed her new SUV. How unfortunate that the vehicle had been repossessed. Why hadn't June called her to ask for a loan?

Shrugging, she walked up to the door, knocked, and went inside without waiting for a response. "Valerie?" she called out.

"She's not here yet," Verna said, bustling from the kitchen and wiping off her hands. For her baby shower, she wore a pretty light pink sheath that showed off her baby bump. "She had an early shift and chauffeured my kids around town earlier. Now she had to run to town to get more champagne." She frowned. "Not that I get to enjoy the champagne."

"That's what happens when you get knocked up," Millie said, grinning.

The place had been decorated in green, yellow, and white streamers with purple balloons. A gift table had been set up near the modern white stone fireplace, and she carried her gift over. "Just how much champagne do you think we need?" she asked, noting three bottles already nestled at the end of the table.

"I don't know." Verna laughed. "I'll end up driving everybody home." Her thick hair framed her pale face.

"Are you feeling up to this?" Millie asked.

Verna pressed a hand to her side. "I am. Just having some Braxton-Hicks today, I think. This kid really wants out."

Millie looked around. Valerie had been very generous with the decorations, brightening the room with color. "Do you think you're carrying a boy or a girl?"

"I really don't know." Verna tugged on a streamer. "Valerie has been bugging me to find out. I wish she'd get her own life. I worry about her."

"So do I," Millie said quietly. It seemed that Valerie lived on the fringes of her sister's life and never acted as the heroine in her own story. Soft music played through the speakers as the river babbled outside. "Where's June?" Millie asked.

"She went with Valerie," Verna said, rubbing her belly. "Why?"

"June wanted to talk to me for some reason."

Verna's phone must have buzzed because she lifted it to her ear. "Hey there, Alex. No way, are you kidding? That's good news.

That would be sweet of you. Thanks. We'll meet you there." She looked up, her eyes sparkling.

"What?" Millie asked.

"Alex found the cat."

Elation whipped through Millie. That morning, she'd called everyone she'd ever met trying to find him, putting the entire town on alert. "Oh my God. Thank goodness. We've been looking all over for him."

"Come on. Alex's bringing him over—he said the animal is a little the worse for wear." She moved toward the doorway to the kitchen, which opened to the path between the twins' homes.

Millie hurried toward the kitchen but stopped cold at the sight of June sprawled on the floor with blood pooling around her head. "June!" she cried out and then halted. Wait a minute? She turned around to find Verna pointing a gun at her. "What in the world?" Millie took a step away from the pregnant woman.

"Yeah, sorry about that," Verna said. She glanced toward the front window and Scott's SUV. "We need to go out the back."

* * * *

Scott clicked off, fully irritated again. He just might fire this bonehead. He mulled over what Wolfe had said as they'd hunted for Kat. Maybe Wolfe had a point. Perhaps Scott needed a change, but if so, what did he want to do? He needed to strategize to keep his mind engaged, and not many jobs actually involved strategy. He couldn't be less interested in the stock market or real property investments.

He peered through the front window of the charming one-story white clapboard cabin and didn't see any movement, not liking the quiet. He really didn't like that June was inside. If she was facing money problems, and if she had truly been dating Clay, then she could be a danger to Millie. Perhaps she had gotten jealous enough to kill him.

Sitting in the vehicle didn't work for Scott.

Knowing that she'd be ticked off, he stepped out of his SUV into the blustering wind, then paused at the sound of voices. They'd moved outside into the chilly day? That made zero sense. He ducked low against the brutal breeze and bolted around the side of the cabin near the greenhouse to where he could hear better.

"Millie?" he called out. If she'd gone outside to speak with June alone, he might just spank her this time. She had promised to stay inside with the other women.

"Scott?" she called out, her voice high-pitched.

He barreled around the corner and stopped cold at seeing Verna Montgomery pointing a gun at Millie. The sight of the obviously pregnant woman in light pink with a deadly Glock in her hand had him reeling.

"What the hell?" He moved to the side, his arm dropping to his hip, close to where his gun rested, nestled at the base of his spine.

The woman looked up, her eyes cold. She edged to the side, keeping Millie between them. "If you have a weapon, drop it," she ordered, her voice harsh.

"I don't," Scott lied.

Millie looked at him, her eyes wide in her pale face. "June is inside," she whispered. "She lay unmoving with blood all around her."

"We'll figure this out. Verna, you haven't hurt anybody yet. I'm sure June will be fine," Scott said soothingly.

"Huh? I cracked her head hard enough that I heard her skull fracture," Verna hissed. "Sorry, but you're in my way."

Scott moved then. She fired instantly. Pain exploded through his chest, and the force threw him back. He landed hard on his shoulders and hips, causing wet mud to squish out from either side of his shoulders.

"Scott!" Millie shrieked.

He fought the darkness, coming in and out, swamped by memories of other bullets impacting his body. Grunting, he forced himself to roll over and shoved himself to a seated position. He wavered, looking around. Red dotted the edges of his vision, and he tried to focus. Where was Millie? He couldn't see her.

The sound of a small motorboat pulling away from the riverbank caught his attention. Shit. He rolled over again to all fours, and forced himself to stand. Pain ripped through him so quickly his breath stopped, maybe forever, but he forced himself to plod along the side of the house toward his vehicle. He wrenched open the driver's side door, using the handle to hold himself upright, and leaned in to scrabble for his phone.

Blood had flowed down his arm to his hand, making it slippery. He pulled the phone out and let himself drop to the asphalt. He pressed a button.

"Wolfe," his friend answered.

"Wolfe, I need backup. Now." He barely got the last word out as he fell to the side. He didn't feel a thing when his head hit the driveway.

Chapter Forty-One

Millie huddled in the bottom of the metal boat, staring up at Verna as the pregnant woman expertly maneuvered upstream. The rain had ebbed, leaving her more conscious of the damp air and chilly wind. "Verna, what are you doing?"

Verna watched the river, the gun casually on her knee and pointed at Millie. If Millie lunged at her, she'd get shot. She was also too far down in the boat to be able to leap over the side without Verna at least getting off one round. "Just be quiet. You're upsetting the baby. We'll be there in a minute."

Millie looked around and didn't see any other fishing boats. The stretch of river between Valerie's and Verna's homes was more rocky and tough to navigate than much of the watercourse, so it was unlikely they'd see anybody else today. The Derby was taking place on the New River, so most anglers would be over there.

Even so, she kept her eye out for anybody who might spot her. She wouldn't make a sound and get someone else hurt. But witnesses might be helpful, unless Verna was as unhinged as she appeared.

"Did you kill June?"

"I don't know. I cracked her pretty good," Verna said carelessly.

Millie studied the woman she'd known since they were children. The wind whipped Verna's hair around, and the sight of the gun so close to her pregnant belly was garish. "June's been your friend for decades."

"Yeah, well, June couldn't keep her mouth shut," Verna muttered, pulling the steering handle toward her.

"Why? Why did you hurt June?" Millie couldn't make sense of this, and she couldn't stop thinking about Scott. He'd been unconscious and bleeding, but hopefully soon the party guests would show up and somebody would see him. He fell at the side of the house, but June remained in the kitchen. Somebody would see her and surely they'd call the police, who would certainly search the property.

But did Scott have that kind of time? Millie clutched the side of the boat with one hand, her teeth chattering from the chill. "Why did you hurt June?"

"June wanted to talk with you. She confronted me first, which was a huge mistake."

Apparently so. "What did June want to tell me?"

"That I had had an affair with Clay. The bitch saw me one night with him, but I swore it was a one-time mistake, and she agreed to keep my secret. Liar." Verna turned into a small cove and expertly ran the boat up on the sandy beach. Using the handle for balance, she stood, having to stretch her back and place one hand on her belly. The other hand remained on the gun. She pointed the weapon at Millie and gracefully stepped over the side, her heels sinking in the sand. "Come on, Mills, let's go."

Millie vaulted over the edge of the boat, her feet landing in the chilly river. She sank a couple of inches and lifted up her kitten heels as she waded onto the wet sand. Verna gestured her to move on ahead. Millie did so and could feel the barrel of the gun pointed between her shoulder blades. "Why did you kill Clay?"

"Hurry up, Millie, or I'm going to shoot you right here."

Millie started toward the house.

"No, go to the right, to the boat shed."

Millie turned. Verna and Alex's boat shed loomed down the beach; she slipped over rocks on the way. "Don't do this," she said.

"Inside now," Verna barked.

Millie opened the door and stepped inside, surprised to see the lights already on. A dismantled motor sat in the corner. Alex had always liked rebuilding motors.

"Get over there, Millie." Verna gestured with her gun toward the motor.

Millie walked over to the motor, looking for any sort of weapon. A wrench perched on a low table, though in her experience, wrenches never beat guns. A plaintive meow caught her attention and she looked down to see a cage behind the motor. "Kat?" she asked, bending down, then turning to look over her shoulder incredulously. "You kidnapped the cat?"

Verna grinned. "Yeah. Little bugger was running around when I dropped Alex off the other day, so I tossed him in the car. I figured it'd be a good way to get you out here if necessary."

"You kidnapped a cat." Millie opened the cage before Verna could say anything and grasped Kat, pulling him out and hugging him. "Oh Kat, are you okay?" He meowed plaintively and licked her neck. "You are sick, Verna," she said, standing with the cat in her arms. He snuggled right into her and purred. "I don't suppose you fed him."

"No, I haven't fed him. I'm going to kill him along with you," Verna said.

Millie gaped at her old friend. "What is wrong with you?"

"I am sorry about this, Millie. But all of this ongoing stress isn't good for the baby. I have to do what's right for her."

The woman was maniacal. "Did you hire that hit squad?"

"Of course."

Millie drew connections in her mind, and it hit her. "Henry Halcomb! That's where I've seen him before." Oh, it had been a good ten years ago, but she'd met him on the river briefly. He had been with a group of anglers, including Verna.

"Yes," Verna said. "I dated Henry when I attended nursing school those few weeks. Oh, he didn't attend school or anything, but we met in town. We kept in touch."

Evilness had nothing on this bitch.

The door opened and Nancy Wilcox walked inside, her belly bigger than Verna's. "I'm here." Her voice shook.

"Good." Verna waved the gun toward the door. "You need to go and hide the two bodies at my sister's house." She rattled off the address. "We don't want nerdy Valerie to get into trouble, do we?"

The world spun around Millie. "Valerie is part of this as well?"

"No." Verna snorted. "Not my innocent sister who wishes she had my life. She'd never have the guts to plan a good future like I have. Come on, Millie. You know Valerie. She lives most of her life for me, and probably still loves Alex from their brief romance in the eighth grade. How pathetic."

Nancy gagged as if she needed to vomit. "Listen. I'll give that money back. Please don't tell the police that I have it."

Oh, for goodness' sake. Millie stared at her. "Are you a part of this? Did you help kill Clay or know that Verna hired Henry Halcomb to kill us?"

Nancy hiccupped. "No. I didn't know anything about my boyfriend's business. I told you that. This lady called me this morning and said I was going to jail because I kept that money you said I could have. I just want to run away."

"No, you're not running anywhere. You need to take my car and hide the two bodies at my sister's house before people show up for that stupid party." Verna waved the gun as she issued orders.

"You mean your baby shower?" Millie asked, her brain feeling as if it was full of pudding. "This is crazy. How could you do this?" The woman was pregnant, for goodness' sake. She sat back. "Does this have something to do with June seeing Clay?" Why else would Verna have tried to kill poor June?

"June never dated Clay." Verna looked at her as if she was dumber than a box of rocks.

"But Valerie said—"

Verna winced and rubbed her belly with her free hand. "I told Valerie that June left the bar with Clay several times. Valerie thought she told you the truth when she gossiped with you. My stupid, sad sister who hangs on my life because she doesn't have one of her own." Verna's eyes gleamed and she held the gun as if she couldn't wait to use it. "Clay and I were soul mates." She patted her protruding stomach. "I have the heir to his fortune right here."

Millie clapped a hand over her mouth to keep from throwing up. When she'd gotten herself under control, she slowly lowered it, still holding the hungry cat. "You and Clay dated?"

"Yes. He had a real future," Verna shrieked. "Not like Alex, who's going to be stuck in this stupid town for the rest of his life, begging for scraps from somebody like you. We had to get married after high school because he knocked me up. I made a lot of mistakes."

Millie's body jolted at the venom spewed by Verna. Alex certainly didn't deserve this. "Does Alex know you and Clay slept together?"

"Of course not. I mean, Alex and I aren't that close anymore, but he thinks we should stay together as a family," Verna scoffed. "But when I became pregnant with Clay's baby, I knew I had a better future. He had an incredible future lined up. He planned to run for office and probably even rise higher than that idiot Skinner. He could have been governor."

Millie highly doubted that, but now wasn't the time to argue. "He never drugged you?"

"No." Verna's lips pressed together. "He promised me when we started dating that he would find a different hobby."

Hobby? The woman considered drugging and raping victims a hobby? "So you knew? You actually knew that he was drugging and raping women and you still dated him?"

"He had changed, or at least he would have once we reached the governor's mansion. I would've made sure of it," Verna said.

She pointed the gun at Nancy. "Get moving. If you don't pick those bodies up before people arrive, we're in deep shit. Go now."

Nancy looked at Millie. "Fine." She stomped out of the shop, tears streaking down her face.

Millie took a couple of steps toward Verna, trying to look casual. "I don't know you at all."

"You never did," Verna said. "You always thought you were better than everybody else, creating those dorky inventions. But you know what? You haven't made a dime from them. Everybody thought you'd be a billionaire by now, and all you do is work with those lugs in the government."

"I love what I do," Millie said, trying to get a step closer. If she was going to take that gun, she needed less distance between them. "So what's your plan now? You're going to kill me?"

"You're lucky I didn't kill you the other night in Clay's cabin."

Millie looked at her, shaking her head. "You're not going to get away with this. You shot the chief of police."

"I had to. He had the VCR tapes."

Millie needed to keep her talking, just in case help was on the way. "What really happened that night?"

Verna eyed the cat. "I went to see Clay at the bar, and he sat drinking with you."

"He drugged me!" Millie yelled.

"I know!" Verna yelled back. "And please lower your voice. You're upsetting my baby." She rubbed her belly with her free hand. "That night? I actually saw him slip the concoction into your beer."

Millie almost took a step back out of shock but forced herself to remain in place. Her knees trembled and the cat stopped purring. She loosened her hold on him, not wanting to strangle him. "You said you saw me get into Clay's truck and scoot over."

"Yeah, that was kind of a lie," Verna said, her teeth gleaming in the meager light from a hanging bulb. "He got you outside and pretty much had to lift you into the truck and shove you over. And he saw me." For the first time, hurt echoed in her tone.

"He saw you?" Millie repeated. "What do you mean?"

Red burst across Verna's face. "He turned and saw me, looked right at me, then got into the truck like I didn't matter." Tears gathered in Verna's eyes. "So I followed you."

"That's what was on the VCR tapes?" Millie asked. "Just you following us?"

"Well, and you passed out in the front seat of Clay's truck," Verna said. "You slept against the window, I think. Anyway, yes, I followed you, and I'm sure those cameras recorded my vehicle behind yours. I had to get the tapes from the chief, and he wasn't expecting to be shot by poor little ole pregnant me."

Fury whipped through Millie and she calculated the distance between them. "Then what?"

"Clay carried you inside through the garage door. He always left his back sliding glass door open, so I walked around the house and entered that way."

"Where was I?" Millie asked.

"He hefted you into the bedroom and had already taken off his clothes," Verna said, "and I just couldn't believe it. I mean, how dare he choose you over me?"

"You were jealous?" Millie spat out. "Are you insane?"

Verna wiped off her mouth with one hand. "No. But I had my future set. I went into the room. I even offered to share you."

Millie gagged as bile rose into her throat.

"And he laughed," Verna finished. "He said no, that he wasn't interested, that he wanted you. So, I don't know. The world went dark and I stabbed him over and over and over again. He fell onto the bed, and when I came back to myself, he was dead."

"Where did you get my knife?"

Verna grinned. "I took that months ago. Thought I'd sell it, but I don't know."

Oh, she knew. "You planned his murder."

Verna shrugged. "Not really, but you know. Just in case he went south, I needed an insurance policy. Now this baby will get everything she should have had if he'd lived. You'll be dead, though."

Millie took a deep breath and faced the cold truth. Verna wanted to kill her. "So then what? You took off my clothes and put me in bed with him?"

"Yep, and I wrapped your hand around the knife," Verna said. "He deserved it."

Millie just looked at her old friend. How had she missed the insanity in the woman? "You pretty much had me framed for Clay's murder. Why hire a hit squad to take me out?"

Verna sneered. "I don't know how well those drugs work long-term. You saw me when I argued with Clay in his bedroom, and I thought you might remember at some point." Pride filled her voice now. "Plus, once you were dead, I could come forward as the star witness and say that I saw you and Clay fight. That you later confessed to me you had killed him."

"So you served as the county prosecutor's secret witness."

Verna snorted. "I surely did."

"You're crazy."

"Ha. I'm brilliant. Now you'll die, and I'll tearfully admit that you confessed to killing Clay." She looked down at her swollen abdomen. "Everyone believes the pregnant chick."

"I don't deserve to die."

"Nobody will really miss you," Verna said. With that, she took a deep breath and steadied her aim.

Kat let out a shrieking squeal, dug his claws into Millie's neck, and launched himself into the air.

Verna screamed as the cat hit her face and raked his claws down her cheeks.

Millie dodged in beneath the cat and tackled Verna by the legs, knocking her onto her back. The gun fired.

Chapter Forty-Two

Scott heard the firing of a gun, and he nearly lost his mind. He immediately lunged toward the door to the boathouse.

"Stop," Wolfe said, grabbing his good arm.

Even so, agony ripped through Scott with a force that nearly knocked him to his knees. He wrenched his arm free. "I'm going in there."

"Let me open the door," Wolfe growled, gun in his hand. "You go low. I'll go high."

Out of the corner of his eye, Scott could see Ian gently lead Nancy to a rock, where she collapsed. The woman shook and cried violently.

Scott took a deep breath and ignored the pain in his shoulder from the bullet wound. It had knocked him out for a few seconds before his friends had arrived. "Go," he ordered.

Wolfe opened the door, and Scott went in low, his gun in his good hand, pointed out.

Millie and Verna struggled furiously on the ground with Verna punching and clawing and kicking for all she was worth, her dress riding up past her hips. Millie dodged each blow and seemed to be trying to subdue the woman without harming her or the baby.

"Millie," he snapped.

She paused and Verna punched her in the cheek, tossing her to the side, so Millie rolled several times.

Verna scrambled for the gun. Scott sprang forward and kicked it across the dirt floor.

Verna screeched and levered herself up, swiping at his knees. He took a step back.

Wolfe was instantly there, hauling the woman to her feet by one arm. Sirens echoed in the distance. "Hold still," Wolfe growled.

The woman snarled at him, then all the fight went out of her. Tears streamed down her face. "It wasn't my fault. This is all a mistake."

"Bullshit," Millie said, standing and holding her cheek. "Scott." Her eyes widened, and she rushed for him.

He held her close with his good arm, pulling her into his body. "Are you okay?" he asked, his voice shaking.

"I'm fine." She leaned back, her eyes wide. "She shot you. I didn't know if you were dead."

"I'm fine. It was a through-and-through, according to Wolfe." Truth be told, his entire right side hurt, but nothing else mattered now except his woman. "I love you. I know it's a weird time to say it, but people keep shooting at us."

Tears filled her eyes, and one slid through the dirt on her pretty face. "I love you too. It is a weird time to make the declaration."

"There you go," Wolfe said. "Happy? Kat." His entire face lit up. The cat let out a strangled meow and leaped nearly across the entire boathouse to land on Wolfe's shoulder. The animal immediately wrapped himself around Wolfe's neck, his mangled ear twitching. Then he snarled and reached out, batting at Verna.

Verna batted him back, and Wolfe pushed her away. "Knock it off. Leave the cat alone. What are you doing here, buddy?" He stroked the animal.

"She kidnapped him," Millie said. "Thought it might be a good way to lure me here."

The look Wolfe gave Verna had the woman taking two more steps back.

"He hasn't eaten," Millie said, sagging against Scott. "How is June? Please tell me she's not dead."

"She's going to be okay," Scott said instantly, tightening his hold even though his gun was at her waist. "Oliver stayed with June to wait for the paramedics. Ian's outside. He has Nancy Wilcox. Care to catch me up?"

She gingerly felt along his rib cage. "Verna planned and executed all of this. She's pregnant with Clay's baby and became angry when he drugged me. So instead of saving me, she killed him. Then she shot the chief so he wouldn't see her car on the VCR tapes. She hired the hit squad to take us out, fearing that I'd remember seeing her that night. I don't. That Henry is one of her exes."

"Worst of all," Wolfe growled, "she catnapped my cat."

Scott disagreed that was the worst of Verna's crimes, but he refused to argue with Wolfe right now. The darkness kept pushing in on him, and he fought it back. "Are you sure you're unharmed?" he asked Millie.

"I am, but I just can't believe it." Her voice softened with sadness. "Alex is going to be devastated."

"Alex is better off." Wolfe said what they were all thinking.

The door opened and two police officers rushed in, guns out.

"We're good," Scott said. "She's the one you want." He gestured with his chin toward Verna.

"No, I'm not." She put her hands protectively on her belly.

"Don't even," Millie retorted, looking at Officer Locum. "She is the one. She shot the chief, killed Clay, and hired a hit squad. The pregnant woman outside is innocent."

Locum moved toward her, taking out his cuffs. She protested all the way out of the boathouse.

Wolfe murmured to Kat, "Let's get you some food, buddy. I'll buy the good tuna fish in a can." They soon exited as well.

Millie looked up at Scott's face. "Let's get you to the hospital."

"Sounds good." He clenched his back teeth together to keep from snarling with pain. This shooting might lead to more nightmares, but he would no longer play it safe or be bored. Life was too fucking short. "You're it for me, Millie. I don't care how long it takes. I was frozen, under water, and you warmed me up. Brought me back to life. We can go slow, we can go fast, but it's going to be you and me."

She slid an arm around his waist and started pulling him toward the door. "I can live with that. I'm more than happy for it to be the two of us." As they walked outside, her gaze caught on Ian standing next to his brother. "Well, and our whole team."

Chapter Forty-Three

Three days after being kidnapped by Verna, Millie fidgeted on a hardwood bench, once again wearing her boring navy-blue suit. She'd spruced it up with a bright green shirt as well as sparkly pink jewelry borrowed from her great-aunt. She sat at one table with Scott and JT flanking her. While her brother didn't belong at the hearing, he wouldn't be deterred.

On the other side sat Special Agent Rutherford.

It was an informal hearing room rather than an actual courtroom, so a three-person panel sat in front of them at a table. Rutherford had finished discussing how badly she and Scott had screwed up the department's case against Werner Dearth.

Scott sat next to her in a charcoal-gray suit with his arm in a sling. His color remained good and as usual, his remarks reached brilliance, so if he endured pain, he masked it well. His phone buzzed and he glanced down to read the screen.

"What?" Millie asked.

He leaned toward her. "Verna admitted to throwing the Molotov cocktails into your house. She's trying for some sort of insanity defense."

Millie sat back. "She'll still do time, right?"

"Oh yeah," Scott said.

Her phone dinged and she reached for it on the table to read a text. Relief filled her. "The chief is out of his coma," she whispered to Scott and her brother. "June is there with him and has already been released with a concussion. They're both going to be fine."

"Excuse me," Agent Rutherford thundered. "Do you mind? I'm finishing my statement."

"What an ass," JT muttered, not so quietly.

Rutherford painted a pretty damning picture of not only Millie, but the Deep Ops team. They weren't exactly conventional, and Tom Rutherford had wanted to get rid of them from the very beginning. He looked polished in a dark brown suit with his perfectly coiffed blond hair combed back from his face, and his argument sounded logical and well thought out.

The back door opened, and she partially turned to see Angus Force stride inside with Nari beside him. While Angus led the team, Nari was their psychologist and overall spiritual advisor, as far as Millie was concerned. Behind them came Malcolm West, their undercover operative, and his fiancée, Pippa, followed up by Wolfe and Dana. Oh, good. Millie was glad to see Dana and knew that Wolfe would sleep better now that she was back within his reach.

Then she caught sight of Wolfe's hands, which held two overflowing latte carriers with mountains of whipped cream and sprinkles. He grinned. "I found a good latte place down the street. It has been too long for all of us."

Angus grimaced.

Brigid walked in, gave her a thumbs up, then reached back for the hand of Raider Tanaka, the most buttoned down of all the Deep Ops team. Their British colleague, Jethro Hansen, strode inside next holding the hand of Gemma Falls, his fiancée. Finally, Ian and Oliver Villan stepped inside and flanked the door as if to protect everybody from some sort of infiltration. Angus stomped up, shoved open the barrier between the benches, and set his stance.

"Angus Force, what are you doing here?" Agent Rutherford asked, his voice rising.

Angus ignored him and looked at the panel. "First, I'm here to say that the FBI just arrested Werner Dearth for a boatload of crimes, including fraud. Brigid compiled enough evidence against him to put him away for decades."

Millie turned and gave Brigid a thumbs up. The woman always performed excellent work.

Angus cleared his throat. "Second, I'm here to make a claim. Millie's part of my team, and she's not going anywhere."

"That's not up to you," Rutherford sputtered.

"It is." Angus looked at him. "You don't seem to understand. This team sticks together." He looked at the panel of two men and one woman, all midforties, all high-ranking at the HDD. "I mean it. I'm making this statement right now. If you fire Millie, you're firing all of us. Where one of us goes, we all go."

Millie gasped. "No, Angus."

He barely flicked her a glance. "It's done. It's decided."

"That's quite the bold statement," the HDD officer on the left said, his eyes a blazing brown. Millie hadn't bothered memorizing their names. She didn't really care. She just didn't want to be fired.

"I agree," Angus said, "but I mean it. If she's out, we're all leaving."

Millie looked at the assembled group. They all were grim, but nobody protested. "You can't leave your jobs just because of me," she said. Again, nobody protested.

"We hope you reconsider that stance, Agent Force," the woman in the middle said. "Not that your declaration carries import in this situation. The evidence supports a reprimand in Agent Frost's file and not a termination of employment."

Hope flew through Millie.

"Excellent," Angus said. "I'd like for her to be transferred permanently to my team with a promotion."

"You can't be serious," Agent Rutherford sputtered again.

Angus gestured everyone toward the door. "Take it under advisement. I'll submit the proper paperwork—again—tomorrow."

Millie found herself scrambling to stand as Scott gestured her ahead of him, both Scott and Angus covering her back. She walked numbly out of the hearing room and rode the elevator to the bottom floor, where the entire group walked out as one.

"You all just offered to leave your jobs because of me," she said, trying to talk sense into one of them.

"We're all in or all out," Wolfe said cheerfully. Kat poked his furry white head out of Wolfe's left pocket. "I cut the inside of the jacket so he can sleep in there if he wants now that he's grown. He likes it there."

Millie reached out and scratched Kat's ears. "I'm glad he's all right."

Wolfe grinned. "Come on. Let's go check out where your house is going to be."

"No, I..." She stumbled.

Scott put an arm over her shoulders. "You kept your job. It's all good."

Her eyes filled. "I can't believe you all would quit your jobs because of me." Millie sucked in air as the wind tried to pierce her jacket.

"And you, Scott," Angus said, motioning everybody toward the parking garage.

"What about me?" Scott asked easily.

Angus slid an arm over Nari's shoulders. "We need a lawyer on board who can also serve as an operative once in a while. What do you say?"

Hope leaped into his eyes but he quickly banked it. "I'll think about it."

"Think about this," Nari piped up. "Every member of the team, except for Angus, has to meet with me on a professional basis. Rumor has it you have nightmares. I can help you with that."

Wolfe and Jethro both nodded. "She really can," the Brit said. "She's the best."

"I am," Nari said, smiling.

Millie could see how much Scott wanted to be part of the group. She figured he'd accept.

"I'll think about it," he repeated. "Millie and I need to speak first."

Epilogue

Scott stood on the piece of property apparently owned by Millie Frost. "This is nice," he said, looking at the mature trees and the space between the houses. Everybody on the team seemed to either have a house, be building a house, or planning on someday building a house. He wasn't so sure about Ian and Oliver, whether they wanted to stay or not, but the rest of the team seemed to be taking it for granted that they would.

He liked it here. He appreciated the big gate at the far end of the road and he enjoyed the fencing and the feeling of safety. "What do you think, Millie?" he asked.

"It's pretty. Angus sweetened the pot with the workshop of all workshops for me." She grinned. "He even agreed that anything I invented would be mine alone to patent and manufacture. However, I'd probably cut everybody in. In addition, I can have as much time as I need every month to go see Aunt Mae and JT, and even help out with the business if I want."

"That's ideal." Scott took a deep breath, and his body relaxed in a way it hadn't in far too long. Being part of the team appealed to him, but it was the woman who came first.

She planted her hand on his good arm. "Are you accepting Angus's job offer? You could still keep your law office and just hire a managing partner."

The idea held definite appeal. "It depends on you."

"What about me?"

He chose his words carefully. "I don't want to push you into anything because it seems like such a great arrangement."

"I love you, Scott Terentson," she said, putting both hands on his chest. "I've loved you from the first second I saw you, even when you said you were a lawyer. Boy, the dreams I had."

He grinned and leaned down to kiss her nose. "Yeah? Tell me about them."

"Maybe. It depends if you stay or not."

"I know it's quick, Mills, but I love you too. I don't want just a maybe, though."

She blinked. "Life is full of maybes."

"Yeah? Marry me." He meant every word. Oh, it didn't have to be tomorrow, but he wanted her for all time, and there was no reason not to make the claim right now. Plus, he'd all but promised Wolfe he could be a groomsman, and he wouldn't want to disappoint the man who seemed to be his new brother.

Pink flowed into her pretty face. "Seriously?"

"Yeah. I figured you could design the coolest rings ever made."

"I do like diamonds," she murmured. "And designing them? Absolutely."

His heart thumped. Hard. "Was that a yes?" he asked.

"That was absolutely a yes." She leaned up and kissed him.

He took over the kiss, taking them both under, enjoying the feel of her against him on the land that would someday be their home. Then he leaned back. "We could have a double wedding with your aunt Mae and Chief Wyatt." The chief was out of the woods and the two had immediately become engaged.

Millie laughed. "I would absolutely love that."

He leaned back. "You sure?"

She grinned. "Yes. Forever."

Printed in the USA
CPSIA information can be obtained
at www.ICGtesting.com
LVHW042145120224
771697LV00034B/301

9 781516 111282